stolen moments

a secret romance is hardest to hide in the spotlight.

a.b. jackson

COPYRIGHT

STOLEN MOMENTS.
Copyright © 2026 by A.B. Jackson.

All Rights Reserved. Printed in the United Kingdom. No part of this book may be used or reproduced in any manner whatsoever without written permission except in the case of brief quotations embodied in academic work, critical articles and reviews.

If anything of the storylines or themes contained in this book impacts you and you require professional help around your own mental health please contact your GP, or if in crisis please contact the Samaritans on 116 123

STOLEN MOMENTS may be purchased for education, business, sales or promotional use. For information, please email hello@abjackson.com

Published by Jackal Entertainment

First Edition

Edited by Dakota Nyght

Cover Design by Rocío Martin Osuna

DISCLAIMERS

This book is <u>loosely</u> inspired by a true story.

Whilst this story is inspired by true events. This is a work of fiction, where certain events and details have been fictionalised for dramatic purposes.

Other than individuals clearly in the public domain, to protect the identities of the individuals in this book, pseudonyms have been used instead.

Any similarities to anyone you may know or can think of, are merely coincidental, and are not intended to represent or defame any individual.

This story extends beyond just this book and series and into the world of song.

If you want to hear the songs that have been created with some of the biggest songwriters and producers in the world for this book, you can check them out on Spotify, Apple, Amazon and YouTube by scanning the QR code below.

DEDICATION

I would like to dedicate this book to Sk8er Boi.

Contents

1. Alexander — 1
2. Christopher — 15
3. Alexander — 29
4. Christopher — 37
5. Alexander — 49
6. Christopher — 61
7. Alexander — 75
8. Christopher — 89
9. Alexander — 101
10. Christopher — 115
11. Alexander — 129
12. Christopher — 143
13. Alexander — 157
14. Christopher — 171
15. Alexander — 185
16. Christopher — 199
17. Alexander — 213
18. Christopher — 225
19. Alexander — 241
20. Christopher — 257
21. Alexander — 273
22. Christopher — 289
23. Alexander — 301
24. Christopher — 313
25. Alexander — 329
26. Christopher — 343
27. Alexander — 355
28. Christopher — 367
29. Alexander — 381
30. Christopher — 393

ACKNOWLEDGEMENTS — 409
ABOUT THE AUTHOR — 411

1. Alexander
Thursday - June 13

Today is not the first time I have sent someone flying toward their death.

But this time, I seem to be flying with them.

I'd barely caught the screech of bicycle brakes over Green Day's *American Idiot* blaring through my earbuds before the front wheel connected with my left leg. My hands and knees hit the hot tarmac as the bicyclist, with his Lycra top and shorts the same green as the crosswalk signal locked in my vision, careened through the air.

Fuck.

I really *am* an American idiot.

I'd managed to escape from my hotel unnoticed, but I've managed to cause a scene in less than five minutes. No wonder my team never wants to leave me unchaperoned, despite being twenty-three and a full-grown adult.

"Are you okay?" I look up to see an older gentleman in a flat cap leaning over me, a concerned look on his face, while a dozen or so other people gather round the motionless bicyclist a few yards from me.

Adrenaline courses through my veins, forcing me back onto my feet. A scuff on my right hand tingles as I pull my black baseball cap down. The last thing I need right now is for people to recognize me.

"Yes, I'm good."

It's a lie, but I need to escape this scene as quickly as possible. I can already see the headlines:

Alexander Morgan Sends Man Flying to His Death.
Alexander Morgan Guilty of Manslaughter.

The old man looks unconvinced, but with everyone else's attention focused on the bicyclist, I'm able to make a clean break and dash down the road. I stop several blocks down outside the Three Falcons, an unassuming traditional British pub.

I crane my neck one last time, sending shooting pains up the side of my neck, to check the street behind me. It's times like these that I wish I were an owl. Not only for its perceived wisdom about staying out of trouble, but its ability to look over its shoulder without discomfort.

I push on the gold handle of the pub door, wincing at the pressure on my scraped palm, and enter. The cool air from the interior hitting my skin gives me the sensation that my sweaty black running top is clinging even tighter to my body.

I pass the wraparound bar, a grandfather clock sitting next to a beaten-up wooden piano, and a collection of rustic wooden tables and stools on my way to the restroom, where I rest my hands on the cool porcelain sink and finally allow myself to breathe. After a moment, I turn on the tap and stick my hands underneath, involuntarily jerking back from the sting as the water hits my palm.

You'd think I'd be used to the pain from all the scuffs and

knocks I've accumulated over the years while skateboarding. But my pain threshold seems to have dropped ever since I had to give that up. Just one more thing my team won't let me do. There's too high of an insurance premium on my face to let me deliberately risk damage.

In the mirror, I look pale and sweaty. My pupils are so dilated that I can barely make out the blue of my irises. I try to reassure myself that I am not at fault.

I had the right-of-way.

He jumped the light.

You're not the one at fault here.

But no matter what I tell myself, the guilt in my chest won't subside. I reach for the paper towels, wet a couple, and dab at my hands and knees to remove the embedded stones and stop the blood.

I always seem to fuck everything up. Me and trouble are on a first-name basis. BFFs, you could say. My ride or die. Except I'm a captive on the ride, and God help anyone who crosses my path.

I've learned to expect the worst and hope for the best.

I look into the mirror again before leaving the restroom, taking a moment to tuck my blond hair under my baseball cap and behind my ears.

Shit.

My left earbud.

My heart rate rises as I scan the floor, glance underneath the urinals, and into the empty stalls and around the sink, but it is nowhere to be seen.

It must have fallen out when I fell.

Is this how it ends? Some CSI detective finds my earbud, retrieves my fingerprints, and then pins the bicyclist's death on me?

I shake my head. That train of thought is the hot mess

express to either hell or disaster. No one will put two and two together, and I've got plenty more Bose earbuds back at the hotel from my brand deal anyway.

As I make my way back into the pub, a chiming sound from the grandfather clock alerts me to the fact it's already 3 p.m.

Great. If I'm lucky, I've got five minutes, ten max, before the team realizes I'm not where I said I was going to be and a crisis unfolds. I pull my phone out from my shorts pocket and look at the lock screen. No new messages from management or security appear, so it seems I'm safe for a little while longer. I breathe more steadily and return my phone to the other pocket.

I exit the restroom and pass a small scattering of people filling a handful of tables on my way to the bar, intent on finding something to squash the ruminating thoughts in my brain. If you were to ask anyone who knows me or of me, they would tell you my professional title is singer. But that is my secondary profession. The first? Professional overthinker.

I'd win an Olympic gold if they turned it into a sport.

The bartender, mixing someone else's drink, looks up at the mirror behind the wall of spirits as I approach and catches my eye, prompting me to adjust my baseball cap once more. I haven't come this far and gone through all of this to have my cover blown now.

In the time it takes for the older woman beside me to pay for her drink and the bartender to wipe down the surface of the bar with a gray towel, I decide what drink to go for.

"What'll it be?" the bartender asks in a Cockney accent, flinging the towel over his shoulder. His eyes sparkle at me as I pause, trying to make sure I understand him correctly.

"A Jameson on the rocks," I attempt in my best British accent.

His eyes narrow, causing my skin to prickle with icy dread.

Does he think I'm underage?

Will he ask for my ID?
Is my British accent that bad?
Has he recognized who I am?

He doesn't look like one of the nineteen thousand people who'll be attending my show tonight, but I've learned not to assume that no one over the age of forty will know who I am.

"Coming right up." The bartender breaks his stare, raps his knuckles twice on the wooden bar, and grabs a glass, filling it with ice before pouring the drink and turning back to me.

"That'll be six fifty."

My phone puts up a fight as I prize it out of my pocket, sending the other contents inside flying across the floor to hit the metal foot of the table behind me.

"Thanks," I say, my cheeks flushing with embarrassment as I tap my phone on the card reader next to the cash register.

Thank God for Apple Pay. One less thing to potentially expose my identity.

As I grab my drink and turn to retrieve my things, a man who looks about the same age as my father picks them up and hands them to me.

"Here you go," he says with a genuine warmth that reminds me why I love London and the people here.

He slides my hotel key card and metal chip medallion into the palm of my hand.

"Thanks," I say, and quickly push them back into my pocket. I'm unsure if he knows what the chip symbolizes and I don't want to draw attention to it, given the drink in my hand. Especially since my team gave it to me just this morning, in honor of my two-year soberversary.

By the time I find a seat in the back corner of the pub, where I'm least likely to draw attention, the minute hand on the clock has already reached five minutes past the hour. With the hotel a good ten minutes from here and a lobby call time at three thirty to head to the O2 Arena, I barely have time to down my drink and sneak back to my room before anyone notices I'm not in the gym.

I cup my hands around the tumbler, the coolness and condensation of it causing another short burst of pain to flicker across my palm. But I'll take everything that's happened today, all of the pain, if it means I can get a moment of normality. These days, it feels like I'll do pretty much anything to get a stolen moment of freedom.

I close my eyes and imagine myself floating across the concrete on a skateboard, but I'm jolted back to reality by a vibration in my pocket. Taking a deep breath, I pull it out, carefully removing all the contents this time. I place the room key and chip next to the cardboard coaster on the table before seeing Paul, my manager's name, flash on the screen.

I can feel disdain etched across my face at the sight of his name.

I allow the call to ring through, knowing I've probably only got ten to twelve minutes max to get back to the hotel before Paul blows his lid. To gain some time, I shoot a text to my assistant, Lucy.

> Just in the sauna. I'll be back in ten.

Lucy is the easiest one of my team to manipulate into getting some me time. Three dots appear as she begins typing a response, then disappear. My chest instantly tightens. They must already know I'm not in the sauna.

The fear of repercussion tightens its grip round my throat, only to ease slightly when the three dots reappear.

LUCY
Okay. Let me know if you need anything.

I'm good.

Lucy thumbs-up my message in acknowledgment, and I slide the phone back into my pocket along with my room key before grabbing my sobriety chip, flicking it back and forth between my thumb and pinkie finger.

Go to rehab, they said. *It will be great.*
Have therapy, they said. *It will help.*
They're all a bunch of dirty, dirty liars.

Rehab and therapy won't bring Samuel back. Won't resolve the issues, including my sexuality, that I still have to hide from the world. The only things that seem to work are running, working out, sex, and drowning myself in alcohol. Well, after two years of trying it their way, I'll be damned if I continue to put myself through hell by digging up the past and ignoring solutions that work.

It's called the past for a reason after all.

My phone vibrates again, forcing me to pull it out of my pocket once more. This time it's a message rather than a call from Paul.

PAUL
Rob checked the sauna. Where are you?

Ugh. Can't Paul get off my back for one minute? Surely that's not too much to ask for, is it?

I take a look at the whiskey in front of me, then back at the chip. I grab the tumbler and down it in one. The back of my throat burns and I instantly feel the alcohol rushing through my veins. The hairs on the back of my neck stand upright. Oh, how

I've missed the taste. How it releases the tension in my body, slows my heart rate down, and calms my brain.

I get up from the stall, leaving the chip behind on the table. Keeping my head down as I make my way past the tables and out through the door onto the street, I begin typing rapidly.

> Tell Rob to wait by the side entrance on Harwood Ave. I'll be there in ten minutes.

It actually takes twelve minutes, because as I pass where the accident happened, I see the cyclist being loaded into an ambulance on a stretcher, and pause. He still seems alive, much to my relief. I finally stop on the opposite side of the street from the hotel and rest my back against a lamppost, facing away from its historic red-bricked exterior, to catch my breath.

Given the wrath I would have faced from Paul and Connie, my publicist, if I'd actually killed the cyclist, I can tolerate whatever awaits me inside. I chance a quick look at the door, where a few fans are loitering.

I momentarily debate whether to wait until they move on or just make a dash for it, when I see Rob's tall dark frame on the other side of the glass. He turns his head left and right, scanning the street, before clocking me and nodding. One of the fans turns to follow the direction of his nod and squeals as she spots me. I dash across the street, weaving through the cars, and somehow manage to make it past the fans and through the door that Rob holds open before they can snap any pictures.

As we make our way along the hallway toward the elevator, Paul intercepts us. He starts to grill me in a lowered voice.

"Where have you been?" A vein in his neck bulges.

"I went for a run around Regent's Park to clear my head." I cross my arms over my chest.

A hotel guest attempts to approach me, pen and pad in hand,

but Rob cuts them off, keeping them at a distance. All I can do is smile and wave while Paul keeps me moving into the elevator.

Once the doors close, Paul casts me the look I fear the most: disappointment fused with anger. It never fails to make me feel small and disobedient.

"We don't have time for you to just go out for a run whenever you want. It's not safe for you to go out by yourself. If you're going to go out, you need to take Rob with you."

"Cause that won't draw any attention. Plus, it's not like Rob can keep up with me." I nudge Rob's belly with my elbow. Rob's brows furrow as he looks down at me. His six-foot three-hundred-pound body overshadows my five-foot-eight frame.

"I couldn't, but one of the local security team could," he says.

"I know how much you value your freedom, but you can't just go out on your own without protection. Especially when there are hundreds of people waiting outside," Paul cuts in. The elevator jolts as we reach the fifth floor, making his glasses slide down his nose.

I feel even smaller, like a child being scolded for doing something any other human—well, one that isn't as famous as I am—gets to do.

"I know. I know. It won't happen again, I promise," I say. I keep my head down, knowing I will no doubt be seeking forgiveness again in the future rather than asking for permission to do anything.

As the doors open, Rob does a quick scan of the hallway to ensure the coast is clear before we exit. We walk down the hallway on the royal blue carpet, passing a table with an old rotary telephone on it and a scattering of framed pictures of trains and railway stations on our way toward the Presidential Suite.

I take a few deep breaths to brace myself, knowing the rest of the team is waiting inside, as Rob taps the key on the card reader.

The fuss starts as soon as I enter. They are all loitering around the long oak table, which is littered with a dozen Brewed coffee cups and enough paperwork to deforest the Amazon jungle. It makes me question whether my tour really is carbon neutral.

Before anyone has a chance to address me directly, I swiftly turn to the right, making my way through the bedroom and into the bathroom, and attempt to shut the door behind me. Paul's hand stops it from closing. Connie stands behind him, in a silk blouse and pencil skirt, holding a can of Diet Coke in one hand and flicking strands of her blond bob behind her left ear with the other.

"Alex, we don't have time for this." He rolls his eyes.

"But I need to shower before we head out." Swirling anger rises in my gut.

"There are showers at the venue," he says, his eyes narrowing.

I know this, but I'll be damned if I don't try to grab at least one more moment to myself before the machine kicks in.

"Surely you don't want the paparazzi and fans outside to see me like this?" I question. I stretch out my hands, showing off the scrape on my palm, and then gesture at my disheveled appearance.

It's the only angle I can think of that will appeal, if not to Paul, then at least to Connie, whose job it is to ensure I look my best when it comes to public exposure.

Paul briefly glances at Connie before returning his attention to me.

"Well, you should've thought of that before you went and did your disappearing act. We're already late for soundcheck, and the doors open in two hours."

Stolen Moments

Paul pushes the door open wider and gestures at me to return to the bedroom.

I drop my shoulders in defeat and follow Connie back into the main room where everyone is now waiting by the door, ready to go.

Leaving the hotel is a military-style operation, complete with decoy cars, additional security guards to back up Rob, and a clear path out—all with the goal of reducing any threats to my safety. It also hammers home the perceived recklessness of my actions this afternoon.

When I emerge from the hotel, the size of the crowd seems to have exploded. It's almost equivalent to those I experienced two months ago on the South American leg of the tour. Fans had camped outside the hotels in Buenos Aires, Rio de Janeiro, and Mexico, singing and playing my songs at all hours of the night.

Thankfully, unlike those hotels, the Landmark has a private road at its front entrance that fans aren't allowed on, which makes getting into the waiting vehicles easier. Lucy, Rob, Paul, Connie, and I get into the first black Mercedes sprinter. The rest of my entourage jumps into two other waiting vehicles.

The radio drowns out the screaming fans outside as we pull away from the hotel and onto Marylebone Road, speeding off toward the O2.

"It seems like the whole of London has come down with Alexander Morgan fever this week, and boy, can we see why!" the DJ says. "Tonight kicks off the first of his seven sold-out shows at the O2, and we'll be there to bring you all the exclusive news. Plus, stay tuned for your chance to win tickets to join me, Abbie McCarthy, and meet the man himself anytime you hear his latest single, *My Anchor*, this week on Capital FM."

Although I've been doing this for ten years now, it's only in the last couple that my career has gone stratospheric. My team has made a deliberate push to move me away from teen sensation to credible solo artist, starting with the release of *It's You That I Need*. It has been a gift in one sense that my music is finally getting the recognition I've always wanted, but it's also a curse, with all the restrictions and added security measures it brings.

While Paul, Connie, and Lucy discuss the schedule, I sink lower into the leather seat, savoring these last few golden moments of calm before the madness starts once more.

The madness of the first show here in London has everyone running round like headless chickens as they try to get me from my dressing room to the stage before the show starts.

Sound check overran by an hour due to technical issues, setting everything else back, including the meet and greet, and now I'm rushing underneath the stage to the end of the catwalk, with my stylist, Laurie. She drops to her knees as we reach the end and stares up at me, panic strewn across her face.

"I can't get the zip to close. Can you try sucking in your stomach in a little more?"

The buzzing sound of the crowd can be heard over the intro video as she frantically pulls at the zipper. I do my best to help, exhaling and trying to shrink my abs and glute muscles so she can button the fly, but all the working out I've done to buff up means my leather pants are so tight they're practically cutting my circulation off. Laurie reaches for the talcum powder by her knees, shoving more on the skin around the waistband.

I hear Freddy kickstart the playback in my in-ear monitors.

Damn. I have less than thirty seconds before the toaster lift springs me up onto the stage in front of nineteen thousand people, who are getting louder with every passing second.

I pull at the waistband, hoping Laurie can snap the buttons in place. A wardrobe malfunction is the last thing I need during my first show in London.

"Just use a safety pin, anything, to hold me in for now," I say. My heart rate soars, not from the adrenaline, but the fear of what will happen if we don't get this locked down quickly.

Nodding, Laurie pulls a safety pin from her fanny pack and quickly secures my fly in place, then jumps off the toaster lift just before it propels me up onto the stage.

I land in one piece, my heart settling slightly, and hold my position for eight counts before the opening guitar riff of *Compare To You* kicks in. I hear the screams, take in the flashes and sound, and then notice a cool draft. It's not coming from the wind machines in front of me, but from down below.

My gaze moves slowly from the crowds in front of me down to my legs. The spotlight reflects off the safety pin on the floor —it didn't withstand the impact of the landing. Neither did the Velcroed side seams, apparently. My black leather trousers are no longer in place around my hips, but are instead hanging halfway down my legs.

Fuck!!!

2. Christopher
Thursday

Could this day be any longer?
I tap away on the door handle with my fingers and feel another wave of irritation rise as the cab continues to wait, despite the traffic light having turned green, for an elderly woman with a walker to cross the road.

By the time we pull up to the Landmark Hotel, six hours later than I had planned, my dinner plans with Stephen cancelled, and out an extra five pounds more than I'd expected to be for the ride, I am beyond feeling pity or compassion for anyone. I reluctantly tap my phone on the card reader, grab my rucksack, and step out of the taxicab, rolling my eyes at the absurdity of the past twenty-four hours.

God, I don't miss living in London.

"Good luck getting your luggage back!" the taxi driver shouts.

The wave of irritation turns into a tidal wave. Damn British Airways.

"Thanks," I manage through a gritted smile.

As I attempt to make my way into the hotel, I pull at the

neck of my brown hoodie. The late-night summer's heat, a rarity in London, is oppressive, and a crowd of hundreds of eager young girls and women, many looking at me with hunger in their eyes, blocks the twenty yards between me and the hotel entrance.

"Are you here with Alexander?" asks one of them.

"Alexander who?" I attempt to edge past her with a stern look.

"Oh my God, you're joking right?" another girl says, stepping toward me.

"Nope, afraid not," I say, trying to keep moving through the growing crowd toward the hotel entrance. If I don't get in before the clock strikes midnight, I'm going to turn into a pumpkin, or even worse, a gremlin, and Lord help these girls if that happens. But a third girl pops up in front of me, stopping me in my tracks.

"He's only the biggest pop star on the planet!" she exclaims.

As I look around, I notice numerous handmade posters.

Alexander, Marry Me.

It's You That I Need, Alexander.

No One Compares To You Alexander.

I politely smile and move again toward the hotel entrance, suppressing the flashbacks to my mum's endless lectures that these women are evoking with their relentless questioning.

The doorman, dressed in a top hat and a long winter jacket that looks completely out of place in this summer night's heat, stops me in my tracks.

"Can I help you, sir?" His nostrils flare; his lips purse. He looks me up and down with the same disdain that I managed to hide from my face when confronted by those girls just now. But I guess, unlike me, his resting bitch face never rests.

"Yes, you can let me pass so I can check into the hotel," I say. I press my lips hard together as I finger comb my unkempt brown hair, unwilling to entertain the power play that he seems keen to act out.

Sure, I look far from my best, but wouldn't anyone whose flight from LA was delayed for three hours and then found out their luggage was still five thousand miles away when they arrived at their destination?

"Sorry, sir, and welcome to the Landmark Hotel." His face softens as the words tumble from his mouth, and he finally pulls the wooden door open and steps aside to let me through.

"Check in is on the other side of the hotel," he says as I enter.

I roll my eyes at yet another inconvenience. Maybe the taxicab driver knew about my preference for the rear entrance. The corner of my mouth lifts at the thought.

As I walk through the halls to the front desk, I breathe in the familiar samphire scent that reminds me of childhood summers with my grandma. The long journey through the corridors, with their mix of marble flooring and Persian-style carpentry, makes me want to shoot myself in the head, until I'm taken aback by the familiar sight of palm trees and a scattering of decorations.

It's almost symbolic, if I believed in such things. My current life in LA, embodied by the palm trees in the atrium. And my former life in northwest London, represented by chandeliers, flower vases, and an old-school landline phone with a rotating dial.

The night manager greets me as I reach the reception desk. Her pearly white smile stands out against her golden-brown skin and black uniform.

"Welcome to the Landmark Hotel, sir. How may I help you?"

"I'm here to check in; Christopher Foster," I say, removing my backpack from my shoulders, retrieving my passport, and passing it over to her. The passport looks even more worn out and beaten-up than I feel.

"Just one moment, sir, while I pull up your reservation."

As the woman looks through her computer, I take a moment to center myself and breathe. I'm here now. The nightmare journey is over.

Yes, I may be sleep deprived.

Yes, I may have missed catching up with my best friend Stephen over dinner.

Yes, I may be without clothes until my luggage catches up with me, but I am here now, and that's all that matters.

"I can't seem to locate your reservation, sir. Could it be held under a different name?"

"Why would my booking be under a different name?" I respond sharply, catching myself as I do. Once again, my mum flashes into my mind, and how she would have reprimanded me for speaking so rudely to someone who was only trying to help.

The night manager laughs. "We tend to have a lot of famous people staying here, and they all stay under pseudonyms. You wouldn't believe some of the names they use. Robert Downey Jr. stayed here as Tony Stark once, and Daniel Craig's team made me put him down as Minnie Mouse."

Her eyebrows rise alongside her smile, immediately diffusing my frustration. I guess I'm not the first angry guest she's had to deal with today, and no doubt I won't be the last.

"I'm sorry, it's been a hell of a day," I say. "I'm here for my sister's wedding next weekend, and her fiancé took care of all the hotel arrangements. The booking may be held under Daniel Reed."

"Ah yes, here we go." The night manager clicks her mouse and prints out a document.

Well, at least one thing of mine has been found today.

"I have one booking here under Daniel Reed for ten nights, which I am assuming is yours?"

"Yes, that's correct."

"Great. If I could just get you to fill out this form, please, and also if I could get a credit card for any incidentals." She slides the paperwork across the counter and hands me a weighted pen as I pass over my credit card and start completing the form.

Surely this should all be automated by now.

After I hand back the paperwork, she returns my credit card and passport and starts going over all the hotel details. I have no patience for it at this ungodly hour. But the nagging voice of my mother, telling me to show some respect, reappears once more, and I force myself to smile and nod along.

"Breakfast is included in your booking and is served from 7 to 11 a.m. in the atrium, just up on your left where the palm trees are. The gym and spa are open from 7 a.m. to 8 p.m. and are located one floor down. The elevator to the fifth floor is just across from us on the right. I've noted the Wi-Fi details down for you on the inside of the room key holder." She hands me the key. "Do you have any questions?"

"I'll let you know if I need anything," I reply. I won't. I can think of very few circumstances in which I'll need her help, but manners don't cost you anything.

A yawn escapes my mouth as tiredness washes over me. All I want to do now is creep into bed and pull the duvet over me.

"Will you be needing any help with your luggage, sir?" She nods at the bellboy standing behind me at the concierge desk.

"I'm good, thank you." I slide the key into the pocket of my brown sweatpants, return my backpack to my shoulders, and muster up the last of the energy I have to make my way across the foyer.

As I press the button for the elevator, I hear a flurry of activity nearby. Muffled screams, coming from outside the hotel, get louder and then quieter again, probably from the doors opening and closing at the entrance.

The lift doors open, and as I make my way in, I feel a looming presence behind me.

"I'm going to need you to step aside, sir, and wait for the next elevator."

As I turn, I'm confronted by a towering, bald-headed Black man with a goatee beard, who is staring down at my not-so-short five-eleven, one-hundred-fifty-five-pound self.

There's a steely determination in his eyes, but this American douchebag picked the wrong person to mess with tonight.

"Excuse you?! I think you'll find in this country that we wait our turn. You can help yourself to the next lift, thank you very much."

The shock on his face tells me he's not used to having people fire back at him, and it's confirmed when I hear a slight chuckle from behind him.

"It's fine, let's just get to the room," I hear another American voice say.

I can't quite make out who it's coming from. The mountain in black takes up my entire field of vision. But I'm guessing it's someone important, given that this guy, who must be security personnel, refuses to take his glare away from me. As four more people make their way in, I'm forced into the right corner of the wooden elevator, right by the golden panel with the lift buttons.

I take note as they squeeze themselves into the space: Another security person with an earpiece in. A petite red-haired woman, struggling under the weight of a dozen items. Yet another bald-headed guy wearing oval-shaped glasses and with a poker face, who looks like he'd be a dab hand at cards. And finally, a blond woman with a bob whose physique is so slim as to be bordering on anorexic. And someone else, the owner of the mysterious voice, in the middle of all of them.

"Which floor?" I ask no one in particular.

"Three." The blond-haired woman, lost in her phone, barely acknowledges me.

"Six," the bald-headed guy with glasses says, in a monotone voice.

The two security guards share what seems to be a coded look as they take in the control board and then me.

"Which room are you staying in?" the big guy asks, deadpan.

"What's it to you?" I retort.

God, these fucking Americans.

My difficult people quota for the day has not only already been met, but exceeded.

"Which room?!"

I tense at his domineering tone.

After a couple of awkward seconds, I reach for the room key in my pocket. The bigger security guard lurches forward, reaching for my arm, stopping just as I pull out the card holder. I open the flap to reveal the number and wave it in his face.

"Room 506. Now, which room are you in?" I puff my chest outward.

I'm not going to cower like I used to when confronted by an intimidating man.

Another chuckle comes from the only person in the lift I still can't make out.

"Not everyone is a threat, Rob. Leave the man be," says the American voice again.

When the lift doors eventually close and the security guard steps aside, I finally see the reason for all the commotion. A strikingly handsome guy, a couple inches shorter than me, stands diagonally opposite in the lift, with eyes so ocean blue they could wash me away.

A handful of sun-kissed golden locks are interwoven through his light-brown hair, which is styled perfectly, sliding backward. A few stray hairs linger just by his left eye. For a shorter guy, he's built like a Greek Adonis. A tight-fitted white T-shirt accentuates his tan and showcases a rippling six—or is that an eight?—pack.

I inhale deeply, realizing that the sight of him momentarily took my breath away, and move my gaze to the framed picture next to him when I catch myself staring a split second too long and his eyes meet mine. I'm relieved when the blond-haired woman cuts through the silence.

"It looks like the outfit malfunction has gone down rather well online. Alexander's big reveal seems to be trending across all the social platforms." She raises one hand to air quote "big reveal," and then continues to scroll through the phone without looking up.

I laugh inwardly to myself. What a world to live in where the only issue of the day seems to be a wardrobe malfunction.

"What's so funny?" The hot guy's ocean-blue eyes catch mine.

I feel like a deer in the headlights.

Shit.

Did I just laugh out loud?

My mouth gets me into so much trouble sometimes. But I'm not going to pander to this guy either, even if he is hot as hell. Especially after the day I've just had.

"Here you all are complaining about an outfit malfunction, and I literally only have the clothes on my back after my luggage got lost today. The woman upstairs is clearly having a laugh at my expense." I shoot my gaze upward to the ceiling.

"What woman?" The confused look on his face is both endearing and compounds my frustration at how Americans so often take things literally.

"God," I say, pursing my lips. That seems to make a smile break out on his face, and I reluctantly force the right side of my mouth to rise.

"Well, seems like we're both having shitty days then."

I ponder momentarily, debating how to respond. Sarcastically, sympathetically, or any of the other –allys? But before I do the lift stops. Both women exit.

"See y'all in the morning." They wave, and the doors close behind them as we continue up.

The bald-headed guy with glasses, who up until this point has only uttered one word and has been typing furiously away on his phone, pipes up.

"I've emailed the day sheet alongside the one printed in your room for tomorrow. Glam is at ten. Call time is eleven. The junket runs straight through till five. Connie's already briefed the journalists that tonight's mishap is off topic so you're not caught off guard." The way he punctuates each sentence gives the hot guy just enough time to nod his head.

As the lift reaches the fifth floor, I go to step out, but the burly security guard stops me, pushing me back to let the hot guy and the others out first.

"Nice to see chivalry is still alive and well," I say, my foot-in-mouth disease catching me by surprise once again.

Sarcasm clearly doesn't land well with either of the security guards or the bald guy in glasses. But another chuckle comes from the hot guy's mouth, reassuring me, albeit briefly, that I'll live to see another day and won't feel the wrath of his security.

Making my way out of the lift behind them, I instantly see why Kelly and Daniel chose this as their wedding venue. The decor is elegant but understated. Sconces adorn the cream-colored walls, held up by golden angel wings. The royal blue carpets are framed by a Versace-style pattern on the perimeter.

I stop briefly at the gold plaque highlighting which directions the rooms are in, and my shoulders drop when I realize that my room is in the same direction they already are walking in. *Great*.

I count each room number as I pass—500, 502, 504—before

I get to 506, and then notice that everyone else has stopped at the next room up from mine, at what I can just make out to be the Presidential Suite.

I retrieve the door key from my pocket and after running my finger over the smooth wooden texture, press it against the card reader. But the key isn't game. Despite several attempts, the door refuses to open. My anger bubbles up as I slam the key against the reader, harder each time. Why must all hotel doors be this difficult to open?

The three of them linger outside their room, staring at me, which doesn't make it any easier.

"By all means, don't let me stop you." I motion with my hand to their door. I'm not here for their entertainment or amusement.

"Here, let me."

The hot guy walks toward me, taking the key out of my hand as if I'm some damsel in distress. He gently slides it over the card reader, unlocking the door on his first attempt. Smugness comes over his face.

If he wasn't so attractive, I would wipe that look right off it.

But my bed is now in sight, and that is all that truly matters.

"Thank you," I say, opening the door wider, as he hands me back my door key. A surge of electricity races across my skin when his hand touches mine.

"I hope you get your suitcase back tomorrow. Did they say where it would be?"

His question stops me in my tracks as I enter the room, making me turn around.

"Still back home at LAX. Thank God I packed my gym gear," I say, twisting my arm behind me to pat my backpack.

He pauses for a beat, catching my eye.

Now I see why all those girls are waiting outside the hotel.

Close-up, he is even more breathtaking.

"You're from LA too?"

A sparkle in his eye shows me there is genuine interest, and I wonder, if only for a fleeting moment, if he might be interested in me, before reminding myself how stupid I sound. The thought that this heartthrob, with hundreds of women outside screaming his name, could be into someone like me is ridiculous.

"Yeah, I moved there a couple of years back," I say nonchalantly, before adding, "I hope you don't have to deal with any more *BIG* reveals this week."

I quickly close the door and slam my back against it, mortified at what I just said. Something sharp in my backpack causes a shooting pain to run through my spine.

What the fuck was I thinking?

Did I see a mischievous smile on his face as I shut the door? Or is my mind playing tricks on me again? I turn and peer through the peephole. He's still standing there, shaking his head. The fish-eye lens makes his face and muscular frame more round.

After what seems like an hour, but is probably more like three seconds, I reach for the door handle. But just before I pull it down, he turns and walks away. The sound of his footsteps on the carpet get quieter before I hear the loud sound of a door shutting.

I let out a large exhale and lean forward, banging my forehead against the door.

What a dick move.

I take off my backpack, placing it on the table beside the television, next to the notepad and guest services folder. Like all hotel rooms, the bed is tidily made, with two bedside tables on either side and lights that match those in the hallway. The golden curtains are already drawn. I fling my sneakers off next to one of the two golden armchairs and remove my socks before reaching across to my backpack and retrieving the miniature toiletries bag British Airways gives out in business class. It was the only redeeming quality of my nightmare travel journey. Bag in hand, I make my way into the bathroom.

The coolness of the marble-tiled floor catches me by surprise. But it's not nearly as shocking as my reflection in the mirror. God, I've seen better days. If I didn't know any better, I'd think I was thirty-seven and not just turned twenty-seven. The dark circles under my eyes are big enough to hold all my physical and emotional baggage and then some. My disheveled, short brown hair, completely void of its usual right-side parting, looks like I've had one too many big nights on the town and am paying the price for it.

I quickly brush my teeth, cursing the overhead lighting as I do so, and strip down to my boxers. I leave my clothes scattered next to the bathtub and grab my phone before making my way to the bed.

The Egyptian cotton sheets caress my bare skin soothingly as I settle in, and I plump the pillows before turning my attention to my phone, ignoring messages from my sister and mum. Curiosity has gotten the better of me.

After firing up TikTok, I go to the search tab, but I struggle to recall the hot guy's name.

Think, Christopher. Think.

As if on cue, I hear the faint chant beyond the curtains.

Alex. Alex. Alex.

That's it.

I quickly type in *Alex*, *London*, and *wardrobe malfunction*.

When the results load up, I am greeted by hundreds of videos, all from different angles. Alex is catapulted into the air and lands on stage with his trousers hanging halfway down his legs.

I scroll through one video, then another, until I land on one that's zoomed in close enough to reveal that he has quite the package. Clearly, the hashtag wasn't lying.

I'm tempted to scroll further and find out more about this Alex guy, or is it Alexander? But I've got a big day ahead tomorrow, and I need all the sleep I can get to face my mother. I roll over to turn off the lamp and put down my phone, hoping that I can get a decent night's sleep. But clearly the day isn't done playing with me just yet.

The squeals and louder chants of *Alex! Alex! Alex!* from behind the curtain get louder, as if the crowd below has been lifted up to right outside my room.

I pull one of the pillows over my head, attempting to drown out the sounds of the screaming girls below.

Please tell me they'll all be gone by tomorrow.

3. Alexander
Friday

Who *was* that guy?!

No one speaks to me like that, not even—nope not going to think about him. I push the name aside to return my focus to those dreamy hazel eyes, limned with a green outer ring. Each word, spoken in that British accent, hypnotized me like a snake charmer.

The sting I'd felt when he slammed the door in my face has been replaced by somersaults in my stomach—and heat rising on the back of my neck.

Ever since I shot to fame ten years ago off the back of a viral video, I've been surrounded by people who pander to my every need. But he didn't seem to give a fuck who I was. And apart from Paul, who tells me what to do, when to do it, and how—which I have to admit is pretty useful for a guy with ADHD—everyone else seems to go along with what I say.

But even then, Paul usually draws a line. He knows where to stop, although it's likely due to fear of losing his job if he oversteps the mark. Yet, elevator guy didn't care.

The minibar underneath the widescreen TV in the lounge

catches my eye, calling out to me like a siren to a sailor in the night. I force myself up off the beige couch. I close my eyes as I grab the door handle, hoping that somehow the cleaning staff ignored my team's request to remove all alcohol from my room and replenished it with some spirits, wine, or heck—even a beer or three.

I mean, surely my need for a drink is understandable, right? With everything I have to hide, what else will push the intrusive thoughts away?

With one strong yank, the door opens, but my hopes are crushed when I open my eyes. A half dozen bottles of Fuji water, two cans of Diet Coke, and a couple of Sprite Zeros stare back at me.

Can't I even get a little sugar to ride out the adrenaline from the concert? I shrug, admitting defeat. I kick the door shut before toeing off my Nike high-tops and collapsing back onto the couch.

The four empty chairs, arranged on either side of the sofa, set off a pang in my chest. They're yet another reminder of how lonely I get after a show. There's a definite letdown to performing in front of crowds of people and then being locked away in a suite all alone. It's like going a hundred miles an hour down the freeway and then making an emergency stop. It's just unnatural. I wince as the faint chants of my fans echo down on the street below. Even *they* get to be all together.

Fine. I have to do something to distract myself. I grab the remote and flick aimlessly through cable channels, hoping to find something that will keep me awake until the adrenaline wears off so I can finally pass out. Not only that, but stave off the intrusive thoughts about the start of tonight's show.

I was so humiliated.

Standing there.

Exposed.

To nineteen thousand people.

I mean it's bad enough when it happens in front of *one* person, but the whole arena saw it and now it's all over socials for the world to see. Maybe I should look on TikTok to see if what Connie was saying in the elevator was true. I drop the remote and reach into my jeans for my phone.

Over the next hour I go further and further down the rabbit hole. First, I watch videos of myself exposed on stage, terror plastered across my face, before my dancers move in front of me to shield my motions as I pull the sides of my fly back up and pin it closed again. Then I get caught up in the videos discussing whether I've had a penis enlargement operation or not.

The whole thing makes my body shake.

The objectification.

The double standard of being an American artist means I need to have a good voice and be physically attractive at the same time. And that's how I got into this mess tonight in the first place. If Paul and Connie hadn't pressured me to bulk up for the shoot with *Men's Health* on Sunday, I would have fitted into my pants and none of this would have happened.

I wish I could magically remove the pressure of needing to have a perfect physique. Eat what I want, drink what I want, when I want, without a care in the world. Instead, I'm stuck on this shitty protein diet. No carbs, no sugars, and definitely no alcohol. It might as well be called the *fuck my life* diet.

And what's worse, the gym isn't even open, so I can't go hardio on the cardio and try to lose some of this muscle. Paul had picked a hotel that only opens their gym during the day, justifying his decision by saying it's one of the best for security in London. Although I hadn't noticed any security cameras in the elevator earlier. Maybe Jay Z and Beyoncé had asked for them to be removed when they stayed here?

"Looks like the only workout I'll be getting tonight is with you," I say to my right hand. I shuck off my white Calvin Klein boxer briefs and begin to rub my shaft.

The guy from the elevator pops into my mind as soon as I close my eyes. I picture him looking down at me with a commanding presence, hazel eyes staring deep into mine, His authoritative voice has me wanting—yearning—for him to take me. I give up trying to edge myself. I can't contain the testosterone coursing through my veins, and instead I pound my hand vigorously up and down my shaft, chasing my orgasm, and climaxing almost as soon as I start. My body spasms momentarily, left leg twitching, until I relax into a state of calm.

As I make my way into the shower to clean myself up, I wonder if the elevator guy is still awake. The monsoon shower washes away the remnants of myself, along with any guilt I had about breaking my sobriety this afternoon. The horror from what happened on stage also recedes, leaving me think about the guy next door and what I can do to get his attention.

I grab a towel after turning off the shower, wrapping it tightly round my waist, and grab another to dry my hair. The mirror light perfectly accentuates my eight-pack and V-line. Maybe all this hard work and restrictive diet isn't that bad. The wry smile on my face stares back at me.

Applying moisturizer to my face, I breathe in the summer flower scent, and instantly begin wondering what the guy smells like, tastes like, feels like. *Shit*. I've only known this guy for five minutes and he's already gotten into my head like an earworm.

He's probably sound asleep and couldn't give less of a fuck about me if he tried. In fact, he had pretty much said so in the elevator. Which only makes me want him more.

Maybe I should go knock on his door?

Didn't he say his luggage got left behind in LA?

Maybe I could offer him some of my gym gear to wear?

No, he said he had some in his bag.

Maybe I could bring him something else. But then what if it doesn't fit? He was a good couple of inches taller than me, and no matter what anyone says, those couple of extra inches matter.

My mind races, remembering other details.

He lives in LA too. When this tour is over, I could actually meet up with him. Then a thought grinds me to a complete stop. I don't even know if he's gay. Come to think of it, his unkempt look, brown hoodie, and sweatpants didn't scream gay to me.

The towel around my waist starts to rise, and I feel the blood pumping through my body again.

Nope.

Don't let yourself get carried away; you need to sleep.

I push my boner down.

Even if there is a remote chance that he is, one, in fact gay, and two, likes you, you need to play it cool. And don't do the usual, fall fast and hard, only for it to all come crashing down.

I retreat back to the bedroom, throw the towels onto the armchair next to my bed, and reach for my phone. I reluctantly set my alarm for 8:15 a.m., leaving me only five hours to sleep. Six if I'm lucky. But at least this allows me to get in an hour workout before glam arrives and I'm stuck repeating myself for six hours on the press junket.

How in the ham sandwich is it already 8:15? I stretch out my arm, blindly trying to shut off the piercing sound of the devil disguised as an alarm clock.

I swear I only closed my eyelids five seconds ago.

The sunlight peeks in through a crack in the blackout curtains, which I clearly didn't draw properly.

The pounding in my head feels like I've been hit by a forklift truck. I try to lift it from the pillow and immediately regret it. What kind of fresh hell is this?

I grab the water bottle next to my phone and swallow it down three gulps, hoping it will wash away whatever this is, then message Rob.

> I'm heading to the gym in ten.
>
> Bring painkillers.

ROB
> Sure thing, boss.
>
> Grabbing the coffees now too.

For all the crap I give Rob and have put him through over the years, he's been a solid guy. He's learned my morning ritual by heart, knowing that I'm intolerable until I've had an iced Americano. And apart from Paul, he's pretty much been there since day one and has witnessed all the mad shit that's unfolded. In fact, he was the first one to find out I was gay when he walked in on me and Samuel. Surprisingly, he was totally cool about it all. It made me check my judgment about the types of people I expect to be homophobic.

After freshening up in the bathroom, I make my way into the walk-in closet to pick out gym wear. I throw on fresh briefs and one of my twenty black Nike running tops. I almost grab a pair of gray shorts before opting instead for tight pink ones with a five-inch inseam. They'd caused quite a stir when I was papped in them a few weeks back. If they don't capture elevator guy's attention and help me work out whether he's into guys or not, nothing will. A grin rises to my lips at the thought.

"Boss!" Rob shouts, the sound of the hotel room door closing behind him.

"Just a minute."

I slide on socks and sneakers and quickly grab a new box of earbuds before making my way out to the living room, where Rob patiently waits in one of the chairs, a packet of ibuprofen in one hand and my coffee order in the other.

"You're a life saver."

Rob smirks as I take the iced coffee and pop two pills, glugging them down.

"Ready, boss?" He pushes himself out of the chair and toward the door.

"Ready, as I'll ever be," I reply, following him out.

As we make our way down the hallway, my heart sinks at the sight of the Do Not Disturb light shining on the gold plaque beside elevator guy's door. So much for potentially bumping into him in the gym. Aside from the cleaning trolley halfway down the hallway, it's eerily quiet in the hotel this morning.

When the elevator door opens, a Chinese family holding their luggage steps to one side to let Rob and me in. Their little girl looks up at Rob and quickly reaches for her mom's hand, as if scared of him. Rob instantly notices this and slides a hand into his pocket, withdrawing a candy and offering it to her. I smile. Rob has a softer side that very few get to see. The elevator stops to let them out on the ground floor, and the little girl waves goodbye. I glance over to see a huge smile on Rob's face while we continue down to the basement.

When we get there, I'm relieved to find there's no one else in the space aside from the three young women checking guests in at the desk, giving me free rein to use whatever equipment I wish. Rob leaves me to it, standing watch inside the pool room and keeping an eye on me through the glass window that looks into the gym.

I step onto the treadmill with a cup full of water and pop in my earbuds as I fire up the speed to nine miles per hour, cranking up *Sex on Fire* by Kings of Leon. Thankfully, the headache has subsided with the coffee and ibuprofen, but a wave of nausea has emerged in its place.

I probably shouldn't work out while feeling like this, but I don't want a repeat performance of last night's inadvertent strip tease, and if that means doing a load of cardio and feeling slightly nauseous while doing it, then so be it.

No pain, no gain after all.

With each successive mile, the nausea gets stronger. Sweat drips from my body all over the treadmill. A cramp forms in my leg when I hit the four-mile mark, and it feels like every stride is pushing whatever's in my stomach up through my esophagus. The burning sensation reaches my throat as the five-mile mark approaches.

I crank the speed up, hoping that if I can just make it another minute the sensation will subside, but my body has other plans.

I desperately reach for my cup of water, trying to hold it steady and drink while my legs run away from me, but I can already tell it's too late. I reach for the emergency stop button, but just as my hand comes down on it, the wave of nausea turns into a tsunami. Dread washes over me.

This.

Is.

Not.

Happening.

Right.

Now...

4. Christopher
Friday

At first, I thought it was just hunger pains. But when I smelled the coffee and saw a short brown-haired woman walk past my room and into Alexander's room next door with a croissant, the pang in my chest tells me otherwise.

I'm sure she's just part of the team, but a quick look at my watch tells me it's just past nine and the bald guy had said Alex's glam wasn't till ten. Shaking my head and closing my door behind me, I try to stop myself from thinking that she, rather than an alarm, is his morning wake-up call.

By the time I make my way down to the elevator, a flurry of activity is happening in the Tower Suite opposite of my room. Three different entrances are being used to load things in— makeup cases, clothes, and a variety of food and beverages, including a tray of pastries and fruit. The gold plaques on either side of the suite's main door scream *Notice Me!* and seem more befitting for a pop star of Alex's popularity than the room next to mine.

But then as my therapist says, when we assume, it makes an ass out of u and me.

When no one's looking, I nick a jam tart and escape into the elevator, smirking at my reflection in the gold-plated doors as they close.

I slide the tart into my mouth. I need all the energy I can get today.

Another yawn escapes my mouth involuntarily as I reach the gym reception, reminding me that the sleeping pills, peppermint tea, and blackout blinds all failed to fight off my jet lag and insomnia and allow me to sleep.

You'd think, given my travel-heavy job in international marketing, that I'd have found something that works by now, but no.

For a hotel, the gym reception seems over staffed. Two women who've clearly spent a bit too much time with a cosmetologist are crammed behind a small white desk. A third hovers against a shelf full of towels, reapplying lipstick. All are preoccupied with each other, gossiping like girls at a prom. They don't notice me until I approach the desk.

"Can we help you, sir?" one asks when I pause, trying to work out where the gym is. She gives me a wide smile.

"First time here?" another asks. She bumps the first girl out of the way with her hip, and throws her a side eye, wiping the smile from her face.

"Yes," I respond bluntly. I'm in no mood for this.

She looks at me, but I only stare.

"Well, let me show you around," she says. She cocks her head toward a door next the desk, waves her key card over the door's reader and then motions me forward.

Just as I'm about to walk through, a dark shadow fills the space, exposing the security guard I'd almost had an altercation with the night before.

Great.

"We need a cleaner in the gym."

His icy tone startles the woman leading me in. She turns and power walks down the hall without uttering another word, leaving me stuck with him.

Maybe I should try being a little more accommodating this time.

"Can I offer a hand?" I force a smile on my face, dialing it back slightly to make it more natural. *See? I can be nice.*

"I need you to stay right there," he says, a hand stretched out to stop me.

A rush of adrenaline goes through me, and I snap back into the snarky tone I'd used last night without thinking.

"Where do you get off telling people what they need to do?" I cross my arms. "Last time I checked, the King hadn't died and anointed you the new king of England. So, if you don't mind, I'm going to get on with my workout."

"I do mind." He moves a step forward, blocking my path. His eyes widen as they stare down at me.

I quickly evaluate my options. Duck under his arm? Knee him in the groin? Before I get a chance to either act or respond, a cleaner appears with a mop and bucket to clean up whatever mess he's made.

Now that the mountain's focus is off me, I'm free to follow them into the gym, where I'm greeted by an overwhelming odor of vomit.

"Bing, bang, bong. Clean up on aisle three. Clean up on aisle three." The words escape my mouth before I think twice about it.

The cleaner and security guard both look over their shoulders back at me. I shrug and wave my hand at the window and treadmill with spew all over them.

It's only when I hear a slight chuckle that I notice Alexander emerging from behind the pillar in the middle of the room. All the color has drained from his face. A hand towel is thrown over his shoulder, and his bare torso reveals abs so defined it's like DaVinci carved him out of marble.

The plastic bag in his hand, holding what must be his gym top, hovers close to the shortest shorts I've ever seen. They accentuate his thick thighs and a bulging crotch that looks even bigger in person. He must have caught me gazing a little too long, because he coughs, bringing my attention back up to his face.

"God, you're a sight for Stevie Wonder's eyes," I say.

"You're quite the comedian, aren't you?" He arches his left eyebrow, and the right side of his lips move in a slight uptick.

I go to take a bow, but he quickly turns his attention to his security guard.

"Could you run this up to the room and bring me down another top?" He holds the bag out.

"Are you sure that's a good idea?" The security guard nods at me.

Alexander hesitates. I see the flicker of doubt appear on his face.

"You heard the man," I say, injecting myself into the conversation.

"I don't take orders from you," he says back. The frown line deepens in his forehead. It's so deep that I momentarily wonder whether Botox would be enough to fix it, or if Polyfilla would do a better job.

"Can you two just fuck and get this sexual tension over with already?" Alexander says, rolling his eyes and shaking his head.

"He's not my type," I say to Alexander, with an *ooo-kay* undertone. "No offense," I say to the security guard, shrugging my shoulders.

"Some taken," he responds, stifling a laugh, and for a moment, I see him softening.

"I'll be alright, Rob, I promise. I just need to finish this workout. And anyway, I'm feeling a lot better now that I've been sick." Some of the color is returning to Alex's cheeks.

"If you're sure? I'll be five minutes max." Rob grabs the bag from Alexander. The two share a knowing glance with each other and then look at me.

"I think I can handle myself if he ends up posing a threat," Alexander says, pointing his thumb at me.

"I'm not so sure. I do have a blackbelt in origami." I place my hands on my hips and arch my brows, triggering another laugh from Alexander as Rob looks on with a perplexed expression.

Clearly his sense of humor isn't as strong as his physicality.

"You know... to fold you into an aeroplane and turn you into a flying fuck I no longer give." I motion flinging a paper plane at him.

Rob opens his mouth to respond, but Alexander stops him, patting him on the chest.

"I'll be fine, and anyway, I could use someone to spot me with the weights." He looks at me to see if I am down, and although I had planned to go for a run to fight off the jet lag and mentally prepare for lunch with my mum, this isn't such a bad alternative.

"Sure," I say, trying to sound as nonchalant as possible to prevent Alexander from getting any inclination that I might enjoy this.

Rob leaves with the cleaner, who's managed to remove all remnants of vomit from the gym, leaving us alone.

There are probably a million people who would kill to be in my position.

Alexander makes his way over to the bench press, grabbing the thirty-two kilo dumbbell weights, and lies back in preparation to lift them, leaving me to follow.

"Big night?" I ask.

There's a nervousness in my tone that reminds me of that

first date feeling. I've never been a fan of small talk, but what do you say to someone with this level of fame?

"Oh, the vomit," he says, pushing the weights up and down above his chest. "No, just woke up feeling crappy this morning. Must be a bug or something."

"Yeah, right," I laugh, rolling my eyes. His exhales get louder with each push up of the dumbbells. My eyes drift down his body, skimming his washboard abs—he definitely has an eight-pack—and pausing on the bulge in his shorts that I couldn't help but dream about last night. "I could barely sleep for hearing those girls screaming your name in ecstasy."

"What girls?" he snaps. He drops the weights and gets up off the bench.

"Calm down, treacle," I say, trying to recover the easy camaraderie we'd just had. "I mean the ones outside the hotel who accosted me when I arrived. They were still chanting your name when I tried to sleep."

I can see why they'd be screaming his name. Those blue eyes, that chiseled jaw, the body that's just the right amount of muscular, all adds up to a breathtaking whole.

"Oh God, I'm sorry. Did they keep you up for long?" He stares intently at me.

I debate whether to tell him the truth: I didn't sleep at all, and that it wasn't helped by the endless videos I had watched of him on TikTok. But I opt for the easier path instead.

"I managed to get off round two-thirty, three. Don't they keep you up?"

"Noise-cancelling headphones," he says, retrieving them from his pocket and shaking them at me. "They're a godsend. You should get a pair."

I feel a wild surge inside from the way he smiles at me. How can a man as devilishly handsome as this be engaging in conversation with me?

"Wanna swap?" He motions to the bench.

"You are joking right?" My gaze is drawn to the dumbbells. "These guns can barely lift ten kilograms, let alone thirty-two."

Before I know it, Alexander is gripping my left bicep leaving me no time to flex to try and save face at how scrawny I am in comparison to him. A surge of electricity rolls across my skin, forcing my body hair to stand upright and my cheeks to flush.

"It's not so bad," he says, letting go. "Here, let me grab you a couple of fifteens, and we'll see if we can get you to bench that."

He heads over to the rack to retrieve the weights, and I find myself being convinced to do something I'd usually never dream of doing. I attempt to make myself comfortable on the bench, adjusting my shoulders as Alexander stands over me, holding the weights in position above my chest.

"Here. Let me just adjust your hands." He twists my wrists forty-five degrees as he passes me each dumbbell.

As I look up, I can almost make out his cock through his shorts.

His abs look like a stairway to heaven, toward lips that could whisper sweet nothings into my ear.

"How does that feel?" he asks, letting go and stepping back slightly.

"Feels great."

I lower the dumbbells toward my chest and attempt to push them back up, trying to keep my attention focused on the ceiling rather than his abs. But the encouraging words I get from Alexander prompt a stirring in my shorts.

Oh no. Not now.

Of all the times I could get an awkward boner, this one is far from ideal.

"That's it. You've got this," he says in that sweet voice of his. Each reassurance makes my cock harden.

"For someone that doesn't like to bench press, it seems like you rather enjoyed that," he says, his gaze drifting from my face to my crotch. My cock is now hard as a rock. Unfortunately, thanks to my boxer briefs, it looks more like the Leaning Tower of Pisa than the Eiffel Tower.

I want the ground to swallow me up. I'd hoped he hadn't noticed, but his line of vision meant it was impossible to not see.

"Well, we can't have you being the only one whose bulge is exposed to the world," I say in a lame attempt to deflect attention away from my growing problem. My reply gives me enough time to quickly get up from the bench and readjust my package.

I turn to face him, trying to think of something else to give my raging hard-on a chance to subside. But as I catch sight of his ripped torso again, I know I'm powerless and will just have to ride this one out.

"You saw that." He says it more as a statement than a question.

Damn. So much for playing it cool.

"No. Only what that woman in the elevator was going on about last night. Some big reveal." I'm unable to keep my eyes from drifting down to his shorts.

The bulge that I looked at from every conceivable angle overnight is now within touching distance. I can't help but wonder even more what it would feel like to get my hands and mouth all over it.

The sound of the gym door opening snaps me back to reality. Rob reappears, brandishing a new black top.

"Here you go, boss." Rob flings it at him, and Alexander grabs it in one quick sweep.

"Cheers!" He sounds slightly uncomfortable as he slides the top on.

Goodbye abs.

"The team are all in the room. They're ready when you are," Rob says. My heart sinks as this brief moment is stolen from us.

I lower my head, but as I look down, I notice a twinge in Alexander's shorts.

No. It can't be.

Did he get aroused too?

I try to shrug it off, but maybe, just maybe, this jock-looking pop star—who seems to be the object of every young girl's fantasy—actually dreams of men instead of women.

"I'm nearly done, just a few more reps, then I'll head up, in say five?" His gaze drifts toward his watch and then back to Rob, before turning to me.

"You good to stick around a few more minutes to offer a helping hand?"

My mouth nearly falls open at the way he says helping hand.

It's all I can do to stop myself from saying, *I can offer more than a helping hand.*

I nod into the awkward silence instead.

"Sure," Rob says, and he moves toward the door, but turns just before he exits. "Want me to order any breakfast to the room?"

"I'm good, but if you're doing another coffee run, I'll get the usual, please."

The usual? What is his usual?

I'm sure the women waiting outside the hotel would know every little detail about him. But before last night, I'd never even heard of Alexander. The only thing I do know right now is that he's an American singer who had a wardrobe malfunction on stage. Oh, and that he could just be the most attractive guy I've ever met.

Alexander snaps me out of my thoughts.

"So, what brings you to town? I realize I don't even know your name."

"Christopher," I say.

"Alex," he responds, offering me his hand to shake formally.

Does he go by Alexander publicly and prefers Alex in private?

His shake, a vice-like grip, sends my mind places that I really need it not to go right now.

"I'm here for my sister's wedding next weekend, so I'm here for all the prewedding shit." I walk back toward the bench press.

"Not a fan of weddings, I take it?"

"Nope. Especially not the family drama that comes with it." I swallow down a lump in my throat, trying to push away the thoughts about why I'm staying here at the hotel and not at my parents' home and why my father won't be attending.

"Families can be the worst."

I briefly catch the pain in his eyes, but I know not to dig too deeply when it comes to family. Alexander slides back on the bench, grabbing the dumbbells to begin the next repetition. The power dynamic changes once more with me towering over him.

"So, why are you here?" I try, tentatively.

"Oh, I'm in town till next Sunday doing a run of shows at the O2," he says. His muscles flex with each thrust, matching the quiet casualness with which he said he's performing at one of the biggest and most prestigious arenas in the world.

Wait.

He's also here for the next ten days? I might get to spend more time with him. My pulse quickens at the thought.

I let out a deep exhale to try and temper my excitement.

"You get much downtime while you're here?"

"Nah, the team's got me working like a dog. I think I might have one day off next Thursday if I'm lucky. When I'm not performing on stage, they've got me doing promo, photoshoots, or recording." His body slumps as if his spirit has left it as he gets back up off the bench.

With a schedule like that, no wonder he looks a little worn down. That probably explains the reason he was sick earlier too.

"Right, I better get back upstairs. Thanks for spotting me this morning. Appreciate it." He goes to shake my hand, but then pulls me in for a hug instead, nodding at Rob through the glass window.

"No problem," I reply. "I should probably head up shortly too, but I think I'll hit the steam room first."

"They have a steam room?" His voice lifts along with his eyebrows.

"Apparently? It's in the changing room." I pause and wonder whether to hedge my bets. "Might be worth you jumping in to sweat out the remainder of the bug that made you sick this morning," I say, walking past him and out the door.

I dare not look back over my shoulder, but I feel his looming presence as I hear two sets of feet follow me. I open the door to the changing room, but my hope quickly turns to disappointment when I see the steam room. It's barely big enough to swing a cat in.

"Looks like there's not enough room to fit both of us in there," he says, leaning against one of the wooden lockers.

I shed my sneakers and remove my socks, shorts, and top by the padded seats in the center of the room, then grab a towel from the rack on the wall and open the door to the steam room. There's a feistiness in him that I just can't help but play along with.

As the steam flows out, I shimmy out of my underwear and hang it up on a hook along with the towel.

"There's just about enough room, if you want to come in," I say, winking.

5. Alexander
Friday

The steam engulfs me, and I let myself be taken completely. Christopher pins me up against the glass room of the steam room, holding my hands above my head. He removes his hand from my left wrist, and slides it down over my abs toward my cock, grasping it firmly.

I am consumed by his touch, his mouth on my neck, when a pounding on the glass snaps me out of my daydream and back to the reality of my hotel shower.

Ugh!

"Didn't you hear me? We need to wrap this up." Rob circles his finger in a clockwise motion while turning off the portable speaker playing Blink 182's *All the Small Things*. This is the second time Rob has ruined my moment with Christopher, albeit this one was in my imagination.

I was already pulling down my shorts to join Christopher in the steam room when Rob had shouted "Bruce!" I know to stop what I'm doing whenever I hear that particular pseudonym. And lo and behold, a second later, two older Eastern European guys had walked into the changing room.

In the aftermath, I'd left without even acknowledging Christopher. It's happened so often over the years that I've been programmed to follow Rob out of the situation and back to safety as quickly as possible. If I had a dollar for every time a moment has been stolen from me in the last ten years, I'd be a very rich man.

"Coming," I say. I turn the shower off, opening the glass door to grab a towel once Rob leaves. Resting one hand on the marble sink, I wipe steam from the mirror with the other. My reflection matches what I feel inside—dejection.

What's a guy gotta do to get his rocks off in this place?

By the time I've popped my Adderall, changed, and sat through Erica working her magic, the transformation is complete. I'm no longer Clark Kent, but Superman, I grab my iced coffee and down the last of it before joining the rest of the team and some of the members of my UK label in the meeting room of my suite.

"What's the agenda, guys?" I ask while walking in. I nod and smile at the familiar faces who look up. Hopefully it will be a short meeting. In other words, pass me the day's itinerary, tell me what I need to do, and then let me get back to daydreaming about Christopher.

I sit down in the only empty seat and ignore what Connie is discussing, instead picking up the call sheet for today. My initialed logo is stamped at the top and a list of media outlets, their reach, interviewer, and interview times fills the rest of the page. At the very bottom, I see that I'm booked to do a TV interview on location and then a late dinner with a film producer at Sexy Fish in Mayfair.

In the middle of the table, an assortment of the daily UK newspapers competes for space with platters of fruit and breakfast pastries. Images of me from last night are plastered across their front covers. My heart sinks as I lay down the call sheet and grab an apple from one of the trays. They all have various takes of the same headline:

Alexander's BIG Reveal.

Alexander's BIG Entrance.

Alexander Arrives in London With a BIG Bang.

I want to be taken seriously as an artist, and have worked hard to transition my music from the pure pop sound that launched my career into a more credible sound to broaden my audience. But headlines like this just objectify my body instead of focusing on the music.

I take a bite of the apple and reach for one of the papers. The story opens with *Teen sensation turned heartthrob wows on opening night of his UK tour.*

I skim through the article. It's void of any references to the evolution of my music or the production values of the show, and is instead focused on my outfits, my looks, and the screaming fans. My chest tightens, my right foot tapping faster with each word I read, until I finally fling the newspaper back onto the table, startling two of the UK promo team members across from me. *Sorry*, I mouth. I smile back at them both when they smile at me and wave away my apology.

"You got that, Alex?" Connie asks. Her eyebrows arch.

"Huh?" I ask, pausing with the apple in front of my mouth.

"The key points to cover," she says. "One, how great it is to be back in your favorite city in the world. Two, *My Anchor* is a shoo-in for number one next week and is your favorite from the album. Three, that you're recording a live album at Abbey Road this week."

"Right," I answer, completing my bite and slouching into the leather chair. I swing back and forth, looking at the 11 p.m. clear time on the call sheet.

That's another twelve hours away, and all I want to do is crawl back into my bed, or Christopher's, and close the door to the world. But I have to remember that this is all I ever dreamed of as a child, to leave behind my small town in Northern California.

In ten days, this touring and promo cycle will be wrapped up. I'll have a couple of months off before the movie we're discussing tonight with the producer is due to begin shooting. Hopefully I'll be able to get some much needed rest.

As the meeting wraps, I quickly hug and say hi to everyone before leaving the suite and walk twenty yards down the hallway to where the press junket will take place. I'm hoping to catch a glimpse of Christopher, but the hall, closely guarded by one of the local security team Rob has brought in, is empty.

Once in the room, I slump into the interview chair, shoulders sagging. My white T-shirt rides up under my open black button-down short-sleeve shirt. The sound guy comes up, passes me the mic pack, and threads the microphone cable up underneath my shirt, attaching it next to the second button.

"Everything okay?" Erica asks as she comes in to do some last-minute touch-ups. Her brown hair is pulled back into a tight ponytail.

I take a deep inhale, pushing myself up and ready to tell her, when the sound guy asks me to test the mic. My shoulders drop again as I run through the usual *one-two one-two testing* script, getting a thumbs-up from him.

Only a handful of people know about my sexuality, and everyone, including my parents and brother, are under a strict non disclosure agreement to ensure it doesn't get out. This image of me, carefully crafted over the years, allows my fans—who are predominantly female and under twenty-one—to buy into the dream that they may one day become the future Mrs. Morgan.

Last night's scandal wouldn't even register on the Richter scale compared to the seismic impact me coming out would cause. According to Paul and Connie, my career as a pop star would be over. I tried to point out that many artists are gay or at least bisexual, including George Michael, Elton John, Freddy Mercury, David Bowie, and Sam Smith. But Paul and Connie dismissed me by saying those artists were all British, came out later in their careers, and didn't always recover from the scandal. "Different rules apply to American artists," Paul had said, "especially when trying to appeal to the Bible Belt of middle America."

So, that was that, and I stay closeted, fearful that everything I've built will be taken away in a moment. I play along with the narrative that the team put out, which includes linking me to a string of women anytime a sniff of my sexuality makes its way beyond harmless fan fiction and into the media.

"And can we expect any other big reveals, while you're here in London?" The male journalist from *The Sun* raises his brows as he leans forward to ask.

I feel my cheeks getting red and I shift my right leg to cross it over my left.

"Carl!" Connie shouts from behind the camera.

Her glare is directed straight at him and would burn a hole through him if it were a laser. That is all it takes to force his brows down and for him to lean back into his chair.

"Sorry," he says, raising both his hands to her before turning back to face me.

"Your fans here in London want to know, are there any exclusives you can share with them while you're here in town?"

I've been playing this game for so long now, I almost kid myself into thinking I'm letting him in on a secret—giving him an exclusive scoop. I lean forward, looking directly into his green eyes.

"I'll probably get into trouble from you-know-who," I say, thumbing over my shoulder at Connie with one hand and covering the microphone with another. "But between you, me, and the English fans, I'll be heading to Abbey Road Studios next week to record a live album, including my latest single *My Anchor*, which my team told me this morning is number two here in the UK."

The sparkle in Carl's eyes tells me he's bought into my acting, and it's reaffirmed when Connie gives him the nod that he can run with what I said on the record.

"Congratulations!" he says. "And I'm sure with the shows this week and everything else, you're on course for your fifth number one single."

"That would be the perfect present to end this tour and my time in the UK with, Carl," I say, leaning across and squeezing his knee. I leave it there a beat longer than I should, just to ensure this line makes its mark and he includes it in the final piece. If he does that, it will mobilize the Morganites, as my fans affectionately refer to themselves, to drive streams and sales of the song all this next week.

But that wouldn't be the best present from this trip. That would be Christopher.

With that, the interview concludes. Carl and I exchange a brief hug and thank you, and we snap the obligatory selfie before Connie escorts him out of the room and readies the next journalist.

"Can I grab five please?" I say, looking at Lucy. Her bright red hair stands out in the darkness where she sits next to Erica by the playback monitor.

"We need to keep moving, we're on a tight schedule today," she says, briefly looking up from her phone. She returns her gaze to the screen, continuing to type away. So much for being the easy one to manipulate.

We're only three interviews down and I've got another nine to go before we have a brief break. I try not to be difficult—I don't want to be accused of being a diva for always keeping journalists waiting—but I need a moment. I opt for the line that always works.

"I'm going to piss myself if I can't grab just two minutes to go to the toilet."

Lucy looks up, dropping her phone into her lap, and nods. "Fine, go," she says. "But quickly." Mission accomplished.

Removing the small microphone and placing it on the seat, I attempt to make my way to the main door in hopes that I might catch a glimpse of Christopher, but Lucy stops me.

"There's a toilet back there." She gestures behind her.

Quick, think on your feet.

I need to take a shit. Nope, too many people here, that'll be too embarrassing.

Ah, that's it.

"I need to get something from my room," I say, though I'm not all that convincing judging by the look on Lucy's face.

"We can send Rob to get it for you when he gets back."

Usually, I'm grateful that Lucy runs a tight ship. She prevents me from getting caught up for too long with people or in situations that I want or need to be rescued from. But this time, her efficiency is working against me.

I force a smile on my face as I walk past the film crew and into the bathroom, but I don't lift the toilet lid. Instead, I sit down, pulling my phone out of my pocket and turning Airplane Mode off. A bunch of messages and email notifications flood my screen. Ignoring them, I scroll to my "I Am Social" folder, where I keep all my social media apps, and open up Instagram.

I hit the search tab and enter Christopher's first name, then realize that's all I have to go on. Other than his name, the fact that he's originally from London, and he's here for his sister's wedding, I don't know anything else. I look at posts tagged with the Landmark Hotel, hoping to catch a glimpse of him, but all I see are a flurry of videos of me leaving the hotel, interspersed with images of guests underneath the palm trees in the atrium or from their balconies. None feature Christopher.

Why do they make it look so easy on TV shows to find information on someone?

I look to the right, where a landline is attached to the wall, next to the toilet paper. It's a strange place to take a call, but a lightbulb moment hits me.

I reach for the phone and dial zero, automatically getting an answer.

"Concierge, how may I assist you today?"

"Hi, yes. Can you put me through to Christopher's room please?" The way the words come out of my mouth makes it sound like I have a stutter.

"Do you have a surname, sir?" comes the response.

"I don't, but he's in the room next to me..." A beat passes while I try and work out the number. "Room 506."

"One moment."

The line goes silent for a moment, then connects, and my heart begins to beat harder in my chest. But after twelve rings, I admit defeat and hang up. I pull myself up off the toilet seat and flush, pretending that I haven't just spent the last couple of minutes acting like a stalker.

Is this what Rob has to contend with? Is this the level my fans go to just to try and get in touch with me?

Rob greets me when I open the door, making me jump.

"Lucy said you needed something from your room?" He rubs his hands together.

I motion him to one side of the hallway, out of earshot of anyone else, and lower my tone to a whisper.

"Not exactly. I need you to find out more about that guy from the gym earlier."

"Is there a problem?" Rob's posture snaps upright and his eyes narrow.

"No. The complete opposite. I was a dick earlier when we left the gym and I want to apologize, but he's not answering his room phone, and I only know his first name, so I can't message him on social media."

"Want me to get the team to run a background check on him, get you all the information you need?" Rob cuts me off, his eyes widening in eager anticipation.

I know it's standard protocol to run a background check on anyone I work with, but it does feel a little too invasive for a guy I've just met.

"Can you just keep an eye out for him in the corridor to see if he returns?"

The eagerness in Rob's eyes disappears.

"That all, boss?" His chin tilts down toward his chest, like a puppy wanting to be thrown a bone.

Maybe I *could* do with a little help. After all, one quick google search by Christopher will bring up pretty much anything he'd want to know about me. It's not like I can do the same for him.

"Whatever you can find would be great. Oh, and I guess we'll need to get something from my room, so Lucy doesn't catch on."

Rob gives me knowing look and a tilted grin, hinting at mischief.

"Sure thing, chicken wing." He elbows me in the side and lets out his infectious laugh as he walks away.

I desperately want to chuck something at him. Damn him and that awful nickname. He still uses it regularly, despite my arms no longer being as scrawny as they were ten years ago. But, next to his, I guess they'll always be puny. And I'll always be that wiry kid he was put in charge of protecting, and a part of me likes that.

As I make my way back to the interview chair, I see Connie sitting on the armrest. She greets me with a half smile before returning to her usual neutral expression. She briefs me quickly before the next interviewer comes in.

"Alison from *This Morning* is somewhat of a national treasure here in the UK," she says. "Her interviews always go viral. They're fun and playful, so you'll be fine. She played Connect Four with Beyoncé and had Ryan Gosling and Harrison Ford in pieces with her jokes." She pats my arm and heads out to the door to get Alison as I sit down and put the microphone back on my shirt.

Although I often give Paul and Connie a hard time, maybe because they still treat me like a child, they do look after me.

Erica rushes over, readjusting my hair and misting me with spray to give me a healthy glow, while Laurie helps readjust the mic.

"Sorry again about last night, babe," she says. "I promise it won't happen again." Laurie's face looks whiter than mine was after I was sick this morning.

"Don't worry about it. At least they got their money's worth," I say, waving off the apology. She gives me a small smile as she backs away.

After another quick test and a thumbs-up from the sound guy, Connie walks Alison in and over to me. Alison's turquoise and yellow dress and gold bangles match her bright megawatt smile as she sits down and greets me.

"In three, two, one…" the cameraman calls out.

"Good morning, viewers! Today we have an extra special guest with us, who's taken time out of his busy schedule while here in London to talk to us about life on the road, his latest single, and more... Alexander Morgan." Alison points her cue cards at me.

And with that, I switch on the charm, turning it up to an eleven.

"The honor is all mine, Alison. I've been looking forward to this interview all week, wondering what games or questions you have in store for me..."

As the camera rolls and the interview continues, I catch Rob out of the corner of my eye. He gives me a thumbs-up sign, and I can't wait for the interview to end. Has he seen Christopher? Has he found out something about him?

6. Christopher
Friday

By all means, take as long as you need. *I just love watching things age in real time*, I grouse to myself.

My gaze burns a hole through the man in front of me, who is carting his suitcase down the broken escalator and taking up the whole width so no one can pass. The tuts and sighs behind me confirm that I'm not the only frustrated.

I finally make it to the underground platform, just to see the tube to Hampstead exit down the tunnel. The next isn't due for another five minutes. I rub my forehead and let out a sigh.

Great.

She's gonna kill me.

Most families would be understanding if I'm running late, and would maybe even offer to delay lunch to be accommodating—especially after all I've been through in the past thirty-six hours and the fact that I still have some work to do later. But the Foster family, or more specifically my mum, is anything but understanding or accommodating. It's her way or the highway.

I collapse on a metal bench, noticing the sweat circles

forming underneath my armpits are staining the new beige polo I'd bought after finishing in the gym.

The mere thought of my gym interlude this morning causes a wave of irritation.

I rest my elbows on my knees, letting my head collapse into my hands.

How stupid was I to think he'd join me in the steam room, like it was a gay sauna?

What a schoolboy error.

A ping from my phone snaps me out of my pity party, and I retrieve it from the pocket of my black jeans.

> **KELLY**
> Please hurry, she's on one today and I can't face her on my own.

I quickly fire back a response before returning my phone to my pocket.

> Stuck waiting for the tube at Euston. There as soon as I can be.

I feel for my sister, even though the upside to this delay is that I am spending less time with my mum. Ever since Daniel proposed to Kelly in Paris eighteen months ago, my mother has turned into a Mumzilla. She's taken over all the planning and preparation, to the point that you'd think it was my mother, not my sister, getting married.

Thankfully, living on the other side of the world shields me from the worst of her qualities. But I still pick up on the passive-aggressive tone in her messages when I don't get back to her quickly enough, check in frequently enough, or support her in a way she feels she should be supported.

I rise from the seat and head down the platform to look at

the passenger information display. As I walk, my attention is caught by a poster advertising Alexander's run of O2 shows. His gaze seductively draws me in, until the ping of the tube doors opening forces me to look away and board the train, right behind a woman with her stroller.

Thankfully, the carriage isn't too busy. I manage to find a seat opposite a man reading a copy of the Metro. Alexander stares back at me from the front page.

God.

Do I really need more reminders of him?

My cheeks flush as I pick at the cuticles on my fingernails.

Twenty-four hours ago, I didn't know Alexander Morgan existed. Now he's there everywhere I turn—except the one place I'd hoped he would be: behind me in the steam room.

The loud sound of the tube rumbling along the tracks sets the baby in the stroller off, its lungs packing a powerful scream. The mum sits there, lost on her phone, ignoring the baby. *Great.* Another neglectful mum, forcing me to ride through purgatory. I shake my head and cut a death stare toward the baby, who catches my gaze and goes silent.

If only that power worked on my mother.

"Finally, he bothers to grace us with his presence," my mother bellows. She puts her wine glass down, shaking her head as the waiter escorts me to the table where she and my sister are seated. Her purple clutch, which matches her dress, sits next to her wine glass on the table.

"Lovely to see you, too, Mother," I say, bending down to lean in for a hug. The embrace is over before it even begins, just like the presence and sudden withdrawing of her love.

I quickly move around the table to hug Kelly, who looks resplendent in a floral summer dress. Her auburn locks are tied back in a loose ponytail, allowing the freckles on her porcelain skin to shine.

"Tread carefully," she whispers in my ear before releasing me.

I widen my eyes at her. *Like I'm not used to navigating the minefield by now*, I think.

The waiter returns, pours another glass of Cabernet Sauvignon for my mother, and looks at me.

"Anything for you, sir?"

I open my mouth to speak, but I'm interrupted by my mother raising her hand.

"We've already ordered food for you since you kept us waiting." Her sideward glance at the waiter says, *Can you believe my child?* "But go ahead, let the gentleman know what you're drinking. I can never recall what it is you like to drink these days." She waves at me, finally giving me permission to speak.

I let out a short exhale, swallowing down my frustration, and look across to Kelly's drink.

"I'll take the same as her," I say, nodding at Kelly.

"It's just a soda," Kelly says, grabbing the glass and sipping through the straw.

"Then I'll take mine with vodka, please." I smile at the waiter as he heads off and then cut a confused look at Kelly, who shrugs my look away and places the glass back down.

"I'm glad to see that *one* of you is still willing to drink," my mother says. Her hand pats the back of mine while she rolls her green eyes at Kelly. Kelly chose to cut back on her drinking after Dad died. My drinking habits stayed the same. My mum's, if anything, increased.

I'd have thought today would have prompted Kelly to have at

least one alcoholic drink to deal with Mum and her constant disapproval. But it's displayed differently to Kelly than it is to me.

By the time the three Caesar salads arrive twenty minutes later, mine thankfully graced with chicken and bacon, my mother has barely taken a breath. She barely notices as the waiter sets the food down.

She's been walking us through the minute details of the next week. Fittings to attend here, final samples to sign off on there. The rehearsal dinner. All of this prompts reassuring nods and *um-hmms* from Kelly and me intermittently. My mum doesn't mind our indifference; she really just wants an audience.

The conversation only stops when she asks me who I plan on bringing to the wedding.

"You know," she begins, placing her cutlery down in the bowl and leaning forward, "I may have come to terms with your sexuality over the past couple of years, but the wider family still doesn't know. I think it's best we keep it that way." She arches her eyebrows and narrows her eyes at me.

I've taken too big a bite of my salad, so I cover my mouth to stop myself from spitting my food at her. I chew instead, buying some time to swallow down my anger.

"I was thinking of renting one of those mail-order brides. You know, to keep up appearances. But apparently there's been problems with getting them in the country since Brexit." I slouch back into the padded chair, crossing my arms.

"That's not funny." Her lips purse.

My mum has always been convinced I have no sense of humor, which quite frankly is ridiculous.

Kelly kicks my shin under the table and widens her eyes at me. Before I have a chance to respond, she jumps in. *Fine*, I think, scowling at her.

"He'll be sitting next to you and Aunt Brenda, so there's no need to worry there." Kelly is ever the diplomat. My mum ignores us both, waving down the waiter and signaling for the bill.

Clearly, we're done here. Thank God for that.

When the waiter comes over with the bill and card machine, Mum insists on covering it, removing her credit card from her clutch. It's all a ruse to look good in front of the waiter, and for once I don't pretend to play along with fighting to pay for the bill. With her though, there is never such thing as a free lunch.

"Christopher, darling…" Ah, there it is. She taps her card on the machine, then slides the card back into her clutch and slowly gets up from the chair. "Would you be ever so kind and order us an Uber to your sister's final fitting appointment?"

I glance at Kelly as I get up, who looks away sheepishly.

Clearly, she hadn't told Mum that I have work to do and won't be able to attend.

Typical. Always avoiding dealing with the issue.

I let out a deep exhale and reach for my phone.

"What's the address?" I ask, looking between the two of them.

"Kelly, give him the address. I'm going to use the toilet." Mum waves dismissively, tottering away in heels a size too big that clink on the tiled floor.

"Really," I say, once she's out of earshot, and hand Kelly the phone to type in the address. I cross my arms, leaning over the back of the chair.

"You'd think I haven't got enough battles to fight, without having to take on yours too," she says, shoving the phone back at me and shaking her head.

Fair enough. I quickly order the Uber and shoot off a text to Stephen while we wait for mum to return.

The Uber arrives a few minutes later, and as we step outside,

Stolen Moments

Stephen calls in response to the SOS message I sent him, right on cue.

"I'm not with my laptop right now, but I can be back at the hotel in thirty minutes," I say, pausing for dramatic effect when my mum turns. Then I continue, "Okay, can you hold a minute?"

I've learned it's best not to lie to her, but be what I call truth-adjacent with a parallel truth. In this case, I do need to work, but no one would be calling me from the West Coast at this hour.

I clutch the phone to my chest, and turn my gaze to my mother, who has rage forming in her eyes.

"I need to get back for work; it's an emergency." My voice rises a semi-octave higher than usual in an attempt to be as convincing as I can.

"You've been here all of two hours, and already you're bailing on us." My mum shakes her head and opens the car door. "Forever the disappointment of this family," she says as she gets in, slamming the door behind her.

A sledgehammer crashes into my chest.

Kelly mouths *Sorry*, as she gets in the other side, before they drive away and leave me on the curb.

I'm winded by the weight of my mum's words. Seeping through my veins. Crippling my broken heart even further. I've mourned the loss of the mother I'd hoped to have, and accept the mother I got instead, but low blows like that still wound me.

I imagine, for a moment, a mum who would be understanding. Who would hug their son tightly. Who would call for no other reason than just to hear my voice. The honking sound of a car horn startles me, and I shake the delusion away, returning the phone to my ear.

"Sorry, you still there? Thanks for that."

"No problem. We still good for drinks later?"

The last thing I want to do is go out after that interaction, but I know moping around in my hotel room is the last thing I need right now.

"Sure, want to come to the Landmark for 7 p.m.? We can grab a drink there and head into Soho after."

"Sounds like a plan. I'll see you then."

Stephen hangs up, and I walk down the high street and back to the underground.

"Mr. Foster. Mr. Foster."

I've barely stepped back into the hotel when the woman who checked me into the hotel last night waves me down, stopping me by an arrangement of pink and purple hydrangeas next to the concierge desk.

"Good news! The airline delivered your luggage to us. I had one of the bellmen take it up to your room for you." Her eyes sparkle with delight.

"Thank you, Imani. I really appreciate that." Today, I see the golden name badge on her uniform. I must have missed it in my tiredness last night.

I instinctively lean in and hug her, and then pause, unsure what has come over me.

Maybe it's her small act of kindness.

Maybe it's the fact that she's around the same age as my mother.

Maybe it's that she symbolizes everything my mother is unable to be.

Kind.

Warm.

Considerate.

"Oh, and a bit of advice. You may want to be a bit more

discrete down in the gym." Her voice lowers to a whisper as a couple walks by and she points to one of the cameras by the stairway to the atrium.

The horror must be evident on my face because she follows up with, "Don't worry, I ensured no one else saw the footage." She winks at me.

"Thank you," I say, quickly turning to make my way toward the elevator.

Is that why Alexander left me hanging in the steam room?

The slow ride up is punctuated by a number of stops that let guests off at the lower floors. I breathe and try to be patient. All I want is to get back to my room and finish up the last few bits of work I need to do.

When I reach the fifth floor, I'm greeted by an eerie quietness. The bustle that greeted me when I left for lunch has disappeared. As I make my way down the hallway, I notice not only a maid's trolley positioned outside my room, but Rob, lost in his phone, leaning up against the wall. He's hard to miss given his towering frame.

When I get closer, Rob notices me, raises his hand and immediately coughs. Panic spreads across his face.

My door is ajar, which is strange considering I had left the Do Not Disturb sign on. Why would Rob be positioned outside my room and not further up at Alexander's?

Rob ignores me, which is fine by me—one less difficult person to deal with today—and I turn into my room, only to bump straight into Alexander.

Ah, that explains it.

"Well, well, well. Look who it is. Houdini himself," I say, crossing my arms. Alexander takes a startled step back, his eyes widening.

"I can explain..." he begins, then awkwardly waits for me to say something.

Although I am no stranger to awkwardness, I am not going to help.

"Go on…" I wave my hand, waiting for him to continue.

I'm intrigued by how he couldn't wait to escape earlier, but now he's in my room.

His gaze darts behind me to Rob, still waiting just outside the door, then back to me and then to behind him. He walks back to the table where my laptop sits beside a notepad and pen.

"I wanted to leave a note for you about earlier." He grips the pad and holds it up to me. It's void of any writing.

"Ah, a note in invisible ink. My favorite kind." I arch my eyebrows.

He shifts uncomfortably, placing the pad back down.

The tension goes on a beat too long. Rob steps inside before Alexander waves him away.

"Okay, I'm not jumping to any conclusions here," I say—I totally am—"but I'm guessing you're not here to write me a note." I sit down on the bed across from him and stop for a second, taking in how handsome he looks.

In the space of twenty-four hours, I've seen him in casual attire and practically naked in the gym. But this casual getup of a black button-down shirt over a white T-shirt, dark-blue denim jeans, and white vans might be just my favorite look yet.

"I was walking back to my room and saw the door open and wondered if you were in…" His blue eyes glance my way, but he doesn't make eye contact.

"Mm-hmm," I say, placing my hands on either side of the bed, leaning slightly back. I suddenly discover another new pleasure in seeing the discomfort rise on his face.

He takes a couple of steps back to rest his bum against the table, almost tripping on the laptop charger as he goes.

"And I wanted to explain about the changing room earlier."

"Right," I say, pushing myself upright. I'm not gonna make

this easy for him. Especially after he left me high and dry. Well, high and wet.

"Rob called out one of my pseudonyms and I left in a hurry." His eyes dart to Rob, waving him away again when he steps inside again at the sound of his name.

"Pseudonym?" I ask out loud.

"Yeah, Bruce," he says, his voice lowering.

Ah, so that's what the random name was.

"Oh, I had you down as more of a Casper myself." I laugh at my own joke.

"Fair." A smirk appears across his face as he twists his watch around his wrist.

"Boss, we really need to go," Rob says, walking in.

Wait that's it? That's all I get?

"I better go," he says, nodding at Rob and lifting himself away from the table.

"In case you're worried, I'm not going to press charges," I tell him, getting up from the bed and gesturing toward the door.

"Press charges for what?" he asks, looking sideways at me.

"Breaking and entering? Trespassing?"

An awkward silence ensues as he walks to the door, then I finally break into a smile.

"Oh, you're joking." His shoulders slump as a smile appears across his face.

I pause for a beat. That smile had me hooked, line and sinker, from the moment I first saw it.

"Well, this time at least," I say, shutting the door on him once more.

God, this really is becoming a bad habit.

Banging on the door startles me awake, and I realize I must've fallen asleep. I grab my phone and glance at the screen, noticing 7:22 on the clock and numerous missed calls from Stephen.

"Sleeping Beauty finally emerges from her coma, I see," Stephen says. He rolls his eyes as he barges past me and into the room, plastic bag in hand. He throws himself down on one of the armchairs, flinging my gym gear off onto the floor.

"Sorry, must be the jetlag," I answer, shutting the door and walking over to the armchair next to him.

"Well, lucky for you, there was a hot guy a hundred and forty-three meters away. He kept me occupied," he says, with a slight shoulder lift and a dirty look. This is followed by a mischievous grin on his face as he leans over and pulls a can of Pimm's out of the bag. He chucks one to me and grabs the remote beside him to turn on the TV.

"What happened to Nico?" I ask, opening the can and taking a swig. I'm barely able to keep up with Stephen's sexcapades.

"Oh God, that one?" he says, scrunching up his face. "He was three guys ago. He was good for my hole, but not good for my soul."

I close my mouth to stop from spitting out my drink.

"Anyway, what about you. When are we going to find you a man? I read your star sign. It looks promising, and the moon is in Venus." He waggles his eyebrows up and down.

"Stephen, I'm not praying to Venus for a penis," I say, waving him off and turning away. I catch sight of myself in the mirror and realize I'm in no fit state to be heading out.

I get up to pull clothes out of my suitcase, when all of a sudden, I hear Alexander's voice coming from the TV speakers.

"London's one of my favorite cities in the world. I'm so glad to be back here. Everyone's been so nice. The fans, the folks at the hotel, right down to the people at the gym who were kind enough to lend me a helping hand."

My heart skips a beat.

He can't be?

He's talking about me on national television.

"Fuck me, he's hot," Stephen says, pulling out his phone from his short shorts.

"You think?"

I try to play it down, but Stephen and I have always had similar types, which has caused issues in the past. At one point we were forced to set an "I saw him first" rule if we both liked the same guy. It gave the other person space to try it out rather than us fighting.

"Don't tell me you wouldn't fuck Alexander Morgan," Stephen says. His attention is split between me and the screen.

I'm half tempted to tell Stephen what has happened with Alexander since I arrived, but I wouldn't even know where to begin.

"Sure, he's fuckable." I shrug my shoulders.

Until I know whatever this thing is between me and Alexander, it's best to keep it under wraps. Stephen always gets way too excited and overinvolved whenever I meet someone new, and it invariably only lasts a date or two. So it's best to avoid even mentioning it.

"With arms like those, he could throw you around the room and break you in two." A smile rises on his face. His gaze is now locked on the screen, watching Alexander, who is sitting alongside other guests on the couch. An actress gushes over him.

"My daughters are head over heels in love with you," she proclaims in a seductive Mrs. Robinson-style tone. She reaches over and touches his leg, making me squirm inside.

But I'm not sure if I'm the only one who is uncomfortable, or if everyone else tuning in feels the same way. I look over at Stephen to check his reaction, but I've lost him to his phone. Pings of Grindr echo from it.

I turn back toward the TV and study Alexander's face to see if he's uncomfortable, but the camera cuts away before I can decipher his expression. All I'm left with is a slimy feeling in my stomach.

Is it envy?

Jealousy?

7. Alexander
Friday

We've barely been off the air five minutes, yet Rita Watson has taken advantage of the opportunity to corner me against a table filled with snacks in the green room. She leans into me, talking loudly into my ear over Nelly Furtado's *Promiscuous*, which is playing from the speaker in the ceiling above us.

"A little dickey bird tells me you're planning to move into acting. Maybe I could bring my girls to one of your shows and we could exchange notes." One of her hands rests on my shoulder. The other grazes past my arm to grab a carrot stick. She dips it in some hummus and seductively licks it off.

My whole body shudders at the thought.

She's almost old enough to be my mother. Except for my mother wouldn't be dressed in a red cocktail dress with a slit almost to her hip and her boobs pouring out. I'm also pretty sure the two girls she's referring to aren't the ones she waved to through the camera lens ten minutes ago.

After my last trip here, when we were thrown together on a

different TV show, I'd thought my polite rebuffs to her advances were enough. Clearly not.

This is a woman on a mission.

And I'm the unfortunate target.

"I'm sure my team can arrange something." I smile politely at her, pulling back from the smell of hummus emanating from her mouth. I turn to look at Paul, Connie, and Lucy all huddled by the drinks table. I play with my watch, slightly longer than usual, until Lucy sees and catches my eye.

Green rooms are meant to be safe spaces. Not places where I'm more vulnerable to predators than I am to the massive crowd waiting outside the studio.

Thankfully, it only takes Lucy a handful of strides to reach us.

"Alexander, I just need to grab you quickly for some idents." There's a determined expression on Lucy's face. The smile slides off Rita's face and turns into a frown.

"It was good to see you again," I offer—a lie—as Lucy links her arm in mine and pulls me away.

"Thank you," I whisper, fearful that Rita may be able to still hear us, despite the song still playing and the buzzing of the two dozen people crammed into this room.

"No problem," she says, stopping halfway down the hall. "Apparently, Rita has quite the reputation around here. I heard two women in the restroom earlier," her head nods toward the restroom behind me, "discussing how when her film producer husband's away, she gets her claws into whomever she feels can further her career. I'm guessing that's how she got to where she is today."

Lucy looks back over her shoulder, where the click of heels precedes Connie's entrance. "She slept her way to... well, she slept her way to the middle." A sardonic smile forms on Lucy's face, forcing me to chuckle.

"That actress said you'd mentioned she could get guestlist passes for tomorrow's show?" Connie's question sounds more like an accusation. Her face scrunches up in disgust as she reaches into her purse to retrieve her cigarettes.

"I guess," I say, letting my indifference speak for me.

Rob appears down the corridor, waving at us to come toward the exit, as Connie lifts the cigarette to her mouth.

What's the worst that could happen?

The car hits a speed bump, sending the iPad Paul is passing to me flying out of his hand. I just barely manage to save it from hitting the floor before the seatbelt digs into my shoulder, snapping me back into my seat.

The shock on Paul's face returns to his usual glare as he readjusts his glasses.

"Jackal Entertainment is a reputable production company, and the producer and director, Alfonso Pena, originally comes from the music industry himself. He previously worked at your label in the production arm."

I scroll down through the web page, skimming over the text and the list of productions they've been involved in. Paul's pause goes on a little too long, prompting me to look up.

He removes his glasses, in a way that I know by now means he's trying to push something across the line. He starts to lean in before the seatbelt pulls him back.

"We could go with a bigger production company, but partnering with Alfonso and Jackal Entertainment allows us to retain more creative control of the film." His eyes gleam.

Ah, that's it.

Control.

It always comes back to control with Paul. It's his second

favorite word, right after visibility. Control over the brand. Control over the projects I do or don't work on. Although in this instance, maybe having more control over my move into acting wouldn't be such a bad thing.

It's true what they say: You never get a second chance at a first impression. I've seen many of my contemporaries attempt the transition from singer to actor, with varying degrees of success. I want to ensure I don't end up like them—ridiculed for my foray into the acting world.

"And where are they at with the adapted screenplay?" I ask.

Kirk, my agent at William Morris Endeavor, had encouraged me when I first floated the idea of moving into acting. He suggested I buy the rights to a few popular books, like some of his other clients and the actress Reese Witherspoon had done, to give me a built-in audience for the film and more control over my acting debut.

Disposed was the book we settled on. It was the only one that had kept me turning pages during the long tour bus rides through middle America last year.

"We've had to change screenwriters a couple of times," Paul is saying. "The scripts were too formulaic. They cast you as the pretty boy who goes on a hero's journey. But the latest guy we've got seems to have stayed true to the gritty storyline and nailed it." Paul slides his iPad back into his leather briefcase before returning his gaze to me.

"Is there anything I can..."

Before I can finish, the car comes to a screeching halt, throwing me forward in my seat. I briefly flash back to the night I lost Samuel.

The car hurtling toward us.

Samuel swerving to miss it.

Then the car hitting a tree, and Samuel's body flung through the windshield.

The rest is still a blur. The call to Paul. The panic about what to do.

I press my hand to my chest, trying to control my breathing, when Paul looks across at me. The air feels like it's being squeezed out of my lungs and I take short, sharp breaths.

I'm safe here.

I'm safe.

But I can't seem to shake the panic as I unbuckle my seatbelt. When Paul leans forward and opens the door, lightbulb flashes start going off.

"Just keep your head down and let's get you in the restaurant," Paul shouts over the paparazzi screaming my name.

By the time I've settled into the round booth at the back of the restaurant and exchanged pleasantries with Alfonso, all I can think about is grabbing a stiff drink—or anything stiff for that matter. The waiter comes by and Paul and Alfonso decide to split a bottle of red, while I get stuck holding a Sprite.

I scan the room for the waiter, who has been burning a hole in the back of my head ever since I walked in. People always think they are being subtle, staring when I'm not looking, but it's a feeling you get—knowing somebody's watching you. I finally catch sight of him and take the opportunity to excuse myself, lifting the napkin from my lap and placing it on the table as I slide out of the booth. Rob, sitting at a table across from us, gets up. But I motion with my hand for him to sit back down.

I catch the waiter next to the swivel door into the kitchen, out of view from the main dining room where all the guests are seated. "Hi," I say.

The waiter, dressed all in black, looks like he's just stepped off the runway. His chiseled jawline, messy dark hair, and gaunt figure is all the rage in Milan and Paris right now.

"Hi," he responds, sliding his hands into his pockets. He looks briefly at me before looking away and then back again.

"I need your help." I stretch my hand out and lean against the wall beside him. "My team has me on this no carbs, no alcohol diet, and after the day I've had, I could really use a *stiff* drink or two. What do you say? Help a guy out, brother-to-brother?" I gently tap him on the shoulder and lift a brow.

Another waiter, balancing four plates on his arms with an assortment of sushi rolls, exits the flapped door. He pauses briefly when he sees me, eyes wide, before continuing forward. I snap my fingers to recapture the attention of the waiter in front of me before digging into my pocket to pull out a couple of fifty-pound notes. I reach over and slide them into his trouser pocket.

"When I order my next drink, would you be sure the barman free pours some Belvedere in?" After a quick nod and a smile from him, I start to return to the table, but then think better of it and turn back. "Oh, and this is our little secret, okay? No need to put it on the bill."

He pauses before nodding reluctantly, bringing a smile to my face.

Good boy.

Paul and Alfonso are deep in conversation about the nuances of the film industry, which frankly, I have no interest in. Especially now that I finally have a proper drink. I open my mouth wide to swallow the last mouthful, the ice cubes clinking against my teeth. Vodka is far from my preferred spirit, but it's the easiest to get past Paul's ever-watchful eye. So it's a small sacrifice to make.

Setting the glass down, I reach for another slice of sushi with my chopsticks, but pause, seizing the chance to take stock of Alfonso in a moment where he's not watching me. There is a kindness in his green eyes as he laughs off Paul's pointed remarks. His navy button-down shirt complements his cropped salt-and-pepper hair and olive skin, giving him a distinguished air. The remnants of his boyish good looks tell me he would have broken a heart or three when he was my age.

My gaze lingers a bit too long, and his head suddenly turns toward me. He looks at me, then down to the Dragon roll where two pieces remain, my chopsticks hovering near one. I nod at him to take the other, as Paul swoops in and grabs the one I was about to pick up.

Typical Paul.

"So, what spoke to you about this book so much so that you wanted to use it to launch your career?" Alfonso's hand covers his mouth, making his words barely audible.

It's so rare I'm actually asked for input into my own career choices that I'm briefly taken aback—both by Alfonso's question and by Paul not immediately jumping in to answer on my behalf.

"Well, the most important thing for me, is to be taken seriously as an actor," I say, unsuccessfully attempting to scoop up some of the black miso cod with my chopsticks. "To not go down the predictable route. I want to go against the stereotype, play a really gritty role people wouldn't expect, and the main character in the book is exactly that." I finally get a grip on the piece of the cod with my chopsticks and lift it up to my mouth.

Alfonso nods and smiles, resting his elbow on the table and cupping his chin in his hand. The way he looks at me gives the weight of my words even more importance, like they're not only being heard and acknowledged, but also understood.

A warm feeling rises inside of me.

So, *this* is what it feels like to be respected.

"And are there any actors or movies that stand out to you?" His eyes lock onto mine, a soft intensity in his stare.

"I really respect the likes of Christian Bale, Heath Ledger.

You know, those actors who really commit to the role." He nods back at me in agreement, and my smile widens across my face.

We're interrupted by the waiter coming alongside the table and setting down another slew of dishes. He grabs a couple of the empty plates before looking directly at me.

"Can I get another one, please?" I ask. I reach for my glass and shake the almost melted ice cubes inside.

"Certainly, sir." He looks across to Paul and Alfonso, who exchange a glance at one another and then at their empty glasses of wine.

"Sure, we'll take another as well," Paul responds. From there, the conversation gets lost in the nuances of what the role will entail and what I'll need to prepare for.

Paul puts his hands down on the table once the bill has been settled and looks across at me.

"Right, we better get back to the hotel, before our car turns into a pumpkin," he says. His speech is lightly slurred, the glazed look in his eyes magnified by his glasses.

The restaurant crowd has thinned out, but there are still enough tables with guests to provide an audience as Rob steps up and helps me out from the booth. The warmth I feel inside, a mixture of the four drinks I've had and the warm chat with Alfonso, has opened me up tonight more than any journalist ever could. Alfonso is ultimately still a stranger, but he's one who has been able to put me at ease. Well, that and the vodka. Still, that's hard to do, given my trust issues.

I've lost count of the number of people I used to know who changed once I became famous. They say fame changes you. Well, I've come to learn that fame doesn't change *you*, it changes the people around you. Which then, by extension, forces you to change.

You never know who's going to sell a story or come out of the woodwork to befriend or reacquaint themselves with you.

They're not interested in who I am, but in what I am. What I can provide as a result.

Yet tonight, with Alfonso, I didn't pick up on that feeling from him. Maybe it's because he's already in the industry and conveyed a genuine interest in what I had to say. And I felt safe with him. That, and I know Paul would never put me in a situation where something could come back to bite me in the ass.

I stumble slightly as I step out of the booth, laughing it off when the others look at me. "All this talk about acting has me giddy with excitement," I say, rolling my eyes.

Alfonso smiles back, while Paul shakes his head and grabs his briefcase, and we all follow Rob to the entrance. Thankfully, the bill came with mints, allowing me to hide the alcohol on my breath. Although, by the look of Alfonso and Paul, I needn't have worried. The two bottles of red they knocked back contribute to their slow meandering through the tables to the door. The delay gives a couple of tables enough time to reach for their phones and slyly try to take a photo, as if I wouldn't notice.

I'm shocked when I see Paul lean in to hug Alfonso goodbye at the restaurant entrance. It's an unusual display of affection for Paul, one that I've not seen in years.

"We'll be in touch soon to discuss next steps," Paul says, patting Alfonso's back.

"Sounds great," Alfonso says, and smiles before turning to me. "It was great to meet you, Alexander. Thank you for your time tonight." He stretches out his hand.

"Thank you for seeing me," I say, ignoring his hand and leaning in for a hug.

I feel my eyes welling up and quickly shake my head to clear the sensation. I pull back and release myself, and Rob nods before opening the door to reveal a small crowd of people and a handful of paparazzi waiting next to the car.

I didn't realize how big my suite was until I began pacing it twenty minutes ago, trying to build up the confidence to knock on Christopher's door. The conversation we had earlier didn't go exactly how I hoped. But thankfully, it didn't go as badly as it *could* have gone if he had walked in thirty seconds earlier and caught me rummaging through his backpack.

The alcohol that loosened me up at the restaurant is starting to wear off, which is unfortunate. I could really do with some Dutch courage right now. I've spent the past hour showering twice and changing outfits three times, finally settling on gray sweatpants and a white vest. I want to give off a cool laid-back impression, but that's a far cry from how I'm feeling right now.

Another glance at the clock above the TV shows me it's 2 a.m. If I don't head across to his room soon, I'll probably blow my chance.

I get up, head over to the tall mirror attached to the wall, and begin psyching myself up, just like I do before stepping out onto the stage each night.

You got this.

You're the man.

I repeat the mantra a number of times, believing it slightly more with each go around. As I grab the room key and my wallet off the side table, I hear the faint sound of chants coming from outside and notice the pile of new earbuds sitting on the table. I grab one of the boxes and slide it into my pocket.

Great.

That'll give me a more plausible reason to knock.

I leave the room, closing the door quietly behind me, and slowly walk toward his door. I stop outside and linger momentarily, taking long deep breaths to try and steady my heart, which has begun beating rapidly against my rib cage.

I hesitate as I reach up to knock, and pull my hand away. He's probably asleep. I turn and start to head back toward my room when I remember the mantra.

You got this.

You're the man.

Before I have the chance to bail a second time, I reach up and knock three times with my fist, then step back slightly in anticipation.

I shake my head in confusion as the door opens and see a guy in a black crop top, short shorts, and white trainers standing there, mouth agape.

Did Christopher move rooms? Had what happened earlier make him have second thoughts about being down the hall from me?

Before I have a chance to ask, the guy starts speaking rapidly in a thick Irish accent.

"Holy fuck. It's... You're...erm. Hi!" His blue eyes widen more with each word.

"Sorry, to bother you..." I begin, starting to turn away, when I hear a familiar British accent and turn back to see Christopher appear, a toothbrush hanging from his mouth.

"Is that room service with our drinks?" He pulls his toothbrush out as his eyes meet mine. The Irish guy still stands there, frozen like a statue.

Well, I guess that answers my question of whether this is still his room and if he's still up. My chest tightens at the sight of Christopher standing behind the Irish guy.

I'm half tempted to make an excuse and quickly leave. Clearly, he's got company and is not interested in exploring anything between us. My shoulders slump and I slide my hands into my pockets, where I feel the earbuds. I grab them and hold them out in front of me in a closed fist.

"Sorry about the noise downstairs. I've been handing these out to each room to apologize," I say, opening my palm to expose the earbuds. "Do you need me to grab another pair?" My attention is now firmly locked on Christopher. He looks incredible in a white polo shirt with gold buttons.

Christopher moves past the other guy, who is still frozen in place.

"Thanks," he says, slowly reaching forward and taking the box from my hand, studying it. "One should be enough." His gaze returns to mine.

"I'd better head to the rest of the rooms." I pat my empty pocket and nod down the hallway. I can't wait to escape the discomfort of the moment. "Have a good night."

My thoughts are racing at a thousand miles an hour.

Did I make everything up in my head?
Was he not flirting with me in the gym this morning?
I was sure I'd picked up on a level of flirtation in his room earlier.
Who is that guy?
His boyfriend?
A hook up?

The lyrics to the nineties classic *Over My Shoulder* pops into my head, encouraging me to turn around as I get to my room and reach for my door key.

But my hope of seeing Christopher walking toward me turns to disappointment when I see the Irish guy's head and not Christopher's peering around the doorframe. He disappears quickly, like a tortoise retreating into its shell.

I rub my hand over my chest. Maybe a run will help dispel the tight clutch of emotion pinching my chest. But I exhale in frustration when I remember the gym is closed. *Damn this hotel.*

I'm just about to turn back to the door, when I notice a hotel staff member wheeling a trolley down the hallway with a silver dome and two bottles of wine on it. I lift my hand, beckoning him toward me. He smiles, willfully obliging, pushing the trolley to my door.

"What would it cost me to take those off your hands?" I say, reaching into my pocket. "Fifty? A hundred? Two hundred?" I retrieve my wallet and open it up to take out four fifty-pound notes.

"Sorry, I'm afraid these are for another hotel guest." His bland expression gives nothing away. "You'll need to place an order with housekeeping."

I shake my head at him.

Can't this guy tell I'm a man in need right now?

"I need discretion, my man. Let's not make this a big deal." I lean against the wall and pull the remaining notes out of my wallet. "What if I double it?"

His eyes widen at the sight.

Jackpot.

Everyone has a price. Even if they don't know what it is.

I slide the money into his waistcoat pocket, return my wallet to my pocket, and grab the two bottles of wine off his tray. I tuck one under my arm to retrieve my door key and place it on the card reader, then stop just as the door opens.

"In fact, while I'm at it, I'll take the food too," I say, sticking my foot in the door to stop it from closing. I set the two bottles down and return to grab the plate from the trolley.

If Christopher's gonna deprive me of him, fine. But I'll be damned if I'm the only one who is deprived tonight.

8. Christopher
Saturday

I can't tell if the pounding in my head is from consuming too much alcohol or the fact that Stephen hasn't stopped talking since Alexander came to my room last night. It feels like the Spanish inquisition, only with an Irish accent.

How do I know Alexander?
Why was he knocking at my door at 2 a.m.?
Do I think he's gay?

His questions come so quickly that I don't have time to answer.

At one point last night, he even fired up Grindr to see if Alexander might be on there as a headless torso. He flung his phone on the bedside table when it turned out the closest guy was roughly two hundred meters away—close enough to potentially be in the hotel—but far enough away to confirm it wasn't him.

Stephen's disappointment is written all over his face. I have to swallow mine down and push it aside. I'm kicking myself for agreeing to let Stephen come back to my room when he didn't want to call it a night—especially after I'd had to miss the previous night due to my travel issues. His sad face had pulled at my heartstrings.

Guilt will be the death of me.

Now Alexander probably thinks Stephen is some random guy I brought back for a pump and dump, or worse, my boyfriend. My stomach churns at the thought.

Even in his sleep, Stephen was talking in between snores, such is his penchant for chatting away whether anyone is listening or not. All of this leaves me hungover, grumpy, and lethargic as we make our way down to the atrium for breakfast.

By the time we sit down, Stephen has finally stopped talking my ear off. Not to give his vocal cords a break, but to begin chewing, if that's what one would call it, the pile of buffet food on his plate. He's loaded his tray with a pile of sausages, bacon, baked beans, fruit, a muffin, and two fried eggs. A slice of smoked salmon dangles off the side.

I slouch into the padded chair, pushing my sunglasses up my nose and pulling down my baseball cap, hoping it will hide the fact that I am on tenterhooks, waiting to see if Alexander will make his way into the dining room. Just the smell of Stephen's food is enough to make me dry heave, let alone the taste of the Taittinger champagne he insisted on both of us having.

I rub the side of my cheek.

God knows how I'm going to make it through my sister's hen do later.

"I wonder if he'll be down here for breakfast," Stephen says between mouthfuls. He scans the room like a hunter on the prowl.

"I doubt it. Especially not with vultures like you trying to swoop in and pick him up," I say. I shake my head as Stephen reaches for one of the strawberries on his plate and chucks it at me. He misses, hitting the woman at the table next to us.

Stephen ducks his head, hiding underneath the spare baseball cap I loaned him, leaving me to face her glare.

He had been insistent that he come down to breakfast wearing what he wore last night. Stephen prefers to call it the stride of pride, rather than the walk of shame, but I insisted he change into a clean black T-shirt and shorts. I admire his confidence in wearing what he does. But there's only so much embarrassment I can take, and last night's attire was not appropriate for a hotel like this.

I twist my neck slightly and see the look of disdain from the woman he'd hit, who is now moving the strawberry onto her empty plate. She and her companion get up to leave.

"I'm so sorry—he's on a trial run in society, and clearly, it's not going well."

My tentative smile dies as the woman shakes her head and walks off. Stephen kicks my ankle under the table, forcing my attention back to him.

"If anyone needs to be locked up in a padded cell, it's you," he says. His nostrils flare as he scoops up another mouthful of baked beans.

"And leave you out here unsupervised?" I furrow my eyebrows and rub my shin.

Stephen may not be a good pitcher, but he can definitely kick.

"Another glass?" the waitress asks Stephen, stopping him from retorting.

Stephen's sour face softens at the thought of more alcohol.

Thank God for small mercies.

He looks at my champagne flute, barely touched, compared to the last dregs at the bottom of his.

"Sure, that'd be grand. And while you're at it, could you rustle up something a little stronger for my friend here? A Bloody Mary perhaps."

The waitress nods and walks away. Stephen reaches across for my champagne and downs it in one before launching into another monologue, simultaneously chowing down on one of his sausages.

I smile and nod, looking down at my untouched sausage sandwich, when Stephen stops talking. I look up, worried that speaking with his mouth full has finally backfired, but there's no food left in his open mouth. His eyes widen as a dark shadow engulfs me from behind.

Weird?

The light pouring in from the glass roof, six floors above us, still seems to be lighting up the rest of the tables and the buffet across the room.

"Is this table taken?"

My heart leaps into my throat as I recognize the Northern Californian accent. Stephen shakes his head back and forth, mouth still open.

Alexander sits down diagonally from me at the table to the right of Stephen and I, forcing me to move my chair slightly to the side to get a better view of him. He's wearing a blue LA Dodgers baseball cap, oversized sunglasses, and a loose-fitted tank that's cut so deeply at the side I can make out his ripped abs.

Damn.

This man is all kinds of fine.

He manages to make even what I'm assuming is hangover attire sexy as fuck.

"Heavy night, guys?" he asks, nodding at the drinks the waitress puts down for us. His voice is raspier than yesterday.

Beneath the table, I twirl my thumbs, trying to hide my discomfort.

As if last night wasn't painful enough.

Now I'm trapped here with him and Stephen again.

"You could say that," Stephen eventually says, like he finally got his voice back from Ursula. It saves me from the growing discomfort rising in my chest as Alexander remains focused on me.

"Let me clear this for you, gentlemen." The waitress picks up the used plates in front of Rob and Alexander. "Can I get you started with a drink, perhaps?"

"I'll take an iced Americano, please," Alexander responds with a smile.

"A black coffee, thanks." Rob says, and his nod sends the waitress away.

"Sorry about last night," Alexander says, switching his gaze between Stephen and me. "I didn't get back till late, and the fans outside seemed louder than usual. I hope those earbuds worked. Wouldn't want you having two bad nights of sleep in a row." The right side of his mouth lifts.

"Sure, no bother." Stephen takes it upon himself to lead the conversation after quickly knocking back another mouthful of champagne. "You wouldn't happen to have another pair, would ya? This one's been keeping me awake for years with his snoring." He points his thumb at me.

The discomfort in my chest instantly turns to irritation, and I lean forward and kick Stephen under the chair.

The cheek.

"What d'ya do that for?" Stephen's brows furrow.

"I'm sure we can get another pair," Alexander says. A smile forms on his face as he looks at the pair of us. Rob, in the meantime, completely ignores the bickering and takes his phone out. Stephen raises his eyebrows at me as he reaches for his champagne again.

"Have you guys been together for a while then?" Alexander asks, waving his finger between us.

Stephen spits his mouthful of champagne all over me.

"God, no! Would you look at him?" His face screws up in disgust. "It'd be like sleeping with my brother, but worse."

I reach for the napkin beside my plate, squeezing it tightly before wiping the champagne from my face and top. I don't know if I'm more angry at Stephen for doing that in front of Alexander, or more relieved that Stephen has ruled out that the two of us are definitely not a thing.

"Sorry, I didn't mean to offend you," he says. "It's just when you said for years, I assumed you were partners." He reaches up for the coffee that the waitress passes to him.

"Oh God, his standards are so low, he's resorted to using a shovel," Stephen says, laughing. He looks away from me toward Alexander.

"Says the man who taught me that desperate was actually lifestyle choice," I shoot back, knocking the smile from his face. I shift my shoulders back and reach for the Bloody Mary, taking a sip and instantly regretting it as immediate heartburn rises.

Touché, motherfucker. Touché.

Alexander lets out a laugh, stopping Stephen in his tracks.

"You two are like peas in a pod," he says, leaning back and reaching for his coffee.

"More like two ice cubes in a glass, trying to be cool, but both due for a meltdown," I say.

Alexander smirks as Stephen cuts me a dirty look.

Fuck.

Did I just say that out loud? I wince.

God, I need to get my mouth wired shut like Kanye.

"You Brits are so funny." Alex puts his coffee back down on the table.

"Irish," Stephen coughs, insulted by the insinuation.

"Right." Alex nods, looking at Stephen momentarily before returning his attention to us both. "What are you guys up to later then?"

"I'm free as a bird," Stephen says, leaning forward. His cutlery scrapes against the plate as he shovels the last of his food onto his fork and almost throws it into his mouth.

I look at him, confused, knowing that he agreed to attend Kelly's bachelorette party today because he won't make the wedding.

"Well, if you guys want, I'm playing at the O2 tonight. Rob can get a couple of tickets for you both if you give him your name and number."

"We'd love to," I say politely, holding my hand out across the table to stop Stephen from talking. "But it's my sister's bachelorette party today. She'll kill me if I don't come." My heart sinks at this new roadblock in the way of Alexander and I spending more time together.

"Look," Stephen says, stretching back in his chair. He reaches for a pen left with a bill on the table behind him. "I'm sure your sister won't mind if we duck out halfway through." He grabs a napkin and scribbles on the corner to make sure the pen works—it does—before writing his name and number on it and passing it to Alexander.

Alexander takes the napkin and then looks up at me.

An awkward pause ensues.

I'm guessing he wants me to throw him a bone, but I don't know what to say.

"Ah, this is an English number," he finally responds, breaking the silence. "Your phone doesn't work with English numbers, does it, Rob?"

Out of the corner of my eye, I see Rob looking dumbfounded before his face changes.

"Right." Rob adjusts himself in the chair, which barely contains him.

"Give him your number," Stephen urges me, waving the pen frantically at me.

There's no chance I'll be able to make the show tonight. But rather than reiterate the point, I grab the pen from Stephen and an unused napkin from the place setting next to me and write down my details. I hand it over to Rob as a little girl approaches Alexander with a piece of paper.

"Can I get your autograph, please?" she asks sweetly, holding out what looks like a copy of one of his albums. Her expression is one of awe.

"Sure!" he says, motioning at me to pass the pen.

My hand shakes slightly as I pass it to him.

Is that nerves? The hangover kicking in?

I reach for the Bloody Mary, sipping at it once more, pushing through the heartburn in hopes that the alcohol will do its job and calm my nerves.

Alexander places the pen on his table, returns the album to the girl, and fiddles with his watch.

Rob gets up as the little girl smiles and runs back to her table near to the palm trees on the far side of the restaurant, and Alexander copies the motion, downing the last of his coffee.

Before they head out, Alexander turns and looks at me.

"We'll leave the passes on the guest list and if you can make it, then great."

And with that he turns and is gone.

Once they're out of range, Stephen leans over toward me. "I think he's into me," he says. The smell of his breath makes me want to vomit.

"Sure," I respond, looking down at the table. "He's *so* into you that he left your details on the table." I slide the napkin back toward him.

"Can you believe it—this one," Stephen gives one of Kelly's friends wide eyes and jabs a thumb at me, "turned down Alexander Morgan offering us passes to see him at the O2 tonight?"

Stephen's been downing drinks like they're going out of fashion since breakfast, at the cocktail-making class, the karaoke bar, and now here at Magic Mike Live. I truly don't know where he puts it. Must be the Irish in him.

"We could be backstage now, lapping it up with Alexander, but instead we're here with a load of middle-aged women, watching some low-rent Channing Tatum wannabe stripping for cheap thrills." He shakes his head as we wait for the next section of the show to begin.

I get his disappointment. I'd wanted to go to see Alexander tonight too. Stephen was like a broken record, begging and pleading, trying to convince me to go. But that's where we differ, morally and value-wise.

Loyalty has never been one of his strong points. Like so many other gays I know, he's noncommittal and likes to keep his options open—just like his legs on a Friday night—in case something or someone that's a better option comes along. In the queer world, monogamy and commitment are seemingly a rare thing these days.

Even if we had ended up going, Stephen would have invariably made it about him backstage, and I know the only reason Alexander invited us in the first place was because of me.

Ignoring Stephen, I take in Kelly, who's a few seats down from us. Two plastic dicks are attached to springs on her headband, and she's bopping away to Blackstreet's *No Diggity*. I can't help but laugh.

I know I made the right decision.

If something is meant to happen with Alexander, it will. But tonight, it's about Kelly. My sister's friends all let out a loud scream when one of the strippers, dressed up in a skimpy police outfit, appears from behind the red curtain. He steps around the lone chair on stage and walks toward Kelly, taking her by the hand and pulling her up on stage.

"What's your name?" he asks, removing the hat and wiping the sweat from his brow.

"Kelly?" She sounds nervous, like she's unsure of her own name.

"Well, Kelly, your friends here tell me you've been a bad girl," he says, gently pushing her down into the chair. "So, I'm going to have to punish you." He removes a truncheon from his leather belt, and starts sliding it up and down on the palm of his other hand, his fingers gripped tightly around it.

Screams erupt from the crowd, and I'm relieved that our mother went home after the karaoke. She'd almost had an epileptic fit when they played Pin the Dick on the Daddy earlier. I can't even begin to think about what she'd say if she was here watching this now.

Ginuwine's *Pony* starts to play, and the guy cuffs my sister's hands behind the chair and starts to seductively gyrate around her. As he straddles her, he rips off his top and encourages Kelly to stick her tongue out, then moves his washboard abs over it before dropping to his knees.

When the second verse kicks in, he spreads Kelly's legs apart, thrusting his head up underneath her skirt. The screams from the crowd are deafening, and even Stephen gets in on the action. He's up on his feet, shouting at Kelly to take it all in.

I guess all it took was the sight of something sexual to get Stephen's mind off of Alexander and onto something else. Yet, every movement of the man on stage makes me think about what I want to do to Alexander.

The stripper works his way around to Kelly's back and uncuffs her before laying her down on the floor gently, in a way that's both kind and dutiful. Then he rips off his trousers to reveal just a G-string, barely containing his privates. Images of Alexander, exposed on stage, flick through my mind.

The stripper grinds down on Kelly, flipping her from missionary style into reverse cowgirl and every position in between. I'm both grossed out at seeing my younger sister being sexual with another man and turned on at the thought of that being Alexander and me doing that to him.

The song is almost finished as the stripper makes one final move—jumping up in the air before skillfully thrusting down on Kelly, and the crowd roars in climax. Kelly stumbles up, disheveled and with a smile as wide as a Cheshire cat across her face, revealing that she's having the time of her life.

Yet, as I'm clapping, all I can do is think about Alexander and what he is up to right now.

9. Alexander
Saturday

The dance moves to *Tonight, I'm Gonna Fly*, one of the few songs I begrudge still having to perform ten years into my career, are so drilled into my head that my body goes into autopilot, allowing me to instead focus my attention on Block 111.

I keep scanning the rows, hoping to spot Christopher. But I can't seem to locate him. Rita Watson, yes. She waves her hand at me like a windshield wiper, having to hold on to the strap of her dress every time she does so as not to expose herself.

I even double-checked with Lucy during a costume change to ensure I have the right block, but she confirmed that's where the seats were with a nod and a vague roll of her shoulders.

With just two songs left and one last look at that block, I admit defeat. I call in my performance for the rest of the show. My voice is beginning to give way again, forcing me to hold out the microphone to the crowd and encourage them to help me sing along. The team had set up an IV drip for me before the show—I'd told them the lingering effects of the alcohol might be a virus—but it's starting to wear off.

Nothing like a hangover to remind me I'm not invincible.

And nothing like a guy not showing up to remind me I can't always get what I want.

I plaster on a smile for the final song, my biggest hit to date, *It's You That I Need*, and hold out the microphone to the crowd, letting them and the backing vocals carry me through. I bow out without as much as a *Thank you, London!*, or *Goodnight!*, keeping my head down and ignoring the crew and guests loitering backstage to speedwalk down the corridors. I just want to retreat into the dressing room.

By the time I've showered, changed clothes, and gotten a fresh layer of makeup from Erica, Rob is there to escort me into the backstage bar. The red-walled room is filled with people standing by the bar or seated on felt couches scattered round the vast space. The dim overhead lighting is thankfully turned down a notch, giving my weary eyes a rest.

"Don't forget to smile," Connie says, greeting us at the door. Her head tilts slightly to the side, waiting for me to put one on my face.

"Happy," I say, giving her a fuck you smile.

Connie rolls her eyes, turns around and moves into the room, clearly expecting me to follow. At my request, Rob goes to check with the box office about Christopher.

It's like I'm being wheeled out for another performance, this time to a bar of friends and family, though neither are present. My parents aren't supposed to come over till next week, and my brother Harrison avoids anything to do with my shows. Instead, the room is filled with a bunch of music industry contacts and their friends and family. And one disheveled Rita Watson, standing with her friend and talking to Paul. Connie does her best to introduce me briefly to everyone, moving me on after exchanging pleasantries and posing for the obligatory selfies.

Boxes ticked.

Hoops jumped through.

Yet no badge or medal at the end of it.

"Sorry boss, looks like he never picked up the tickets," Rob says, leaning in, just as we get to Rita and her friend.

His words wipe the fake smile from my face.

I knew Christopher coming was a long shot, but it's a double blow when I'm confronted by Rita in her skimpy green dress.

"Why so down?" Rita says, like she's speaking to a baby. She stretches her hand out, thumb and index finger extended, to lift the corners of my lips upward. A flicker of irritation forms in my chest when no one comes in or tells her to move her hand away.

"I'm sure I can find a way to turn that frown upside down," she says, giving me a wink. She removes her hand once I force the smile back on my face and drops her right shoulder, letting the strap slide down and almost exposing herself once more.

The mere thought of being in bed with her sends a shudder down my spine.

Have some class.

Connie cuts me a sideward glance. *Play nice*, I can hear her saying.

"Glad you could make the show. I hope you enjoyed it," I say, shaking away my disdain to once more become the consummate professional. Smile, exchange pleasantries, take the obligatory selfie, and move on.

"Oh, we definitely enjoyed it," she responds. She briefly looks at her friend, lost in conversation with Paul, and then turns back to me. "Especially those moves in *Tonight, I'm Gonna Fly*." She raises her eyebrows suggestively before letting her eyes drift down to my crotch.

"Excuse me, I just need to make a quick call," I say, suddenly filled with such loathing that I know if I don't remove myself right now, I will cause a scene. I nod toward the door for Rob's benefit, so he knows to ensure no one bothers me as I leave.

Once I'm out of the room, with Rob following behind me down the hall, I let out a sharp exhale. No longer in performative mode. Not sacrificing my needs to appease everyone else. I reach for my phone and instantly feel my chest tighten again at its reluctance to slide out of my jeans pocket. The frustration rises up to my throat as the facial recognition fails to recognize me.

Damn makeup.

I attempt to rub it away with the palm of my hand as I hold the phone up to my face again. This time it opens, right as I enter my dressing room, and I slump into the white leather couch. I open up iMessage, scrolling back past new messages from the family chat, a friend back home, and Paul, to the message I sent Christopher earlier.

> Hope you have a great time at your sister's bachelorette party. Robs left two tickets under your name if you change your mind.

A wave of fear hits me when I see there's no "delivered" notification underneath. But I know I took down the number right. I'd checked the napkin three times when entering it in.

Maybe his phone's dead?

Maybe he doesn't have roaming set up, and his phone only works on Wi-Fi?

God, I wish my head would give me a break sometimes.

But I need to know the answer.

I click on his contact icon and let my thumb hover over the call button. I take in a sharp inhale, hold my breath and close my eyes, and press the call button. It goes straight to voicemail.

Hi, you've reached Christopher Foster. I can't get to the phone right now, but if you leave your name and number, I'll get back to you.

The sound of his voice hypnotizes me briefly before a rush of panic hits. I hadn't thought about what I would say to him on a voicemail, let alone if he actually answered. I manage to hang up just before the beep sounds.

What would be a good reason to follow up? I tap my fingers on the arm of the couch. I don't want to come across as desperate, and sending another message when he hasn't even read the first one would be just that.

But I do want to see him. To hang out with him.

A thought pops into my head, and I redial, this time leaving him a voicemail.

"Hey, so a few of us are heading to Tape for a personal appearance I have to do, just in case you want to swing by. They've got me a table and a load of free drinks, so you, your sister, and all her friends are more than welcome to come. Let me know."

Rob opens the door, and the flash of lightbulbs hits me.

"Wait!" I yell, over the bellowing from outside.

Rob slides the door back and I reach for my phone, checking once more, but there's still no message from Christopher. My gaze darts around the car, traveling from Rob to Lucy to Connie, and then on to Paul.

"I need to put Christopher plus guests on the guest list."

Paul looks at me with a concerned expression, then toward Rob.

"Who's Christopher?" Paul asks.

I gaze at Rob, whose expression remains steadfast, then at Lucy, who shrugs, and sigh. They're the only two who know about my interactions with Christopher. At least they've respected my right to privacy, but I know what this means with Paul.

I take a deep breath and say, "Just some guy from the hotel.

His sister is having her bachelorette party tonight and I thought they could swing by."

Paul shifts in his seat, leaning forward slightly to study my face, just like he would a painting in a gallery.

"Do we have a nondisclosure agreement in place?" His expression is deadpan.

"Come on," I laugh, shrugging him off. "Not everyone I interact with needs an MNDA."

"I'm already running a background check on him," Rob says, breaking the awkward silence. Paul stares at him as if to say, *We'll talk about this later.*

"Well, we'll still need to get an MNDA in place. We all remember the mess that Roy got us into." He shakes his head as he looks at Rob's hand, which is still gripping the door handle.

Memories of Roy flash through my head.

He was a gaunt Australian artist on my label. In the months after Samuel died, he had pretended to care for me, like he knew what it was like to lose someone close. He had enabled my drinking, helping me spiral out of control, and made a move one night. Even though I didn't find him attractive, I caved after months of longed to be touched by another human. When I pulled away afterward, he didn't take it well. He started insinuating that I was using him when he was promoting his album during interviews. As rumors began circulating online, Connie and Paul got my lawyer involved to silence him and pay him off.

Ever since then, MNDAs have been mandatory. But in the haze of the last three days, the thought of getting Christopher to sign one hadn't even entered my mind.

"Alex?" Paul snaps me out of my disassociated state.

"Sure. Do what you need to. Just ensure he's on the list," I say, as Rob opens the door again and escorts us through the paparazzi and into the club.

The pounding music reverberates through my body, shaking

the ice and empty bottles of Belvedere in the bucket on the table. I reach for one of the mixers in carafes—it barely contains any apple juice, typical—and pour the last of it into the glass, all under the gaze of the crowd that surrounds our VIP table.

Why they insisted on putting us in the middle of the club and not at one of the VIP tables lining the walls is beyond me. My attention turns to Paul, but he's deep in conversation with Rita's friend, who's somehow managed to worm her way into our group and is straddled up beside me. Thankfully, Lucy sits on the other side of me, keeping a watchful eye out, while Rob stands at the edge of the booth next to Connie.

"You think if I asked the DJ, they'd play *Fat Lip*?" Lucy shouts in my ear over the music.

"Not a chance," I say, chuckling and rolling my eyes at her.

The track blasting from the speakers is a far cry from the music both Lucy and I bonded over when I interviewed her to become my personal assistant: Sum 41, Green Day, Foo Fighters, and Avril Lavigne.

A gaggle of bleach-blond women, all in gold pants and matching white vests tied up in knots to reveal their midriffs, approach the table with three new bottles of Belvedere, complete with sparklers.

Anyone in the club who wasn't already looking in our direction definitely is now.

The DJ cuts the music, jumping on the mic.

"Everybody give it up for my boy, Alexander Morgan, in the house tonight!"

I feel my cheeks flush as the crowd erupts. I stand up, lifting my glass in acknowledgment as the DJ turns the music back on. He segues into a remix of *My Anchor* that the UK label dropped today. All of this is a bid to get me to number one on the singles chart.

I feel everyone's eyes on me, like they're expecting me to

jump on the mic and do an impromptu performance, but thankfully that wasn't part of the PA agreement.

"Want a glass?" Rita asks, waving the Belvedere bottle at me, her eyes widening.

A flicker of hope rises in my chest. Not because of her, but at the thought of alcohol.

Of course I want one. But everyone else won't let me, and it's not worth the risk of getting caught drinking so publicly.

"I'm good, thanks," I say, brushing away the flicker of hope and crashing back down to reality. I wave my glass of apple juice at her.

"You know," Rita says as she finishes pouring herself a drink, "I've got someone looking after my children tonight. We could take the party somewhere else after this." Her words are a statement rather than a question, and her hand slides onto my ass, pinching it. The left strap of her dress finally loses its fight to stay up and falls, exposing her nipple.

She waits for me to look at her, which is something I'm determined not to do, but end up doing anyway, and I pull away just enough for her to stumble into the table. I don't want to be caught in a photo with her in such a state of undress.

She looks surprised as Rob helps her back up. She pulls her strap back up, shakes her head, and straightens her hair.

My pocket vibrates, and I quickly move to the other side of Lucy, out of harm's reach. My phone slides out easier this time, thankfully, and I unlock it to reveal a message from Christopher. My heart trips over itself as I read it.

> CHRISTOPHER
> Sry battry dead. Bck t sistrs hse. Gym tmr?

I rub my eyes, reading the message three times and trying to decipher his spelling.

The disappointment weighs heavily on my shoulders when I

realize he's not coming and won't be at the hotel when I get back.

I immediately start typing out a response, then stop myself.

I've got rehearsals tomorrow for the live album recording at Abbey Road, then the *Men's Health* photoshoot and another show at the O2. I'm not going to have time to get into the gym, as much as I want to before the photoshoot.

"Let's go," I say to Lucy, sliding my phone back into my pocket and then rubbing my hand over my watch so Rob sees.

Rob lifts a small flashlight to get the attention of the venue manager by the stairs, cuing the security to clear a path for me to exit the building.

"Where are you going?" Rita drunkenly asks, downing the last of her drink. She scrunches up her face at the aftertaste, grabs her bag, and slings her arm over my shoulder.

"I've got an early start tomorrow," I say, keeping my attention focused forward as Rob removes her arm from around me. I nod at Paul to take care of Rita as we head toward the door.

The darkness of the club is immediately replaced by the flood of all-too-familiar camera flashes of the paparazzi. A commotion breaks out behind me. As I turn around to see what's happening, I see Rita lunging toward me, pushing herself free from Paul, and trying to make her way into my car.

Rita, Rita, here! The shouting of the paparazzi gets her focus long enough that she turns briefly to pose for the pictures, giving Rob enough time to shove me in the car.

I stumble inside, landing lengthwise on the seat, and slump my head into my hands. I can already see the headlines all over the internet and in the papers tomorrow.

Rita Watson spotted leaving London hotspot with Alexander Morgan.

"Let me order you a car," I hear Paul's voice say from outside, as Connie, Lucy, and Rob get in, shutting the door behind them and leaving Paul with her.

Great. Just what I need.
Another scandal.

Sunday

"Do you know how many people would kill me for this job?" Erica laughs.

Her hair is scraped back and her dark top is covered with splashes of the baby oil she's been applying to my body for the last fifteen minutes. I stand topless in some dark fitted Lululemon shorts, which she's covered with paper towels to prevent them from staining.

The photography team is adjusting the lighting around a bunch of different gym equipment, setting up the third and final look for the *Men's Health* shoot.

"And yet, neither one of us gets anything from it," I say, winking at her.

Erica's been with her partner Suzanne for fifteen years now, and is the only other LGBTQIA+ member of my travel party.

"Do you reckon you'll get to do this for a gay magazine one day?" Erica steps back to look at my body, spots a dry bit, and grabs the baby oil bottle to apply more to my arm.

"Maybe," I say, shrugging. I look over at Connie, who is talking with another woman.

I'm lying to myself. I know the answer is a no.

Connie had shut it down when I'd asked a couple of years back. She didn't want to fan the flames or set me up to be outed by a journalist.

That leaves Erica as one of the only people I can talk openly with about my sexuality. With Paul, Rob, and Lucy, it's almost a don't ask, don't tell situation. And Connie avoids it all together, unless she needs to shut down a rumor.

Erica steps back one last time, giving me a once over, and nods in approval.

"With a look this hot, you'll break the internet."

Her smile widens as I whack her arm, and then I'm called over to where the photographer waits by the makeshift gym.

He leans forward on one of the weight machines, showing me how he wants me to pose. He holds his hands above him, exposing a hairy belly underneath a worn-out KISS T-shirt.

"Can I get you to start in this position? And we'll go from there."

"Sure," I say, moving myself into position. Erica ruffles my hair to give it that unkempt, messy look. The music starts again, Nirvana's *Smells Like Teen Spirit*, to help loosen me up as I hold the first pose.

"Great."

"That's it."

"Chin up for me."

"Look slightly to your left."

"Amazing."

"And tense your abs slightly for me."

"Perfect."

"Now if you can just tense those biceps of yours."

"You've got it. Now hold it."

The camera continues to snap away as the photographer shouts out commands like an army general, and I couldn't feel more objectified if I'd tried. Does everyone who appears topless on the cover of *Men's Health* feel the same way? Or is it just me?

The younger version of me clearly bought into what they are selling. I'd begged Erica to buy me copies of any magazine that had someone looking like I currently do gracing the cover. In the safety of my room, I'd masturbate vigorously two or three times in a row over them.

But as I've got older, my tastes have changed. I no longer find the Greek Adonis physique that's so revered by the gay community attractive. Especially now that I know how much hard work it takes, not only to gain the muscle in the first place, but to maintain it.

After what seems like an eternity, Connie wraps the shoot. We've already fallen behind schedule due to the live album rehearsals running over. So she's arranged for the *Men's Health* interview to take place in the car on the way to the O2.

I still feel sticky, despite Erica's attempt to wipe me down as we left the shoot. The white T-shirt I threw on is covered in oil marks.

I see the journalist waiting in the car as I get in with Connie and Erica.

"Alexander, this is Claire from *Men's Health*."

"Great to meet you," I say, extending my hand to greet her. She's dressed in head to toe workout gear, blond hair scraped back into a ponytail. A pang of envy rises in my chest at the fact that her job allows her to wear comfy sports attire, while I find myself changing into new looks multiple times a day.

"Well, look at you, you great big hunk of spunk!" she says in a brash Australian accent. Clearly the women here in London are not shy about being forward. I shudder again at the thought of Rita's clumsy overtures last night, before batting the thought away.

The shift in Connie's body language tells me she's picked up on my discomfort, and she reaches for a box of donuts next to her. "We got your favorite," she says, opening the box to reveal a dozen Red Velvet donuts. I stare at all that sugar, wrapped up into a heavenly package that I've been craving for weeks.

Who said you couldn't fall in love at first sight?

And who said it had to be a person?

But before I allow myself to reach in and take one, I look at Claire.

"Don't worry, Claire's been briefed that this is strictly off the record," Connie says. Claire nods as Connie pushes the box toward me. I take one before Connie passes the box to Erica, who grabs one, and then to Claire, who waves it off, patting her flat stomach.

"Simon showed me some of the raw shots he took before we left, and I think this could be our biggest selling issue since Beckham," she says.

A smile rises on my face, not at the thought of the sales, but at the exact cover she's referring to. Oh, I know that one too well.

"Really?" I ask. I take a bite of the donut and the cream bursts into my mouth. God, I really have been missing out these last couple of months.

"Yeah, you look incredible."

I shake my head, dismissing the compliment. It's amazing what restricting your diet, working out, makeup, and good lighting can do. I've always been told how attractive I am, but I still see a spotty teenager in the mirror.

"Let's begin by walking our readers through what workout program you use to get in such incredible shape." She reaches for her notepad and clicks the top of her pen.

"Donuts," I say, letting out a laugh and then taking another bite.

I want to tell Claire and the readers that it's hell. That this physique comes at the cost of my sanity. But I know this is all part of a carefully curated PR plan, led by Connie, to start positioning me as a leading man in Hollywood. To move beyond the teenybopper image and grow and expand my audience, rather than letting them outgrow me.

"I've been working with a personal trainer called Nick Garcia for the past few years now, and he's really helped me understand my body frame. He created a bespoke workout that targets each body part to get the results I want."

Then the words just fall out of my mouth, as I fill Claire in on the grueling workouts Nick puts me through. The alternating cardio to weight days. The four-one-three-one-four-one on-off schedule I adopt on a fortnightly basis. How I've been able to keep up the workout schedule, even though Nick headed back to LA two weeks ago for the birth of his baby.

"And is there anyone who gets to take advantage of this physique?" Claire asks slyly. A smirk rises on her face. Connie jumps in before I can say anything, telling Claire that personal questions are off the table.

My mind immediately goes to Christopher and I remember that I never responded to his message.

"Can you just give me a second? I forgot something I need to respond to." I grab my phone from my pocket, and quickly open his message, deliberating what to say.

It needs to be light, fun, maybe even sarcastic—like him.

I can feel everyone's gaze on me. As the silence becomes deafening, I shoot off the first thing that comes to my head.

How's your head? You around later...

After sliding my phone back into my pocket, I return my attention to Claire.

"Sorry, where were we?"

10. Christopher
Sunday

Nothing says "Sunday tradition" in the UK quite like stuffing your face with a Sunday roast in a pub and instantly regretting it. The succulent chicken. The roast potatoes cooked in duck fat. The Yorkshire puddings, smothered in dollops of gravy. And of course, a side of vegetables, which I always assume are placed there for decorative purposes.

Kelly lets out a burp as she finishes her last bite and places her cutlery on the plate.

I've become so familiar with her burps over the years that I can infer what each one means. This one is satisfaction. Not to be confused with the one of regret, which Daniel lets out as he rubs his belly.

Both of us wish that we had also opted for the kids-sized meal Kelly had ordered, but then we don't have the digestive issues that have plagued her since childhood to justify ordering it. I shove the last of my roast potatoes to the side, having already pushed my stomach to its limits, and down the last of my beer, hoping it will help the food move through my system as quickly as possible.

I guess this means another thirty minutes on the treadmill tomorrow morning.

Across from me, Kelly and Daniel look like the picture-postcard of love. Daniel gently wipes away a drop of gravy that lingers on the corner of Kelly's mouth with his napkin, pulling at my heartstrings. Her green eyes dance at his kind gesture and she leans in to kiss him. Nothing too PDA, just a tender kiss. A token of appreciation for always looking after her.

How she's even functioning is beyond me. But then she barely drunk last night, and love is the perfect hangover cure. Me, on the other hand—I somehow passed out on their sofa at whatever o'clock and woke up with a neck stiffer than a preacher's dick at a whorehouse.

It doesn't help that I'm wearing one of my future brother-in-law's tight-fitted Abercrombie T-shirts. I pull at the collar, which is slowly cutting off the circulation to my throat.

"Fancy another one?" Daniel asks, nodding at the empty pint in front of me.

I really shouldn't. Ideally I'd have something stronger. But this quaint old man's pub frowns upon the vodka skinnies I'd usually be having right now.

"Go on then," I say, reluctantly pushing the glass across the table.

I barely manage to cover my mouth as a burp tries to escape from it.

Kelly nods yes to another coke and Daniel makes his way to the bar, leaving us both at the round wooden table, tucked away by the window. Thankfully the afternoon sun is no longer shining directly on us.

"What are we going to do about you?" Kelly asks. She adjusts her chair and moves closer to me, placing her hand on top of mine.

"Probably write a tragic novel featuring my sad story and sell it for a profit," I retort, pulling my hand away and laughing off the discomfort rising in my chest.

"Can you be serious for a moment?" Kelly shoots back, grabbing my hand. "I see the way you look at me and Daniel. I see the pain in your eyes. But you've got to stop living in the shadow of Dad. He's gone now. And you've got to stop punishing yourself. You deserve love just like anyone else."

Her eyes give me the look I hate more than any other: pity. A lump forms in my throat and my eyes go misty.

"But you weren't the one that killed him." I reach for the napkin, dabbing my eyes with it.

"The alcohol killed him. Not you. The alcohol." Her nostrils flare, her eyes swirling with anger, not at me, but our father. Kelly has never held me responsible for his death in the way that I do, or that our mum does.

I force down a wave of guilt. If only Ryan hadn't given me an ultimatum about our relationship, forcing me to come out to my parents. If only I hadn't told my dad mid-match, when Arsenal was losing the game. If it hadn't been for those things, he'd still be here. He wouldn't have gotten stinking drunk at the pub and knocked himself unconscious falling down the stairs.

I close my eyes, reliving how we'd made it to the hospital and found that they'd already switched off the machine, pronouncing him dead, and how my mum had beat her fists against my chest.

You did this to him. You did this.

She left me there in the hospital hallway as the nurse escorted her away.

And then I withdrew.

From Ryan.

From love.

From the world.

I opted to get as far away from everyone and everything as

possible. An internal company transfer to Los Angeles made it possible to create a new life for myself. But it isn't one that includes or allows intimacy.

"You deserve to be happy, Chris," Kelly says, reaching for my hand once more, squeezing it tightly. "Have you reached out to Ryan since you've been back?"

The sheer mention of his name sends a shiver down my spine, like nails down a chalkboard.

"Not interrupting anything, am I?" Daniel cuts in. He pointedly glances at Kelly's hand on mine as he places the drinks down on the table, while I wipe a tear from my eye.

"I was just asking Chris about Ryan," Kelly says, lifting her eyebrows at Daniel.

"Ah yes, Ryan." He takes a sip of beer and wipes the foam from his mouth. "Whatever happened to him? You two made the perfect couple."

I almost choke.

We were far from the perfect couple. It was more like I was agreeable to his coercive ways. He was my first boyfriend and I was a newbie in the world of relationships. I was his third after two prior long-term relationships.

Kelly cuts me a look, checking to see if I'm okay talking about it or if she should change the subject. She's looking out for me, the way we always have for each other, in the absence of parents who rarely if ever did.

"Last I saw, he's deeply in love with some Spanish guy," I say with a tinge of envy, not at Ryan's situation, but at the fact that everyone around me seems to be in loving relationships. Yet here I am, living in LA, chasing after unavailable men, and reliving a pattern that my therapist tells me is a symptom of the unavailability my father showed me.

Great. What am I meant to do with that?

"His loss, buddy," Daniel says, hitting me on the shoulder.

"There's plenty more fish in the sea, or sausages in the frying pan. If you get what I mean," he says, with a wink and a nudge, laughing at his own joke.

I glare. *Really, Daniel.*

Daniel is many things, but emotionally aware isn't one of them.

He means well, but he isn't the guy you go to for a heart-to-heart. It's probably the lawyer in him. It is a complete 180 from Kelly's compassionate demeanor, which she employs daily in her job as an art schoolteacher.

"Who was that Alexander guy your friend kept on banging on about last night? I vaguely remember something about him being at your hotel? He invited you to a show?" Kelly pulls a hairband from her wrist and ties her hair back.

A wave of fear hits me.

Shit, I'd texted him last night. Did he reply? I go to grab my phone, but stop. Kelly and Daniel both stare at my hand hovering above the pile of devices. Whoever gives in to temptation first has to pay for dinner. It's a way to keep us all present.

Fuck it.

I cave. I grab the phone and turn it over. My heart skips a beat when I see an American number show up in my notifications.

"Looks like dinner's on Chris," Kelly says, smiling and nudging Daniel as he rubs her back.

I ignore them both, reading the message Alexander sent.

ALEXANDER
How's your head? You around later... 😈

He sent it just under an hour ago.

I twirl my thumbs over the screen, wondering how to respond, when Kelly snatches the phone out of my hands.

"Give it back!" My voice is loud enough to have the table

next to us turn and cut us a disapproving stare. I reach toward Kelly to retrieve my phone. But she leans back just enough so I can't reach, and then passes it across to Daniel so he can read the message.

"Sounds like someone's got a booty call," Daniel says, his eyebrows waggling up and down like a Mexican wave.

I can feel myself going red from embarrassment as I slide down into my chair. But maybe he's right. Maybe tonight is finally the night something happens.

My attention snaps back to reality when I see Daniel's thumbs rapidly tapping away.

"What are you doing?" My voice is even louder this time.

The woman at the other table turns around again, tutting this time. I snarl at her. My eyes tell her in no uncertain terms to *Fuck off and mind your own business*. My glare quickly makes her turn her neck back to her own table partners.

"You're welcome," Daniel says, and hands my phone back to me. He leans back and places his hands behind his head.

I look at the message, feeling mortified.

> Not had any complaints. Yeah, I'm around. Your place or mine? 🐻

What is Alexander going to think? I mean sure, I've been dropping not-so-subtle hints. But this? This is taking it to the next level. The anger at Daniel causes a burning in my chest. Or maybe it's just heartburn.

"Why would you write that?" I ask, lowering my tone so the woman won't turn around again, and placing my phone back on the table.

"Oh, come on. Rodrigo at the office shows me his Grindr messages all the time. You gays don't beat around the bush. You get straight to the point." Daniel lowers his hands from behind his head and reaches for his pint to take another sip.

"Right, 'cause all us gays are the same, aren't we." I shake my head disapprovingly.

Daniel decides to double down. "Well, you do all use Grindr like Drag Race, get a little over-dramatic at times, and worship at the altar of various divas—do you not?" There's not a hint of sarcasm lining his face or in his words.

"Hold on, let me just consult the manual of how to be a gay man," I say, reaching into my pocket to pull out an imaginary book. I lick my finger and start flicking through imaginary pages. "Oh God, I skipped that chapter!" I pretend to put the imaginary book down. "What would us gays do without straight guys like you out here to remind us how to be?" I mock bow down to Daniel.

"Come on guys," Kelly says, trying to mediate our escalating stand-off. She reaches for her coke, taking a gulp.

"My bad," Daniel says, holding his hand out for a truce.

"It's okay. Us gay guys are used to straight guys and their correctile dysfunction," I fire back, batting his hand away with a smirk. Kelly laughs, spraying the coke she's drinking out of her nostrils.

"What does this Alexander guy look like anyway?" Kelly asks, putting down her glass. She grabs a napkin and wipes her face with it before retrieving her phone and firing up her internet browser. She stares at me expectantly, waiting for me to reveal Alexander's full name.

There's no point in fighting Kelly on this. She's like a dog with a bone and will only do this later without me if I don't give in now.

"Morgan," I say, grabbing my glass and downing the rest of my pint in one.

"As in *THE* Alexander Morgan?" Her eyes widen, like I know of more than the one. She immediately types his name into the search bar, bringing up a handful of images of him.

Daniel leans over to get a better look before looking at me.

"Go on, my boy," he says, grabbing his napkin and throwing it at me. His raised eyebrows quickly drop back down as Kelly scrolls and clicks on a link.

"Ohhhhh..." he says. They share a concerned look before looking over at me. Kelly slowly hands her phone to me, almost apologetically, as if hating to be the bearer of bad news. And as I look down, I can see why Daniel's eyebrows dropped. My heart falls to my feet as I read the headline:

Rita Watson Caught Leaving London Club with Alexander Morgan.

I've been berating myself for the last half hour. I'd tortured myself on the forty-minute tube ride back from Hampstead by looking at videos and posts of the incident on social media. Then, as if that wasn't enough, I'd opened my laptop as soon as I got back to the hotel, opening tab after tab. Now, I'm pacing up and down in my hotel room, looking across the room at the multitude of tabs on my web browser.

Of course he's fucking straight!

Why must I always go for the unavailable ones?

Or the straight ones.

Or both.

My thoughts continue to spin as I throw off Daniel's top and remove my jeans, socks, and boxers, leaving them spread across the floor. I grab my pajamas from my suitcase and head into the bathroom.

"It'd be so much easier if I were straight," I say out loud, looking at my worn-out face in the bathroom mirror. I reach for my electric toothbrush and toothpaste and start scrubbing my teeth viciously.

If I were straight, I wouldn't have had to come out. Dad would still be alive. And Mum wouldn't resent me for Dad no longer being here. I'd be able to date without having to hide it from my extended family, and I wouldn't be in this position right now.

A knock on the door startles me. I switch the toothbrush off, placing it next to the handwash, and grab the towel to wipe the toothpaste from my mouth before looking at my watch.

It can't be.

He's got a show tonight, and he won't be back for at least another couple of hours.

Another knock sounds as I make my way toward the door.

Peering through the peephole reveals a bald man with glasses, wearing a smart buttoned-down shirt and chinos, standing on the other side. A folder is clutched in his right hand.

He looks like one of the guys I saw in the lift the night Alexander arrived, which must mean he's someone important on Alexander's team.

I take one quick look in the mirror—my pajamas aren't the best outfit to greet him in—and slowly open the door.

"Christopher Foster, right?"

I'm immediately taken back by his forthrightness. How does he know my full name?

"Can I help you?" I ask. My shoulders tighten as he looks me up and down.

"Yes. I'm Paul, Alexander's manager. I was hoping you might have a moment."

I grip the door more tightly, keeping it slightly ajar.

"What's this regarding?" My confusion and irritation merge into one.

"Would you mind if I come in?" he asks, stepping forward. "It's a rather personal matter and I'd rather not discuss it out here." He looks both ways down the hallway before turning back to me with a harried look on his face.

I'm guessing that look is quite common for managers, based on my limited exposure dealing with talent through the creative campaigns I oversee at work, but I don't relish seeing it directed at me.

I debate for three beats whether to let him in, but curiosity about the folder he holds firmly in his hand gets the better of me. I pull the door open and wave him through to the room. I flinch as he walks past me, and I close the door a little harder the necessary.

Paul steps over my clothes, which are strewn across the floor, making himself comfortable in one of the armchairs, and I quickly pick them up and throw them in the suitcase before I join him, sitting down in the other.

"What is it you want to discuss?" I ask, trying to regulate my breathing. Suddenly it feels as if I'm in some sort of trouble.

Paul places the folder down on the table between us.

"It's been brought to my attention that you've had some, erm, how do I put it, *interactions* with Alexander since we've been here in the hotel."

The way he says interactions has me shifting in my seat.

His gaze is locked on me. He's clearly waiting for me to respond, but I don't know what to say, so I sit in silence, waiting for the discomfort to pass. After an awkward silence, he continues.

"As I'm sure you can imagine, someone with Alexander's level of visibility brings a lot of attention and speculation with it."

Shit. My body tenses and my gaze immediately darts to my laptop screen, prompting Paul to stop and follow the direction

I'm looking. I let out a slight sigh when I see my screensaver staring back at me.

I don't need Paul to think I'm adding to the problem.

I readjust myself in the chair and look down at the folder and back up at him.

"It's my job, as his manager, to ensure that I protect him," Paul says. He reaches for the folder as his eyes stay locked on mine. His stare is magnified by the lenses in his glasses.

"I see," I say, nodding my head as he opens the folder.

My body relaxes slightly as I get a sense of where this is heading.

"If these interactions are to continue, we need some assurances that you will not disclose the details of those interactions to anyone." He retrieves some of the papers inside, placing them down on the table.

Ah! I knew it. They're trying to keep me silent.

I sit up in the chair and the power shifts in the room as I pull my shoulders backward and lift my head higher.

"And if the interactions were to stop?"

I have no intention of being Alexander's plaything, either to appease his sexual curiosity or his urges whenever he's horny and Rita Watson isn't around.

"Then I will need you to agree to the terms set out in this document." Paul reaches for a second document and neatly lines it up next to the other one.

I pause for a beat. My stomach lets out a gurgling sound, making me wince as I pick up the papers.

MNDA is spelled out at the top of both of them.

Mutual Non-Disclosure Agreement.

I've heard about these things before. I even signed one once at work, promising not to reveal company secrets for one of our clients. But I've never had to sign one to cover a relationship that, frankly, doesn't even exist.

As I make my way through the first document, Paul taps his fingers impatiently, as if that's going to speed up the process. I try to make sense of each clause in the agreement and what is being asked of me.

I'm not sure they can even hold me accountable for half of the things in there. Certain points, like using a pseudonym to communicate, I've already broken.

My eyes widen as I get toward the end and see a statement that if I disclose the nature of our relationship to anyone, I'll be held liable and will have to pay damages of ten million dollars.

My stomach knots up at the mere thought.

Thank God, I've already sworn Kelly and Daniel to secrecy.

The second agreement is a much shorter one-page document. Basically, it buys my silence if I immediately cease all communication with Alexander. The price? Twenty thousand dollars.

Once I've finally finished reading both, I look up and am greeted by an impatient look across Paul's face.

"So...." he says, not beating around the bush.

"When do you need a decision by?" I place the papers back down on the table.

"Before I leave the room," he says, reaching into his pocket to retrieve a pen. He sets it down, strategically, on the contract that buys my silence.

Like it's a test.

Like he's *encouraging* me to end all interactions immediately, rather than continue getting to know Alexander.

There's no expression on his face as he studies me, like a poker player trying to read my hand, but I hold all the power here. So, I throw caution to the wind and ask the question that's been on my mind all evening.

"And this Rita woman. Has she signed one of these?" I rest my hand atop the documents.

Paul shifts in his chair, crossing his right leg over his left. "That's on a need-to-know basis."

"Well, if you want me to sign one of these before you leave the room, then I need to know." I can feel my forehead wrinkling.

He pauses momentarily, as if weighing up whether to share something or not. Opens his mouth, then closes it. He adjusts himself in his seat and inhales deeply.

"If you're trying to ask me if Rita is his type, then I think you already know by virtue of the fact that I'm in here asking you to sign one of these documents."

My gaze goes to the laptop again.

So, all of that isn't true. Everything I read was fabricated?

I can't believe I just wasted the last couple of hours spiraling. Thinking that Alexander and Rita were hooking up and that everything that's happened in the past seventy-two hours was all a figment of my imagination.

I look back at both documents one more time. The easy way out is on the left. The road less traveled is on the right. I take two deep breaths, close my eyes as I reach for the pen, and grab the stack of papers, filling out my details at the top and signing the bottom of each page before handing it over to Paul. I catch a brief look of ire on his face, gone in the blink of an eye, before his poker face returns.

Did he not want me to sign that document?

Did he expect me to take the money and run?

"Right." Paul slaps his knees, slides the paperwork back into the folder, and stands up, signaling the end of this meeting. "I'll leave you to it."

"Will I be getting a copy of that?" I force myself up from the armchair and point to the document, now tucked away in the folder again.

"No need," he says, making the short journey to the door

and letting himself out without another word. The door closes quickly behind him.

A pang in my stomach instantly appears, and a wave of regret washes over me. I rush to the door, opening it, but a quick look in both directions reveals that Paul has already disappeared.

I close the door and put my back up against it, sliding down to the ground. I drop my head into my hands.

Did I just sign the wrong document?

11. Alexander
Sunday

PAUL

You were right.

I can hear Paul's voice in those three words, spoken through gritted teeth. There's a distinct coldness, a reluctance to admit that I was right and he was wrong.

I should stop this car, run into the art gallery opposite, and have them print the text out so I can hang it in the window for all to see: Paul O'Neil admits he is wrong.

My whole body is giddy with excitement. Paul's text confirms what I thought: Christopher is interested in *me*, not in the money.

It's horrible to have to put these things in place, but I had to start questioning everyone's intentions after my popularity skyrocketed. It began with family members and friends who were selling me out to make a quick buck, but then escalated when unfinished tracks were leaked online before they were ready to be heard. The situation with Roy was just the cherry on the top.

At one point, I couldn't work out who was leaking stuff to the media, so Connie came up with a plan. I adopted a dog and told everyone who asked about it a different name—keeping its real name under wraps. But when an article appeared in the press saying the dog's name was Bailey, I was heartbroken. Of all the people to sell me out, I had never expected it to be my younger brother.

I confronted Harrison about it, and at first he denied it. But I had evidence this time. When our parents made him log into his bank account, we saw regular deposits of not insignificant amounts of money.

That was four years ago, and the relationship has never recovered. Our parents try not to get in the middle of things, but it's hard not to fight when I'm home over Thanksgiving, Christmas, and during the little breaks from work I do get.

I want to spend those moments with my family. Pick up my skateboard or surfboard and just be little fourteen-year-old Al again. But Harrison still lives at home, so there's always tension whenever I return. And all I want is to have my little brother back. To be a happy family once again.

As I sit pondering this, I remember that I have to reply to my parents. They've been asking about coming to London to see the last show of the tour, but I haven't sorted things out yet. And now the last show is only a few days away.

A feeling of overwhelm rises in my chest as I scroll through my phone. There's countless unread messages, emails, and voicemail notifications.

I haven't listened to my voicemails in a good couple of years. I'm sure there are important things on there, but if anything is crucial, I'm sure that Paul, Connie, Lucy or my parents will tell me.

I quickly fire off a message to my parents, letting them know

I'll talk to Lucy to get their flights sorted out, and am about to close the app when I see a new message from Christopher.

> **CHRISTOPHER**
> Not had any complaints. Yeah, I'm around. Your place or mine? 😈

My post-concert adrenaline was starting to taper off, but I feel another surge rush through my veins. Like a B-12 shot in the ass. It makes me want to jump right out of the car, run straight into the hotel, and rip Christopher's clothes off, devouring him completely.

Concentrate, Alex! Concentrate.

I shake my head to bring myself back to the present.

Damn ADHD.

"Lucy, can we look into flights and a room for my parents to come into town?"

Lucy turns her attention to me, away from the twinkling building lights shining against the backdrop of the dark night outside. She opens the hood of her black sweatshirt slightly, revealing loose strands of her red hair tied back underneath.

"Of course." She reaches for her phone. "When do they want to come in?" She opens up her notes app and stares expectantly at me.

"They want to be here for the last show, so I guess maybe get them in a night or two beforehand?" I shrug my shoulders uncertainly.

I don't need them here before then, bothering me.

"And do you know when they'll want to leave? If they'll want to stay on beyond the last show? Go somewhere else in Europe?" Lucy's fingers type away at her phone.

So many questions.

I close my eyes briefly, shaking my head, pushing away my resentment at being the intermediary.

I wish my parents would just book their own travel plans, but they tried to a few years back and got the show dates wrong while also somehow landing in Berlin instead of Hamburg, so now it's just easier for me to deal with it.

"We're back in LA the next day, right?" I try to picture the printout of the schedule on the desk back at my suite. There's recording of the live album tomorrow, and more shows Tuesday, Wednesday, Friday, and Saturday.

"Right," Lucy acknowledges with a nod as I open my eyes.

A man on a late-night walk with his dog catches my attention outside, hitting me with a pang of jealousy. I don't get to do those simple things these days. It had broken my heart when I'd given Archibald—my dog's actual name—up to a friend because Paul said I couldn't take him on the road with me. My lifestyle just doesn't allow me to be responsible for another being.

"Alex?" Lucy asks.

"It's a long way to come for just two nights, so maybe book them a couple of extra nights here after the shows are over. Check with my mom, and then book whatever they want. But, whatever she says, don't get them out here earlier than Wednesday."

If my mom had her way, she'd be out here for the whole tour.

Lucy nods, typing away to put things in motion. I find myself focusing on her in awe, like I sometimes do. I don't know what I'd ever do without her. She's been great ever since she came on board after Samuel died. He was great, too, but he also wasn't the most on top of things when it came to organizing my life. Then again, I was often distracting him when he needed to get things done, so I can't really blame him.

"Anything else you need?" she asks, looking up, and tucks one of the stray strands of red hair behind her ear.

I'm sure there's a million things I need, but right now all I can think about is seeing Christopher for more than a few fleeting moments.

"What time do we need to leave tomorrow?"

"Midday." Lucy clearly doesn't need to look at the schedule. She probably has it memorized.

My gaze drifts to my Rolex before I realize that it's set to LA time. That does nothing to help me figure out how much time that gives me this evening until I look at the clock on the dashboard at the front of the car: 11:37 p.m.

Great, twelve hours. That should be more than enough time to hang out with Christopher for a bit uninterrupted.

I envy Lucy's ability to retain information. My brain is like a sieve. Information is like sand. I only manage to retain the big stuff. But I'll remember the call time. Because it buys me a chance of normality.

By the time I make it through the noisy swarming crowds waiting for me outside the hotel and back to my suite, it feels eerily quiet. My brain, however, is not.

I've brushed my teeth three times, more thoroughly than usual. I rinsed my mouth out with mouthwash and took another Adderall to try and get my brain to focus, though the medication is taking its sweet ass time to kick in.

I even showered twice, letting the last of the water on my body get soaked up by the soft-white Egyptian cotton towel as I run another one through my hair.

My right leg twitches as I stare at the phone beside me on the bed, wondering what to message Christopher or if he's still even up. The last time, I had Dutch courage in my system to help me force myself to knock on his door. But I'm sober tonight, a deliberate decision I made to prove to myself I can take alcohol or leave it—I *can* leave it—and now I don't know what to do.

I finally pick it up, take three deep breaths, and type away.

> Is that so? Mine's probably better.

I can't bear waiting for a response, so I throw my phone back on the bed and get up, heading to the walk-in wardrobe, dropping the towels on the floor. I'm picking out some shorts and a vest when I hear a pinging sound.

It can't be. That was too quick.

But it has to be him. Not only because I've just messaged him, but because I set my phone to Do Not Disturb and set a rule to only allow notifications from Christopher.

I almost stumble over the towels in my excitement.

CHRISTOPHER
> Are you back? I could head over in five...

> Cool. Knock four times so I know it's you.

Shit.

This is really happening.

I'm instantly turned on by the thought of being alone with Christopher in my room. But I want to play it cool. *Need* to play it cool. Yet I'm second-guessing every thought that enters my brain.

Should I tidy my room or leave it messy?

Should I change into something else or keep what I have on?

Should I spray on some of my Creed aftershave, or would that come across as trying too hard?

I move from the bedroom into the lounge area, turn the TV on with the remote, and slump into the couch. My heart rate feels like it's going about as fast as my finger flicking through the channels. I impatiently check the clock in the corner of the screen.

Maybe I could do with a drink?

Seven minutes have passed when I hear four knocks at the suite's entrance, and I jump straight up. Somehow, I stop myself from rushing to the door, taking long deep inhales to gain some composure. I pause at the video screen next to the door to ensure it's Christopher.

My heart skips a beat.

He looks breathtaking in a white polo shirt, blue jeans, and brown boots. His brown hair is parted down the right side and he's twiddling his thumbs. I take one last look of my reflection in the hallway mirror, running my hand through my hair and adjusting my shorts, before pulling open the door.

"Hey," I say.

"Hi." He drops his hands to his sides.

An awkward silence permeates in the air as I take him in.

God, he really is beautiful.

"Wanna come in?" I ask, opening the door wider.

"Okay." Christopher steps inside as I quickly look down the hallway, making sure no one has seen him enter, and close the door behind me.

"Fuck me!" His voice echoes around the suite.

Wow. He doesn't beat around the bush.

I turn around to see Christopher taking in the vastness of the room.

"A girl likes to be wined and dined a bit before dropping her panties for a man," I laugh, trying to hide the grumbling in my stomach.

Christopher turns back to face me. His hazel eyes pierce into my soul.

"Oh. Erm. I mean... Fuck me, this suite. It's massive." He slides his hands into his pockets.

The stuttering of his speech instantly settles my stomach.

He's nervous too.

"Oh yeah, right. Want a tour?" I ask.

"Sure, if you want." He shrugs his shoulders.

The tension feels palpable as I walk through the lounge area, pointing out all the features. I get the sense that Christopher's trying to play it cool. But maybe this is what he's actually like when he's on his own.

Gone is the witty, sarcastic Christopher I've encountered so far. This is a far more reserved and cooler version.

I walk to the window, pulling the curtains open to reveal the main road below. The view is slightly blurry from the rain droplets against the window, but the faint sound of my fans still echoes below, still there come rain or shine. The night lights of the skyscrapers across London shine in the midnight sky as Christopher edges closer to me.

"If you look over there, you can just about make out the BT Tower." I point to the left, recalling the sights on the skyline one of the hotel staff showed me.

He steps up, pressing himself gently into me, and I feel the warmth of his body against mine and his legs straddled to either side. As he leans over my shoulder, I feel his semi-erect penis through his jeans, rubbing up against my left ass cheek.

"Where did you say?" His minty-fresh breath passes by my left ear.

The smell of the sandalwood from his cologne fills my nostrils as I reach for his hand, pulling it up to the window to point toward the tower. My hand fits perfectly on top of his.

"Right there." I push my ass back ever so gently into him, and I feel his cock grow harder with every passing moment.

He leans in even closer, his breath shallower. His mouth is mere millimeters from my left earlobe.

"So, you're saying you'd be the girl in these *interactions*?"

My body stiffens and he pulls back. I read the subtext of what he's insinuating, but I'm thrown by the comment.

It's been a moment since I've last been intimate with a man and had a conversation about what role I take sexually. But interactions? That's a funny word to use, and then it dawns on me—that's Paul's code word.

I make my way back to the couch, noticing the sheepish look on Christopher's face as I motion him to follow. I pick up the remote to mute the TV. He keeps a slight distance as we sit down, a pillow separating the two of us. I yearn for his body to be touching mine again, but we should talk about what he's just signed.

"Thank you for signing the document, I appreciate it." I rest my hand on the pillow as I wait for his gaze to meet mine.

I want to address our sexual preferences, but I can feel my avoidance kicking in, and this low-hanging fruit feels easier to navigate.

"Well, just to be clear, my lips are sealed, but my facial expressions are under no such obligation." He arches his eyebrows when he finally meets my gaze. "And actually, come to think of it, there are a couple of things I need answering…"

His right leg comes up under his left as he adjusts himself on the couch to directly face me. He sounds like a detective about to launch an interrogation, sending my heart rate soaring for all the wrong reasons.

"Shoot," I say, fighting back the lump in my throat.

He's already in the room. He's already signed the contract.

"The name I need to save you in my phone under. What should I use? Houdini? Casper? Big Reveal?" His gaze drifts to my crotch as a smirk rises on his face.

"Alex is fine." I shake my head at the question's randomness.

"I can't save your actual name in my phone, according to the MNDA I just signed."

Ah, right.

I turn my head away, toward the TV. Avril Lavigne's *Sk8er*

Boi video is playing out. A smile forms on my face as I remember how I used to think she was singing the song about me.

"Skater Boy," I say, turning back to Christopher.

"Okay...?" A look of bewilderment appears on his face as he pulls his phone and room key out of his pocket. He places the room key next to the remote, and holds the phone in his hand. There's an awkward silence, as if he's waiting for me to explain why.

"I used to use Avril Lavigne as my pseudonym when checking into hotels because I loved that song," I say, nodding to the TV. "Then someone worked it out. I never thought someone would think I'd actually use another artist's name. Now I'm stuck with whatever name Paul or Rob sign me in under."

"Ah okay." He nods his head as he types the name into his phone, before returning it to his pocket. "And if someone asks me how we know each other?"

"We can figure that out later," I say, sliding across the couch.

I want—need—to be closer to him, but his hand stops me from getting too close.

"And am I the only one signing an MNDA about interactions?" The intensity of his stare makes me move back slightly.

"Yes," I say, catching the sharpness in my voice.

The Rita issue has been following me all day. Connie says she's handling it, but why does everyone think I'm such a love rat?

"Yes, you are the only one," I say softly, my hand resting on the pillow.

He slips his hand over mine and cups the bottom of my chin with the other. "And are you saying that you want me to be the man in this relationship?"

I want him to be whatever he wants to be.

I want him to throw me all around this room and dominate me.

I want him to own me.

But I don't want to scare him off. So instead, I lean in and kiss him.

His lips are soft, and with each subsequent kiss I lean in more. His tongue parts my lips and slides into my mouth, intertwining with mine.

He leans back into the couch, and I stretch my left leg over him. Straddling him. Kissing him more passionately, more deeply, with every breath.

I lose myself in the throes of passion as he flips me onto my back, pushes me down onto the couch and gets on top of me. He takes control, pinning my hands against the arm of the couch as his mouth goes to work on my neck. Biting it slightly. I wriggle away.

"Too much?" His hazel eyes hover just above mine.

I want him to eat me whole, but I also need to ensure that there are no visible marks that show.

"No...just..." I stutter, trying to catch a breath. "Just not where they can see."

He lifts himself up above me, his hands to either side of my shoulders, like he's doing push-ups over me. The light from the TV captures his biceps as he holds his position. Observing me as I wait impatiently for his next move.

"What?" I ask, as the right side of his mouth rises.

"There you are," he says. "The real you..."

His eyes widen and, in that moment, I feel so vulnerable.

So exposed.

He lowers himself back down, but this time, instead of finding my lips, he kisses my forehead, my nose, the scar on my left jaw from the car crash. All the things about myself that I'm insecure about. It's like he knows. Each kiss is more slow, more meaningful. The pause between each kiss is slightly longer than before.

When he finally finds his way back to my mouth, I'm ready. Waiting. I lean ever so slightly forward, lifting my head off the couch to meet his lips, and as I do, our mouths intersect, our tongues collide. I jolt upright, bumping my head into Christopher's as the sound of the fire alarm starts ringing through the suite.

"Sorry," I say, as he rubs his forehead.

"It's okay." He moves away to sit upright.

"It's probably just a false alarm." I shrug my shoulders.

"Yeah, someone probably just leaned on the fire exit and set it off." He turns back toward me as I grab his polo shirt to pull him back in.

My mouth is ready for another taste of him. The alarm continues, but the wailing sound falls into the background as I lose myself in Christopher once more.

I barely hear the door open.

"Boss. Boss, we need to leave!" Rob's voice is elevated.

Christopher quickly pulls back, letting me swing my legs around and stand.

"What do you mean, leave?" I ask as Rob comes toward me. His eyes scan the room as I adjust myself, pulling my vest down and sliding my hand down my shorts to rearrange my raging hard-on.

"We can't have you go outside like that," Rob says, heading through to the bedroom and into the walk-in closet. He returns with a hoodie and a pair of vans. "Put them on."

"What do you... Erm?" Christopher looks at me, then to Rob.

"It's best if you make your own way out, sir, and follow the hotel's instructions." Rob folds his arms while I push my feet into the vans and slide the hoodie over my head.

Christopher looks at me, his forehead crinkled.

"You better go... I'll message you once whatever this is is dealt with."

Christopher makes his way to the door, looking back over his shoulder while I tie the laces of my shoes, and exits.

Damn that fire alarm.

There'd better be a good reason for it.

12. Christopher
Monday

My body shakes as I attempt to pay attention to Imani, the night manager I've crossed paths with a few times now. She's using a megaphone to update the growing crowd of hotel guests, mingled with Alexander's fans, on the ongoing situation.

I look like a drowned rat. When I'd run out of the hotel earlier, fearful of a fire engulfing the building, I'd instantly been caught by the downpour. I'd made my way to the back of the hotel, squeezing myself underneath the marquee-style roof that extended from the door to the railway station, along with at least fifty other guests. If I had known we'd be stuck out here this long, I'd have grabbed something warmer and more waterproof from my room.

"Thank you for your patience, everyone. We've contained the issue, and it's now safe to return to your rooms," Imani announces. Audible sighs come from the crowd. "Please have your room keys ready to show the doorman as you reenter the hotel." She drops the megaphone down beside her and turns back into the hotel.

I take a look around as the crowd starts moving toward the hotel entrance, trying to locate anyone from Alexander's team. But I don't notice anyone who might be part of his entourage. Rob clearly isn't here. He'd be impossible to miss, even if Alexander was able to blend in. Which means they're not here.

Maybe they kept him inside?

"Escuché que uno de esos fanáticos irrumpió en el hotel!" a woman in front of me says to her partner, as we slowly edge closer to the door.

My Spanish is terrible, but from the look of contempt on her face, it's clear that she believes one of the fans is responsible.

Maybe that's why Alexander isn't here. It wasn't a fire; it was a threat to his safety.

"Excuse me, sir," she says as she shows her room key to the doorman. "Was there a break-in at the hotel?"

"I'm not at liberty to say, ma'am," he says, opening the door for her. She shakes her head, mumbling again in Spanish while following her partner through.

"Room key, sir," the doorman says, closing the door behind the couple. There's a solemn look on his face.

"One moment." I step aside to let the other guests pass as I rummage in my pockets, trying to locate it.

I'm sure I had it with me when I left my room for Alexander's.

I remove my phone and turn my wet jean pockets inside out, but nothing other than a couple of one-pound coins appear.

"I must have left it upstairs," I say, pushing my pockets back in and tucking my phone inside.

The last of the hotel guests are making their way back in, leaving me outside with a dozen or so fans. They seem blithely unaware of the rain, drinking cans of whiskey and coke and Pimm's and playing Alexander's songs through a mini speaker.

"Sir, you'll need to make your way round to the front and

speak to reception to verify that you're a guest." The look on the doorman's face has been replaced with one of contempt.

"You're joking, right?!"

I've not been out here in the cold and wet for over an hour just for some douchebag to make me walk back to the main entrance through the pouring rain.

"I am not joking, sir," he says, his hand still firmly on the door handle.

"You could at least offer me a brolly." I nod toward the handful of umbrellas just to the right of him.

"These are for verified guests only."

I realize I'm fighting a losing battle, and every moment stuck here playing "whose dick is the smallest" is a moment that I could be back in the warm hotel. Sleeping. Or with Alexander.

I sprint for the front, and by the time I make it to the front entrance, I've gone from looking like a drowned rat to a wet mop that lost its will to clean.

I hit a similar snag with the doorman at this entrance but, this time, thankfully, I catch Imani's eye through the glass panel of the door.

"Ask Imani, she knows I'm staying here." I struggle to get the words out as I catch my breath. I just see the doorman's head turn and Imani's head nodding.

After a brief pause, I'm finally allowed through. Imani greets me when I walk into the lobby.

"You poor soul, you're soaked through to the bone!" She places a warm hand on my arm. Her dark eyes look weary. "You haven't been stuck out in the rain all this time, have you?"

I shake my head *No*, as I try to slow my breathing down. And I try to push down my anger at the doormen for being assholes. I have a mind to put in a complaint, but I don't know how close Imani is to them, and I don't want to cause more issues for her. She's probably had a hell of a night.

"They wouldn't let me in because I didn't have my room key. Made me walk all the way round to the front." I exhale and drop my shoulders.

"He did what?" She turns to look back at the door as we reach the concierge desk. She shakes her head before turning her attention to her colleague.

"Can you get this gentleman a towel and a room key? It's Room 506, right?" she asks me.

"It is."

As I reach across the desk for the towel her colleague passes over, I'm taken aback by how Imani recalls my room number. She seems to know everything, so I take a chance with her while waiting for a new room key to be activated.

"You haven't seen Alexander return yet, have you?" I start rubbing my hair dry, before wiping down my arms and clothes.

"Who?" Her forehead crinkles as her eyes narrow.

"Alexander Morgan," I say, lowering my voice to a whisper.

"Oh, sorry. I know him as Avril Lavigne."

The mere mention of the name puts a smile on my face. I guess his team is back to using that pseudonym again.

Her brief pause gives me the sense that there's something she wants to tell me, but can't. Her colleague holds up the door key and hands it over. I mouth *Thank you*, and hand the towel back.

Imani inhales deeply and motions me forward toward the elevators on the opposite side of the lobby.

"You promise to keep this between us?" She widens her eyes at me.

It seems like today is a day full of being asked to keep secrets.

"Yes," I say emphatically.

"You know the actress, Rita Watson?" I nod again as a cold shudder runs straight down my spine.

"Well, she came into the hotel tonight demanding to see Avril— I mean Alexander." Imani shakes her head. "Poor Sheila over there," she points her thumb at the staff member who handed me the towel, "tried to calm her down. But she seemed to be in a drunken rage. When Sheila refused to let Rita know what room he was in, she stormed away. Next thing we knew, the fire alarm was set off."

Jesus.

No wonder Rob was so concerned when he burst into the room earlier.

"Please tell me she's not still here."

"No," Imani says, stopping by the round table. The faint scent of the hydrangeas makes its way through my bunged-up nose. "One of our security team managed to detain her. They kept her out of harm's way until the police arrived."

Just as my muscles begin to relax, the hotel entrance bursts open. Rob comes through, followed by Alexander, his head lowered and the drawstrings pulled tight on his hoodie, and five other people, including Paul.

I start to call out Alexander's name, but stop, not wanting to draw attention. Rob catches my eye.

"You coming?" he asks, though it's more a command than a question.

I sheepishly follow, almost knocking over the flower vase in the process, mouthing *Thank you* to Imani as she smiles back.

Inside the lift, Alexander pulls back his hood, and his face instantly lights up when he notices me.

"Have you been out in the rain all this time?" The puppy dog look in his eyes melts away the coldness I'm still feeling from being stuck outside for so long.

I take a quick look at my reflection in the golden elevator doors, instantly regretting it. I really have seen better days.

"Long story," I say.

As we reach the third floor, the red-headed woman leaves the elevator followed by the blond-haired woman.

"Night," they both say in unison.

"Night, Lucy. Night, Connie," Alexander says, a faint smile rising on his face.

I try to file away their names.

Lucy. Connie. Lucy. Connie.

Who am I kidding? I'm never gonna remember them. I shake my head.

"Night," Rob adds in a monosyllabic tone.

Clearly, Rob is just as tired and pissed off by this whole fire alarm situation as I am. I wonder if they already know the real reason the alarm went off.

At the fourth floor, the remaining two women exit—a brunette and a woman with a pixie cut who is nearly as tall as Rob.

"Eleven a.m. at the suite right?" the tall one asks, turning back once out of the elevator.

"Yes," Paul says, looking up from his phone. The closing doors prevent him from saying anything else. Though, from our interaction earlier, he seems to be a man of few words.

Finally, the elevator reaches our floor, but as I go to step out, Rob stops me, placing his hand firmly across my chest. He nods at a security guard waiting opposite us.

"Hold fire for a second. We all clear?" he asks to the security guard.

My discomfort has me reaching for a funny one-liner, but I stop myself. This is not the time for humor.

"Affirmative," the guy responds.

Rob motions Alexander forward, and the security guard moves ahead of him down the hallway as Rob exits. I motion for Paul to exit before me.

"I'm on the top floor." Paul's nostrils flare.

Fine. Be a dick.

I shake my head as I exit. Alexander and the security guard are already halfway down the hallway, and I get the feeling that maybe Alexander and I won't be picking up from where we left off.

I hover by my door momentarily, retrieving my new room key, before Rob comes back down the hall toward me.

"What are you waiting for?" Rob points toward Alexander's suite.

Maybe I've got Rob wrong. There's a firm but kind side appearing tonight.

Maybe the rudeness I experienced during those first twenty-four hours was actually him being overly protective of Alexander, rather than anything to do with me.

"Oh, okay," I say, sliding the key back in my pocket and heading down to Alexander's suite. The other security guard opens the door once I arrive.

"Night," Rob says.

Night?

What does he mean *night*?

Does he assume I'm staying the night?

As I enter, Alexander comes out of the bedroom, towel in hand. He's already removed his hoodie and sweatpants. His white vest and boxer briefs are all that's left.

"Here." He chucks the towel at me forcefully while making his way past the two armchairs to where I'm standing. I grab it in one swoop, impressed that I have any strength left with how exhausted I am, and start to pat down my clothes.

"Let's get you out of these and into something more comfortable." He reaches for the bottom of my polo shirt, but I pull back. A wave of fear rises inside.

He lowers his hand as confusion floods his eyes.

"Sorry, I'm just a little..." The dryness in my mouth stops me from continuing.

I've always been uncomfortable with guys seeing me naked. Especially ones with physiques like Alexander's. And Kelly had called me "pigeon belly" as a teenager, cementing my paranoia. I'd spent a lot of time in the gym, working hard to get a flat stomach, but I always fell short of achieving that toned, ripped abdomen.

"It's okay," Alexander says, like he can read my mind. "I can get you something else to change into if you want." He walks back toward his bedroom, motioning me to take a seat on the couch where just a couple of hours ago we were in the throes of passion.

"I'd appreciate that."

He smiles as he disappears into the bedroom. I quickly yank my top off and wrap the towel around my torso like a dress. My arms stretch to turn out the lamps on either side of the couch. The glare through the orange lamp shades makes my eyes strain.

"Sorry, all I've got is this," he says, reemerging. He throws me a scrunched up black T-shirt. This time, I miss my grab, and it falls onto the table next to the remote and a room key.

Ah, that's where I left it.

I pick up the shirt, opening it to reveal an image of Alexander plastered on the front, and his name printed underneath.

"The only thing that's missing are the words *Property of*," I quip.

Alexander lets out a laugh as I pull the T-shirt on over my head, wriggling it down over the towel and then pulling the towel out from underneath once the T-shirt covers my torso.

I stand up and look at him.

"How do I look?" I stretch my arms out wide and give him a twirl.

A mischievous grin appears across his face as he steps toward me.

"Uh-uh. Not so fast." I wave my finger at him as he reaches for the button on my jeans. "Rob seems to think I'm staying the night." I step back and sit on the couch.

"You don't want to," he says, his smirk collapsing into a frown.

"It's not that I don't want to, I'm just intrigued by the assumption."

Alexander hesitates, opening and then closing his mouth to speak, before opening it again.

"I don't want to be alone tonight," he finally says. He moves toward the couch, moving the cushion that is still there from earlier, and sits right next to me.

"Is it because of Rita?" I ask, using my hand to lift his chin up. His ocean-blue eyes meet mine.

"You already know?" I can feel his body begins to tremble and I immediately shoot my arm around him, pulling him in tightly.

"Yes, the night manager told me." A pang of guilt hits my chest at breaking my promise to Imani so quickly. "You're okay now. Rita's been taken care of." I rub my hand up and down his arm.

"Has something like this happened before?" I get the feeling this isn't his first rodeo.

"I've had a few stalkers over the years," he says. "One broke into my home in LA while I was asleep. Thankfully he didn't cause any harm. Samuel was able to distract him while I called the police, but I've struggled to sleep ever since. Tonight brought all of that back up, even if it wasn't a stalker." He hangs his head low, playing with the drawstrings of his shorts.

Samuel?

I've not heard a Samuel mentioned before.

Maybe he's one of the security team members back home.

I continue to rub Alexander's arm as his shaking begins to subside. The skin on his bicep is smooth and the light hairs on his forearm tickle the palm of my hand.

"Sometimes I just wish I lived a normal life. One where I can walk down the street unnoticed. Go to a skate park and ride my skateboard, without having to worry about people noticing me."

He lifts his head to look at me and pushes himself upright, then grabs my head and kisses me with a passion and intensity that throws me off guard.

Part of me wants to pull back, to make sure he's okay, but the stronger part of me takes over. I lean into it, taking him in. Before I know it, I'm pulling at his vest, yanking it off and momentarily pausing to take in the rock-hard abs that I remember trying not to stare at in the gym. I don't bother trying not to now.

He leans back in, devouring my mouth, running his hands up through my hair and down my back. He stands up to let me quickly unbutton my jeans and then pulls them off with one strong tug. He encourages me to remove my boxers too, which I pull down and fling off with a flick of my leg. There's a passion and intensity burning in his eyes that has my exposed cock throbbing and begging for attention.

Alexander does the same, removing his briefs to reveal his juicy, thick-cut cock pointing at me, and I pull him back down to me. He kneels over me, straddling my thighs and rocking his ass back and forth along my shaft. The throbbing intensifies with every thrust of my hips.

I lower my mouth to his left nipple, flicking it with my tongue, then move across to his right as he lets out a moan. His hand pushes my head harder into his chest. I respond by gently biting and his moan gets louder. He takes away his hand and spits into it before reaching back and sliding his hand over my shaft.

The mere touch of his hand, the vice-like grip as it begins moving up and down, makes my balls swell. Alexander locks his blue eyes onto mine as he strokes me, a smirk appearing on his face.

"You like that, huh?" he asks. His mouth meets mine before I can answer.

He reaches back up to push me back against the couch, then stops and looks down at the T-shirt I'm wearing. He reaches for the hem to lift it off, and I hesitate, but let him do so. I lift my arms up as he pulls it over my head and flings it behind us, hitting the lampshade. He pauses for a moment, as if capturing the image of me in a picture, before jumping off of me, off the couch, and going down onto his knees.

His mouth goes straight to my chest and he works his way from my belly button down my snail trail as his hand returns to caress my cock. He grabs it with the same intensity as a fighter pilot flying their jet. He steers my cock toward his mouth, taking it so deeply that he gags on it, and then comes back up for air.

"Someone's a big boy," he says, inhaling deeply before returning to my cock. I guide him back down onto it with my hands and then use my hips to thrust my cock in and out of his mouth. His gagging becoming further and further apart as I push deeper and deeper.

He stops, getting up from his knees, and looks at me.

"I wanna feel you inside of me." The passion swirling in his eyes ignites a wild desire in my chest as he climbs back on top of me and rubs my cock between his ass cheeks.

"You wanna ride it like a cowboy?" I ask, biting my bottom lip.

He goes to grab my cock, getting ready to guide it inside of him, but stops and lifts himself up slightly above me.

"You're clean right?" he asks, his head tilting slightly to the right.

The inevitable question we ask other guys when hooking up.

"Yes, I'm negative and on prep. You?"

"Same," he responds.

He grabs my cock and starts to lower himself back down, but I stop him.

"You sure you don't need lube?"

"Oh, right," he says, "Stay there." He jumps off and runs into the bedroom. A heartbeat later he's back, tearing a sachet open with his teeth and squeezing lube out into his hand. He reaches behind and rubs it into his ass.

My cock is still standing at attention as he comes back to the couch and squeezes the rest of the lube out into his other hand, sliding it all over my cock before slowly lowering himself onto it.

Sweat beads on his brow as I patiently wait for him to take it in. The discomfort on his face slowly turns to pleasure as he takes all of me inside of him.

"Let me ride it slowly to start," he says, both of his hands placed firmly on my chest.

"Okay," I say, breathing hard.

Alexander goes to work, rocking back and forth in a slow rhythm that has me almost instantly ready to explode inside of him. As he continues, his cock rubs up against my stomach. I spit in my hand, taking his cock in it, and use my wrist to go to work as his rocking picks up momentum.

"I'm already close," he says, leaning in to kiss me again.

"Want me to fuck the cum out of you?"

His eyes widen, and he nods as his mouth collides with mine.

A moan leaves it as our tongues wrestle, this time with less haste and more passion. His response ignites a fire within me, and I begin to thrust my hips upward. His ass bounces up and down on top of me. Removing my hand from his swelling cock, I grab the back of his head to forcefully drive my tongue deeper into his mouth. He takes his hand from my chest and rapidly strokes his cock.

I feel my balls swell, and I know I'm getting close.

I pull my mouth away from his.

"I'm gonna cum," I say.

"Cum inside me," he says, not taking his eyes off me as his hand works even faster up and down on his cock.

Three more thrusts and the cum explodes out of my cock, shooting deep inside of him. My hips continue to buck as my warm load continues shooting out, his ass muscles tightening around my shaft each time.

"Fuck," Alexander says, biting his lip as his eyes roll back. His hand is now putting in overtime, moving with such speed that I worry he will sustain an injury.

I continue to thrust as his ass cheeks grip me even tighter. His whole body stiffens as his load shoots out and all over my chest. A second load hits my chin, and a third arches over my shoulder onto the couch.

Alexander sinks into me as we pant together in unison.

His hand scoops up the cum on my chest and he shoves his fingers into his mouth, before moving toward my mouth. I oblige, taking the cum from his mouth into mine and swallowing it down.

"Fuck me, that was hot," I say.

The post nut clarity allows me to take Alexander in. His skin glistens with beads of sweat.

"I've never had someone fuck me like that," he says, leaning forward to kiss me before lifting himself off and grabbing the towel. He wipes the sweat from his forehead and body and then throws it at me.

"You gonna jump in the shower?" I ask, wiping my body down before standing up.

"No." A devilish smirk appears on his face. "I wanna keep your babies deep inside of me." He bites his bottom lip in a way that has my cock instantly hard again before he turns away from me and into the bedroom.

"You coming or what?" he says from over his shoulder.

I shake my head in disbelief at the fact I've just fucked the hottest guy I've ever met and now he wants to go again.

He doesn't have to ask twice.

I throw down the towel and follow him, ready for round two.

13. Alexander
Monday

It's been so long since I've shared a bed with someone that I'd forgotten what it's like to wake up, roll over, and find a person there beside you.

Their smell.

The warmth of their body, radiating between the sheets.

The slight sound of their breath as they inhale and exhale.

Sure, I've had casual hook-ups in the past. But never do I let them stay. I always make up some reason, some work commitment, that means they need to go.

Last night was different.

Christopher is different.

I needed someone to stay with me.

To hold me in their arms as I fell asleep.

To feel safe.

As Christopher held me tightly, securely, as I snuggled into him—my little spoon to his big spoon—I felt the world just fall away. It was me and him. Safe in the confinement of this bed.

That was until I woke up an hour ago, my dreams shattered

by the recurring nightmare of the stalker breaking into my home, and I turned to Christopher, thinking he was Samuel.

The guilt hit me like a sledgehammer when I realized it wasn't. Nearly three years on, and I still feel as if I'm cheating on Samuel. Like somehow, he's still here and we're still in a relationship. I'm sure he'd want me to move on. He'd probably even like Christopher and his sense of humor. But I can't help but hate how Samuel was stolen from me. Just like how everything good in my life is stolen from me.

My freedom.

My trust.

Before last night, even those intimate moments with Christopher.

When I get like this, my team encourages me to channel my feelings into a song. I turn over at the slight sound of Christopher rustling in the sheets. The rise and fall of his chest lulls me into a hypnotic state, the same state I often find myself in when riding the ocean waves or down at the skatepark.

A warm feeling rises inside as I study Christopher, his dark-brown hair, the mole on his back. It collides with the painful memories from the past, intertwining and dancing into a melody in my head. Words appear in front of me. Almost as if they're flowing through me from some higher power.

I'm so familiar with using rage, hurt, and disappointment to fuel my creativity that I'm confused by this additional emotion of joy, but I don't want to lose it.

I slowly lift the covers, trying not to wake Christopher, and slide out from the bed. I stretch my hands above my head to let out a yawn before grabbing the pad and pen on the bedside table and heading to the bathroom. Throwing them to the side, I pee and wash my hands vigorously before closing the lid to sit down, and then I let line after line pour out of me onto the paper.

I saw your face on a Thursday,
You were cool as an ocean breeze,
Turned me into a nervous wreck
And my mouth began to freeze.
I thought about it all Friday,
What I could have done differently,
Need to get myself out this mess
And bring you back to me.
I got to find a way to your heart,
Don't want this to be over before it starts.

Within ten minutes, I've jotted down a whole song. The lyrics are scattered across three pages, now lined up on the marble countertop in front of the sink. My heart does cartwheels as I look at my widening smile in the mirror. I never smile this early in the morning. I'm normally catatonic, pre-coffee.

I quietly make my way back through the bedroom and retrieve my phone from my discarded shorts before returning to the bathroom, where I hum the song's up-tempo melody into my voice memo app. The sound echoing off the white marble walls provides the perfect reverb and gives the song an uplifting vibe.

I dance around with glee when I finish, and I instantly dial my musical director, ignoring the fact that it's barely 8 a.m., and he probably doesn't have to get up for another hour before we hit Abbey Road.

He answers on the third ring with a yawn, and I immediately run through the song, looking down at the lyrics by the sink. More harmonies form in my mind as I sing it to him, the track blossoming in my mind like a tree in spring. By the second chorus, Freddy is humming along with the melody, creating little riffs with his voice.

"Damn, Alex, that song is dope!" he responds as soon as I finish.

"You think?" I briefly wonder if he's telling me what I want to hear. I never truly know when I write songs if they're any good. I often think they all are, only to realize that most are mediocre when I listen to them being played back. This time though, I instantly feel connected.

"Yeah, man, you gotta get that track down," Freddy says, seemingly sharing my enthusiasm.

A thought pops into my head, and I blurt out the words before the critical part of my brain jumps in and prevents me from saying it.

"You think we could work it into today's recording?" I fiddle with the sheets of notepaper.

"Err...sure." The hesitation in Freddy's voice makes me question my thought, but I know it's a good idea. I reach for the pen, turning the top back and forth, the tip appearing and disappearing like a tortoise's head.

"We could do a really stripped down version, just me on guitar and you on percussion. It'd be a great bonus track for the fans. They've been begging for new music for a year now." I return my attention to the mirror.

Freddy isn't the one I'm trying to convince right now. That would be Paul. He'll likely spout off something about not wanting to put it out just yet. That we're in the middle of renegotiating the record deal.

I tell Freddy I'll send him the voice note of the melody so he can listen to it and work on it. Then I hang up, take a picture of the lyrics, and send them over too. I switch over to the thread with Rob before closing the app.

I'm too wired to sleep now, even though I barely got three hours after Christopher and I had finished fucking for the third time. Rob will have to come through with the goods instead.

> Morning, can you grab me the usual with an extra shot please?

ROB
> You got it boss. Nothing for your guest?

In the excitement of finally being inspired to write again, I'd forgotten all about Christopher still in my bed. I peek around the door to see him still scrunched up under the duvet, sound asleep.

I don't dare wake him, but I don't know his coffee order. Or, come to think of it, what he does for a living or what his schedule is like. I quickly try and rack my brain to recall what he was drinking when I saw him in the atrium downstairs. Then I remember it was a Bloody Mary, and I'm sure they don't serve those here in London at Brewed.

> Can you grab him the same please?

Rob thumbs-up the message and I automatically start to slide the phone into my pocket before I realize I'm stark naked.

Boy, do I need that coffee. I shake my head at my reflection in the mirror, and wipe sleep from the corners of my eyes.

I head back to the bed, the cool air from the air conditioning unit making the hairs on my body stand up on end. I place the phone on the bedside table and slide in under the covers, reaching out to drape my left arm across Christopher, who is still lying in the fetal position.

I could breathe him in all day. The lime blossom and orange scent from his hair reminds me of a late summer afternoon, lying in the park, staring up at the sky and watching the clouds go by.

Christopher wiggles slightly, reaching for my hand, and pulls it more tightly across him. I adjust my right hip to snuggle in more tightly and raise both of my legs to come up under his. This time my dick presses up against his ass.

I've learned to appreciate slowness when I have a chaotic day ahead. My mornings are sacred, especially before coffee. But this is an addition to my routine that I could get used to.

Just as I allow myself to get lost in the thought, I hear the main door close.

Must be Rob with the coffee. That was quick.

Christopher mumbles something inaudible and I kiss the back of his head, remove my arm, and get up. I try to locate my boxers, but quickly give up. Rob's seen me naked a million times by now, and it's not like I've got anything to be ashamed of.

"Thanks, you are a miracle worker," I say.

Rob removes his order—*hot and black just like me*—as he passes over the cup holder with my usual—*cold, dark, and often unavailable*—times two.

"No problem, boss." There's a weariness in his eyes. The heavy-set bags under each one are a clear sign of sleep deprivation.

"You been up all night?" I ask, removing one of the drinks and taking a sip.

"We've been taking it in turns." He nods toward the door.

I'm assuming he means that there's another security guy standing guard on the other side.

"Oh, right. Well, I best let you rest a bit before we have to leave."

"No gym this morning?" He arches his eyebrows.

"I've got my own workout back in there." I wink at him and Rob shakes his head as he turns back to the door and lets himself out.

I reenter the bedroom. Christopher has turned over in the bed and pushed himself up slightly against the headboard. My name is emblazoned across his chest on the T-shirt, peering out from under the covers.

"Do you always greet people naked?" he asks. He rubs his eyes as if they're deceiving him.

"Only for special deliveries," I say, waving the coffee at him. I set the cupholder down on the bedside table, and switch on the lamp so I can pull out his drink. Christopher instantly reaches for his eyes.

"You could give me a heads-up before you turn the light on," he says. He slowly lowers his hands, his face still all scrunched up underneath.

Clearly, Christopher isn't a morning person either.

"I didn't have you down as a vampire," I say, a smirk rising across my face. I hand the iced coffee over to him.

"I prefer to get my morning vitamin D in other ways." He nods at my penis as he takes the cup. "What's this?" He hesitates, then brings the drink to his mouth and takes a sip. "Jesus." His face screws up. "This shit could resuscitate the dead."

"I guess you're not a coffee drinker?" I lift the duvet to slide in next to him.

"I'm more of a Red Bull guy," he says, placing the coffee down on the table.

Between all the sex and sleeping, there's still so much I don't know about him. There's so much I want to know.

"Can I ask you some questions?" I ask, taking a sip of my coffee.

"About?" He turns on his side to face me. His hazel eyes lock onto mine.

"About you... There's so much I still don't know about you. Like, what you do for work?"

"I work for a creative marketing agency."

"When did you come out of the closet?" I ask, taking another sip.

"I didn't." Christopher pauses as I stop mid-sip. "I came out of the cupboard because I," he pauses for emphasis, "am a snack." A smirk appears on his face and I snort.

"What's your body count?" I blurt out the intrusive thought before I can filter myself. Chris answers before I can apologize.

"As in the number of guys I've slept with, or the number I've put in therapy?" He lifts an eyebrow.

"Oh wow, am I gonna need to find me a therapist?"

"Let's just say, I'm single-handedly keeping gay therapists in business." He stretches his hands above his head as he lets out a yawn. "And you?"

My heart skips a beat.

What to do. What to do.

I half the number, then half it again, and it still feels too high, so I half it once more.

"You don't have to tell me if you don't want to." He rests his hand on my arm.

I take the opportunity to pivot the conversation.

"What do you have going on today?" I'm hoping he says nothing so he can spend the day with me.

"I need to do some work later, but apart from a Zoom meeting around seven I'm pretty flexible. You?"

"I'm recording a live album at Abbey Road today." I can't help the smile that spreads across my face.

"That sounds pretty cool."

"It is. I've always wanted to record there. It's the holy grail of recording studios. We even get to record in Studio Two, where the Beatles recorded a load of their albums."

I'm so busy working, moving from one thing to the next, that I rarely get to stop and appreciate the amazing things I've achieved or get to do. If you'd told my fourteen-year-old self he'd be recording at Abbey Road Studios someday, midway through a seven-night sold-out run at the O2 Arena, he'd never have believed you.

But as I've gotten older, I realized that while these moments are great, none of them matter unless you can share them with someone.

"Do you want to come with me?" I ask.

The silence goes on a beat too long, and I can feel the ground opening up beneath me. These days it takes a lot for me to be vulnerable, to put myself out there. My cheeks redden.

"I wouldn't want to get in your way…"

"You wouldn't be," I say, almost a little too quickly, cutting him off.

It's not often that I get rejected, but the feeling is one you never forget. The shame that burns inside the pit of your stomach. The tightening of the heart, like someone squeezing the life from it.

"You sure I won't be too much of a distraction?" That mischievous look reappears on his face as his hand slides under the covers, between my legs and onto my cock.

"Oh, I'm hoping you will be…" I say, rolling on top of him.

I turn the shower off and hand Christopher a towel, then grab another for myself. I exit and lift my leg onto the bathtub opposite, next to Christopher's clothes, and start to dry off.

"God, you're insatiable," I say. My cock is still throbbing as I turn to face him.

"Must be something you put in that coffee." His reflection in the mirror winks back at me.

It's barely been seven hours since we returned to the room last night, and we've already fucked on the couch, twice in the bed, and now in the shower. The last time was even hotter than I had imagined and jerked off to the night we met.

He'd pushed me up against the glass door, pinning my hands to either side of my head, and using his right foot to spread my legs wide apart. After he slid himself inside me, he started pounding away, completely destroying my ass. My cum splattered all over the glass door while the steam engulfed us.

I'm half tempted to drag him into the suite's meeting room and let him fuck me on the table, then into the walk-in wardrobe to do it again. My mouth goes dry as I imagine him pushing me up against the window and down into the bathtub, but I need to conserve at least some energy for the recording and filming later.

My body is craving him, like I crave alcohol, and I can't get enough.

"What's this?" Christopher grabs one of the sheets of paper and holds it up, turning to face me.

"It's nothing," I say, grabbing it from his hand. I scoop up the other two sheets and tuck them into the pocket of the bathrobe hanging on the door.

"Doesn't look like nothing." His brows arch.

"It's just some lyric ideas." I wave him away and wrap the towel around my waist before reaching for my toothbrush and toothpaste.

"Is it about me?" His eyebrows are still arched. He sets his hands on his hips.

Instantly, I feel a burning sensation in my face. Like I've been caught with my hand in the cookie jar. It's one thing to stand here naked in front of him. It's another thing entirely to expose my inner thoughts and feelings.

"It is, isn't it! Am I your muse, like Marilyn Monroe was to Andy Warhol? Like the skater boy to Avril Lavigne?" He pushes at my shoulder playfully.

I ignore him, trying to swallow down the embarrassment, squeezing toothpaste onto my toothbrush and hitting the On button.

"Well, either way. I don't mind being your muse," he says, turning and winking at me. "As long as you don't tear me a new asshole in your songs, like Taylor Swift does to her boyfriends."

I press stop on the toothbrush.

Did he say boyfriend?

Shit.

Does he want to make this more serious?

Calm down. He was just joking.

"I think you're the only one round here tearing assholes," I say, reaching for my prescription bottle. I take out an Adderall and swallow it down whole.

"By the sound of it, I think you enjoyed me tearing it apart." He grabs my butt cheek.

"I do. But we probably should get ready if you're going to join me at the studio today." My body is really hating me right now for not letting Christopher have his way again.

"Oh, I thought you just rocked up at the lobby at twelve?" Christopher scoops up his clothes and walks out.

There was a time when I could do that. Just wake up five minutes before we need to leave, throw on some clothes, and head out. But ever since *It's You That I Need* came out, along with a provocative video of me scantily clad, it's no longer just fans outside the hotel, but the paparazzi too.

"I wish. But I need to get ready. Styling, hair, and makeup. I use a humidifier to warm up my voice." I follow him into the bedroom.

"Maybe I should leave you to it," he says. His face is lowered as he bends over to put on his boxers and jeans. Dejection underlines his words.

"You've got some work to do right?" I ask. "Why don't you

head to your room, then meet me downstairs in the lobby at midday. I'll message Rob and Paul to let them know you'll be joining us." I reach for my phone on the bedside table.

He holds out the polo shirt in front of him. Damp patches are still visible on the shoulders and neck. He throws it down on the bed and bends to pick up the T-shirt on the floor.

"Can I borrow this to go back to my room?"

"Keep it. It looks good on you," I say, laughing.

"Right, I best leave you to it," he says. Christopher throws the T-shirt on, grabs his polo shirt, and heads over to me. His soft plump lips meet mine before he makes his way out.

"See you downstairs, fanboy." I say, and wink as he heads to the door.

"Just don't go writing any more songs about me," he laughs back.

"Someone's in a good mood this morning!" Erica matches my smile in the vanity mirror as she applies more cream under my eyes to hide the heavy-set bags that look like they've been tattooed there the last couple of months. The Veronica's *Untouched* is playing out from the mini speaker behind us.

"I am. I'm feeling really inspired and happy this morning. I haven't felt like this in, well…" Another pang of guilt hits my chest, but I push it down.

"That's great, Alex. You deserve to be happy." She squeezes my shoulder lightly.

I'm almost ready to go, having already done my vocal warm-ups. Laurie pulls together a cool rock outfit for me to wear: ripped black jeans, a white T-shirt, and a black leather jacket.

"Everyone ready?" Paul asks, entering the room. Rob is a shadow behind him.

"Yep." Erica removes the brush, allowing me to put my black Ray Bans on.

"Paul, can I get a quick word before we go?" I lift myself out of the chair.

I want to ask him about including the song I wrote in today's recording. He hadn't responded to my email earlier, no doubt writing it off as another one of my ideas that he doesn't want to entertain. Sometimes his delaying tactics work and I give up. But this time I'm certain that I want to do this.

"Sure, what's up?" Paul turns away from the door and sits down in an armchair, placing his iPad down on the table. He runs his hands down his black trousers and pulls up his striped socks, then motions for me to sit down and join him.

"Did you get the song I sent through earlier? I really want to record it today for the live album." I plop down in the armchair opposite. My expression is safely hidden behind the sunglasses as Paul leans forward to scrutinize me.

"Sorry, I've been slammed this morning. When did you send it?" Paul reaches for his iPad, opening it up, and scrolls through his inbox.

"Here, let me play you the voice memo I made earlier." I pull out my phone, reconnect it to the Bluetooth speaker, and press play.

Paul does his usual. He leans back, eyes closed, and folds his arms as the song plays out. My leg taps, not to the melody, but in nervous anticipation of his feedback. His praise, like all praise, is another one of my addictions. The problem is that the more I get of it, the more I need just to stay even.

His eyes open as the voice memo ends.

"That's a great melody and hook you have there." He rubs his hands together and, grabbing his iPad, gets up from the armchair.

Warmth spreads in my chest, like warm honey over toast.

Thank God, he likes it. Now for the difficult part.

I take a deep inhale and get up.

"So... we can record it today at Abbey Road," I say, more as a statement than a question.

Before he opens his mouth, the look on his face tells me what I already assumed.

"We don't have enough time, Alex. Plus, the band doesn't know the parts. And that's a raw demo."

I let out a sigh, but I'm prepared for his push back. I've already done my homework.

"Freddy's already got the track, and I've discussed the arrangement with him. He's working on it as we speak." Paul starts to speak, but I raise my hand to stop him. "Plus, Morgan Wallen did it for his own live album from Abbey Road, with that song *Lies, Lies, Lies.*"

Paul's stare burns right through me.

It's like pistols at dawn.

But this time, I'm not going down without a fight.

14. Christopher
Monday

"Can I help you, sir?"

The bellman turns to face me after he returns a luggage trolley to the concierge desk. Which happens to be right next to the chair I've resorted to sitting in while waiting for Alexander to come down for the last ten minutes.

"I'm actually waiting for—" I pause, unsure of what I should say. I sort through my options and their consequences.

The lobby area bustles with people checking in and out. A Middle Eastern family has so much luggage it looks like they're moving in. A few people are loitering for no apparent reason. And a couple of twenty-something scantily clad women, seemingly more dressed for a night out than a late-Monday morning, hang out near the flowers, probably hoping for a glimpse of Alexander.

"I'm good, thank you," I finally say. The bellman nods and turns his attention to the laptop on the counter.

I've been trying to calm myself down since coming down. I opted to sit and take deep breaths after pacing the lobby attracted too much attention. Every part of me wants to run back to my hotel room.

I mean it's weird, right? Going to someone else's place of work when you have no reason to be there? It almost feels like the "bring your child to work day" that we have once a year at the office back in LA. Inevitably, the kids always get in the way, and I don't want to do the same.

A sudden flurry of activity starts in the reception area, the number of staff almost doubling in a matter of seconds, and I take it as my cue that Alexander must be coming. I lift myself out of the seat, throw on my backpack, and head toward the door.

The sound of the screaming fans increases dramatically as one of the doormen opens the doors to the main entrance, clearing a path to the three cars waiting outside.

My heart starts beating out of my chest as I see Rob turn around the corner. The sweat patches under my armpits almost double in size and my back suddenly feels like it has become Niagara Falls.

Alexander emerges behind Rob, looking effortlessly cool. His hair is slicked back and his sunglasses sit perfectly on his cheekbones. The fitted white T-shirt he's wearing showcases his enviable physique, and the look is topped off with a silver chain, black ripped jeans, and a pair of black biker boots. He looks like a painting from the Tate Modern come to life.

Before I know it, they're at the entrance, and the two scantily clad women briefly stop Alexander to get a picture. Paul comes toward me, a disapproving look on his face.

"You're in the second car with them," he says, pointing back to three women behind him. He doesn't bother to stop as he follows Alexander, Rob, and a short red-haired woman dressed head to toe in black, out into the first car.

I catch another glimpse of Alexander as I pass the first of

three state-of-the-art Mercedes people carriers, but he doesn't seem to notice me, so I slide inside the second car after the other three women sit down. Fuji-brand water bottles line the cupholders in the sides of the doors, and there's a light aromatherapy scent. The air conditioning is a welcome relief as I remove my backpack, placing it between my feet.

"Who's this?" a tall blond woman asks. She lowers her sunglasses to take a better look at me.

I momentarily freeze.

I was expecting to be in the car with Alexander and Paul, not in one with three women I barely know and have only seen in the elevator. I look at the door, wondering if I should make a dash for it, but the door begins closing, leaving me trapped inside.

Guess I'm stuck now.

"He's the dialect coach we've brought in to help Alex prepare for the upcoming film," another blond woman sitting diagonally across from me says as she reaches for a Diet Coke from her bag.

It seems like this woman wants to control the narrative, and I'm more than happy to play along. The less I say, the less reason there is for the story Alexander texted me to be questioned.

Dialect coach. Film. New Mexico accent.

I shake my head at the excuse. The closest I get to American accents is my poor attempt at LA Valley girl, an even worse Southern drawl, or a slightly above average New Jersey accent.

I'm just hoping no one asks me to demonstrate.

"Oh cool, so everything's moving ahead?" a brunette woman next to me asks.

"Paul got the revised script this morning, so looks like it."

"What accent are you teaching him?" the first blond woman asks, removing her sunglasses. "No. Wait. Let me guess." She puts the tip of the glasses arm into her mouth as she studies me.

"Russian," she says, pointing her glasses at me.

"No, it's not Russian." The pitch of my voice elevates to a level it hasn't been at since my balls dropped over a decade ago.

"Leave him alone," the brunette woman beside me says, reaching over and whacking her on the leg. She turns back to me, stretching out her hand. "I'm Erica. Nice to meet you."

"Christopher. Nice to meet you," I say, meeting her smile with my own.

My stomach settles slightly, grateful for the conversational pivot.

"You're English too," the woman opposite says. "Laurie, by the way. I'm Alexander's stylist. Erica there," she points at the brunette, "is hair and makeup. and I guess you already know Alexander's publicist, Connie." Laurie's hand meets mine as I pull it away from Erica's.

I nod, though I didn't have a clue who Connie was, and quickly try to remember their names.

Connie. Erica. Laurie.

"Where you from?" I ask, trying to make small talk, although I'm certain she's from Birmingham based on her Brummie accent. I may not be an actual dialect coach, but I can at least decipher where people are from.

"I'm from Birmingham originally, moved out to LA a decade ago. You?"

Looking at her tanned skin, green eyes, black crop top, and black jean shorts, I'd never have placed her as someone from this side of the pond. I guess that's what LA does to you. Her accent is the only giveaway. There's not a hint of America laced in it.

My accent, on the other hand, started to slip as soon as I moved there. The constant need to change the pronunciation of words like water and mum, or replace words completely, like changing over from lift to elevator and toilet to restroom, slowly eroded my North London accent into a more mid-Atlantic one. Now I'm stuck somewhere between the two.

"I'm from North London originally. Moved to LA three years ago for work."

Keep your answers short. Concise.

No need to give them a monologue.

"Have you ever thought of Botox?" Laurie asks, deadpan.

Jesus. Talk about forthright. I know I looked rough this morning, but what a way to knock a guy down when he's already feeling uncomfortable and insecure.

"For your armpits, I mean." She points her sunglasses at my pits. "It does wonders. Stops sweat stains from forming."

Oh. *Oh.*

My instant relief turns to discomfort as everyone turns to look.

"Thanks for the tip. I'll have to look into it," I say. Heat rises across my face.

"Are you also staying at the hotel?" Erica asks.

Connie removes her glasses to look at me with a pointed stare. Clearly, she's not one to be crossed. I feel a lump come up into my throat.

"Err, yeah. It was easier than staying with my family, while I'm here. My sister's—" I stop myself just before I reveal the true reason I'm in town. Connie's eyes widen.

"Why don't we leave the poor man alone," she breaks in. "He's got enough to contend with. Plus, we're nearly there." I smile a *Thank you* at her for saving me, but she doesn't respond in kind. She turns her attention out the window instead.

An unnerving feeling rises inside once more.

Did I do or say something wrong? Did Paul tell her something that's causing her to act this way?

Thankfully, we're at Abbey Road Studios mere moments later, and I'm startled as a hoard of fans surrounds our car, banging on the sides. They press their hands against the windows, trying to peer inside.

As we pass through the gates and onto the gravel drive, the banging stops, but the loud sound doesn't seem to abate. Instead, it gets louder as the car door slides open. The three women get out and I grab my bag and exit the vehicle.

There must be hundreds, if not thousands, of people beyond the gated wall. Alexander stops at the top of the stairs, turning briefly to wave at the crowd before heading in. The rest of us follow him inside into the reception area, where everyone seems to congregate.

I take in the record plaques scattered across the walls. They feature an array of artists, including the Beatles, Oasis, Amy Winehouse, and nearly a hundred others. Alexander's attention finally drifts toward me after he hugs and high-fives a bunch of guys and a woman, who I assume must be his band.

"Guys, this is my dialect coach, Christopher," he says, reaching his arm across to drape over my shoulder.

The mere mention of the word *dialect* brings up a nauseous feeling in my stomach and I shudder. Alexander removes his arm.

I wish he had picked something, anything, other than a dialect coach.

A nutritionist. A personal trainer perhaps. But a coach?

"Nice to meet you," I say, plastering a smile on my face. I shake their hands as Alexander introduces them and what they do. I try in vain, once more, to commit their names to memory.

Andy, Aidan, Lola.

"And this is my musical director, Freddy. He's the one who's been helping me with that new song I mentioned earlier." He arches his eyebrows.

"You convince Paul to let you record it yet?" Freddy asks. His tall, broad frame and shaggy dark-brown hair differentiates him from the clean-shaven and straight-haired look of the rest of the band. But they all wear the same outfit. Black T-shirt. Black jeans. Black sneakers.

"Yeah. As long as we nail the other tracks. No pressure, guys." Alexander lets out a different kind of laugh than the one I've become familiar with.

His attention turns to me as the band starts to discuss arrangements.

"Everything okay traveling here?" He turns his back on the band and lowers his voice. "They weren't too hard on you, were they?" He nods his head at Laurie, Erica and Connie, who are standing next to Paul, Rob and a red-head—Lucy?

"Yeah." I hesitate, taking a slight breath and keeping my voice low to match his. "But Connie seems a bit off with me, and I'm not sure how long I can keep up this dialect coach facade."

"Oh, don't worry about her. She's like that with everyone. And you'll be fine." Alexander waves away my worry.

The rumble of discomfort bubbles up again.

I'm not sure how to feel about how quickly he pushes away my concerns.

Paul coughs loudly, then motions everyone to follow him down the hallway and into a small control room. It looks exactly like how I envision a recording studio. A large soundboard stretches across the room beneath a glass window, which overlooks a large room already set up with various instruments. A tall stool sits in the middle, a mic in front of it, and an acoustic guitar rests nearby on a stand.

"Lucy, will you look after Christopher while I go down and start recording?" Alexander slings his leather jacket on the couch, squeezing my arm.

"Sure." She turns her attention to me. "I don't think we've properly met. I'm Lucy, Alex's assistant. I've heard *all* about you." A grin forms on her face.

"Is that right?" I say, following her lead. Alexander twitches as his attention darts between the two of us. "You'll have to tell me more."

I take off my backpack and sit down on the couch as Lucy does the same, moving Alexander's jacket to the end.

Thank God. I'm not going to be stuck here all day pretending to be a dialect coach, and Lucy seems to know the truth.

I'm already regretting getting the Carbonara. I rub my hand against my chest, fighting off the indigestion. My eyes really are bigger than my belly these days.

The dining area at Abbey Road is only half full. His team is spread out at the various plastic tables in the center of the room. Other studio employees line a couple of the tables up against the wall, further down the room. Connie and Paul stand outside, Connie animatedly talking away between drags of her cigarette.

"Want some?" I slide my plate toward his bowl of salad and chicken.

"I don't do pasta," he says, pushing it back toward me.

His mood has been off ever since we sat down to eat ten minutes ago. But there's no need for that type of blasphemy.

"No pasta? What's next? You kick puppies? Hate dessert?" I elbow him in the ribs as I eye the cheesecake on the table across from us.

I could google the answers to all the things I still don't know about Alexander, but I'd rather learn about them from him. At the same time, I don't want to interrogate him. I don't want to be like one of the journalists he complained about earlier.

Alexander forces a smile on his face, but drops his gaze to his salad.

The silence makes me fidget in my seat.

Fine, let's talk about something else.

"What's with all the black. Did someone die or something?" I hold his startled stare for a moment before moving my gaze away.

"Oh, it's a tour thing. To ensure everyone blends in when it's dark on stage. The last thing you want is someone wearing a bright shirt or white trainers walking on stage and ruining the suspense." He reaches for another bit of chicken with his fork.

"They must all have a lot of black clothes then," I say, picking up my lemonade. Maybe it will wash away the indigestion.

"Yeah, fifty shades of black," he says, biting into the chicken.

"I heard you're more a fifty shades of gray kinda guy."

Alexander almost chokes on the chicken as Paul and Connie walk back through the patio door. He raises his right hand to flag them down as he grabs a napkin with his other hand and spits the chicken out into it.

"Have you two got a minute? I wanted to follow up on what we were discussing earlier before I go back in to continue recording." I see a flicker of irritation cross his face.

"Sure, why don't we head up to the control room, where it's more private?" Paul says, looking at me coldly.

"Here's fine." Alexander points to the two empty chairs at the table.

"I can leave you all to it if you need," I say, grabbing my plate and pushing my chair back.

"Stay," Alexander says, gripping the back of my chair.

I get the feeling that neither Paul nor Connie like me, judging by the looks of disdain on their faces as they reluctantly draw the chairs back to sit down. Paul removes his glasses and places them on top of his iPad while Connie tucks her skirt under her legs.

I've always wanted people to like me. I've actively gone out of my way to do things to make people like me more, unless they piss me off like Rob did when we first met. But I have to remember what my therapist said: *Ten percent of people will never like you no matter what you do.* And maybe these two fall into that ten percent.

"Before you start," Connie begins, "we've just spoken to the head of the label and we're at number one in the midweeks with *My Anchor*."

"Congratulations," I say, but the other three remain silent. Paul gives me a brief sideways glance and shakes his head. It reaffirms that my role here is to stay quiet. I lower my head and reach for my lemonade instead, silently telling myself to shut up.

"The issue is, it's tight at the top, and the label wants to give it another push beyond the remix that they dropped Friday," Connie adds.

"Get to the point..." Alexander says, pushing the cutlery together in his bowl and scowling.

"The label wants you to do some more promo tomorrow, before the show, to create enough of a gap to ensure you land the number one slot. They've got Radio One's *Live Lounge* on hold, along with some big podcast interviews lined up. *Chicken Shop Date*, *Table Manners*, and one with that pop star Lily..." Connie looks up at the ceiling as if trying to pull the name from thin air.

"Allen. Lily Allen," I offer, when the silence goes on a beat too long.

"Yes. That's the one." She nods at me before returning her gaze to Alexander. "I need to go back to them in the next few minutes to lock it all in."

Alexander's finger circles the rim of his glass, clockwise then counterclockwise, seemingly weighing the decision.

"What do you think?" he says, turning his ocean-blue eyes to me.

"Er...." My gaze drifts from him over to Paul and then Connie.

Whatever I say here, I'm going to put my foot in it.

Connie and Paul have measured expressions, but I can feel their frustration at Alexander batting the decision to me.

If I side with Alexander and tell him not to do it, both of them will hate me. They will label me another Yoko Ono, as if I'm trying to get into all his affairs. But if I side with Connie and Paul, then I've ignored what Alexander told me about no one looking out for what he really needs. My heart beats rapidly against my rib cage.

It's a lose-lose situation.

I take another sip of lemonade to draw out my response, working out how to be Switzerland in this discussion.

"I think Paul and Connie are the best placed to answer in regard to what you should do. I don't have a clue about these things." A lie—given my marketing background—but right now isn't the time to discuss that. "Though I will say, *Live Lounge* is pretty iconic and the *Chicken Shop Date* show always seems to go viral online."

Once again, I catch a micro-expression on Paul's face, this time a smirk, before it returns to a neutral expression. Connie gives away no such clues. Alexander adjusts himself in his chair.

My heart rate begins to settle. Seems like I managed to navigate that minefield without setting anything off.

"Right," Alexander says. "I'll do it, but on one condition."

"Name it," Paul says.

"You guarantee *Stolen Moments* makes it on the live album, and that we record it today. You do that. I'll do the promo." He folds his hands across his chest, looking proud of himself, as he leans back into the chair. Paul and Connie exchange a brief look.

"Deal. Let me call up the label and let them know," Paul says, pushing back his chair to stand. Connie gets up with him. "Oh, actually before I forget, a couple of other things. Alfonso has sent through the revised script. I've had it printed off and will leave it in your suite."

"Okay, and the other?" Alexander's head tilts upward to meet Paul's gaze.

"We got the untouched pictures back from yesterday's shoot," Connie says, gesturing at Paul to open his iPad. "I want to get one of the images out to the press tonight to help with the push. Can you go through them now and let me know which ones they should start touching up?"

Paul retrieves his phone from his jacket and begins typing away as Alexander scrolls through the gallery. I lean back ever so slightly to try and see. There's a variety of topless pictures of Alexander, all buff and brooding and in positions that remind me of our second meeting in the gym. I feel my temperature rising, and I scrub my hand across the back of my neck.

"Which one do you think?" Alexander asks. He turns the iPad toward me, flicking between two almost identical images.

I move my hand from my neck to under the table, readjusting myself. The discomfort that my now semi-erect cock is causing in my jeans matches the discomfort in my chest, as Connie and Paul wait impatiently in front of us.

"That one," I say, returning my hand to the top of the table, stopping the gallery at a topless image of Alexander staring broodily into the camera. His tanned, oily skin is lit to accentuate every single muscle as he stands tall in front of a weight machine.

Thank God, we're sitting down. My cock is now fully erect. I rock back and forth, trying to adjust myself without making it obvious. Alexander must notice, because his hand slides under the table, grabbing my leg to stop me.

"That one it is," he says, handing the iPad back to Connie, who nods as Paul lifts his head from his phone.

Alexander's hand slides up my thigh, stopping when he reaches my cock. A smirk rises on his face.

"The promo's all locked in, we're good to go," Paul says, waving his phone.

"And the track?" Alexander asks. His hand fiddles with the button on my jeans.

"The label has agreed. They're drawing up a side agreement now to carve out the song as a stand-alone deal, and I'll have John look over it."

"Great," Alexander says, punctuating the conversation with a full stop while attempting to pull my zipper down.

Paul and Connie turn and exit the restaurant, their heads close together and whispering about something.

"People might see," I whisper, pushing his hand away. I frantically look around, scared someone might notice, but everyone seems lost in their own conversations.

"Well, let's go somewhere quieter then," he says. A smile reappears on his face as he stands up.

15. Alexander
Monday

"Let's run that one more time," comes the engineer's voice from the control room.

My back stiffens in frustration. Freddy shrugs his shoulders and reaffirms what I'm already thinking. We nailed that take. Everyone had their parts perfectly down. Andy played the melody note-perfect on guitar. Freddy used just the right amount of percussion for this stripped-back version of *Compare To You*.

And if anything, my voice has gotten better throughout the afternoon.

The mild irritation in my chest quickly moves beyond frustration and into anger.

Since lunch, everything seems to be moving at a slower pace. We've done numerous takes of each song. Repositioned the microphones. Got through trade union-mandated breaks for the hired musicians.

I have the feeling that the team is delaying things. Paul is running down the clock, using every possible stalling tactic he can so we run out of time to record *Stolen Moments*.

"Let's take five. I wanna hear the playback."

I jump off the stool, sliding my headphones off and hanging them over the mic stand before heading up to the control room. My mood darkens with every step I take up the wooden staircase where so many of my idols have climbed, where I see the engineers and Paul standing alongside my A&R guy Nathan Watkins, who's flown over from LA.

"Can you run that last take back for me," I say as soon as I open the door, skipping the formalities or even a greeting for Nathan, who arrived only half an hour ago.

The engineer, who wouldn't look out of place playing with the Strokes with his gaunt frame and long dark hair scraped back into a ponytail, pulls up the Logic file, hitting the space bar to kickstart it.

"Turn it up a little."

He slides the volume up on the sound desk as I move over and sit down in one of the free chairs. I lean back and close my eyes, allowing the sound to wash over me. Of all the tracks I've recorded, *Compare To You* is one of my favorites. Other songs have been more commercially successful, but this one was the game changer for me. And it was the first song I wrote after Samuel died.

My eyes well up at the thought of him.

When the track finishes, I rub my eyes and then open them, turning my attention to Paul and Nathan, who seem to be joined at the hip. Nathan takes a drag of his vape and then picks at the label on the empty plastic bottle in his hand.

"Sounds perfect to me. What's the issue?" My forehead crinkles as I study them.

Nathan moves his hand to his nose, fiddling with it like he's done one too many bumps. Discomfort is written across his aging face. For a forty-year-old, he looks closer to fifty.

Paul remains silent, letting Nathan lead the conversation.

"The vocals were slightly behind the musicians in the second verse," Nathan says, averting his gaze. He looks over to the couch where Lucy and Connie are seated, working away on their laptops.

"Pull that up for me, will you?" I ask the engineer. I get up from the chair and move closer to the sound desk.

The engineer skips to one minute twelve, hitting the play button. I lean in next to the speaker, listening intently. I try to pick up on the delay Nathan is referring to, but I don't hear what he's talking about.

"Doesn't sound out of time to me." I turn back to face Nathan, crossing my arms over my chest.

What do they take me for, a fool?

Nathan gets fidgety, takes another drag on his vape and looks down at his sneakers.

"Paul?"

Clearly Nathan doesn't want to be made to walk the plank for whatever is going on here, and he's obviously following Paul's command, who, once again, always has to be in control.

"I know you've got a better take in you," Paul says. "Once this is out there, it will live online forever. You don't want anything out there that's less than perfect, right?" His eyes narrow, while speaking to me in a patronizing tone that grates on me like nails down a chalkboard. Like he thinks I'm still fourteen and unable to see through his manipulation.

Nathan chucks the plastic bottle at the bin but misses. He walks over to the bottle, picks it up, steps back a few feet, shoots... and misses once again.

Ugh.

I tap my foot on the floor while I wait for Nathan to pick up the bottle and place it in the bin properly. I feel my anger get bigger with every tap of my foot.

"Where are we at with the side agreement?"

"We're still waiting for the label lawyers in LA to get back to us," Paul says, pulling his phone from his pocket as if checking for an update.

I look at my watch. It's 11:15 a.m. over there. At times like these, I'm glad I leave my watches on LA time.

"What's the hold up? It's been hours since we agreed to this." I'm unable to keep the bitterness out of my voice.

"These things take a moment, Alex," Paul says, volleying it straight back at me. His voice is elevated, causing both Connie and Lucy to look up from their screens and the engineers to look away.

His words hit me right in the chest.

Scolded like a child, humiliated in front of his class.

I shrug my shoulders, refusing to take my gaze from his.

This is not how this conversation is going to end. Not on my watch. Not this time.

"You're telling me the label can secure all that promo for tomorrow in the space of a couple of hours, but their lawyers and mine can't knock up a standard one-page side agreement?"

The room falls eerily silent.

Check.

"It's not as easy as that, there's terms to discuss," Paul says, breaking the silence and rolling his eyes.

"Don't roll your eyes at me," I say. My nostrils are flaring like a dragon ready to unleash fire. "Like the terms we agreed to for doing the promo tomorrow, on the condition I get to record *Stolen Moments* and include it on the live album?"

How dare he try and make me look a fool.

This is my career he's messing with here. Not his.

The fire is no longer swirling in my stomach but is rising into my throat.

"Let's call up the UK label boss. Let's tell her tomorrow's promo is off, because you and Nathan couldn't get the promo down. In fact, better yet," my attention turns to Nathan, "let's get Nathan's boss on the phone right now, and tell him we've decided not to renew my record deal with them. That we'll be going with Sony instead."

Check. Mate.

A look of terror washes over Nathan's face as I return my gaze to Paul.

Paul looks at me, as if to call my bluff, but I reach into my pocket for my phone, bring up the CEO's number and wave it at him.

I don't care if everyone in this room thinks I'm a petulant child throwing a temper tantrum. I'll be damned if I continue to march to the beat of Paul's drum.

"Let me chase up the lawyers now," Paul says, turning and heading for the door.

Nathan gets up out of the chair to follow him, but I'm not done yet.

I need something to take the edge off this rage.

There's no gym here. I can't go out for a run with all the work there is left to do. And I can't see Christopher to do the only other thing that settles this swirling mixture of emotions. Which leaves only one other option.

"Nathan. A quick word." I motion him toward me.

He looks back and forth between me and Paul and starts to step slightly toward Paul, but my stare intensifies, and he reconsiders. Paul shakes his head, closing the door behind him.

"You want me to renew this deal, right?" My voice lowers, as I sling my arm over his shoulder.

"Of course I do," he says, his voice wobbling.

"Well, I'm going to need you to do me a favor. I'm going to need you to get me a couple bottles of Belvedere."

"But..." Nathan stops me, turning his head to face me.

Nathan knows I'm in recovery, but I hold all the power right now.

And I am going to take advantage of it.

"It's just for this week. You know the deal with the pressure. I'm just taking the edge off of things. If anyone can understand that, it's you." I rub my nose for effect to acknowledge his habit, which these days seems more like an addiction than a bump here or there.

"I don't know, Alex. You got yourself into pretty bad shape last time. Do you really think it's a good idea to open that box again?"

I have a flashback to the intervention in my home before I push it away.

Nope, not going there.

I can control my drinking now. I went all yesterday without a drop.

"All things considered, I think anyone would have been in a bad shape given what I went through. I'm good now. The tour is coming to an end. The album's outperformed even our wildest expectations. *My Anchor* looks like it will hit number one this week. I can handle my liquor. I just couldn't handle what happened. But I've dealt with that now."

The rumble in my stomach contradicts me. I'm lying, both to him and myself. But I've dealt with it the best way I know how. I put it in a box and filed it away in a dark room at the back of my mind. Alongside everything else.

Nathan turns to me once more, and I give him the same smile that drives all my fans crazy. The corner of his mouth lifts slightly.

I've got him.

"That's my man," I say, patting his chest twice with my hand. "Oh, and this is between you and me, okay?"

"Okay," he says, nodding in agreement.

"Now go get that deal across the line," I say, slapping his ass as he trots off to find Paul.

I head across the room to the couch, where Lucy and Connie are sitting. There's a Christopher-shaped hole between them. Lucy looks up as I tower above her. Connie doesn't give me the same courtesy.

"Where's Christopher?" I ask, rubbing my chest with my hand. The anger inside is starting to subside.

"He said something about jumping on a Zoom. Took himself off to find a quiet space." She closes her laptop, slides it inside her bag, and pushes herself up off the couch.

"Do you know where?" I ask, my gaze dart to the door when I see a figure passing by the window.

"I don't, but I could go find him if you want?"

"Please." I nod at her when she turns back to face me.

"He seems like a great guy. I can see why you like him." Lucy's smile and approval acts like a Tums, settling my stomach.

I'm momentarily distracted as Connie makes an inarticulate noise, smirking and shaking her head.

I shake off the need to ask her to clarify her response. Her opinion holds a lot of weight alongside Paul's in business affairs, but when it comes to affairs of the heart, I defer to Lucy and Erica and, at a push, my mom.

Just before I begin the third take of *Stolen Moments*, the blue doors in front of me open. Christopher walks through with Lucy. Thank God I'm sitting down on a stool, otherwise the sight of him would have sent me stumbling.

There's something about the way he carries himself—like he's slightly uncomfortable in his own skin, but imbues his posture with confidence to counter it—that has me enraptured.

"Alex, you ready?" the engineer asks through my headphones.

The distraction of Christopher and Lucy made me miss the cue, and I'm snapped back into performance mode. I slide my fingers back into position on the guitar.

"I'm ready," I say, nodding as if the engineer can see me.

"You said that with some determination. Okay, we're recording. Whenever you're ready."

I nod to Freddy, who in a matter of hours has managed to bring this song to life. He created a percussive arrangement that goes far beyond what I envisioned when I wrote it this morning.

My gaze drifts from Freddy back to Christopher as I begin to play out the chords in C major, and hold the intro for four bars rather than two. I adjust myself slightly to get closer to the microphone.

I saw your face on a Thursday,
You were cool as an ocean breeze,
Turned me into a nervous wreck,
and my mouth began to freeze.

With each successive line, I feel the room disappear around me. It's just Christopher and me, alone in the room. Me, serenading him on the guitar. Vulnerability seeps into my tone, in a way that counters the up-tempo poppiness of the song.

Christopher's gaze doesn't leave mine.

Just before I get to the final chorus, another intrusive thought about Samuel comes, snapping at me out of my memories. The symbolic embodiment of him manifests in front of me. Lucy on the left professionally, and Christopher on the right, at least sexually, if not romantically.

I try to shake the thought away, but I can't push it out of my head.

My fingers stumble on one of the chords, forcing me to stop.

"Sorry guys, I lost my focus. Can I take a minute before we go again?" I ask.

I need to find something to distract myself.

I slide the guitar into the stand and jump off the chair, but get yanked back by the headphone cord. I quickly remove them, leaving them over the mic stand, and make my way to Christopher and Lucy as the thoughts become stronger.

Samuel's voice echoes in my head.

You think you can replace me.

You think I don't know what you're doing.

Samuel's words, the last conversation we had before the crash, swirl around in my brain.

And what he accused me of is now true. Chris stands right in front of me.

"That was great," Lucy says, although I can't bring myself to look at her, at them.

I look at the clock above the door instead.

Will I forever be haunted by Samuel's ghost?

Am I condemned to live a life of suffering?

"No seriously." She reaches for my arm as I tuck my hands into my jean pockets. "That song is really something." She lifts up on her toes, trying to catch my eye.

"Appreciate it," I say, finally. I drop my gaze to meet hers, once I manage to push the thoughts of Samuel away. "I could really do with a drink right now."

"Sure, what do you want? I'll run and get it for you." She waits for my response

"Nathan was going to head out and grab me a drink. Can you go get him to make it for me?" I ask, ignoring her look of confusion.

"Okay...?" My response obviously doesn't make things clearer for her, but she turns, exiting the room to go chase down Nathan.

"What did you think?" I ask Christopher, who is standing awkward and silent in front of me.

I usually restrict myself to asking my team for opinions about my music, or the fans who consume it. I learned early on not to listen to the critiques of snobby music journalists. I even framed a few of those reviews, and hung them up in one of my bathrooms back home:

Listening to this felt like bad sex—lots of buildup, zero climax.

This song lasts longer than most of my exes, yet somehow still left me unsatisfied.

If foreplay felt like this song, I'd fake a headache every time.

But since I wrote this about Christopher, I'm desperate to hear his thoughts.

"Sounds like this muse has managed to cast a spell on you," he says, chuckling.

"Is that right?" I arch my brows as I step toward him.

It's way too easy to play along with him. To avoid asking for what I want. For what I need. But right now, what I need is not sexual innuendo, but reassurance. Reassurance that this song is good. Great even.

But I'm still not ready to let him in fully.

Sure, he's already been inside me, but that's what I always do. I let guys into my ass before I think about letting them into my heart.

It's easier to dance around the edges. To speak in metaphors than ask outright.

"And what do you think this muse would sing back if it were a duet?" I'm keen to get inside his mind, to know his thoughts. Especially since I've exposed myself through these lyrics.

"Well... I guess they would be flattered and might feel the same way." The right corner of his mouth lifts into a semi-smile.

Might.

Might feel the same way?

Does that mean he might not?

Is he only interested in hooking up with me?

Is he just using me to say he hooked up with a celebrity?

I catch myself before I go too far down the rabbit hole. I take a deep breath, and follow it up with a long exhale.

"And how do you reckon the muse would move from *maybe* feeling the same way, to *actually* feeling the same?" I ask.

Christopher stares at me, as if mulling over his choice of words. I've noticed his ability to stop and form his thoughts before expressing them. It's a trait I'm beginning to envy.

"I guess he'd continue to do what he's already doing, and maybe move from something that's been mainly physical to something more intimate." He rubs the back of his neck, shifting his weight from his left leg to his right.

"Intimate?" A flicker of irritation rises in me.

"There's still so much I don't know about you. That we don't know about each other," he says. His hazel eyes study me with an intensity that makes me reach for my watch. "The questions you asked in bed earlier didn't offer much insight, and I didn't really get to ask you anything."

Gone is his usual sarcasm. It's replaced instead by vulnerability.

I lower my head as I continue fiddling with my watch.

He's right.

The blue doors swing open and Nathan walks through, drink in hand. He reaches out to hand it to me.

"Thanks, Nathan." I say, grabbing it, as he looks at Christopher.

I'm unable to move quickly enough. I take a gulp to push

away all my feelings. The alcohol burns my throat as it goes down, forcing me to cough out loud.

"Wrong hole," I say, trying to deflect the concern on Nathan's face.

"I can go get more Manuka honey if you need." He reaches for the door.

"You're good. I should probably just sip it."

Nathan looks at his watch, then back to me.

"Right. Well, better get back upstairs. We're running tight on time." Nathan taps his watch and makes his way back out, leaving me to turn my attention back to Christopher.

"Maybe the artiste would be open to being more intimate tonight?" Christopher asks, as Freddy calls me back to resume recording.

"Maybe..." I say, turning and heading back to the stool.

"Maybe" buys me more time.

"Maybe" gives me some time to fill up with enough Dutch courage to remove some of the barbed wire around my heart and allow myself to be more intimate.

More vulnerable.

More exposed.

"Solid work today, Alex," Paul says.

I'm still raging about the stunt he tried to pull earlier. For the fact that I had to strong-arm him into getting him to do what I asked for. Especially after I'd conceded to giving up my free time to do the promos.

"Thanks," I say through gritted teeth, keeping my eyes focused out the car window.

"They're gonna bounce the tracks over to LA tonight to be

mixed and mastered. We should have something before we wake up in the morning to approve and sign off on."

At this point, I barely care about anything.

The alcohol is working its magic. Nathan gave me two additional drinks in between filming the live videos to accompany the live EP release. Not only has it reduced the intrusive thoughts and feelings, it's also greatly reduced the number of fucks I give.

My gaze briefly drifts to my bag, where two bottles of Belvedere are wrapped up in my leather jacket. Hopefully the car ride is smooth, with no sudden jerks to make them clink.

"Cool." My voice is drained of all energy, and my body feels like it's shattered and running on empty.

All I want is my bed and a decent night's sleep.

My insomnia is bad at the best of times, but this schedule, coupled with the fact that I barely slept last night, has me yawning repeatedly. So much so that I'm fogging up the window.

Paul takes the hint that I don't want to talk. The rest of the drive back to the hotel is cloaked in silence. Paul turns on his iPad, and Lucy and Rob tap away at their phones. Lord's Cricket Ground catches my eye as we drive past. I wonder if the cricket players there have a schedule as relentless as mine.

The usual kerfuffle greets me as we arrive back at the hotel, and I'm quickly swept through the back entrance and into the small elevator on the right that barely fits the four of us.

I'm assuming Christopher and the rest of the team aren't far behind and will make their way up in another elevator. I keep my head lowered as we exit and walk through the maze of hallways, past a couple of guests and a room service trolley, back to my suite. One of the local security guards standing by my door opens it, letting me through.

"Thanks guys," I acknowledge.

I ignore the folders and paperwork strewn across the table, close the door behind me, and make my way into the bathroom. I toss the backpack on the counter, strip out of my clothes, and turn on the shower.

"Alex?" The sound of Christopher's voice drifts through the suite.

My smile rises as I step under the warm water.

I like the way he pronounces my name with his English accent. And the fact that he calls me Alex, not Alexander. Maybe we are getting more intimate as we get to know each other more.

"Just jumping in the shower, make yourself at home," I shout back.

I let the water wash over on me as I pump the shampoo into my hands, applying it to my hair. Before I finish, I turn the handle as far to the left as it will go. Ice-cold water shoots out, forcing a shudder through my body. It's a habit I've gotten into to help calm my nervous system down.

Just as I reach to turn the water off, the bathroom door bursts open.

"What the fuck is this?" Christopher shouts.

His hand pushes a folder up against the glass. I squint through the condensation, trying to make out the word written across the front.

Christopher.

16. Christopher
Monday

"Are you fucking kidding me?"

Saliva shoots from my mouth like venom. Fury courses through my body. Alexander stands frozen in front of me, water dripping from his naked body.

It was bad enough being made to sign an MNDA, but this?

A criminal background check. My resume. A list of previous addresses I've lived at. A scan of my passport. A bank statement. Several screen shots of social media posts. My father's death certificate. Key information on each marked with a yellow highlighter.

It's a whole new level of invasive.

"Let me explain." Alexander's wet hand reaches for my wrist.

"Keep your fucking hands away from me." The growl in my voice echoes off the marble walls. He pulls his hand back, his pupils dilating.

All evening I've been thinking about getting to know him better, how to be more intimate, only to find out he already has all he needs to know about me in this folder.

"Let me get this right," I start, taking a deep breath. "First, you make me sign an MNDA, which won't stand up in a court of law by the way, just so you know. And now you've got a dossier on me." I wave the folder in his face.

My heart pounds against my chest, and I take another deep breath to temper my anger.

"You've got to understand—I'm doing this because I like you," he says. There's tension in his voice, matched by tightness in his shoulders. As I watch, he twists his fingers, then seems to realize he's doing it and stops.

Oh no. I'm not falling for that.

Twisting it round and blaming me.

I've been gaslit far too many times by my mother, father, and Ryan, to fall for it now.

"Bullshit." I throw the file down to the ground. The pages scatter across the floor, all over Alexander's clothes and the bathmat.

I can feel the grip on my anger slipping out of my hands, but I need to stand up for myself. I don't care if he's famous. If he lacks trust. That doesn't give him a free pass to do whatever he likes without repercussions.

"You know trust is earned, not commanded, right? Banging on about not being able to trust people, yet here you are doing the same exact thing. Sneaking round, trying to find information about me behind my back."

My mind drifts back to when I'd found him in my room.

Was his innocent explanation about leaving a note really why he was in there?

I shake my head, not wanting to lose my focus on the issue at hand.

"It was management who wanted me to vet you before anything happened." His voice fades away to a whimper as he begins to shake. He reaches for the towel hung up beside him, flinging it over his shoulders, but leaves the bottom half of his body exposed.

Is he mocking me?

"Stop blaming everyone else." I cross my arms over my chest, for a little extra bolstering. "They may have wanted to, but you could have said no. You could have come and asked me whatever you wanted to know, but you didn't. You went and hired God knows whom to dig up all that stuff on me instead."

I nod at the papers scattered across the floor.

I'm still dumbfounded by how they managed to get ahold of everything.

"You have no idea what it's like to be famous. Not knowing who's selling stories on you. How paranoid I get, wondering if people want to know me for who I actually am or for who they see in their phones. For what they think I can give them."

Alexander reaches for another towel, gripping it tightly as he wraps it round his waist. He sniffs hard as he brings his hands up to his face and wipes at his eyes.

His actions pulls at my heartstrings, but then I wonder if this is all an act. After all, there was a movie script next to the dossier folder on the table outside.

Is he trying to act his way out of this?

Is he trying to garner my sympathy vote?

"I couldn't care less if you were a unicorn named Bob. Do you think I care about all of this?" I wave my hand around at the expansive bathroom, double the size of my own next door. "Five days ago, I didn't even know you existed. I'd never even heard a song of yours."

Alexander lifts his head, wiping at his nose. His eyes make intermittent eye contact with me, finally turning into a sustained stare.

"And that's one of the reasons I'm so attracted to you." He takes a step toward me, then another when I don't respond. But the third step sets me off. Not only has my privacy been invaded, but now my personal space has too. His body is mere inches from me.

"Stop. Just stop, Alex. You can't just talk your way out of this." I turn to leave the bathroom, going out into the bedroom, through the lounge, and toward the door.

Alexander grabs at my shoulder as I reach for the door handle.

I jerk my shoulder upward, knocking it away.

"Don't go, Christopher, don't leave me." He drops to his knees, his deep blue eyes looking up at me like a dog not wanting their owner to leave.

A pang rises in my chest like a balloon, whispers at me to give him a chance, but I pop it with a pin. I need to get out of the room before he breaks me down. Before I regress into my old ways of letting myself get walked over.

I open the door to the suite, startling Rob, and walk past him toward my room. Alexander follows me out, barefoot, the towels the only thing covering him. I remove my room key and hold it up to the reader.

"Please Christopher..." His voice carries down the hallway as he approaches. Rob follows behind him. I push open my door when the green light appears.

"No," I say, walking into my room. I slam the door shut behind me and bolt the lock. I storm past the desk and over to the minibar.

I'm half expecting Alexander to bang on the door like a crazy person, but I get the feeling, from the look in Rob's eye, that he wanted to get Alexander out of the hallway and back into his suite before anyone saw him.

I pull the refrigerator door open, retrieving the half bottle of wine left over from Friday night, and knock it back in one. I plonk the bottle next to my laptop and pull out my phone. I start scrolling through my call log, needing to speak to someone, anyone, just to make sure I'm not crazy. That Alexander getting a dossier on me is way beyond reasonable.

I stop myself from calling Stephen, knowing he won't be able to comprehend anything beyond the fact I've been hooking up with Alexander. I also skip past my housemate Andrew back in LA. He wouldn't be much help either. Yes, he's great with advice, but what could I say? I already signed the MNDA, and I don't fancy being sued for defamation if Andrew ends up spilling the tea to someone.

My finger stops on Kelly's contact. She already knows about Alexander, but she's getting married in five days and the last thing she needs right now is my drama on top of everything else.

Maybe Alexander has a point after all. It's hard to know who you can trust when there's potential money to be made. The love of money is the route of all evil after all. I fling my phone onto my bed.

Ugh.

Well, I guess I might as well put that journal my therapist told me to get to good use. I retrieve it from my bag before collapsing onto the bed, pull out the pen, and open it to the first page.

Tuesday

Hours later, I wake to light streaming through the drapes. I reach up to cover my eyes, the journal still open across my chest. God, my back aches.

I must have passed out from a combination of tiredness, a depletion of the adrenaline and cortisol pumping through my body, and the half bottle of wine I necked.

I roll over, the journal falling off my chest, and reach for my phone, but it doesn't turn on. Damn iPhone batteries. I lift my wrist, but my watch isn't faring any better, probably because I haven't charged it since I arrived.

It takes three attempts to lift myself up off the bed, unstrap my watch from my wrist, and retrieve the cables from my bag. I plug them into the wall and then to my phone and watch before grabbing the TV remote, turning on the TV, and collapsing back onto the bed.

The first channel is BBC Breakfast, broadcasting a segment about the importance of Pride Month for the LGBTQIA+ community and being true to who you are. That's ironic, given my current predicament.

I catch the time on the screen, 9:17 a.m., and flick the TV back off. I really should be getting up and on with my day.

I head into the bathroom, removing the clothes I fell asleep in, and brush down my hair, which is shooting out in all different directions.

A wave of guilt hits me for what happened last night. Journaling made me consider Alexander's point of view just as much as my own. But I'm also proud that I stood up for myself and for what I felt was right. I'm a relatively open book, and I had meant what I'd said at Abbey Road about being more intimate. I want to learn more about who he is—who we both are. But not from Google or a dossier, but from each other.

They say you should never go to sleep on an argument, but I needed the night to cool off. To allow my anger to subside. To be able to speak to Alexander rationally about what happened, rather than emotionally.

After freshening up, I consider going down the hallway to Alexander's room, but there's no point. He's likely left already for his Radio One Live Lounge performance, and I can't text him as my phone still hasn't turned back on yet. The charge is taking forever.

Maybe I should head to the pool, do some laps to stretch out this kink in my back, while my phone powers up. I can always message Alexander when I get back to the room.

I put on my swimming trunks, a T-shirt, and my Nike sliders, and grab my door key. As I pull the door open, I'm almost sent flying backward by two paramedics shooting by me.

Panic grips my heart, the same feeling I experienced with my father, and I turn to follow them. They run into Alexander's suite, where Rob holds the door open for them.

I go to follow them in, but Rob blocks me from entering.

"What happened?" I look past him into the suite, but there's no sign of Alexander or the paramedics inside.

"You need to leave," Rob says, his commanding tone addressing me as if I'm some kind of nuisance.

"But what's happened? Is Alex okay?" Panic seeps into my bones. My thoughts start to race as I fear the worst.

I just need to know he's okay.

"Don't make me tell you again," Rob says. I can tell from the look in his eyes that he isn't in the mood to deal with me, but he's also afraid. Afraid of what, though?

He steps inside, closing the door behind him, and leaves me alone in the hallway.

I stand shell-shocked for a moment before making my way back down the hallway, past my room and to the elevators. There's a churning discomfort in my stomach, the same feeling from four years ago when I entered the hospital looking for my father. That time, I couldn't stop replaying the last words I'd said to him, thinking I'd caused his accident.

I don't think I could live with myself if the same thing happened again.

By the time I reach the pool, I've tried every calming technique I know.

Mindfulness. Word association. Breathwork. But nothing

pushes away the sheer state of terror gripping my body. Each lap I make in the pool seems to pass quicker. I keep trying to work my way through the notion that something terrible has happened to Alexander. For each intrusive thought that comes up, I try, unsuccessfully, to counter it with an opposing viewpoint.

Surely if it was that bad, the paramedics would have come with a stretcher rather than just a medical backpack? I finally settle on a plausible reason to believe that things aren't as dire as I fear when I lift myself out of the pool.

When I finally make it back to the fifth floor, after a quick pit stop in the atrium to pick up some fruit and a chocolate croissant from the breakfast buffet, the hallway is deadly silent. There's no sign of Rob or anyone outside Alexander's suite.

My knock on his door goes unanswered, and after three rings of the doorbell, I head back to my room. I go straight to the phone on the bedside table, dialing reception. But when they answer and I give them Paul's name, I realize I don't know his surname, or any of Alexander's entourage's surnames.

"I'm afraid that unless you have their full name I can't put you through, sir."

I hang up in defeat, sighing.

My hope rises again when I see a notification light emanating from my cell phone.

Heading across to the table, I unplug it to see a load of email notifications, a couple of messages from my family group chat, and three voice messages from Alexander. The last one was left at 2:10 a.m.

I'm sorry, Chris. Please talk to me, I need you.

His speech is slurred to the point that I almost don't recognize that it's him.

I immediately call him back, but it goes straight to voicemail, and I hang up. There's no point leaving a message. I don't want

Stolen Moments

to say anything that someone might come back and use against me.

Think, Christopher, think.

I tap my fingers on the table.

That's it.

The *Live Lounge*.

I lift my laptop open, pull up Radio One on my web browser, and click play on the livestream. Sabrina Carpenter's *Espresso* blasts out when it finally stops buffering.

It's 11 a.m., and I'm assuming Alex would have to be there by now if he is still going to be on the show.

That was Espresso *by Sabrina Carpenter, and we've just had word from downstairs that Alexander Morgan has finally arrived in the building. Stay tuned for a* Live Lounge *you won't want to miss.*

I pull out the desk chair and collapse into it.

Thank God, he's okay. Thank God, he's alive.

The tension in my body finally leaves as I stretch my legs out.

I wait anxiously for the next twenty-five minutes until I hear Alexander's voice.

My time in London so far has been great, he says to the host, his voice horse and slightly distant. I try to imagine what he looks like right now. I can't view him on the video stream; it was disabled just before he came on air.

And you were at Abbey Road yesterday, recording a live album. Is there anything you can share with us, a little exclusive perhaps? the DJ asks.

We're going to drop the album on Friday, and fans have been begging me to release new music, so I've included a new song I wrote just the other day while here in London. His voice starts to sound slightly more like the one I know.

A new track… Can you give us a title? The DJ probes for more.

I lean forward into the laptop, intrigued by what he might say.

You'll have to wait until Friday when it goes live.

Well, you heard it here first. Alexander Morgan is releasing a new live album and a new track Friday. Now before we let you leave, it's a tradition for artists to perform a cover, so without any further ado, take it away, Alexander.

The opening chords to Sabrina Carpenter's *Please, Please, Please* play out, a tune I've become familiar with due to Kelly playing it nonstop over the years. As the song goes on, I wonder if he intentionally chose it after our argument last night.

Surely it's not a coincidence.

When he gets to the second chorus, my suspicion is confirmed when he changes a line in the lyrics to *Don't bring me tears, when I'm standing here just trying to clarify*. With that, I know he's talking directly to me.

I want to run to him. To slap him for what he did.

But also, to hug him. To tell him we'll work things out.

"Where are we at with the deck?" Pietro asks me over the Zoom call.

Given the distractions over the last forty-eight hours, I've barely had time to work on the slide deck for our newest client, Brewed. I've been tasked with outlining a creative marketing strategy for their upcoming Christmas campaign.

Pietro, my boss, was kind enough to allow me to work from London this week, so I didn't have to take it out of my annual holiday allowance, but now I'm feeling the pressure.

"Microsoft's been playing up on my laptop and I haven't been able to format the slides to send it through." Once again, I'm being truth-adjacent, but Pietro doesn't need to know that.

"I've got an appointment with the Genius Bar right after this call to fix it, and then I'll get it straight across to you."

"Okay, but we need it in the next two hours," Pietro says firmly.

I start to breathe out a sigh of relief, when Tony, another account manager at the firm, unmutes himself.

"You could always use Canva," he says. He smirks and adjusts his Harry Potter-shaped glasses.

Not helpful Tony, not helpful.

Tony and I have never seen eye to eye. When I was initially transferred to the LA division of Elemental Creative, he was quite standoffish. Then last year, when they brought in a new assistant, Sara, he became quite possessive of her.

Turns out that possessiveness was actually him hooking up with her on the down-low. It's a sackable offense if the powers that be find out, but I let it slide, holding on to that information for a rainy day.

I inhale deeply and adjust myself in the chair.

"Thanks, Tony. I'm not that adept with it, but maybe Sara could help teach me when I get back." The smirk quickly disappears from his face as I fight off the one trying to rise on mine.

Touché, motherfucker, touché.

With the meeting wraps, I close Zoom, relieved I've bought myself another couple of hours to finish the project. But that also means I'm going to be late to the theater, with Kelly, Daniel, and my mum.

I grab my phone and quickly fire off a message to the family group chat.

> Crisis at work. I'm gonna have to skip dinner.
>
> I'll meet you at the theater. x

Two messages appear almost simultaneously, contrasting in both tone and understanding.

> **KELLY**
> Hope it's nothing too crazy. We'll leave your ticket at the box office. x

> **MUM**
> Can you not prioritize your family at least once, Christopher Foster!

Water off a duck's back. Water off a duck's back.

I shake my head at my mum's response, repeating the mantra to myself out loud. I won't let her words impact me. And of course I'm going to prioritize work over her—especially if it affords me the ability to stay out in Los Angeles and far away from her.

I look at the time on my phone: 5 p.m. If I can power through the presentation now, I'll have it done by seven and will still make it to the theater before curtain call. And even better, that timing means I will see mum, complete my duty as a son, and won't have to listen to her moaning. One of the many reasons I love going to the theater.

Just as I put my phone down, Alexander comes to mind, and I lift it back up. Throwing caution to the wind, I try once more to call him, but his phone rings through to voicemail again.

I know he's okay. I'm certain he's okay. I heard him on the radio. But I just want to see him to make sure. To settle the discomfort in my chest that's stayed with me since this morning.

I fire up TikTok, type in his name, and scroll down through several posts. One of them stops me in my tracks:

Alexander Morgan Found Unconscious in Hotel Suite.

My heart jumps into my throat as I click on the video. An American woman under the handle Hollywood Exposed starts to discuss details of what happened. *Rumors are circulating that paramedics were called to the Landmark Hotel in London this morning, when pop star Alexander Morgan was found unresponsive in the bathroom of his hotel suite.*

I instantly close the app, my whole body stiffening.

A nauseous feeling forms in my stomach.

That can't be true. It can't be.

Can it?

17. Alexander
Tuesday

Everything is too loud, too bright, too overwhelming.

I dial down the brightness and sound on my laptop. I'm being forced to engage via Zoom with Amelia, aka my sober coach, aka Captain-no-fun, back in the US. I've known her since the last time I relapsed and left rehab. Today, Paul insisted that it was speak with Amelia or rehab—no third option of a day off, much to my frustration—but now I'm thinking rehab would have been a better option.

I might take Amelia more seriously if it weren't for her electric blue hair and the garish multicolored dress that screams *Notice me*. She's been lecturing me for the last fifteen minutes, telling me I'm crying out for attention, when everything about her is doing the same. Like she is the famous person, not me. She is trying, in her condescending, holier-than-thou way, to get me to acknowledge the seriousness of what happened.

Sure, Rob found me in a semi-state of unconsciousness. Sure, my phone was smashed on the floor with two empty bottles of vodka on either side of me. And yeah, there was vomit all over the bathroom. But tell me, what pop star or rock star hasn't gone too hard on the liquor one night, only to regret it the next day?

The last thing I need right now is more judgment from other people.

"What caused you to relapse?" Amelia asks, finally coming up for air. I try and fail to get a read on her emotional state.

My inability to read her expression is not because of my stinging eyes or the poor Wi-Fi connection backstage in my dressing room, but from the copious amounts of Botox preventing her eyebrows moving an inch. I know this because she *loves* talking about *all* her appointments.

I go to answer, but my throat is dry and painful. The aftertaste of bile lingers despite three swigs of mouthwash. I reach for ginger tea with Manuka honey in it, hoping it will soothe my throat and buy me a second to think of an answer.

The truth? Christopher's words cut me open. Not like a scalpel, but like a butcher's knife, and then I quickly spiraled through the four levels of desperation.

Lying.

Pleading.

Drinking.

Defeated.

Or the other truth? That the boxes I've filed away in the back of my mind keep coming back to haunt me. Samuel. The crash. Roy. And further back, my teacher.

Placing the cup down, I opt for the easier third answer: work. I don't want to give Amelia an excuse to push for more sessions.

"Everything was just getting to me. All the demands, the lack of time off, the pressure to always be on, the inability to do what I want."

Amelia nods while the reflection of my face solemnly stares back at me on the screen.

Yes, I may be lying, but it's a plausible lie, and it is a

contributing factor. The last ten months have been relentless. My agent added an additional twenty-seven shows to the original proposal, due to overwhelming demand. Then management kept slipping in promo here and there and everywhere—including the bits today that Connie convinced us to keep to counter the online rumors that I'd been found unconscious.

No wonder I'm exhausted.

No wonder Michael Jackson relied on propofol to get some rest.

I wonder if he started to feel less and less like a human and more like a product. A cow no longer just being milked, but bled dry. My team is determined to get every last bit out of me before they sling me out to pasture. Or worse, to the slaughterhouse.

"Have you been able to voice that to anyone?" comes Amelia's voice. It's the first sign of compassion, if you could call it that, she's shown since jumping on the call.

I can feel Rob's eyes on me from where he's sitting on the other couch in the dressing room. I'm unable to look at him without feeling guilt for what I put him through. Usually I'd be left alone for something like this, but ever since Rob found me, he hasn't left my side. And Paul has mandated I be watched around the clock.

"Nobody listens. I'm always told to just get on with things. That I should be grateful for everything, but I can't talk about —" Amelia's eyes widen as the anger rises in my chest, but I catch myself before going any further. The two forbidden S-words, Samuel and Sexuality, nearly fall out of my mouth.

I reach for the cup to take another sip, swallowing the words down with it.

"I can't talk about the downside of what it's like to be a pop star." I put the cup back down and reach for the laptop. I rest it on my legs as I lean back into the couch.

Again, not a total lie.

"With all that pressure on you, it's no wonder you ended up relapsing. Maybe you should consider heading back to a treatment facility?" Amelia's face moves closer to her screen. Her brown eyes flicker with judgment, sparking more anger in the pit of my stomach.

"I don't need a treatment facility. I need a break." I shove the laptop back up on the table. "A break from touring, a break from pretending to be someone I'm not, and a break from this." I slam the laptop closed.

When will everyone realize that my drinking is not the problem? It's what's causing me to drink that's the problem. My face begins to burn as I push myself up off the couch and head to the fridge to retrieve a bottle of water. I splash some out onto my palm and rub it over my face.

The rehab facility two years ago didn't understand what it was like to be me. The pressure I was under. How, before I even wake up, I have seventy-eight people to pay for every day on tour. A hundred thousand dollars to pay out for wages, travel, and accommodation. And unlike in a band, where the show can still go on if one member is ill, if I don't show up everything gets cancelled. And I'm the one left footing the bill.

But they didn't get it; they didn't get me.

You need to move toward the discomfort. Embrace it. Like I hadn't been through enough already—the discomfort without any progress. Why would I seek out more? Why would I voluntarily put myself through that again?

"Do you mind if I turn off the lights, try and get some rest before the show?" I ask, opening the fridge again. I pull out an eye mask and head to the light switch, still unable to look at Rob.

"Okay, boss," Rob says, with a heavy sigh.

A lump forms in my throat at his response.

I hit the switch, swallowing down my guilt and shame, and

head back to the couch. I lean back into the cushions and pull over the mask over my eyes. The coolness helps bring down the heat radiating from my forehead and cheeks.

I just want this all to be over.

One of my dancers repeatedly taps on my cheek and brings me to, as another dancer thrusts a bottle of water in front of me, urging me to drink it. I push myself upright with my left hand, head spinning, eyes struggling to focus.

Dancers.

Stage.

Screams.

The air is squeezed out of my lungs as dread washes over me.

"Where are we at in the set?" I ask, before sipping the water.

"You dropped to the floor halfway through Tonight, I'm Gonna Fly," another dancer adds. All five of them are creating a protective circle around me at the end of the catwalk, away from the crowd still chanting my name.

Four songs left to go. *Great.*

I take another sip of water, and do three deep inhales before grabbing the hand of one of the dancers, who helps me to my feet. A cheer erupts from the crowd. My feet are wobbly as I take the microphone back from one of the dancers and try and head back into the starting position for Tonight, I'm Gonna Fly, but I already know I can't carry on.

I hold my hand up in the air, to stop the dancers and band from starting, remove my in-ear monitors so I can hear myself, and turn and slowly walk back up the catwalk to the stage. Rob and another security guard track me on the sides the whole way up, alongside the spotlight.

"Kill the spotlight," I say into the microphone. The light is burning on my shoulders and back, not helping.

It swoops to my right and then goes out. The darkness is a relief. The faint light from the LED wall at the back of the stage continues to play out the video montage that accompanies *Tonight, I'm Gonna Fly*, which is just about bearable for my eyes.

I turn and face the crowd, a rising discomfort in my body forcing me to tense up, and I will my muscles to relax. This is so embarrassing. First I was exposed on stage, and now I've fainted.

"Sorry about that little fall over there, everyone," I begin. The crowd is still chanting my name. One little girl waves vigorously at me from the front row. I give her a little wave back, which has her squealing and hugging her mom. "I'm just a little overwhelmed by all the love in this room tonight."

The screams erupt, almost blowing the roof off the arena, and it brings a smile to my face, which only causes the crowd to get louder.

"There's been some rumors flying round online today that I was found unresponsive in my room this morning. And I'm sure that what you saw just now won't do anything to squash those rumors." My leg is beginning to twitch, so I walk to Freddy's drum kit, grab a bottle of water and take a couple of gulps.

The crowd falls eerily silent as I put down the water bottle and grab the towel next to it, wiping my brow. I deliberate what to say next.

Do I tell them the truth?

Reveal what's behind the curtain like in the Wizard of Oz?

My fans aren't stupid. In fact, many of them have picked up on the relentlessness of my schedule. Ever since the Free Britney movement, it seems like they are checking in on me more. Like they realize that I, too, am a human, not just a robot wheeled out as and when needed.

Stolen Moments

But I'm not sure I'm ready to reveal everything right now.

I turn back to face the crowd, throwing down the towel.

"The truth is, this tour has taken its toll on me, and I'm exhausted. But I never want to let you all, my fans, down." Another cheer erupts. "I appreciate that you've come to see a full show, but I don't think I can make it to the end, so I'm wondering if I can make a deal with you all. Would it be okay with you if, instead of performing the last four tracks, I give you the world premiere of my new song, *Stolen Moments*, that drops on Friday?"

The screams have me reaching for my in-ear monitors. I shove them in, not to hear the music and the clicker that keeps me in time, but to protect my eardrums from bursting.

A warm feeling brews in my chest.

Thank God they agree that this trade-off will be a win-win for everyone.

A crew tech rushes on stage with a stool as Andy switches his electric guitar for an acoustic guitar. Freddy maneuvers himself out from behind the drums and moves across to the percussion stand.

I hoist myself up on the stool and grab hold of the mic stand, sliding the microphone in the holder. My heart sounds almost as loud as Freddy usually does on the drums while I wait for everyone to get ready.

Was this a good idea? Other than the band, my team, and a couple of people from the label, no one has heard this song live. What if they don't like it? What if everyone who's heard it is wrong, and the people who really matter, my fans, hate it?

My head turns to Freddy as he nods at me, setting off the clicker in my ear. No backing track to accompany us. Just Freddy on percussion, Andy on acoustic guitar, and me on vocals.

I take one final breath as Andy plays the opening chords and I say a little prayer.

Please don't let me fuck this up.

Paul's voice hits me like a fire hose as soon as I come off stage. It immediately extinguishes the pure joy I felt from the insane reaction to performing *Stolen Moments* for the first time.

"I can't believe you performed *Stolen Moments*," Paul shouts at me as Rob guides us straight to the waiting car.

"What was the alternative? Stop the show completely? You already told me we had to go ahead with the show. Despite me wanting the day off, despite the paramedics telling us that I needed rest." My body tenses up as I reach for the seatbelt and strap myself in.

"We had a whole plan to launch this track—which I didn't want to put out, by the way, you did—with the DSP's, Spotify Billboard in Times Square, Apple Music takeover. And now, we'll likely have lost all of that coverage, thanks to your decision." Paul reaches for a bottle of water, opening it and squeezing it tightly as he gulps from it.

If he wants to go there, then *hell*, am I ready to go there.

"Well, I wouldn't have had to resort to that if you'd actually postponed or canceled the show." The tension in my shoulders moves to my head, causing it to start throbbing.

Paul's forehead crinkles as his eyes narrow.

"Sure. We cancel the show. You're left footing the bill. Not only for what it costs to keep this machine running, but for all the refunded tickets." Paul crosses his arms, crosses his legs, and lets out a disapproving sigh.

The disapproving sigh, the condescending tone, all of it acts like a red flag to a bull.

"First, I'd only have to pay back the advance to the promoter. Second, that's why we have insurance, in case things like this happen. Third, anyone would think this is your money, not mine. It's like you care more about the money than me." My chest rises and falls in rapid succession.

How fucking dare he.

"That's not…" Paul leans forward, but I cut him off, indignant.

"I haven't finished. If you keep pushing me, there'll be no shows. What happened this morning wouldn't have happened if you hadn't kept pushing me, and I've had enough."

Paul falls silent, as if he can sense what's on the tip of my tongue.

I'm tempted to say it right there and then, but we're still twenty minutes from the hotel, which would give him time to fight his cause, and I need to weigh my options. What would I do if I actually fire him?

One day, I tell myself, my parents will work out how to use FaceTime properly.

"Alex, baby." My mom's chin greets me as I answer her call. Their departure gate is visible behind her. My dad says hello, out of shot.

Thankfully, Lucy was able to pick up a new iPhone to replace the old one. So I don't have to do this on my iPad and carry it around the suite. My old iPhone lays on the table, its cracked screen staring back at me. A glaring reminder of what unfolded this morning.

"I'm okay, Mom, I'm okay. You know not to believe what you see on social media." My hand reaches for the back of my neck, as I look out of the window.

"I know when you're lying to me, Alex, you always rub your neck when you lie." My mom's face finally appears on screen. Her nostrils flare.

Why must she insist on doing video calls?

It's so much easier when she can't see me, can't read my body language.

"I'm exhausted, Mom. I just want to get these shows done and go home." I drop my hand from my neck and let out a yawn to help sell the narrative.

"Are you sure you can't come back tonight? We can wait for you here, pick you up?" She attempts to give me a once over.

"I could, but I just want to get them done and out the way. That way I can take a proper break from everything." My thoughts drift to the skatepark and just being free to ride my board once again.

Oh, how I dream of that life.

"Well, your father and I will be there in a few hours. You rest up and we'll see you when we get to the hotel, okay?" Her face disappears off the screen again.

"Okay Mom. Love you. Love you, Dad."

My dad's face reappears next to my mom.

"Love you, son," they both respond in unison before hanging up.

I tap my phone into my hand as I peer out the window.

The argument with Paul in the car continues to play out in my head. Maybe I should speak to my lawyer, John, to get the ball rolling and explore my options. But that only addresses one of my problems. Christopher is the other. And a lawyer isn't going to provide a solution there. In fact, hiring people to help me with Christopher is what got me into this mess in the first place.

I stop tapping and hold the phone up to my face to unlock it —intending to call him—when I remember that I don't have Christopher's number. When Lucy updated my phone, the last backup was from a week ago, before all this started.

Rob had knocked on Chris's door for me when I got back,

but there was no answer. And he didn't pick up when I tried to call his room on the landline.

I want to apologize to him.

To tell him I never should have let the team go through with compiling the dossier on him.

How amazing the response to *Stolen Moments* was tonight.

Just have him hold me in his arms again.

I've already lost Samuel forever. I don't want to lose the first guy I've truly cared about since. But there's nothing more I can do. Nothing but wait and hope that Christopher reaches out. That he will forgive me.

My stomach gurgling is a stark reminder that not only have I not eaten anything all day aside from a packet of nuts, but that room service is taking forever. My gaze drifts to the side table where the packets are stacked, weighing up whether to have another when a knock comes from the door.

"I've got it," I say, almost running to the door as Rob reappears from the bathroom.

"Finally," I say opening the door.

But it's not room service that greets me.

18. Christopher
Tuesday

I'm stunned into silence.

Of all the responses I'd anticipated from Alexander, *Finally*, was not one I was expecting.

"Oh God. I thought you were room service. I'm sorry." Alexander is rapidly blinking, his body freezing momentarily, before he takes two steps back and ushers me in.

I'm taken aback when I see Rob occupying one of the armchairs in the living room. Well, that explains in part why there was no one on guard at the door after the Rita incident the other night. His dark-chocolate eyes scan me from head to toe.

"Rob, would you give us the room, please?" Alexander motions me onto the couch, and picks up a packet of peanuts from above the minibar before joining me.

"I'm under strict orders not to leave you alone," he says. Rob's glare makes me fidget uncomfortably.

Does he think I'm responsible for what happened last night?

Am I considered a threat to Alexander's safety? Like the fans downstairs? Like Rita?

"I'll be fine, I promise. Look, he doesn't have anything on him."

Rob gives me another once over before pushing himself up out of the armchair.

"Okay, I'll be in the meeting room, but the door *will* be staying open." He looks back at Alexander, who shakes his head, before leaving us alone.

I reach for the pillow, the same one that I threw off the couch two nights ago to get closer to Alexander, and settle it on my lap as a layer of protection.

"Christopher," Alexander says, his deep blue eyes widening as he looks at me. He reaches over and sets a hand over my knee. "I'm so sorry about everything. The MNDA, the dossier... I never meant for you to feel like I didn't trust you."

The warmth radiating from his hand as it meets my knee sends a surge of electricity through my body. My grip loosens on the pillow.

I catch myself wanting to go down the old familiar path of using sarcasm to fend off my feelings, and stop before the words come out of my mouth. I take a deep breath instead, and I see Alexander's jaw clench in response.

"This whole dating a pop star thing, it's a completely different world to me," I say, slowly. "I even looked it up online, but there's no instruction manual, no how-to guide. So I'm shooting blind here. I don't know what the norms are, or what expectations come with this." I lift my hand from the pillow and wave it in the space between us.

Alexander's jaw relaxes and squeezes his hand more tightly on my knee.

"I get it. It's a lot. I appreciate that, and I don't blame you for reacting the way you did. Heck, I'd probably have reacted even worse if it was the other way round." The corners of his mouth lift.

The warmth in his eyes melts away the residual resentment that I didn't realize was still there.

Maybe I underestimated him.

Maybe he can take responsibility and ownership of what he did.

Unlike my father. Unlike Ryan.

"I actually owe you an apology too," I say, removing the pillow from my lap and spinning to face him. "I've been worried sick about you all day. I tried to call, but you didn't pick up. I thought I caused all this, and that you didn't want to speak to me."

Alexander shifts back slightly, extends his arm, and grabs his phone off the table next to us, handing it to me.

"I smashed it in a drunken rage last night," he says. I take in the shattered screen. "I only got a new phone after the show, but the backup didn't restore your number. I actually thought that *you* didn't want to speak to *me*."

His hand trembles slightly as I pass the phone back to him, and I see a slight purple bruising on the back of it as he sets the phone on the table again.

"What happened?"

He follows my gaze down to the mark on his hand.

I guess this is the real test.

If he will open up. Tell me the truth. Be more intimate with me.

After a long pause and a deep breath, he begins.

"After you left, didn't return my messages, I started to spiral. Everything from my past came flooding back and I couldn't deal with it, so I kept drinking. I wanted to quiet the thoughts. Numb the pain. Next thing I knew, I was waking up next to a puddle of vomit with a light in my eyes and a drip in my arm."

I go to reach for him, to comfort him. But I pull back.

Would I be comforting him or am I just trying to quell the tension in my muscles?

The guilt swirls in my stomach.

His eyes are still locked on the table.

"What came flooding back?" I ask, when he finally lifts his head. He turns his face toward mine. His eyes well up, and I wonder if I've gone too far. "I'm sorry, you don't have to talk about it if you don't want to."

"No, you deserve to know. And I need to talk about it, to get it out." He lets out a heavy sigh and rubs his eyes before continuing. "I lost my old assistant, Samuel, in a car accident. It was my twenty-first birthday and we were out celebrating. Everyone thinks it happened after he dropped me off at my house, but I was in the car with him." There's a lost look in his eyes as his gaze drifts from me to the window. It's one I know all too well. "We were having an argument, and he wasn't paying attention to the road. A car came at us, he jerked the wheel, and we collided with a palm tree."

Alexander's chest begins to rise and fall quickly, and he reaches for his eyes again. Tears start to roll down his cheek.

"The rest was a blur. The way I handled it was all wrong. I left him there to die. Paul said—" he pauses, but doesn't finish the sentence. "The guilt has consumed me ever since, but I couldn't talk about it to anyone. So, I started drinking instead."

Jesus.

The poor guy.

I lean across, putting my arm behind him, and rub his back reassuringly.

There's a steady stream of tears falling down his cheeks now.

"Eight months later, my team lead an intervention when my drinking got out of control. I'd been sober ever since. Up until last week, when my team gave me a two-year sobriety chip. Everything came flooding back. Then when we argued last night and you left, and I thought I'd lost you too." He wipes his eyes again.

"You're the first person I've actually cared about since Samuel. I've already lost one person who can see beyond all the pop star business and see the real me. I don't think I can handle losing another."

His words set off a number of fireworks in my chest simultaneously.

Fear, hope, excitement, trepidation.

I'd assumed this was just a tour romance for him.

That I was just a quick hookup.

That he probably had a different guy in every city.

But judging by the longing in those blue eyes, I'm starting to get the sense that this, whatever this is, means more to him than just a casual fling. And I also get the feeling that Samuel must have been more than just an assistant to Alexander.

I hesitate, debating whether or not to ask about Samuel, when the doorbell rings.

"That must be room service," Alexander says, rolling his eyes before pushing himself up from the couch.

Rob emerges out of the meeting room, but Alexander waves him off.

"I got it," he calls. He checks the mini-TV screen at the side of the door, quickly rubbing his face before opening the door.

"Sorry for the delay, we're short-staffed tonight." Imani wheels a trolley through the entrance, making me slightly less frustrated at the interruption. Two plates, covered by silver domed lids, sit on top, along with some cutlery and a range of condiments.

"Where would you like me to put them?" she asks.

Her eyes briefly meet mine, and a soft smile appears on her face before she turns to Rob. A pang of guilt hits me. Maybe I shouldn't be here. I'm not sure if I should try to justify it…

blurt out that I'm Alexander's dialect coach, but Rob steps forward and pushes the guilt away with his movement.

"You can place the rib eye down there, and I'll take the rest in there," he says, nodding at the office behind him.

"Do you want anything?" Alexander asks me as Imani puts the dish down on the table. She lifts off the lid, and the smell of steak hits my nostrils.

"I'm good, thanks," I say, as he returns to the couch.

Rob retrieves a fifty-pound note from his pocket and hands it to her. He shows her out of the suite before returning to the other room.

Alexander digs into his meal, bypassing the knife like so many of my American friends do, and using the side of his fork to cut the steak. He inhales it, barely chewing before swallowing it down and then grabbing a handful of fries, scarfing them down too.

And I thought Stephen was bad when it came to food etiquette.

I'm unsure where to pick up. Doubt lurks in the suburbs of my mind.

Where do I start? Should I reassure him he hasn't lost me? Clarify who Samuel is? Acknowledge my own guilt that I've been living with? Or explain why I was so triggered by the trust issues?

I tap my fingers on my knee, and realize that if I'm expecting him to be more intimate and open with me, then I need to be too. I readjust myself on the couch.

"I know what it's like to live with the guilt of feeling like you're responsible for someone's death," I say.

Alexander almost chokes on a french fry. I immediately reach over to pat his back as he coughs it out. Rob comes racing out, only for Alexander to hold up the offending food item.

"Just a fry," he says, waving it at Rob.

"Eat slowly," Rob admonishes him. He scowls, shaking his head as he returns to the room.

Clearly I'm not the only one who has noticed that Alexander's eating habits are carnal.

"Some people choke under pressure—you choke on carbs." The wry smile on my face gets a side eye and a shake of the head from Alexander.

"Too soon?" The smile drops from my face.

"Too soon," he says, grabbing another french fry, this time chewing more slowly. "How do you know what it's like to feel responsible for someone's death?" His brows furrow as he cuts another piece off of his steak.

"The night I came out to my parents, it didn't go too well. My dad told me, in no uncertain terms, *I'll not have a faggot for a son living under my roof,* and then stormed out. That was the last time I saw him alive. He went to the pub and ended up falling down a flight of stairs. He was dead by the time we got to the hospital." My shoulders slump and I let the air out of my lungs.

Alexander holds his fork up to his mouth, pauses, and returns it to his plate.

"He said that to you? I'm so sorry." He shakes his head in disbelief.

I nod in affirmation.

"Yeah, and what's worse, my mum blames me for his death. It's not bad enough that I feel guilty as it is. She had to stick the boot in. *If you'd only kept your mouth shut, your dad would still be here,*" I say, mimicking her tone. A pang in my chest forces me to draw a breath before continuing. "The rational part of my head knows it was my dad's drinking that caused it. But the brain isn't rational. No matter how much therapy I've done, I can't seem to stop blaming myself and my sexuality for it."

There's a stinging sensation in my eyes as they cloud over.

"That's why I broke up with my ex, Ryan. Why I took the

company transfer to LA. I've realized I can't outrun my problems. They invariably catch up with me. But I do know this." I wipe my eyes as I turn to face Alex. "The solution to the problem isn't at the bottom of a bottle. As fun as it is to escape your mind or lose your inhibitions, it doesn't help in the end."

A look of remorse comes over Alexander's face as he begins to fidget with his watch.

"I know," he says. His gaze meets mine before drifting back to his watch. "I am swearing off alcohol. I just need a break from everything." His shoulders slump like the weight of the world is on them.

And I don't want to add to it.

To make this conversation any heavier than it needs to be.

"I get why you have trust issues. I would too if I had everyone wanting to know my business. I don't truly blame you for getting that dossier done, which was pretty extensive by the way." I lift my left eyebrow. "I just hope that moving forward, if you need to know something, you'll come to me first. That's all I ask."

I reach for his chin, lifting it and turning his face to meet mine.

"I will. I promise," he says, lifting his hand to cover mine.

And for some reason, I let myself fully relax. The touch of his hand, the tenderness in his voice, shifts something inside of me.

Like the turning of the tide.

Like I'm being pulled toward him, rather than pushed away.

And if I let myself, I know I'll get swept up in him.

That this could be the turning point in our relationship.

"So, who's this Ryan guy then? Do I need to be concerned?" Alexander breaks the moment to grab one of the last remaining french fries.

"Of Ryan?" I shake my head at the mere notion of Alexander

being jealous of him. "Sure, I really enjoyed the thrill of the weekly emotional breakdowns he put me through."

I've had years to perform an extensive postmortem on our relationship, and the results come back conclusive every time: poisonous.

Wednesday

My vision slowly comes into focus as I feel the weight of Alexander's arm across my chest. It's a feeling that's oddly comforting, given my penchant for wanting my own space in bed. He looks so peaceful, his eyes flickering underneath his eyelids, the stray blond highlights in his hair shooting in all different directions, that I don't want to disturb him. But I need to get going.

I remove the noise cancellation earbuds he lent me, and stretch out my arm to reach for my phone. The slight movement wakes Alexander.

"Morning." His voice is sleepy in my ear as he kisses the back of my head.

"Morning," I say, rolling over. I fire up my phone as he shifts himself upward to meet me against the headboard. He kisses my cheek before resting his head on my shoulder.

"Is that your sister?" he asks.

My home screen features an image of Kelly and I underneath the Hollywood sign, taken during her trip out to LA last summer.

"Yeah," I say.

"She's the one getting married, right?" He lifts his head from my shoulder to look at me.

"Unless I have any other siblings I don't know about, then yes."

My laugh doesn't get a response from Alexander.

"I'd like to meet her," he says, pushing himself upright. "You should both come to my show tonight." A wide grin appears across his face.

Wait? What?

I know I wanted him to open up more. To be more intimate. But this feels a bit too fast even for me. And, given the MNDA, I thought this needed to be kept a secret from everyone. Even if Kelly is somewhat aware of our relationship.

Alexander must notice the reaction on my face, because he slumps slightly against the headboard.

"Or not."

"Sorry… I'm just … the MNDA." I'm still trying to wrap my mind around what he's asking.

"Do you trust her to keep this a secret?" He waves his finger between us.

"Yes," I say emphatically.

"Then I trust you," he says. He puts his hand on my chest, resting it right on my heart.

Damn.

Those four words hit me like a sledgehammer.

I'm trying hard to go slowly. Not to rush in like I did with Ryan. Not to let myself get carried away with what this could be.

But when he says stuff like that, it's hard not to allow my thoughts to run away with themselves. To picture a future with us together.

"Plus, my parents are flying in today. So, if you are going to meet them while they're here, then it's only fair that I get to meet your family too." He hits my chest twice before pulling his hand back, a smirk on his face.

"Your parents?" There's mild discomfort rising in my chest, although not from the sting of Alexander's handprint, which has left a mark on my left breast.

Jesus.

This is all becoming a bit too surreal.

Like someone accidentally sat on the remote and fast-forwarded through all the other initial milestones you'd normally go through before meeting the family.

"Yeah, they're coming in for the final couple of shows. They'll be at the show tonight. You can meet them then." His puppy dog eyes tug at my heartstrings, making it hard to say no.

Of course I want to come and see the show. To see him do his thing.

But am I ready to go all in? To lay all my cards out on the table?

"I'll have to check with my sister, but I guess this muse should see you perform at some point while you're in town," I say, adding a cheeky wink that prompts him to bite his lip.

He leans in to kiss me, the taste of steak still lining his tongue as it slides into my mouth, and I try desperately to not lose myself in him. I've got so much work to do today that I really can't afford to be distracted right now.

"I really need to get back to my room, to get on with my pitch," I say, pulling back slightly and placing my hand on his chest.

"Come on, we can be quick." The force of his chest pushes my hand back as he moves forward to bite my bottom lip. His hand slides down toward my belly, causing me to flinch.

"Why do you always shift when I touch you there?" he asks. He pulls back, removing his hand and placing it next to my hip.

"I don't like my stomach." My gaze darts away from his.

"I don't get why." He moves his hand back over it gently.

"Says the guy with the most perfect physique." Envy laces every word.

I've never been able to get anywhere near Alexander's physique. A two-pack was the best I could muster six months into LA, when I tried to fit into the WeHo standard.

"This?" he says, looking down and pulling at his abs. "I'd trade my body for yours any day of the week. The pressure to keep this up is relentless."

I'd never have thought someone with a physique like that could be envious of a body like mine. Normal as it is. I've been brainwashed into thinking that all gays want and desire the Greek Adonis physique.

The muffled sound of my phone comes from under the duvet, and I reach for it. Alexander mouths *Get it* at me when he notices Kelly's name appear on the screen.

"Hi," I say, putting the phone to my ear as Alexander disappears under the covers.

"What are you up to?" Kelly asks.

"I'm just in bed, and you?" My voice rises as Alexander slides down my body, taking my cock into his mouth. One hand cups my balls and the other pushes the duvet back so he can meet my eyes with his.

"Mum's insisting we go over all the wedding plans this afternoon. Wanna join?"

"And be subjected to another psychological takedown? I think I'll pass."

"Ask her about tonight," Alexander whispers, momentarily coming up for air. My cock begins to swell as he swallows it whole again.

"Remember that artist I mentioned that's staying at the hotel..."

God, he's good at this. My cock is already throbbing as Alexander's head bobs up and down. He starts working away at the bottom of my cock with his hand, cranking up the electricity coursing through my veins.

"Alexander Morgan." Kelly's voice is hesitant.

"Yeah, that one." My hips begin to buck. "Well, I ran into

him, and he invited me to the show tonight. I'm wondering if you'd be down to join."

I've never been one for premature ejaculation, but there's something about the way his tongue slides over the tip of my cock. The way it dances around my foreskin, while his warm hand cups my balls and the other rubs up and down, that sets me on fire. It's barely been a minute and I'm already close. Alexander pauses momentarily, waiting for Kelly's response. There's a hunger in his blue eyes.

"I'm not sure, I have so much to do before the wedding. What time is it?"

"Err, I'm not sure what time..." I say, looking down at him.

Alexander mouths *Seven p.m.*, and returns his attention to my cock.

"Seven p.m. at the O2 Arena."

After a long pause, Kelly agrees. "Okay, but you owe me."

I smile down at Alexander to acknowledge that Kelly will come.

His eyes widen with delight as he speeds up his wrist and mouth movements. He's devouring my cock, gagging on it with an intensity and ferocity that's almost primal.

"Right, I better go, I need to finish off something..." I hang up before Kelly gets to say goodbye. My voice crescendos, and I feel the cum shoot out of my cock straight down his throat.

Alexander's eyes are locked on mine as he drains my dick dry.

I throw down the phone as my eyes roll backward in my head, losing myself in the aftermath of the orgasm.

"I could get used to that," I say, as Alexander crawls up toward me. I feel his throbbing dick rubbing its way up my body as he comes up to reach my lips, but pauses just shy of them.

"Could you now," he says, wagging his eyebrows up and down.

I've been working nonstop on the deck for Brewed for the last several hours, and I keep losing track of where I am in Pietro's extensive notes. He wants me to adjust the plan to put more emphasis on the global activations around their Christmas campaign. Add more competitor analysis in different regions there. Expand the various KPIs, and so forth. Irritation creeps in like a cruel mistress in the dark. I'd expected the revisions to take half the amount of time it has.

Having the opportunity to lead the creative marketing strategy on an iconic brand like Brewed is an amazing career opportunity that I don't want to mess up—even if the timing is far from ideal. Pietro has been breathing down my neck to get this across the line, but after this is done I can switch off for a few days, get through the wedding, and pick it up again next week.

My phone pings, and I look across, seeing a message from Kelly pop up.

> **KELLY**
> What should I wear?

My irritation at work transfers to her and the situation.

Like I need to be thinking about any more decisions right now.

I don't even know what I should be wearing, let alone what Kelly should wear. I mean, it's one thing to dress for Alexander. It's a whole other thing dressing to meet his parents for the first time.

Another ping emanates from my phone, causing the irritation to engulf my body.

For God's sake Kelly, can you just give me a minute?

But when I look at my phone, it's not Kelly who has messaged me.

RYAN

Hey. Heard you're back in town. We should catch up. Ryan. x

19. Alexander
Wednesday

"And this is in recognition of your album going double-platinum here in the UK," the head of the UK label says.

The plaque is impressively heavy as she hands it over to me. Underneath the glass, embossed with my logo in gold leaf, there are two platinum-colored vinyls set against the backdrop of my artwork. The inscription on a small gold plate reads:

> *Presented to Alexander Morgan in recognition of 600,000 units consumed in the UK.*

All of this is encased in a black frame.

"Thank you," I say, forcing on my camera-ready smile as the photographer lines up in front of us. Everyone from the UK label seems to tower above me as they position themselves to pose. They all dress similarly, too, in black or white shirts and jackets, and jeans rolled up above their ankles as if they're expecting a flood.

In contrast, Erica and Lucy stand out in their blue T-shirts and jean shorts.

"Someone's twinning tonight," I say, once the obligatory photo is out of the way. Erica and Lucy place the plaque down on the bar beside me. The UK label people disperse to the black couches, built into the alcoves of the backstage area. They take a moment to glance at each other and smile before turning back to me.

"Did you hear about Rita?" Erica asks in a lowered voice, her brows furrowing.

"Rita?" My voice is a little too loud as I shake my head, causing a couple of people to stare.

Erica takes two steps forward, motioning Lucy to do the same.

"I overheard one of the label guys over there talking about her." She tilts her head toward a mullet-haired mustached guy. "Apparently, she's at the box office kicking up a fuss, claiming she's on the list." Erica spins her finger in a small circle by her head.

I take in a deep breath, fighting back the tension clawing at my shoulders.

It's just one thing after another. Can I not catch a break for one day?

I scan the room for Rob, who's nowhere to be seen. I automatically reach for my watch.

"Don't worry," Lucy says, placing her hand on top of mine and loosening my grip on the time piece. "Security is already on it to ensure she doesn't get into the building or backstage."

Lucy is somehow reading my mind.

I don't need that woman near me again, causing yet another scandal.

"There you are!" The sound of my mom's voice makes me jump out of my skin.

My face gets hotter with every tottering step she takes toward me. It's like she's cleaned out the merchandise store.

She's wearing a black hoodie with my logo emblazoned on it, and has tucked her brown hair under a baseball cap—also adorned with my logo. She's carrying so much merch in her hands that she's barely able to wave hi to the various label people as she passes them.

I let out a deep sigh.

It's like she goes from one extreme to the other.

She hides things at home from Harrison so as not to make him feel bad about my success, but then she overcompensates when she's out on the road and he's not around.

"You look exhausted." My mom dumps the various bits in her arms down on the bar before pulling me in and squeezing the life out of me. Erica and Lucy take their cue to leave me, after saying a quick hi.

"Thanks Mom." I shake myself free from her grip.

She hasn't been here for five seconds and she's already smothering me and criticizing me in the same breath. She'd be a perfect case study for helicopter parenting.

"Give him a break, Carla." My dad shakes his head as he steps in and gives me a brief squeeze. I leave a slight makeup stain on the fabric of his blue shirt as I pull back.

"Bulking out, I see." He reaches into the bowl of candy behind me.

I force a smile, not having the energy to push back on his criticism.

"What's this?" My mom leans toward the bar, trying to pick the plaque up before she realizes its weight. She lifts herself up on her toes to see it instead.

"The label gave it to me for the album. You can have it for your house if you want?"

As great as plaques are, I'm running out of space on the walls of my office and bathrooms back home.

"Would it not be better at your place? We have to be mindful of your brother." She lowers herself back down and rests her hand on my forearm.

Ugh.

They're always protecting him. Wrapping him in cotton wool.

Even after he sold me out, they stuck up for him.

And now I have to play down my success so he doesn't feel emasculated.

What about me? Can't they be proud of my success in front of him?

Or does it always have to be done away from him?

"Right. Right." I shake my head as I pick out some of the fizzy cola bottle candies and shove them into my mouth.

"Are you feeling better?" My mom puts the back of her hand to my forehead, feeling for heat.

"I'm getting there," I manage to say between chews.

I still feel exhausted, but knowing that I only have the show today and nothing tomorrow is helping. Well, that plus three vitamin IV drips in three days.

"Maybe you and I can have a spa day at the hotel tomorrow? What do you say?" She drops her hand from my forehead and sets it on her hip. There's an expectant look on her face.

"I thought we were going to check out the sites?" My dad scowls at her.

"That can wait," she says, waving away his look.

Seeing my parents quarrel never gets any easier. And though I'm mostly shielded from it these days since I'm away so much, it still leaves me feeling unsettled.

Thankfully, my attention is diverted by the sight of Rob's towering frame entering the room. Everyone seems to naturally move out of his way, such is his command of any space he finds himself in. The heavy feeling of my parents' spat instantly lifts when Christopher steps out from behind Rob, along with a woman that I'm assuming is his sister.

"Hey," I say.

"Hi," he responds.

Fireworks go off in my chest.

Just hearing that one word leave his mouth makes me feel giddy like a teenager. Katy Perry's *Teenage Dream* plays out in my head. It's like his British accent flips a switch inside of me. And ever since last night, it feels like something else has shifted within me too. He's more than just a craving.

I take a moment to absorb how handsome he is. Tonight he's got a prep look going on with a baby-blue button-down shirt, sleeves rolled up to his elbows, khaki trousers, and brown boots.

"This is my sister, Kelly," he says. His hand brushes her long wavy auburn hair as he reaches around behind her to rest his hand on the back of her green dress.

"Great to meet you. Christopher tells me you're getting married this weekend. Congratulations!" I lean in for a hug.

He looks so much like her. She has the same hazel eyes, the same flick at the end of her nose. The freckles on her face are the only difference.

"Aren't you going to introduce us?" My mom looks down her nose at me.

In the daze of seeing Christopher, I'd almost forgotten that she and my dad were there.

"Oh yeah," I say, whacking my forehead to appease her. "This is Christopher and his sister, Kelly. Kelly, Christopher, this is my mom and dad, Carla and Bruce." My hand waves between them.

"Nice to meet you," Christopher says, holding out a hand for my parents to shake. My mom bats that away, pulling both of them in for a hug.

"What do you do round here, Christopher?" Her eyes are like a scanner, moving from head to toe.

In the midst of everything else, I haven't had a chance to tell her about Christopher yet, about who he is. She wasn't the most welcoming when it came to Samuel. It almost seemed like she was jealous that he was spending time with me and taking time away from her.

"I'm Alex's dialect coach," Christopher says. A look of confusion appears on his sister's face.

"Oh my God. I've always wanted to speak like that old woman in Downton Abbey. Can you teach me?" My mom's giddy excitement almost knocks Christopher off his feet. She grabs hold of him, and I can't tell if the discomfort on his face is because of my mom's grip or his inability to play along with the role. His eyes dart toward me—*Help me*—etched in them.

"It's okay," I say, looking at Christopher and then my mom. "He's like Samuel."

I choose my words carefully. A couple of the people lingering in the background, helping themselves to another drink at the bar, seem to be hovering a bit longer than one would expect.

"But Lucy was just here? Is she leaving you?" My mom's forehead wrinkles.

She's never been one to pick up on a hint. Her naivety is both a blessing and a curse.

"No. Not like Samuel in that way." I shake my head.

"Oh. Ohhhhhh." The penny drops and she takes two steps back to take Christopher in fully.

"Well in that case, scrap the old woman from Downton Abbey. I need to know everything about you." She interlinks her arm with his, attempting to pull him away.

His widening eyes scream *Rescue me!*

I do love my mom, but sometimes she gets too involved in

my life. Almost as if she is living vicariously through me. Like she's making up for a life she didn't get to lead.

"Mom, can you give us a moment first, please?" I reach for her shoulder.

"Come on, Carla, let's give the kid some space. And anyway, we need to go find Paul and sort out replacing our tickets." My dad motions her away as she releases Christopher.

"Why do you need to replace your tickets?" I ask, letting out a sigh. I already know about my mom's penchant for helping fans out. They beg and plead with her to help get tickets or pass on fan mail to me. She's always been a sucker for a sob story.

"Your mom gave them away to some actress at the box office outside." My dad shakes his head in disbelief.

"Yeah, poor woman, was meant to be on the guest list, but it seems Paul left her off."

My heart leaps into my throat.

"Please tell me you only gave her your tickets and not your backstage passes too?" My gaze quickly darts to both my parents' chests to ensure they have their triple-A passes on them. My ass cheeks clench together.

"No. Why?" My mom's quizzical expression does nothing to abate the rising fear inside me.

I take a deep breath and motion Rob over with my hand.

"We've got an issue," I say, looking at my mom. "They've given Rita their tickets." Rob bends down to hear my lowered voice, noticing my hand playing with my watch.

"Shouldn't we have? She seemed so genuine." My mom's voice trembles.

Rob bites his lip. I hear an exhale coming from his nose.

"Okay. Leave it with me." He nods and escorts my parents away to ask them questions.

And this is why I tell her not to be so helpful.

"Sorry about that," I say, shaking away the irritation and the tension in my shoulders. I file the issue of Rita away in the back of my mind. Rob's got a grip on that now.

Christopher starts to speak, but Kelly gets in before him.

"Does everyone in here work for you?" she asks, her gaze taking in the various huddles of people in the room.

"Pretty much," I say, grabbing another handful of candy.

Thankfully, I'm locked away in my dressing room most of the time. It can be lonely there, but it provides some peace. It's a space where people aren't bothering me.

"Is it always like this backstage?" She reaches for the bowl of candy, but stops when she notices the plaque. "Wow, this is so cool. Can I?" She puts her hands on either side of it to lift it up.

"Sure," I say, smiling as she lifts it up to study it.

"She's an art teacher, a sucker for design work." Christopher says.

"You can have it if you want?"

I'm so keen to make a good first impression that I feel myself overcompensating to win her approval. As if giving her this plaque will buy me some brownie points.

"I couldn't possibly, it's yours." She puts the plaque back down on the bar.

"I've got hundreds of these back home. Honestly, you'll be doing me a favor."

If my mom won't take it, at least it can go to good use elsewhere.

"Told you I should have brought a bigger bag!" Kelly elbows Christopher as she smiles and thanks me.

"Shall we head somewhere a little quieter?" I offer, starting to feel claustrophobic. It'll be quieter back at my dressing room, and that way I can get to know Kelly and spend time with both of them without prying eyes watching my every move.

"Sure," Christopher says, nodding.

"So. Tell me more about your brother," I ask, leading the way to the door. "What's the most embarrassing story you've got?"

I shoot Christopher a side glance, the corner of my mouth lifting.

"Don't you dare," Christopher responds as he follows behind.

The audience is still screaming as I pause to take a sip of water.

"Last night, I performed this next song live for the first time," I say. I take in the banners in front of me.

Marry Me Alexander.

I want a Stolen Moment With You.

"The crowd was great, but I have a feeling that this song will go down even better tonight."

The crowd screams even louder as I look across to Block 111. I'm relieved to see Christopher and Kelly seated next to my parents, giggling away. Rita Watson is nowhere to be seen. Rob thankfully located her before the show started and got the venue security to escort her from the premises.

"This is *Stolen Moments*."

The crowd roars as Andy starts playing the intro. Christopher looks away from my mom and toward me. Our eyes connect as I begin to sing, and it's as if the other nineteen thousand people have drifted away. I'm performing to an audience of one.

As the chorus kicks in, I pull out my in-ear monitors to hear the audience singing back the words to me. Warmth engulfs me from inside. The track doesn't even come out for another twenty-six hours, but they already seem to know the words.

I wish I could capture this moment right now. Bottle it up and keep it. Freddy raises an eyebrow when I look across to him.

Surely this is a better way to launch the track than as an exclusive first play on a radio show, or a banner on a digital streaming platform.

By the time I've worked my way backstage, after taking a quick moment to wipe myself down with a towel in my dressing room, the VIP bar backstage has already filled up. The room is buzzing with energy. Half of the people hold plastic cups with beer and wine in them. Clearly the request to keep backstage completely free from alcohol fell on deaf ears.

Nathan, who I've managed to avoid since Monday night, greets me at the door, surrounded by several other label employees. He introduces me to many I already know, and a few I don't, from Spotify, Apple, and Amazon.

"That new track is a *hit!*" Nathan says, pulling out his phone.

"Yeah, it's a great track," a tanned guy with a Liverpudlian accent says.

"Thanks," I say as enthusiastically as possible. I try to keep my focus locked on them, knowing that schmoozing is an important part of the gig, but I want to locate Christopher. To find out what he thought. Ask what he and my mom were laughing about.

"Look at the numbers on TikTok." Nathan waves his phone around at everyone. "There's already thirty thousand people using the snippet we delivered earlier today."

They collectively raise their eyebrows, clearly impressed at the statistic.

Nathan has many flaws, but he's always had the gift of the gab. He could sell sand to an Arab.

The brief reprieve allows me to look around the room, and I notice Christopher and Kelly lingering awkwardly at the bar.

"Would you excuse me? I need to go and sort something out," I say, placing my hand on Nathan's back. "Was great to meet you all and thank you so much for coming tonight." I shake everyone's hand before shooting off to the bar. I pat down the Velcro on my stage trousers, which I didn't get to change out of before coming in here.

"Let's head to my dressing room," I say to them both, nodding toward the door.

As we head down the hallway, the ringing in my ears starts to subside. A few of the crew acknowledge me as they move in and out of the various dressing rooms for production and management.

"What did you think?" I ask, turning to them both.

"That was *insane*. I've never heard an audience so loud in my life!" Kelly says, her eyes widen as she almost bumps into one of the flight cases.

I want to prolong the conversation, to ask more questions, but all I really care about is what Christopher thought.

"Is *this* your dressing room too?" Christopher says as he notices the sign above the door. It's the second of two rooms allocated to me backstage. This one is just down the hall from the other one we sat in before the show started.

"No. It's Brad Pitt's," I say, shaking my head as I reach for the handle.

"Oh right. Sorry. I guess one room's not big enough to fit your ego in." I look back to see a smirk across his face.

"I guess the dry wit has come out of retirement," I say. I push the handle down to open the door and motion them to go through. I slap Christopher's ass as I enter behind him.

"Oh honey, there you are. You were great." My mom gets up from the couch, giving me another vice-like squeeze, ignoring both Christopher and Kelly.

"Thanks Mom. Glad you liked the show." My dad gives me the thumbs-up as he heads to the fridge to retrieve a Gatorade.

I'm desperate to know what Christopher thinks, but I'm not

going to get any oxygen in here. Not with my mom taking over the show.

"Could you look after Kelly for a minute?" I ask her. "I just need to discuss something with Christopher." My gaze darts between the two of them.

Before she has a chance to respond, I motion to Christopher to follow me.

Thankfully, I know of a place backstage where no one will disturb us. There's a secret bar hidden behind the wardrobe, just down the hall from my dressing room.

"What's this?" Christopher asks as I open the wardrobe doors.

"Our own little private space." I give him a cheeky wink as he enters.

"Is this where you bring all your muses?" I pull the doors closed behind me and turn to meet his lips.

God, those lips. I could stay attached to those plump pillows of his forever.

"Oh no," I say, pulling back and grabbing his hand. "I take them to the one at the end." I lead him to the bookcase at the end of the bar and motion to him to pull down one of the books. The hidden door opens to reveal a small snug room with a padded couch.

"Aren't I the lucky guy?" he says, his brows rising.

He pushes me down on the couch and starts to kiss me passionately.

Usually I'm the one initiating sex, even if he's the one that ends up dominating, so I'm instantly turned on by this. But I really want to know what he thought.

I push him back, lifting my head slightly.

"Tell me, what did you think of the show?" I prop myself up on my elbows.

"Well," he says, his hazel eyes staring deeply into my soul. "Maybe I could be a fanboy after all…"

"Could you?" I narrow my eyes as a smirk forms on my face.

"Well, maybe not a fan boy. I'm not sure I'm willing to build a shrine in my room and convert to the cult of Alexander." He gives me a wry smile as his hands grip at my trousers, pulling them down. The Velcro comes undone on the sides.

"Oh fuck," he says, letting go. The wry smile is replaced by a gasp.

"Don't worry, they're meant to do that," I say, standing up. I tear them at the sides to show him, and discard them on the floor.

"Nice to see you putting in maximum effort for minimal mystery." He claws into the back of my neck with one hand as the other pulls down my briefs to release my cock.

This time there's less haste and more passion as I tear the clothes from him. Our mouths are insatiable, like we can't get enough of each other, like this is the Last Supper and we are devouring every mouthful.

I ignore the faint sound of my name coming from outside as Christopher pushes me down on the couch and covers my mouth with his hand. He spits in his other hand and rubs his saliva all over my cock before slowly lowering himself onto me. His pupils dilate as he bites down on his lip, pauses to adjust his hips, and then begins a rhythmic movement back and forth.

His ass muscles grip my shaft tightly as he begins to pick up speed.

He keeps his hand over my mouth as the sound of my name gets louder. His hips do all the work, his cock rubbing up and down against my abs. His thrusts get harder and faster as he rides my dick like a cowboy trying to control a bucking bronco.

He has the same dominant look in his eyes as when he's fucking me. As he continues to pound down on me, he takes his hand away from my mouth and begins working on his cock with the same intensity.

I fight back a moan as I hear my name from outside the secret room get louder. Christopher shakes his head at me to not respond, while refusing to stop. He's clearly turned on by the whole situation. His ass muscles grip my cock even tighter with each successive thrust.

I can feel myself getting close when my hips start to buck upward. There's a clapping sound from the downward thrusts of his hips meeting my upward thrusts, which send him higher above me. The sound of my name is now right behind the door. And I can finally make out who it is. Rob.

I raise my hand to push Christopher off me, trying to fight back how close I am to climaxing, but it's too late. Rob bursts in just as I explode inside of Christopher. He has a devilish grin and I turn to see Rob's eyes darting away, unsure of where to look.

Rob has barely been able to look at me the whole drive back to the hotel.

Christopher laughed off the whole thing as Rob left us to sort ourselves out. I'm sure Rob just wants to get me in my room and then head to his own room to forget the whole thing happened.

I give a brief wave to the fans, once we pull up to the front entrance and exit the car, and then I enter the hotel behind Rob. I'm instantly hit with an eerie feeling that makes the hairs on the back of my neck stand on end.

The staff and a couple of hotel guests linger in the foyer looking at me, before turning their attention to their right when an almighty shriek sounds. Rob pushes me back, just as I hear another shriek that could probably be heard ten blocks away. My leg catches Lucy's, who almost stumbles to the floor before Paul manages to save her.

When I turn back, I make out Rita, storming down the stairs from the atrium toward us. She's laser-focused, a fire in her eyes. Her blond hair is disheveled and her white blouse is completely open, exposing her bra. Her black leather skirt looks more like a belt.

"Where is he?" Her voice echoes around the foyer as I duck behind Rob.

"Take him to the elevator," Rob says under his breath, standing firm, as the rest of us follow the local security guard.

"Alexander. Alexander." The first is a plea, the second is outright anger.

I lift my head and instantly regret it. Her speed picks up from a stride to a jog.

"Keep your head down," Paul says sternly, as Rob blocks her path.

I duck my head again, noticing a couple of people holding their phones up as I do.

What is she doing back here?

Is she delusional? Does she actually think we're in a relationship?

"Alexander! Why are you ignoring me?"

"You need to step back, ma'am," Rob says, blocking the hall down to the elevator. The local security guard frantically presses the button.

"Get your hands off me!" she screams, causing me to turn and look at her.

She claws upward at Rob's face, her red nails landing on his cheek. Rob grabs Rita by the waist and pulls her up over his shoulder.

"Get off me. Get off me!" she screams. She starts whacking Rob's back with her fists as he begins to walk away.

My chest tightens at the sight.

I snap my head around as the dinging sound of the elevator arriving sounds and the doors open.

Just get in. Just get inside.

I take one step forward, before I'm compelled to look back one more time.

"Alexander, don't do this. How dare you betray me in front of all these people. After everything we've been through!" Her face contorts like she's been possessed by a demon.

Paul pushes me into the elevator when my legs refuse to move, and I collapse against the wooden wall as the door closes.

What the fuck was that all about?

20. Christopher
Wednesday

The hotel lobby seems like a crime scene when I enter the hotel. There are police standing to either side, talking to hotel staff and guests. They're taking notes in their notepads, looking at the guests' phones.

My heart rate immediately spikes and my mind goes to the worst-case scenario. But there's no trace of blood on the floor. No ambulances outside.

I keep my head low, taking long deep breaths and head toward the elevators. I avoid eye contact with everyone and quickly pull out my phone.

> Everything okay?
>
> SKATER BOY
> Yeah, I'll explain when you get to my suite.

Alexander's immediate response helps me push down the growing dread that has begun clawing its way into my throat, like a zombie pulling itself from a grave.

Once I hit the fifth floor, I turn and head down the hallway. I breathe a sigh of relief at the familiar sight of Rob standing guard by Alexander's door.

"Jesus, what happened to you?" I try to take in what I'm seeing.

Rob lowers a towel with ice that he's holding up to his cheek. There are scratches all across his face and neck, some that have drawn blood.

Someone really did a number on him.

"You don't want to know," he says, pulling the door key from his pocket and tapping it on the reader to let me in.

"After you," I say, my hand outstretched to let him in first.

"I've got to head down to the lobby," he says, shaking his head disapprovingly.

The door closes behind me, and I hear Alexander call my name from the bedroom. After flicking my shoes off by the door, I grab a bottle of water from the table, parched from the long tube ride back from the O2, and make my way in to him.

I open the bottle and begin drinking it. Alexander is lost in his phone.

"She looks psychotic," Alexander finally says, looking up as I reach him at the bed. He passes his phone to me as I sit down beside him.

Who looks psychotic? A fan? What have I missed?

The video begins to play again on loop, and I rub my eyes. I watch it a second time, just to ensure my eyes aren't deceiving me.

"Damn, you're not wrong." I pass the phone back. "She looks possessed."

"Right."

The way Alexander's leg twitches underneath the blanket tells me that this has rattled him more than he is giving away.

The poor guy.

First the TV interview. Then the nightclub. Then the alarm

on Sunday night, and now this. Clearly, this Rita woman is not all there. She's clearly delusional if she believes she's in some kind of relationship with him.

Or have I missed something?

Is there something going on here I don't know about?

"Don't tell me this is what happens when people start catching feelings for you. They start going crazy." I reach for his leg under the blankets and shake it, forcing a smile to his face.

"Only the British ones," he says, winking and lifting the cover, motioning for me to join him. His gaze is expectant.

"Lucky I've been possessed for decades already then. Even the Devil himself wouldn't get a foothold in here." I point to my heart as I unbutton my shirt and trousers, removing my phone from the pocket before joining him in bed.

I lean over and he opens his arm, allowing me to snuggle up into him. The stubble from his cheek rubs up against mine as I kiss him before I lower my head to his shoulder.

The glare of light from my phone pulls my attention to my hand, and I raise it to my face to unlock it.

KELLY

He seems like a keeper to me.

I can't move quickly enough to hide Kelly's message from Alexander's view. He drops his phone on the duvet and snatches the phone out of my hand.

"A keeper, hey?" He raises his eyebrows.

My cheeks instantly burst with heat as my heart jumps to my throat.

She's not wrong. I get the feeling that this really is developing into something more serious. Sharing the same bed for three of the last four nights is definitely more than just a booty call.

But I don't want to feed his ego any more than I already did after tonight's show.

"Don't get ahead of yourself," I say, snatching the phone back. I stretch to put it on the bedside table out of reach. "Kelly's never been a good judge of character. If there was a sport for poor judgment, she'd have enough to start her own team."

"Is that so?" he asks, smirking, and leans over to kiss my forehead in a way that instantly sets butterflies off in my stomach.

It's like every kiss, every touch, removes another brick from the wall built around my heart. It still feels too early to let him all the way in, but enough bricks have fallen over the last six days for him to be able to see over the wall to the vulnerable side of me.

"Talking of family members, I'm intrigued to hear what your parents thought of me." I roll over, resting my arms on his chest, my chin atop the back of my hands. I stare deeply into his eyes.

I haven't cared this much about anyone since...

Nope.

Nope.

You're here with Alexander.

Stop thinking about him.

Ryan has slowly been clawing his way back into my thoughts with a fishhook ever since his text the other night. Even earlier at the venue, when I was riding Alexander's cock, I closed my eyes momentarily and for a split second I pictured Ryan and not Alexander beneath me. Thankfully, Rob bursting into the room snapped me out of it, but the bitter aftertaste of the image still lingers.

"Earth to Christopher," Alexander says, snapping his fingers in front of my eyes.

"Sorry, what was that?" I shake my head.

"The reviews have yet to come in, but I haven't seen my mom laugh like that in forever." His smile produces a dimple in his right cheek.

It's a dimple I could fall into and stay lost inside of forever.

"You saw that?"

Given how big the O2 is, I'm surprised he could make us out.

"I couldn't take my eyes off you all night." His deadpan response makes me question whether he's being serious or not.

"I just thought that was your lazy eye." I allow my eyes to cross as I stare at him. I'm hedging my bets on the latter.

"Do you always joke around when someone is trying to be serious with you?" he asks.

The muffled sound of his phone ringing breaks the awkward silence, giving me more time to ponder my response.

Maybe I do?

Maybe I just want to keep him at arm's length.

I know how hard I can fall when I do allow myself to catch feelings. That's why I always say *Catch phrases not feelings*.

"What's up?" Alexander says, putting the phone on speaker and resting it on his chest. Paul's name appears on the screen.

"Connie's on the call too," Paul shares.

"Right, what's going on?" Alexander's leg starts to twitch again under the duvet.

"Well, the police are dealing with Rita. They have her in custody and have gathered all the witness statements, but it seems to be blowing up all over social media," Connie says.

"I've seen." Alexander shakes his head at me.

"It's going to be all over the news by morning. I've been fielding calls from journalists nonstop for the last hour." Connie sounds unamused.

Is this what his life is like?

Is this what I'm signing up for?

"I've spoken with Rita's publicist, and they're going to have her admitted to rehab. Get her professional help. Apparently, her husband filed for divorce after the images in the press Sunday, and she's been AWOL ever since."

"Thanks for letting me know. What am I meant to do with that?" Alexander's leg now looks more like an Irish dancer's. I reach down to calm it, and start rubbing gently to try and soothe him.

"Well, the media are going to run with the story whether we like it or not. They're insinuating you've been having an affair. There's even speculation that your new song is about her."

"Right." Alexander pushes himself upright against the headboard. The phone drops into his lap as his shoulders stiffen.

"We want to be respectful to Rita and her family, allow them to lead on this, especially given the sensitivity of the matter. But the speculation is actually helping to drive interest in the new live album and especially in *Stolen Moments*. Nathan forwarded the latest Spotify presaves for the album, and you've nearly broken Taylor Swift's record." There's an awkward pause as Connie clears her throat. "We think we should let the speculation play out and have you lie low in the hotel until then."

The hesitation in Connie's voice is clear.

Alexander had mentioned wanting to get out and do something normal on his day off, and since I'm not required for any family obligations until Friday evening and work is now parked till Monday, I'd planned to surprise him and go to the skateboard park in Alexandra Palace. His mom had said it was a great idea.

But I can feel that plan slipping through my fingers, quicker than grains of sand.

"But I've made plans." Alexander folds his arms across his chest and lets out a deep exhale.

"It's already like a circus outside, Alex. The paparazzi are swarming the building like vultures, and this situation will probably have thousands of fans descending on the hotel come morning," Paul chimes in.

Alexander's shoulders drop as he lets out another deep exhale.

This must be what his life is like all the time.

Held prisoner in his own room. Not free to live a normal life. Like a caged animal in a zoo. Let out to perform for everyone watching before being locked away again, only for the cycle to repeat the next day and the day after that.

"Fine," Alexander says, hanging up the phone and chucking it on the bedside table.

"Looks like we're stuck here," he says. His face is downcast as he turns back to me.

Part of me knows we could make the most of the situation, but I know how much he was looking forward to getting out and about for the day. To see the city rather than going, as he put it, *from hotel, to studio, to venue, repeat.*

My gaze drifts across the room to the walk-in wardrobe as I reach for the noise cancellation earbuds. Then it dawns on me.

"Fuck that. I've got an idea."

"Really?" Alexander's face lights up.

"It might be crazy," I say, looking at the suitcases before turning back to him. "But let me sleep on it, and then we can discuss it in the morning."

My idea might be high risk, but then, if you don't take a risk, you don't get the reward.

Thursday

After trying three different suitcases, we finally landed on one that can fit Alexander's broad frame. He contorts his body bringing his knees right up to his chest, to fit inside. For someone who is three inches shorter than me, he can certainly pack a suitcase.

"Right, have you got enough room in there?" I ask, my hand on the zip.

He nods back at me, his face wearing the same excited smile that was there when I told him the plan two hours ago.

Understandably, he had to tell Rob about the plan, and I thought he was going to pooh-pooh the idea. But Rob actually chipped in, helping us find a suitcase big enough and promising to keep it secret from Paul, Connie, and Lucy. All of this, of course, with the provision that I check in with him every hour.

I take one final look at Alexander, who looks strange wearing my clothes. My gray hoodie and black running shorts are almost too tight for him. Thankfully, we are at least the same size sneakers. But Rob had insisted that the less he looks like himself, the more likely he'll go unnoticed.

"It'll only be fifteen minutes, twenty tops," I say, grabbing a bottle of water from the table and throwing it to him.

"I'd happily be stuck in here for an hour if it means I get to leave the hotel," he says. I zip the suitcase closed as he opens the bottle.

I grab my backpack, filled with a change of clothes and toiletries, and wheel the suitcase to the door. We've timed our departure to coincide with the hotel's check out time. Hopefully the busyness of the hotel will make it less conspicuous when I leave.

Concierge had offered to help me with the bags when they brought up the luggage trolley. I'd thought that getting their help made sense, but Rob didn't trust any of them. He did, however, agree it would be weird for me to push the luggage trolley out to the taxi on my own.

Thankfully, Imani was still in the hotel, and agreed to help. She greets us at the door with a cheery smile.

"You should have seen what Princess Anne used to make us smuggle in and out of the hotel," Imani says, laughing as Rob helps me to get the suitcase onto the trolley. The wheel of the metallic suitcase clips the gold bar as we finally wrestle it into position.

"I can only imagine," I say, my eyebrows raising. As I chuck my backpack on top and wave goodbye, Rob whacks me on the back and reminds me to text. Imani and I work our way down the hallway and into the elevator.

"Hold the elevator!" Two women strolling down the corridor shout at me as the door opens. They're the same two women from that I saw stop Alexander for a photo before we headed out to Abbey Road.

But this time they've swapped their cocktail dresses for sporting attire.

"Do you think he'll already be in the gym?" one of them asks the other. She pulls a lip gloss from her shorts and leans into the elevator doors to apply it.

"Maybe," the other says, without lifting her head from her phone. She's scrolling through a load of social media posts, all of them with Alexander in them.

Talk about obsessed.

I shake my head when I catch Imani's gaze. Imani rolls her eyes, forcing me to fight back a chuckle.

By the time we exit on the ground floor, the women have outlined their whole plan for how they're going to approach Alexander. They bicker over which one they think he'll prefer and how they'll ultimately share him if need be.

"Are they always that crazy?" I ask, loud enough for Alexander to hear.

"That's nothing," Imani says as she pushes the trolley toward the exit. "You should have seen the lengths Michael

Jackson's fans used to go to. Makes those two look like amateurs."

The mere thought sends a shiver down my spine.

Imani nods to the doorman and he opens the door, whistling for a taxi. There's a sea of fans and paparazzi waiting outside. They slowly clear a pathway to allow us through.

"Have you seen Alexander?" one girl asks.

"Who?" I respond. I take my backpack and place it on my shoulders. My response is the easiest way I've found to deal with these fans.

"Alexander Morgan. You don't know who he is?" Her face fills with disgust.

Finally, a taxi pulls up. The doorman opens the door, and I carefully slide the suitcase into the backseat, then climb in after it. I thank both Imani and the doorman, handing them each a twenty-pound note. The doorman graciously accepts, but Imani waves it away, telling me not to be so stupid.

The fan still eagerly waits by the taxi for an answer.

"I don't know her," I say to the girl, slamming the door behind me.

A smile rises on my face as Mariah Carey's *Obsessed* plays out on the radio.

Mariah would be so proud.

"Where to, mate?" the taxi driver asks, looking at me over his shoulder.

"Hundred and forty-six, Tufnell Park Road," I say. I sink back into the leather seat, my heart pounding against my rib cage, as the taxi pulls away.

We did it.

We did it.

Several road diversions and thirty minutes later, we pull up opposite my sister's apartment. I tap the card reader with my phone before opening the door.

One last hurdle.

Getting out of the taxi is harder than expected. The suitcase is heavy and I'm trying to be as gentle as possible. Thankfully, it has four wheels, which makes it a little easier to move. I slip my backpack back on and close the door behind me.

"Almost there," I say, tapping the suitcase as the taxi pulls away.

He taps back twice in acknowledgment, just as a hipster walks past, who cuts me a weird look. Ironic, given that his hair looks like his mum put a bowl round it and his cardigan lost a battle to a group of moths.

I do a quick scan of the road to ensure that I haven't been followed before pushing the suitcase across. Adrenaline courses through my veins at lightning speed. I haven't felt this pumped since the day Stephen and I bunked off school to go to Thorpe Park.

I reach the entrance and enter the code in the padlocked box outside my sister's apartment. Her keys fall out and I unlock the door. With one final push of the suitcase over the skirting, we're finally in the clear.

I let out a deep exhale and unzip the suitcase. Alexander almost falls out before getting to his feet and lunging toward me.

"That is the most romantic thing anyone has ever done for me," he says. His arms are locked around my neck, and he leans in and kisses me passionately. Sweat drips from his forehead.

"God help you when you find out what I've got planned for you next then," I say.

"What?" His face lights up as he grabs the suitcase and follows me up the stairs.

"A coffin box," I say, craning my neck back when I get to Kelly's door. His nostrils flare and his smile disappears as I slide the key in the door and open it.

Kelly's studio apartment is small, but cozy. It's enough space for Kelly and Daniel to live in, but just barely. The beiges, whites, and browns used for the walls and furniture give the place more of a beach vibe than a place in Central London.

It seems weird to have their bed in the same place as their couch, which I've spent more nights sleeping on than I'd like to remember. But I guess you don't get much bang for your buck in London these days. Thankfully, they'll be moving out into a two-bedroom house after their wedding and then I'll have my own room to crash in.

I head into the kitchen, throwing the keys on the small round table, and grab two glasses, filling them with water. I hand one to Alexander, who chugs it in three gulps.

"The thirst is real," I say with a smirk.

"You try being stuck in a suitcase for nearly forty minutes and see how you get on," he fires back, placing his glass down on the table.

"Fair point," I say, taking another gulp myself.

"Where are we going then?" Alexander asks, rubbing his hands together.

"All will be revealed in good time," I say, taking one last gulp, grabbing his glass and placing both in the sink before heading back into the main room.

I grab the car keys off the bedside cabinet next to the alarm clock, and pick up a box, topped with a bow, that Kelly left lying against the couch for me this morning. Then I open the front door and motion him out.

We head out onto the main street, closing the building door tightly behind us, and across to where Daniel's black Fiat Punto sits.

"Wrong side," I say to Alexander, as he goes to open the door on the driver's side.

He hits his head with the palm of his hand as he lets out a laugh and then runs around to the passenger side.

I chuck the box in the back and adjust the seat, strapping myself in, and slide the key in to start the engine. I curse under my breath that Daniel drives a manual rather than automatic before reminding myself that I should be grateful to even be able to do this.

"What's that you've got?" Alexander asks, twisting backward to retrieve the box from the back. A little tug-of-war breaks out. I know he's stronger than me and could easily pull it away, but he concedes.

"Patience, Alex. Patience."

I've only seen a picture of what Kelly did to Daniel's old skateboard, and though I think it looks great, I'm not sure if he'll like it.

His puppy dog eyes stare at me, guilt-tripping me into relenting. "Okay fine," I say, handing back the package to him. He tears off the bow and pulls open the box.

My heart races as he opens it.

What if he thinks it's shit?

What if he doesn't get the design?

I close my eyes as he lifts it out, unable to look at him.

"Do you like it?" I slowly open my eyes and watch him. His eyes are locked onto the skateboard, studying every detail Kelly painted onto it. They're all references to the stories Carla had shared with me last night.

The palm trees that line their street. A man holding a surfboard. A half-pipe, and the expression emblazoned across the middle: *You can call me Al.*

"How did you…" The puzzlement in his eyes as he turns to me quickly gives way to realization. "My mum told you, didn't she."

"Yeah, how you were convinced a Paul Simon song was about you," I say, and laugh.

"Well, I guess that makes you my Betty then," he laughs back, and leans in to kiss me.

Betty?

Guess I should have listened to the song.

The skatepark seems relatively quiet for a Thursday afternoon. There's just a couple of guys in grunge-style clothing flipping their boards, skating and grinding on the pipes around the sides. I imagine it will get busier when the kids get out of school, but it still gives us roughly an hour for Alexander to let loose on the skateboard.

"You want a go first?" he asks, waving the skateboard at me.

"I'm good being Avril Lavigne in this situation," I say, making myself comfortable on top of a graffiti-covered wall. Alexander drops the skateboard and heads off, going up and down the ramps.

The look of sheer joy on his face as he works his way round the skatepark, completing tricks with relative ease, settles my stomach. All the planning, all the hard work to get him out of the hotel, getting Kelly to design the skateboard and Daniel to let us borrow the car—it was all worth it to see him be free like this.

My heart skips a beat when I see one of the guys approach him. But then I hear them talk about some random skate terminology that I have no idea about, and my heart resumes beating once more. Alexander's British accent is surprisingly convincing.

Maybe *he* should be the dialect coach.

It's amazing how I take things like this for granted. I have the ability to do pretty much what I want, when I want. Yet for Alexander, it's so rare that he gets to do things like this. With that perspective, I can now appreciate how fortunate I am. How life on the other side isn't always greener.

My phone pings, and I retrieve it from my pocket. It's an email from Pietro with the subject line: URGENT. I'm torn on whether to open the email or not, especially since I've put my Out of Office on and he knows I'm going to be in wedding mode, but curiosity gets the better of me.

I scan through the email. Pietro says the Brewed team wants to talk through my proposal ASAP, and would I be free at six my time to jump on a Zoom with them.

With what we've got planned for the day, I feel like I should just ignore it, but a read receipt notification pops up. *Fuck.* A flicker of irritation runs through me. Now Pietro will know I've read it, and I need to at least acknowledge it.

I guess I could do it in Kelly's apartment when we get back, while they're all out for the BBQ she has planned.

I draft a reply.

Hi Pietro.

Any chance we could make it after 7 p.m. UK time? I'm out with my family arranging the last few bits and won't be available before then.

Best,

Christopher

Just as I hit send, I hear a loud thud, followed by a commotion.

"Bro! Are you okay?" one of the skater guys asks as I look up.

I look down into the half-pipe and my heart jumps up into

my throat. Alexander's eyes are panicked when they land on mine.

Shit.

21. Alexander
Thursday

"Well, the good news is that your wrist isn't broken, Christopher," the doctor says.

I let out a sigh of relief. The bones of my right hand stare back at me from the X-ray screen. I shouldn't have tried to land a gnarly varial flip earlier—I'm such an idiot.

"Christopher?" The doctor's hand on my shoulder brings my attention from the X-ray screen back to him. I nod, remembering Christopher put me down under his name rather than mine, so as not to draw any attention to myself.

"The bad news is, it looks like you've sprained it. Quite significantly. There's some pretty severe ligament damage. There will be a looseness in your wrist joint you'll need to be careful of, and you may experience a loss of function," the doctor says matter-of-factly. He turns to the cupboard, putting down the clipboard, and removes some items.

Everything sounds more serious here in London, or is it just the accent?

In California I was in the hospital so often with cuts and bruises, a sprained this, a torn that—either from surfing or skateboarding—that the doctors and nurses knew me on a first-name basis. Here it seems extremely clinical.

"You're going to need to rest your wrist for at least three to five weeks. Ice it regularly with a cool pack and keep it wrapped up with this bandage." He unravels the bandage, applying it to my wrist.

Three to five *weeks*?

They're gonna kill me.

The knot in my stomach tightens as the doctor pulls the bandage tight, securing it with the safety clip. A throbbing pulse intensifies in my wrist. But the pain is nothing compared to the tongue-lashing I'm bound to receive from Paul for being so reckless.

The only relief is that Christopher is standing beside me. The fear in his eyes earlier from when he came over to help me up from my fall is still tattooed in my head. The rush to the car, driving at lightning speed to the hospital. The wait to be seen, almost as excruciating as the pain itself. Thankfully, no one here has recognized me. I guess in a large part that's because the majority of people back in the waiting area were senior citizens.

"I'm going to write you a prescription for some anti-inflammatory tablets," the doctor says, retrieving his clipboard and removing the pen. "Other than that, you're good to go."

"Thanks doc, appreciate your help."

His pen hovers above the prescription, his brows furrowing at me.

Christopher's eyes widen as I turn to face him.

Damn.

I slipped back into my own accent. I managed to keep up my British accent the whole time and fell at the last hurdle.

What an idiot.

"Come on, let's get you out of here," Christopher says, cutting through the awkward silence. He offers me a hand to slide off the bed as the doctor completes the prescription and hands it to me.

"Thank you for all your help," Christopher says, turning to the door. He opens it, motioning me forward, as I slide the prescription into the pocket of my hoodie and pull the hood back up over my head. I tighten the drawstrings. Not to hide myself from being recognized, but because the embarrassment is making my whole face blush.

We've barely taken ten steps out of the room when a loud voice echoes down the hallway.

"Clear the corridor!" a paramedic shouts.

An emergency unit flies toward us with a stretcher on wheels. A person lies motionless on a gurney in a neck brace, blood splattered across his clothing. Christopher and I jump sideways, backs against the wall, as they charge past us and into the emergency unit.

A sharp pain hits my chest. Like an arrow through my heart.

Was this what happened to Samuel? To that bicyclist?

Did the paramedics rush them in to save them?

Were they even conscious when they arrived at the hospital?

The nausea churns in my empty stomach, the guilt from both incidents all-consuming.

The flashbacks alternate in my mind, overlapping and merging into one. My chest tightens as I struggle for air. I'd thought my PTSD symptoms were behind me.

I am trying to focus on the five senses exercise when I turn and notice Christopher, who is crouched down on the floor. His hands are on either side of his head and he's hyperventilating.

"Chris? What's wrong?"

I immediately shove my thoughts of Samuel and the bicyclist aside.

His breaths come fast and shallow, the color drained from

his face. I grab his hands and instantly regret it. Pain shoots up my arm, but I refuse to let go.

"Follow my breath," I say, bending down in front of him and locking my gaze onto his.

Our chests start to rise and fall in unison, one deep breath following another. Christopher's dilated pupils start to shrink, the hazel irises appearing once more.

"I need to get out of here," he says, jumping up and marching toward the exit.

I take a moment to reconcile that he's left, but I know better than to call out his name and draw attention to myself. By the time I make it outside and to the car park, I've fallen fifty yards behind him.

Christopher is already getting in the car and starts the engine as I speed up to get in beside him.

By the time we pull out of the car park and stop at the third set of traffic lights, I've tried and failed several times to find a way to speak to Christopher. The sound of Jay Z and Linkin Park's *Numb/Encore*, the only rap song I can tolerate thanks to its hybrid nature, offers a distraction from the silent tension.

Finally, I take a deep breath and turn to face Christopher.

"What happened back there?"

Christopher's eyes are locked on the road ahead, his hands gripping the wheel tightly.

"That's where I found out my dad was dead." His tone is void of any emotion.

"Baby, I'm so sorry." I reach across to rest my hand on his lap. He flinches as I set it down, and I see a wall go up.

Fuck.

I've been so lost in my own needs since I fell that I didn't stop to think about Christopher, other than noticing the terror in his eyes and feeling gratitude to him for taking command and looking after me.

I'm so selfish. So absorbed in my own shit.

"It's okay, we're out of there now," I say, removing my hand from his leg as we drive down the road. Christopher remains silent as the radio starts to play SWV's *Right Here*. But I don't feel we're out of whatever this is. It feels like this is gonna be right here for a while.

"So, are you guys in a relationship?" the mousy blond guy asks, waving his finger between Christopher and I. We're sitting on the couch, opposite of Daniel and Kelly on their bed.

"Daniel!" Kelly shouts, whacking him in the bicep.

For a petite woman, she seems to pack quite the punch. Daniel grabs his arm and cowers into the pillow before lifting himself back up again.

"Sorry about Daniel. He was born with his foot in his mouth." Kelly shakes her head and rolls her eyes. Daniel goes to lift his foot up, before reconsidering when Kelly cuts him a look.

"It's a good question, Daniel. What are we?" I ask, turning to Christopher.

His mood has softened since we arrived back at his sister's apartment, but there's still some tension between us. The sound of traffic below comes through the window, the only noise filling the lingering silence in the room. Everyone's attention is on Christopher.

"We're at that stage between fun fling and future therapy session," he says. His sarcasm is delivered with such coldness that it sends a shiver down my spine.

Does he really think that? What's the in-between stage? A relationship?

Kelly cuts Christopher a menacing stare.

I must be wearing my emotions all over my face, because Daniel leans forward on the bed and looks directly at me.

"Trust me, you'll grow used to the Foster humor. They use it to deny their feelings. This one took two years to break down." He points his thumb at Kelly.

"Three," Christopher and Kelly say in unison.

A smile appears across both their faces as Daniel shakes his head.

"So, what do you do for a living, Alex?" Daniel takes the opportunity to change the topic, seeming to sense my growing discomfort as I tug on the drawstrings of the hoodie.

I can't tell if he's bluffing, or if he hasn't put two and two together. Does he not realize that the plaque I gave Kelly last night, which is resting against the chest of drawers behind the bed, is me?

"Daniel, you can drop the pretense," Kelly says, noticing the direction of my gaze.

"What pretense?" Daniel looks back and forth between us, his hands raised.

Christopher looks pissed, but I'm actually enjoying this interaction. I lean back on the couch to soak it all in. It's been a while since I've been solely surrounded by people my own age. Everyone on my team is at least ten years older than me, bar Lucy.

Kelly nods her head backward to the plaque. Daniel cranes his head to look before turning back to face Kelly.

"I thought I was meant to pretend I didn't know who he was. That he's not the guy Christopher's been banging on about."

"I give up," Kelly says, lowering her head into her hands.

"Yeah, that's me," I say to Daniel, turning to look at Christopher.

Redness is forming in his cheeks.

"Not cool, Daniel, not cool." His eyes are locked on Daniel's in a stare so deadly I'm surprised he's not already buried six feet under.

Maybe Christopher does think about me as much as I think about him. And maybe Daniel's right. That Christopher's humor is a deflection from allowing his true feelings to show. I feel the fear that's been with me since we left the hospital fade away.

The smell of the barbeque, set out on the rooftop, drifts in through the kitchen window and lingers in my nostrils, making my stomach grumble.

"I don't know about you guys, but I could murder some food," I say, slapping my legs and immediately regretting it. I try to shake away the pain from my hand. This whole wrist injury is going to take some getting used to.

"Me too," Daniel says, jumping up from the bed. "I'll grab the meat from the fridge."

"Need a hand?" I ask, as Daniel heads out of the room.

"Looks like you're the one who needs a hand," he says, his head turning back toward me like an owl.

"I don't think it's a good idea to leave you alone with Daniel," Kelly says, adjusting her dress.

"It'll give you both a chance to catch up," I say as I head toward Daniel, who has stopped in the doorway. "And that way, I can get to know my future brother-in-law better." I pat Daniel's back with my good hand, the corner of my mouth rising.

I catch the look on Kelly's face, her eyes widening as they dart from me to Christopher, and I know the seed has been planted. That it will give them something to talk about in my absence.

Christopher's been pacing up and down the kitchen for the last fifteen minutes, talking on his phone. His half eaten burger is going cold on the plate beside me.

"Do you think everything's okay?" I ask Kelly.

"I'm sure it's nothing too bad. He's prone to overreacting." She takes another bite of her burger.

I hope she's right, but from the way he's moving, I get the sense that something bad has happened. I turning back to face the window, watching as he hangs up the phone and steps back out onto the deck, Corona in hand. He takes a swig and lets out a deep sigh as he sits back down next to me.

"Everything okay?" I ask, passing him his plate.

"Not really. My boss just went to town on me. I missed an important meeting with one of our clients earlier."

"But you're on holiday?" Kelly's forehead crinkles as she lowers her burger back onto her plate.

"I know, but Pietro insisted on putting in a meeting today. He wanted to lock in this campaign and I agreed to make myself available. But then Alex fell at the skate park, and I completely forgot." He reaches for the burger and takes a bite.

An elixir of guilt and shame swirls in my chest.

I feel awful. If I hadn't fallen, hadn't needed to go to hospital, Christopher wouldn't have been distracted. He would have made that call. Wouldn't be in this mess right now.

I'm such a fuckup.

The sight of his Corona as he reaches for it and takes a swig is so tempting.

"I'm sure it will all work out."

"Easy for you to say," he snaps back. "If I lose this job, I need to find a new job within six weeks, or I can kiss goodbye to my visa and to Los Angeles." Christopher chucks the paper plate down on the brick wall, gets up and heads back inside through the window.

I start to speak, but Kelly shakes her head and raises her hand to stop me.

"He just needs a few minutes to cool off. You couldn't have known this would happen. It'll all sort itself out." She grabs Daniel's empty plate and slides it under hers.

But what if it doesn't?

What if he does lose his job because of me?

My chest tightens with every subsequent thought.

"Surely there's something I can do to fix it. Ring his boss maybe? Tell him it was all my fault?"

I'm desperate to right this wrong.

To make it all okay.

"Sometimes you've just got to let things fix themselves," Kelly says. Her gaze drifts to my wrist.

Christopher eventually comes back out to join me, his energy calmer, as the stars twinkle above us. Kelly and Daniel cleared away the food and brought out a blanket and some pillows, and then tactfully gave us some space, closing the window.

"I bet Tony's sitting there smug as can be right now. Coming in on his horse, the knight in shining armor who saves the day." Christopher shuffles around, getting set up with a pillow under his head.

"Tony sounds like a right dick," I say. I turn on my side, using my elbow and hand to prop up my head, to watch Christopher's chest rise and fall.

"He is. He's a smug little prick who thinks he knows everything. Clarissa from the New York team even filed a complaint about him after he tried to take one of her clients behind her back." His nostrils flare as his mouth fights against the bitterness of his words.

"I can set Rob on him. Have him taken out." This prompts a smile, followed by a laugh from Christopher.

His laugh is like music to my ears. And that smile is everything I've longed for all evening.

"In-laws," he says, lifting himself up, before matching my posture on the blanket.

"Between fun fling and future therapy session," I counter.

The silence continues for three beats, matching the avoidance of what we're both not saying.

"So, what happens between a fun fling and a future therapy session?" I finally ask, caving to the discomfort.

"I don't know. What do you want to happen between the two?" His eyes narrow.

It feels like a game of chicken.

Who's going to break first. Who's going to ask the question that's been circling in my mind for the last two days.

I take a deep breath and exhale before continuing.

"Well, some would say a relationship."

"Do you want to be in a relationship?" His eyes widen.

"Do you?" I start to fidget, moving my legs restlessly to fight off the butterflies forming in my stomach.

"Well, I wouldn't *not* want to be in a relationship with you," he says, skirting the question.

One of us has to jump in the deep end, and my anxiety is getting the better of me.

"So does that mean you want to be my boyfriend?" I push myself upright to stop my legs from fidgeting and swing around to face him, crossing my legs.

"Do you want to be mine?" he asks, lifting himself upright.

The tension bubbles up in my chest.

Just jump in.

Just.

Jump.

In.

I take another deep breath, and blurt out the words.

"I do."

The smile across his face as he pulls at my hoodie, drawing me over to him, sets off a confetti cannon inside. Pure euphoria floods my body as he says *I do too*, before pulling me on top of his chest to kiss me.

There's a softness to him that I haven't experienced before as he removes his hands from my hips and pulls up the hoodie. I extend my hands upward as he flings it off, back toward the window.

The lust and intensity of our usual encounters is replaced by a tenderness. He gently lays me down on my back and lowers himself down across my body. His mouth skips across my chest and abs as he pulls down my shorts and briefs, and his tongue greets the tip of my cock.

My whole body tingles in pleasure as he circles the tip, while the palm of his hand cups my balls and he stimulates my hole with his finger. His tongue is the ultimate weapon to disarm me, rendering me completely useless.

His tongue makes its way down from my cock to my hole as he lifts my legs upward. He makes me moan as he circles my hole in clockwise movements, before spitting on it and thrusting his tongue in and out. He buries his mouth deep, his five-o-clock shadow rubbing up against my ass cheeks.

"I want you inside of me," I say, unable to take any more teasing.

His head comes up between my legs as he rests them on his shoulders.

"I don't have lube with me," he says.

"Just spit on your cock and go slow," I say, eager to feel him inside me.

My eyes widen as he follows my command. He grabs both my legs as he spits on his hand, rubbing his right hand over his cock and then slowly guiding himself inside.

I push against his leg to slow him down as I adjust to the pain and allow my ass to loosen up.

By the time he's fully inside me, his right hand has returned to my legs, pulling them apart more, and I can see his face. Pleasure is etched all over it as he starts to build up a rhythm. He lowers himself down to kiss me. Gone is the tenderness; it's replaced with more intensity, more passion as he begins to thrust more deeply.

I claw at his back and down his ass, pulling him in more tightly, wanting to feel every inch of his thick throbbing cock obliterate me.

His thrusts gain momentum, as if he's shifting through the gears. His tongue is more forceful in my mouth, engulfing me with a passion. I move my hand from his ass and begin stroking my cock with the same intensity as his thrusts.

"Don't come before me," I say, and his head nods. He spits in his hand and brushes mine away, picking up my strokes with the same intensity.

He stares down at me with his hazel eyes as he glides in and out of me, like waves on an ocean shore. His rhythm is better than any bass guitarist. My balls begin to swell as I feel myself getting close. His eyes widen as my hips lift upward.

"Who's a bad boy," he asks, biting his lip as he picks up the rhythm.

He leans back down into me, refusing to slow down his hand movements as my head lifts up to meet his lips. His tongue barrels into my mouth as his cock does the same to my ass.

My back arches upward as I feel myself getting close. I nod at him, and his eyes fill with passion as his hips thrust even faster. His thick cock bounces in and out of my hole, rearranging my insides with each thrust, and as he pounds down one more time, his load explodes deep inside me, just as mine shoots out of my cock.

The warmth of his cum inside me matches the warmth in my chest as my load shoots up on his chin, his T-shirt, and over my vest.

Christopher sighs and pulls out, rolling over as we begin to breath in unison. I reach for his chin, wiping the cum off it before shoving my fingers in my mouth and swallowing it.

"I didn't have you down as a cannibal." His hand wipes the sweat from his brow.

"Well, I want your babies and my babies to meet inside of me," I say, smirking.

"Save some for me," he says, wiping up the cum from my vest and licking his fingers like a KFC advert.

The light from the moon and stars shines down on us as we take each other in. He pulls me in tightly, his leg sliding over mine. Two people intertwined in this perfect moment. A smile rises on my face.

"What are you smiling at?"

"At the fact that this time a week ago, I was jerking off to you in the shower, and now I'm jerking off over your body, while you blow your load inside me." My smile turns into a laugh.

"Well, now that I'm your boyfriend, I can help you with that more regularly," he says, winking as he leans in to kiss me.

My heart skips a beat at the mere mention of the word *boyfriend*.

I want to shout it from the rooftop.

"Christopher Foster is my boyfriend!"

Christopher's hand immediately shoots across to cover my mouth.

"Shush." But he's smiling, and he removes his hand and kisses me again.

I catch a person in a window opposite twitching their curtains, but they're unable to see us from this angle. They pull their window down and draw the fabric across the glass.

No one else seems to hear, and for now, it's only the moon, the stars, and the nosy neighbor that know I'm in a relationship. Not with Rita Watson, but Christopher Foster.

Friday

Paul woke me up an hour ago, his call pulling me from a deep sleep snuggled in Christopher's arms, pissed that I left the hotel without him knowing. I can only imagine how much shit Rob got in when Paul found out.

I don't dare let him know what happened to my wrist, only that I'm safe and that no one has spotted me—the most I could get out between the barrage of words hurled at me.

He asked that I do a live stream to promote the album this morning, but instructed me specifically not to address the Rita news. Christopher leaves me on the roof, heading inside to shower now that Kelly and Daniel have left. They've headed to the hotel to check in for their wedding.

"What's up, Marianne?"

I acknowledge a few fans who are leaving comments, but the messages are flowing so rapidly that I can barely keep up with them. I've set myself up so my bandaged hand is holding the phone, to hide the injury, and my other hand pulls at my hood to hide my bed hair.

"I'm so excited for you guys to hear the live album that's now available on Spotify, Apple, Amazon, or wherever you listen to your music."

My gaze drifts down to the building opposite me, where the same person who looked out the window overnight pulls open the curtain. I step back, just in case they're watching the livestream too.

Will you be playing Stolen Moments at the O2 again tonight? Cat123 asks.

"Yes, I'll be playing *Stolen Moments* in the set tonight and tomorrow night for my last show on the tour."

Is Stolen Moments about Rita?

Rita Watson's a bitch.

Rita is a cradle snatcher.

I lift my hand to rub away the aggravation in my chest caused by the influx of Rita comments.

I've not been online since yesterday morning, and I sense that the internet has gone into overdrive speculating about our alleged affair. The comments continue to come in thick and fast between questions.

"I've just put the kettle on, do you want a cuppa?" I crane my neck back to see Christopher's head sticking out the window.

"I'm good, thanks." I turn my head back to my phone and the live stream.

Who's that?

Is that one of the dancers?

Who is that guy?

My aggravation is immediately replaced by dread as a text message from Paul pops up on the top of my screen.

PAUL

End the live stream. NOW.

22. Christopher
Friday

I stare at the blank page before me, struggling to find the words to write down all I want to say about Kelly and Daniel. If Dad were still alive, I wouldn't have to worry about all of this. I wouldn't have to walk her down the aisle, or give the obligatory father of the bride speech.

I could have just kicked back and enjoyed the wedding, without all the stress that's now resting on my shoulders. The various tabs open on my browser, pulled up while searching *How to write a wedding speech*, have offered me absolutely no help whatsoever.

Make it witty.

Make it personal.

Use anecdotes.

No shit, Sherlock. I even attempted to use ChatGPT to write the speech for me, but it came out with something so nauseating and disingenuous that I just wanted to throw my laptop at the wall and hide under the covers.

The meeting invitation I received from Pietro this morning hasn't helped. The subject line reads *Brewed Meeting Follow-up*.

It's set for Monday. Less than twenty-four hours after I land in LA.

Even worse, there's a name on the invite that I don't recognize, though a quick search on LinkedIn revealed her to be a HR representative for the company. Great.

All of this is taking up unnecessary headspace when I just need to get this speech written and done with. It also didn't help that Paul was berating Alexander about me being in the background of his livestream earlier.

It took everything within me to temper my anger and not snatch the phone from Alexander's hands, to not give Paul what for. Alexander's a fully grown adult after all, and it wasn't like you could actually make out who I was.

Thankfully, Alexander seemed fully equipped to handle Paul. He defended me and actually called Paul out on having to hide his sexuality. Part of me was proud of him for standing up for himself, but the other part was petrified. I've now seen the abuse thrown at Rita over the mere speculation that she and Alexander are dating.

His fans and trolls have torn every part of her to shreds, from her looks, to what she wears, to her career. I don't think I could handle that. It's even making me question whether I made a mistake last night in saying I'd be Alexander's boyfriend.

But then I remember how happy I felt today being with him. Waking up next to him. The way he reached for my hand and held it as we walked down the street to get brunch when no one was around. How he fed me some of his avocado toast, and laughed when I spat some out because the hot sauce hit the back of my throat. Then he tried to convince me to join him in the toilet, not just to clean up the mess on the hoodie, but to make our own mess.

Alexander lifting my chin up to kiss me goodbye when the car pulled up at my sister's apartment to pick him up and take him to the O2. I haven't felt like this since Ryan, and maybe not even then.

The ping of my phone distracts me, and I reach for it, seeing a message from Stephen pop up.

> STEPHEN
>
> Cheeky drink or three in Soho later, before I head to Ireland and your sister's big day tomorrow?

I could really murder a drink or three right now, and if I don't see Stephen tonight, I won't see him again before I return to LA. But I need to get this speech nailed. Plus, I've got that bloody dinner.

> I'd love to but I've got the welcome dinner at the hotel my mum's insisted on doing tonight.

> STEPHEN
>
> Well, if you get bored, or finish early, we'll likely be in Circa. X

I guess if the dinner ends at ten, and Alexander said he won't be back until midnight, I could pop into Soho for one drink, maybe two.

Right. No more distractions. I throw my phone down on the table, pick the pen up and return to the pad. I write *Wedding Speech* at the top of the page and underline it twice.

Maybe I'll start with the time three-year-old Kelly decided to marry her rabbit.

I flick the pen up and down between my index and middle finger.

A ring of the doorbell, followed quickly by a knock, distracts me and instantly makes my blood boil.

Ugh.

Can't housekeeping see the Do Not Disturb light that I left on for them?

"One sec," I say, swinging my legs around and heading toward the door.

"Oh, thank God," Kelly says, immediately pushing past me. "Mum's driving me insane already and we haven't even gotten to the rehearsal dinner yet." Her cheeks are red and she's clearly flustered as she pulls her hair up, removes the hairband from her wrist, and ties her hair into a ponytail.

"Don't mind me, I was just thinking my personal space felt too respected." I close the door behind me and make my way back into the room. Kelly puts her hands on top of her running shorts, pursing her lips. She's unimpressed and unamused.

"Why do you think I avoid her like the plague?" I ask, as she heads to the window.

"It's a lot easier for you to do when you live on the other side of the world. I'm stuck here with her. It's like she's got nothing better to do than sit around and complain." Kelly pulls at the curtains to look out at the road below before turning her attention back to me.

Shots fired.

I clutch my chest, pretending to be hit, and fall to the bed, laughing at her.

"It's not funny, Chris." She kicks my leg as she rolls her eyes.

"Well, where is she now?" I push myself back up.

"Where do you think?" Her hand returns to her hip as she heads to the desk.

Of course. The bar.

She's likely with other members of the family, downing a drink or three.

"You still haven't written your wedding speech?" She lifts up the pad and waves it at me, her head cocked to one side.

"Well, as you might have seen, I've had other issues to

contend with, you know... work... Alexander." Irritation flickers across my skin.

The last thing I need right now is Kelly critiquing me.

I don't want her to add herself to my rolodex of misery. It's already overflowing with people: Pietro, Tony, Mum, Paul, Ryan, and countless others.

"Did I hear Alexander shout that he was your boyfriend last night?" she asks, putting the pad back down. She turns the chair round to face me and sits down.

My heart jumps again, like a kid in a playground with a skipping rope, at hearing Kelly say the word *boyfriend*. I'm barely getting used to it myself, and the thought that I'm actually back in a relationship after nearly four years.

"Yes," I say, feeling my cheeks redden.

"Oh my God. Chris. That's amazing!" Kelly leaps toward me, knocking me back against the bed as she squeezes me tightly. "Wait," she says, rolling off me. "Does that mean I need to make an extra space for him at the wedding?"

"You know that can't happen." My heart sinks faster than Rose dropping the Heart of the Ocean back down to the Titanic.

How lovely it would be to have him sit next to me at the wedding.

To dance with him on the dance floor.

And this, of course, is the reality I now face.

That we as a couple will never exist outside of the confines of four walls and places where Alexander can go unnoticed. Kelly's thumbs twiddle away in her lap, her upside-down smile reaffirming my painful reality.

"Let's get out of here," she says, whacking my knee as she rises out of the chair.

"The room?"

"No, let's go for a run. The weather's nice and Regent's Park is just behind the hotel. Plus, I need to shift the last couple of pounds, and I don't dare go to the gym, in case any of the other family members are there."

I'm already regretting agreeing to Kelly's idea.

I'm absolutely cream-crackered from the lack of sleep and I can barely keep up with Kelly's pace.

"Come on, pigeon belly," she shouts back at me.

"Fuck off, fatso," I shout back.

She extends her middle finger as I attempt to chase after her round the pond. The ducks waddling along the bank get in my way, and Kelly worms her way between a group of Chinese tourists queuing up to get into the paddle boats.

I swear she was a ninja in a previous life. Either that or an assassin, such is her ruthlessness and ability to duck and dive, avoiding anything and everything that confronts her. It's a skill I've only half managed to perfect when it comes to communication.

The sight of the ice cream van offers a welcome relief. Kelly stops a few yards in front of me, and I rest my hands on my knees, bending over to catch my breath.

I really should have spent more time on the treadmill this week.

The sweat drips from my pink Nike top and forms a small puddle underneath me.

"What do you fancy?" I ask, turning to Kelly once I've caught my breath.

"I better not," she says, tightening her ponytail.

"Come on, we've earned it," I say, snaking my arm over her and moving into the queue.

I take in the list of options on the side of the van. The man in front of us, currently getting two cones from the vendor, looks remarkably like our father.

"What will it be?" the vendor asks, leaning forward.

"I'll take the screwball," I say, looking at Kelly.

"I'll have a lemon ice lolly."

The vendor nods and head to the back of the van to retrieve our selections.

"Did you just see that guy?" My head nods over Kelly's shoulder, forcing her to turn.

"What guy?"

I point out the guy who was in front of us, now walking along with his jumper tied over his shoulders and holding hands with a woman wearing a straw hat and blue summer dress.

"That one over there. I had to do a double take. He looks exactly like Dad did when we were kids."

Kelly raises a hand over her eyes to protect them from the glare of the sun as she squints to get a better look.

"I can't see," Kelly says, turning back and reaching for the ice lolly as the man hands over our order. I pull out a ten-pound note and tell him to keep the change.

"Do you miss him?" Kelly asks as we begin to walk away.

"I just left him two hours ago," I say, using the plastic spoon to scoop up the ice cream.

"Not Alexander. Dad." Kelly shakes her head as she tears off the wrapper and takes a lick of her lolly.

"Oh."

I'd be lying to her if I said I didn't miss him. In fact, I'd been dreading coming back to London. Less because I'd have to see Mum, and more so because London reminds me so much of Dad.

Everywhere I turn, I see reminders of him. The pubs that he'd drag Kelly and me into as kids so he could have a pint with his friends, while throwing us money to get squash and play pool. The rides on the tubes and buses that he'd turn into adventures. But the pain of that last interaction with him wiped those memories away.

And I've been running from them ever since.

I couldn't even bear to be at his funeral. Everyone was coming up to me, offering their condolences, telling me he was a good man. A good man, who was just about to disown his son, if those stairs and his drinking problem hadn't taken him out.

"Sometimes," I say, letting out a sigh. "Do you?"

"I do." Kelly lowers her head. "If he was here right now, he'd be able to calm Mum down. Tell her to wind her neck in and just let me get on with things." Her voice is tinged with bittersweetness.

"Maybe we can slide an Ambien or two in her drink later to shut her up," I say, laughing.

But Kelly is too lost in her thoughts.

The ice lolly drips down her fingers and onto the ground.

"Do you mind that it's me walking you down the aisle and not Dad?" I ask, as we exit the park and follow the road back to the hotel. Kelly chucks the ice lolly into a bin.

I look down at my screwball and pull out the chewing gum at the bottom, throwing it in my mouth and the cup in the bin.

"You know I don't buy into that bullshit. A man giving me away to another man, as if I'm someone else's property to bestow upon another human. But I do wish he could be here to see me tomorrow."

I get it.

I do.

I wrap my hand around her shoulder as the back entrance of the hotel comes back into sight. There's a small gaggle of girls sitting on the pavement, talking among each other. Their signs are strewn across the floor.

No One Compares To You, Alexander.

You can be My Anchor.

They all look up in unison as we step over their cardboard signs.

"You're with Alexander's team, aren't you?" One of the girls gets up, the others quickly following suit.

"Yeah, he was at Abbey Road," another says.

My heart begins to beat more loudly as the doorman nods at us.

"How do you know Alexander?" a third questions, rushing around to stop in front of us.

Kelly instantly grabs my hand and drags me through the pack of girls.

"Leave my boyfriend alone!" Her voice carries as we enter the hotel.

Alexander's publicist stands in front of us as we enter, a dumbfounded look on her face.

I drop my hand from Kelly's. My whole body stiffens as she takes me in from head to toe.

"Boyfriend?" She reaches into her bag and pulls out a packet of cigarettes.

Quick.

Think.

She knows I'm gay, but this won't quell her growing suspicion of me. Like a judge on a reality show, she's clearly not amused at what she sees in front of her.

"This is my sister. I don't believe you met her at the show the other night. Kelly, this is," I desperately try to recall her name, "Bonnie." I squeeze Kelly's hip tightly, to ensure she doesn't put her foot in it.

"Connie." The woman instantly corrects me. Her face looks like a gremlin halfway through sneezing.

"Nice to meet you," Kelly says, holding out her hand.

"Sure," Connie says, looking at Kelly's clammy hand and opting to pull a cigarette out of her pack instead.

"Suit yourself." Kelly walks away, pushing the button for the elevator.

I force a smile on my face and follow Kelly as Connie exits the hotel.

Why must I be so bad at remembering names?

"Who was *that* bitch," Kelly says, leaning up against the wall when the doors close.

"Alexander's publicist." I roll my eyes.

"Wow, she puts Miranda from the *Devil Wears Prada* to shame," Kelly laughs as she attempts to do her best impression of *That's All*. She waves her hand at the elevator door.

"So, have I been bumped off your home screen yet?" She reaches into my shorts pocket, trying to get at my phone.

"Get off me," I say.

I push into her belly, forcing her back against the elevator wall, and Kelly immediately clutches her lower abdomen. The look in her eyes as she meets mine is not one of anger, but fear.

"You're not!" I say, as the elevator doors open on the third floor. I hold the doors open as Kelly slowly moves forward.

Kelly's a good liar, but she's never been able to hide things from me. The way her nostrils flicker and her eyes shoot up to the right is a dead giveaway every time. That's why it was always so easy to beat her when we played board games as children.

"It's early days. We're only six weeks pregnant."

A smile forms on her face as she slowly lowers her hand.

"But I thought you couldn't? That the doctor said it wouldn't be possible with your condition."

My mind flicks back to that night nearly ten years ago, when she found out that the root cause of her crippling menstrual pain wasn't her digestive issues, but endometriosis, and that there was a strong likelihood she'd never be able to have children.

"That's what I thought," she says, stepping outside, and I follow. "But I peed on five sticks and all of them came back positive." She shrugs her shoulders as she lifts her hands up.

"Oh my God, congratulations!" I say, being more careful this time as I embrace her. Then I catch our mother walking down the hallway toward us.

"Congratulations? Why on earth are you congratulating your sister? And why the hell aren't you both dressed and downstairs for the welcome dinner." An impatient sneer spreads across her face as she reaches us. Her teeth are bared like a pit bull ready to attack.

The sound of my mother's disdain makes my toes curl.

"Give it a break, Mum. We're not due down there until six, and it's barely a quarter past five." Kelly waves her away dismissively.

Thankfully, Kelly's ninja skills extend to avoiding awkward questions and deflecting conversations, preventing our mum from probing any further.

"Well, you better get a move on, I don't need either of you bringing the Foster name into disrepute because of your tardiness." Her gaze locks firmly onto me.

Once.

It was *once*.

Okay twice. If we include lunch and the theater.

My forced smile pushes down the growing anger inside as she steps into the elevator and disappears.

"Right, I better head up to my room," I say, reaching for the elevator button.

"Okay." Kelly nods at me.

"I can't believe I'm going to be an uncle!" I do a little jump for joy, like a fish out of water.

"Stop it!" Kelly whacks my arm and shakes her head as she makes her way in the opposite direction.

I immediately reach into my pocket to share the news, not with Stephen like I usually do, but with Alexander.

Less than three minutes later, I'm back in my hotel room, and I turn on the radio via my laptop. Alexander should be finding out about now if he is indeed number one.

I carry the laptop with me into the bathroom, the familiar sound of the Capital FM DJ Abbie McCarthy's voice counting down the top ten songs as I strip out of my clothes and turn on the shower.

"Only two records remain in this week's battle for the top spot. Will it be pop superstar Sabrina Carpenter with her latest single? Or will man-of-the-moment Alexander Morgan climb into the number one spot with his summer hit *My Anchor*?"

I can feel the tension building in my chest as I pull a towel from underneath the sink and hang it up next to the shower. I stick my hand inside and adjust the tap to turn the head down slightly.

"I can exclusively reveal that this week's number two and runner-up on the UK singles chart is…"

23. Alexander
Friday

"It's been quite the week for you here in London, hasn't it?" Abbie McCarthy says over the phone.

Paul, Lucy, and Rob are squeezed onto one couch, Lucy on the arm rest, while my parents sit to either side of me on the other couch. Paul stares at me intensely to ensure I don't fuck up, making me fidget with the bandage on my wrist.

As always, Abbie's been briefed on topics she can't discuss, including Rita Watson, but that doesn't always stop journalists from trying to get that headline for the clickbait. Thankfully, I've known Abbie for a while now, having interviewed with her a few times over the years, which makes me feel more confident that I won't have to worry about being tripped up.

"It really has. I'm doing my sixth of seven sold-out shows at the O2 in London tonight. I got to record my live album at Abbey Road, which just dropped today. And now my single *My Anchor* is number one on the charts. It's been the best week of my life."

And I mean it. It really has been. But not for those reasons.

It's been great because Christopher has reminded me what it feels like to love again.

And to fight for what I believe in and see it through.

All these career milestones are amazing, but I've felt empty for the last two and a half years. I was looking to alcohol, sex, fitness, and shopping to fill a void that seemingly could never be filled.

"Why don't you go ahead and introduce your brand-new number one single," Abbie says.

"Sure," I say, wiggling forward and grabbing the phone. My mum squeezes my leg with her hand, a smile radiating out from her face. "Hi, I'm Alexander Morgan, and you are listening to my number one single *My Anchor* with Abbie McCarthy on Capital."

The song begins playing and I start to hang up, but Abbie stops me.

"Alex, you gotta do something to celebrate the song going to number one, man." She's continuing our conversation from before we went live, when I told her I had no plans to celebrate.

It's become so normalized that I never seem to stop and celebrate when I have a number one or reach some career milestone. In fact, this time, it feels like I am being actively stopped from celebrating. I'm being punished for drinking, for escaping the hotel, for spraining my wrist.

As if I'm some teenager that's been grounded.

"Where's good to go here in town?" I ask. Just like in LA, it seems like every time I come to London there's a new spot that's the place to be.

Paul jumps up from the couch and tries to grab the phone from me, almost knocking my wrist in the process. Fear claws at my throat at the sight of him. But I sink back into the couch, holding my phone tightly against my chest before he can grab it.

"The Box on a Friday night is the place to be," Abbie says.

I need to get Paul off my back, his face quickly turning crimson, his glasses framing the fury in his eyes. His hand rests on the mini fridge at the end of the couch.

"Great, we'll be there. Paul, can you speak to Abbie? Sort out the details?"

I finally pass the phone to Paul, who lets out a sigh and reluctantly takes it. He turns off speaker phone and leaves the room.

"Congratulations, baby." My mom's arms go around me, squeezing tightly. The latch of her bracelet gets caught on the back of my T-shirt.

"Well done, son." My dad helps detach the bracelet, then ruffles my hair.

"Thanks," I say, slumping back into the couch.

I'm grateful for the acknowledgment and approval that I yearn for, but I'm conditioned to play it down so I don't upset my brother. Even though Harrison isn't here.

"What's this club we're going to later?" my dad says.

"I don't think they'll let you in like that," I laugh.

My parents look like your typical Americans abroad. They wear matching white T-shirts, with the word *London* and a British flag printed across the front, and beige shorts. Their pink and blue crocs are the only item differentiating the two of them. But they are convinced crocs look cool because Justin Bieber and all the hip people wear them.

"Says the guy in a T-shirt that's more like a crop top." My dad pulls at my black T-shirt, two sizes too tight for me, that exposes my belly button.

"It's Christopher's." I bat his hand away, shaking my head at him as he raises his hands and mouths *Ooooh*.

I swear sometimes he acts like more like a child than I'm told I do.

"What do you think you're playing at?" The door bursts back

open. Rob immediately lifts himself up before seeing it's Paul, and sits back down.

The energy completely shifts in the room, like a dark storm rolling into town.

He throws my phone back to me, and it lands in my lap. His nostrils flare as his forehead crinkles, forcing me to clench my fists and push myself upright.

Paul has been indignant for the whole afternoon. He lashed out at Rob and Lucy for leaving me unguarded for twenty-four hours. And at me for going skateboarding while on tour. And he read me the riot act for how they'll have to change the setlist now that I can't play any instruments.

"You do realize I'm a human, right? Not a robot that you can control." My nails begin to dig into my palms, trying to temper the anger bubbling inside. "God forbid I be a human who wants to celebrate something I've dreamed about as a kid, without any financial remuneration you get a commission from. Who needs a break from all of this for twenty-four hours to cool off."

Paul moves toward me, looming over me like a vulture, pausing for a beat as if deciding whether I'm worth the effort.

"Do you have any idea all the work Connie and I have to do to keep this train on the tracks? To ensure your image and reputation stay intact?" He looks at me the way a cat looks at a knocked-over glass, equal parts disgust and inevitability.

My dad leans forward, but I push him back.

This is my battle; I don't need anyone else fighting it for me.

I push myself up, using my mom and dad's legs as leverage, and meet Paul's glare. The table between us is the only thing keeping us apart.

"And whose fault is that? I didn't want to do promo here, but you insisted. You put me on that couch that Rita was on. I didn't want to do the club PA, but you insisted. Even though you know being in those environments isn't good for my sobriety. And that led to all of this." I pause briefly, allowing my saliva time to help stop the dryness in my throat. "You were the one who wouldn't let me speak out that there's nothing going on with Rita because it's 'good publicity' for *Stolen Moments*." My fingers make air quotes at him.

My ears start to burn up as the rage takes over.

God, it feels good to let this anger out.

To not swallow it down with alcohol and keep it all bottled inside.

Yes, Paul is responsible for helping build my empire, but he seems to be mistaking himself for the emperor, and it's time to remind him of that.

"We're handling the situation. The Sun is running a story in the morning with the blessing of her family that will address the issue and stop the speculation from continuing." Paul reaches for his phone as he lets out a sharp exhale. "In fact, all the speculation led to massive exposure for *Stolen Moments*." He passes me the phone, and I can see that *Stolen Moments* has 17,450 people simultaneously listening to the track, according to Spotify for Artists. "That number is your biggest number ever, and you're on track to reach the top three globally with the song tomorrow."

My heart jumps for joy at the thought, before I remember that Paul actively tried to prevent me from recording and releasing it. My gaze drifts back up from the phone to him. He has a cheesy grin, showing off his veneers, and I want to knock them right out of his mouth.

"The song you didn't even want me to record," I say flatly. "In fact, you actively tried to stall so we would run out of time in the studio." I throw his phone back at him, and he stumbles trying to catch it.

"Look, I was wrong with that, but we don't always get what

we want, Alex," he says. His grin has been replaced with a stern look as he slides his phone back into his pocket.

Before I can respond, I feel my dad's hand on my shoulder as he steps up beside me. My mom gets up on the other side to join him.

"I think you need to remember who works for whom here, Paul," my dad says. He leans over and pushes a finger into Paul's chest, forcing him to take a step backward.

"Come on, son, let's get you out of here and hit up catering." My mom shakes her head at Paul and motions at Lucy and Rob to follow us, leaving Paul in the room alone.

Her tight squeeze makes me feel all warm inside.

Maybe they don't stick up for me against Harrison, but they do defend me when it matters most. And for that, I need to be more grateful.

"Thank you," I say, squeezing her back.

Two more shows. Two more days.

Two more shows. Two more days.

I keep repeating the mantra to myself, trying to push away the last of the anger, while my mom goes up and grabs some food from catering. She insisted that I wait at the table, while Rob, Lucy, and my dad sit at another table to give us some space.

The catering room is set up like a school cafeteria. Tables and chairs are scattered around the room. Servers are positioned behind the three options for dinner: grilled chicken, rice, and vegetables, vegan curry, and battered fish and chips. There's a whole wall dedicated to deserts I can finally eat, now that the *Men's Health* shoot is in the bag, and a fridge stocked full of water and sodas.

My mom makes her way back over, two plates of fish and chips in hand.

"Mom," I sigh, as she hands me my plate. "I asked for the chicken."

"God, Alex! Live a little!" She shakes her head as she puts her plate down and pulls out the seat next to me to sit. "Apparently it's tradition here in the UK to eat fish and chips on a Friday." She unfolds the napkin and tucks it into the top of her T-shirt. "Who are we to mess with tradition?"

To be fair, she's right.

The tour is coming to an end. I have no other commitments to stay in shape for, aside from the film, which reminds me that I really do need to read that script.

"Is he always like that these days?" She scoops up some of the mushy peas with her fork.

"Like what?" I ask, used to Paul's behavior. I cut into the battered fish.

"Righteous. Indignant. As if he's the one who runs the show, not you."

I start to defend him but stop myself. My bad habit is second nature.

I'm so used to silencing my own voice that it's been nice to allow my thoughts space to breath.

"Anyway, enough about Paul. I wanna hear all about this Christopher guy," she says.

Just the sound of his name from her lips makes me smile.

"Do you like him?" I ask, cutting up another mouthful of the fish. The flaky cod melts instantly when it meets my tongue.

I'm wondering if this time she'll give her seal of approval. I'm not sure why I'm so desperate for it, given that she never really liked Samuel. I've often thought that there was a small part of her that was relieved when he died. Maybe in part because she got to spend more time with me again once he was no longer around.

"He seems like a keeper to me. He's funny, smart, and quite

handsome too. If his father looks anything like him, maybe you could put in a good word for me." She elbows my arm, knocking the fish from my fork.

"Mom!" I'm almost sick at the thought, before the sickness turns to fear.

Is Mom not happy with Dad?

Are they no longer getting along?

Is she thinking of leaving him?

Ugh. I shake my head, wishing I could find the off switch and stop my thoughts from spiraling.

"But in all seriousness, Alex, if you don't snap him up, I will." Her witch's cackle makes me grab the napkin beside me and throw it at her.

"Good thing I asked him to be my boyfriend then." I raise my eyebrows as I grab a steak fry.

"You did?!" My mom drops her cutlery and grabs my arm with both hands. "What did he say?" There's eagerness in the ocean-blue eyes that I got from her.

I reach for a handful of steak fries, enjoying keeping her in suspense.

"Come on, son, spit it out!" She releases her grip and whacks my shoulder.

"He said yes."

My mom lets out a squeal that has everyone in the cafeteria stopping to turn around and look at her.

"Jesus, Mom! Keep it down." I put my hand to my forehead.

"Can't I be excited for my own son to find happiness? You've been so down every time we've visited you on the road. It's actually nice, despite all the Paul and Rita issues, to see you happy for a change. And if this Christopher guy is the reason for it, I want him to stick around." She pulls her hand away from mine to lean back and look at me.

It's true. I have been down a lot since I've been on tour this time. In the past, Samuel was always with me, not just as my partner but as my assistant. But on this tour there's been a lot of lonely nights in hotel rooms. A lot of alone time with my thoughts and feelings. Christopher is the perfect remedy to that —the perfect escape.

"Have you guys talked about what happens after you come off tour?" She picks her cutlery back up, using her fork to cut into the last bit of her fish. "He lives in LA, right? Or did I get that wrong?" The scratching sound of my mom's fork on her plate grates against my ears, making me wince.

"Yeah, he does." Which actually makes it a lot easier than when I started seeing Samuel, because he lived in Manhattan. "We haven't actually discussed that. It's all been a bit of a whirlwind to be honest."

My mom misses her mouth with her fork, and the fish falls beyond the napkin around her neck and lands just beneath, staining her top. Both of us look down at it as I shake my head. Clearly she is who I get my eating habits from.

Freddy approaches our table, and my mom reaches for the spare napkin opposite, licking it and dabbing at her T-shirt.

"Congrats, brother. Paul told me the news." Freddy grabs my shoulder, jerking it back and forth.

"Thanks man," I say, motioning to him to pull up a seat.

"We need to get in a studio ASAP to record the studio version. Strike while the iron's hot," he says, sitting down and grabbing a steak fry from my plate.

"The studio version?"

My Anchor is the studio version.

"*Stolen Moments*, brother!" Freddy clarifies.

"Ah yes." I bump my head with the side of my hand.

I'd actually forgotten about following up with a studio version of the track. No doubt the label will be insisting on one now. They'll want me to jump on the momentum and have me push out a fully produced version to keep the ball rolling.

But then that means a video, more promo.

That's the last thing I want to think about right now.

"Should I look into a studio we can hit up while we're still here?" Freddy reaches for another fry.

"Talk to Paul, he takes care of all that stuff."

"Great. I'll go find him." Freddy gets back up, taking off as quickly as he arrived.

"Is that track about Christopher?" my mom asks once Freddy's out of earshot.

"Yes."

"You really like him, don't you?" Her arm nudges me, causing me to blush.

"I do. And the best part is, he doesn't care about any of this. He didn't know who I was when we first met. He just wants to know me. Alex."

"When you find one like that, you need to hold on to them." My mom goes to grab my hand, but stops when she sees the bandage. She pats my hand gently instead.

I'm relieved that she seems to like him as much as I do. That she's invested in our relationship. Thankfully, she's okay with the fact that I'm gay. Even if I have to keep it a secret from the rest of the world.

I don't know how Christopher does it. It's almost worse that he can be out with the world, but his parents aren't, *weren't*, accepting of it. I reach into my pocket to retrieve my phone, but it's not in either of them.

"Have you got my phone?"

"No. You must have left it in the dressing room."

I get up, emptying my remaining food into the trash, and place the cutlery and plate to the side before making my way back to the dressing room. I'm hoping Paul has left and returned to the management dressing room. I could do without seeing him right now.

Thankfully, no one is in the room when I enter, and my phone is lying on the couch. I head over to pick it up and instantly smile when I see a message from Christopher, who I've saved in my phone as Betty.

> BETTY
> Congrats on the number one skater boy. I'm heading down to dinner now, wish me luck. X

I immediately fire back a response.

> Thanks Betty. Hope the dinner's going okay. Oh, and you've got my mom's seal of approval. X

24. Christopher
Friday

"Who's mum's approval? And why are they calling you Betty?" My mum slurs her words, keeping her hand firmly on my shoulder as she looks down at my phone screen. It takes two deep breaths before I can stop wanting to just shrug her hand off.

I'm surprised that she can even read my screen with the amount of alcohol she's consumed. She must be on her fourth glass of wine, and dessert has only just been served. You would think that the death of my father would have curtailed her drinking habits, but no. If anything, it amplified the problem.

Thankfully, I hadn't saved Alexander's number under his own name, owing to the extensive list of requirements outlined in the MNDA. And my mum won't get the Skater Boy reference, the pseudonym I've rather come to like for Alexander.

"Oh it's no one, Mum. Nothing to bother yourself with." I slide my phone back into my pocket. and dip my shoulder intentionally, so her hand slips back to the table.

There's roughly forty people here, both from our side of the family and Daniel's, scattered across ten tables in the ironically named Winter Garden restaurant. Everyone is smartly dressed in cocktail dresses or button-down shirts and trousers. Daniel's family is much more reserved than ours. They mostly stay at their tables, while our family drifts from one to another. Aunt Brenda almost knocks over a waiter when she ricochets off one of the palm trees.

"Will you have a word with your sister? She's doing herself no favors eating that cheesecake the night before her wedding." My mum says this loudly and without a trace of irony as she sticks her fork into the cheesecake in front of her.

Other family members turn around to see what the commotion is.

"Leave her alone, Mum. It's her wedding, not yours. She can do what she wants," I say, lowering my voice, but it falls on deaf ears.

"At this rate she won't fit into her dress." Her voice rises as she takes another bite.

My mum was never going to win Mother of the Year award, but this running commentary is completely uncalled for.

"That's rich, coming from the hungry hippo herself."

My mum drops her fork on the plate and turns, slapping me across the face.

"How dare you!" Her face is so tense, I half expect her jaw to shatter from sheer rage.

The sting across my cheek is nothing compared to the sheer embarrassment of everyone in the restaurant now looking at our table. Kelly quickly gets up from her seat and marches over to us. She glares at me like I've just told her there's no Wi-Fi.

"A word," she says, grabbing my arm and pulling me over to one of the alcoves, past the baby grand piano. The guy sitting at it continues to hammer out the chords to Rascal Flatt's *What Hurts The Most*.

A lump forms in my throat.

I don't know what hurts more, my cheek, or my heart for having that woman for a mother.

"Can you not keep it cordial for one night?" Kelly flicks her hair behind her ear.

"I tried." I cross my arms over my chest.

"Well try harder," she says, poking me with her finger.

"I was defending you!" I bat her finger away. "She was telling me that I need to stop you from eating. That you won't fit into your dress."

Kelly swallows hard, takes a deep breath, and sighs.

"Thank you," she says, allowing her stance to soften. "Look, we just need to get through the next twenty-four hours. If we can keep her away from the alcohol and bite our tongues, everything will be okay."

"Alright," I say, sighing as I hear the clinking sound of a glass coming from the restaurant.

My deepest fear is realized when I crane my neck around and notice my mum standing up, trying to get everyone's attention.

Great.

Another scene ready to unfold.

Kelly holds her fingers to her head and pulls the trigger, making us both laugh as we make our way back to our tables.

"Everyone, a moment please," my mum commands.

I want to hide behind the palm tree. I don't want to be exposed to whatever's coming next, but I just need to keep calm and pray she doesn't do something too embarrassing.

"As you all know, Kelly's father isn't here to celebrate with us tomorrow. And given it isn't the custom for the mother of the bride to speak at the wedding," she casts a sideward glance at me, "I thought I would give a toast this evening to Kelly and Daniel. Where is she?"

My mum scans the room for Kelly, her hand shading her eyes.

"I'm here, Mum." Kelly waves her hand like a windscreen wiper as she returns to her seat.

"On behalf of the Foster family, I just want to thank you all for coming to my daughter's wedding." My mum's words are suddenly a lot more coherent. "I had expected this one to be the first to get married." She stretches her arm out at me. "But if I've learned anything over the years, it's not to expect anything from men."

Oh Lord, here we go.

My mother's favorite pastime is shamelessly taking digs at people, including the people she gave birth to.

I grab my drink and take a long gulp, trying to swallow down my anger and avoid everyone else's gaze.

"But you, Daniel, you've come along and made my Kelly so happy. And I'm so excited to have you be a part of the family. To be the son I've never had."

I feel the eyes in the room burning a hole straight through me, but I can't bring myself to look up. To take my hands or eyes off my glass. I've learned to accept that my mum sees me as a disappointment. So much so that her words barely register with me anymore. It's the pity and sympathy from others that I can't stand.

"I can't wait to welcome you into the family and for you both to make me a grandmother. To the happy couple, Kelly and Daniel."

I automatically raise my glass as the rest of the restaurant does the same.

But wait. A grandmother?

How the hell does she know? I thought Kelly said it was a secret?

I lift my head to find Kelly throwing daggers at me with her glare. I shake my head vigorously. I definitely haven't told Mum. Maybe she guessed. Or maybe she's just speaking figuratively.

"Don't just leave me standing here!" My mum waves her glass at me, ready to clink them together, even as she stares still down at me disapprovingly. Like she hasn't just thrown me under the bus. You know, like all loving mothers do.

I get up from my seat, glass raised, but my mum, in her eagerness to drink, combined with her heavy-handedness, smashes her glass into mine. They both shatter and the liquid sloshes over me.

"Great," I say, shaking my arms and reaching for a napkin to dry myself. Her red wine is barely noticeable on my dark navy shirt, but it's also splattered all across my beige trousers and brown boots.

"Can you clean this mess up?" My mum snaps her fingers at one of the waiters.

I stare at the shards of glass and red wine and vodka soda sloshed across the floor. I've promised Kelly not to cause another scene, but I've done my duty. If I don't get out of here right now, the fury inside me is going to cause some lasting damage.

I turn to walk away, but my mum reaches out to stop me.

"Where do you think you're going?"

"To change," I say, turning around and holding my hands out, so she can fully take in the mess she created.

"I didn't think we'd get you out tonight," Stephen says, passing me a vodka soda.

"Neither did I," I say, gently tapping my glass against Stephen's and his housemate Ciaran's, who seems to be on something. Sweat is dripping profusely from his face, and his fingers constantly rub at his nostrils.

I had no plans to go out after I got back to the room and

showered. But when I headed back to the notepad to try and finish the speech for tomorrow, I found myself too angry to write anything. I just needed to get out of the hotel.

"Spotted any hotties tonight?" I take a sip of my drink through the straw and take in his shirt.

Looking for a Sugar Daddy is printed in block letters across the top. Underneath that is a check list with all his demands.

His short shorts have already attracted attention from a number of the older guys who line the walls of the dance floor.

"Jeez, he's been like the Tasmanian devil," Ciaran remarks. "He's been working his way through the crowd, trying to find a sugar daddy."

"I have not," Stephen says, whacking Ciaran's arm. His mouth locates his straw and he sips through it, acting innocent.

"Seems like your problem is you keep finding sugar-free daddies," I say. My gaze drifts around the bar, noting the lack of potential. "Maybe it's time you try looking for a diabetes daddy instead." Ciaran snorts, and some of his drink flies out of his nostrils.

"That's what I said, we need to go to some hospices in Mayfair, find ourselves a daddy on death's door." Ciaran wipes away the drink from under his nose and licks his hand.

The opening bars of Nicki Minaj's *Starships* starts to come out of the speakers, and I instantly know I've lost Stephen for the next three and a half minutes. He clears space for himself as he moves through the crowds and struts toward the huge disco ball hanging over the DJ, so he can showcase his moves.

I leave him and Ciaran to it, having never been a fan of dancing, and make my way up through the seated area and downstairs to the toilets. It's a tight squeeze as people wait to use one of the two cubicles, but thankfully I only need the urinal, and can skip the half a dozen people waiting in line.

By the time I've peed, zipped myself up, and made my way

back to the sink, the line seems to have doubled. As I bend down to splash my face with water, a familiar voice speaks.

"I thought that was you."

I lift my head and catch Ryan's reflection in the mirror.

I slowly reach for a paper towel to dab at my face, buying valuable seconds to reconcile my thoughts, and breathe deeply into the sheet of paper.

"Oh hi," I say, turning to face him. I rub my hands together, still coming to terms with the fact that he is really standing in front of me.

He hasn't aged a day since I last saw him, nearly three and a half years ago. He still has the same blond hair, green-eyed look, and his tall toned frame is complemented by a white T-shirt, stonewash jeans, and the familiar Tom Ford scent he always wears.

"Didn't expect to see you here tonight. Who you here with?"

"I wasn't planning on it, but Stephen convinced me to come here. You here with Marcus?" It's a veiled dig at the guy he moved on with after I broke up with him.

"Err, can you move?"

A rude effeminate twink pushes me back into the sink, trying to get past us and to one of the urinals.

I start to reach for the back of the guy's shirt but think better of it, clenching my fist instead.

"Wanna wait for me upstairs? It'd be good to catch up properly." Ryan grabs my shoulder, his touch sending a bolt of electricity around my body.

I want to say we're heading elsewhere, but I know I won't be able to drag Stephen away from the dance floor. So I'm stuck here.

"Sure," I say, unclenching my fists. "I'll wait outside in the smoking section."

A couple of minutes later, Ryan steps outside to join me. I

hold onto the golden pole that ropes off a space on the pavement for smokers and vapers to congregate.

"You're looking good." Ryan touches my arm as he steps toward me.

I'm not sure if it's the cool air outside or his touch, but another surge of electricity charges through my body.

"Thanks, so do you," I say, instantly regretting my words.

"So. How's LA?" He tilts his head sideways, widening his eyes.

I remember when I used to get lost in those eyes of his, before my dad's death forced me to take off my rose-tinted glasses and see Ryan for the man he was.

"It's great. The weather's perfect. Work is going amazing, and I can't wait to get back." My truth-adjacent nature is kicking in, but I'm not going to disclose my issues to Ryan, of all people.

"Don't you miss London?" His eyes narrow as he waves the smoke away from the person vaping next to us.

I wonder if he means London, or more specifically *us*.

"Sometimes. Especially the food. But also not really. So much has changed since I was here last."

"But some things don't," he says, leaning forward to kiss me.

I don't know whether it's actual shock or the alcohol, but I surprise myself when I don't instantly pull away. I am momentarily frozen before I not only remember that I am in a relationship, but all the reasons that I ended it with Ryan.

His control.

His persuasive nature.

His ability to make me feel like I was the one to blame for all our problems.

"There you are," Stephen exclaims, as I pull back from Ryan. "Oh my God, I'm not interrupting anything between you two old flames, am I?" Stephen's brows rise as he pulls a vape from his pocket and takes a draw.

"Well..." Ryan begins before I interject.

"Not at all." I pull Stephen in, but wave his vape away when he offers me a drag.

Stephen may be on the wrong side of tipsy, but I'd take that over being left alone with Ryan. Right now, I feel unable to trust my body to comply with my rational brain.

"I heard you and Marcus broke up," Stephen says, taking another draw of his vape and tilting his head upward to blow the smoke up.

Stephen has never been one for subtlety.

"Yeah, a couple of weeks back. It wasn't working out." Ryan's gaze darts from Stephen to me.

"Hear that, Chris, he's single too." Stephen chides me with his elbow.

Maybe I'd actually be better off without Stephen here after all.

I rub my hand across my chest to calm the flicker of irritation inside.

"I'm actually in a relationship," I say, removing my grip from the golden pole and standing upright. Almost as tall as Ryan.

"Since when?" Stephen scratches his jaw, cutting me a look of disbelief.

"Since yesterday."

"Well, I think you should ditch whoever that guy is and get back together with Ryan." Stephen winks at Ryan and grabs his bulging bicep.

I want to high-five Stephen, around the face, with a chair. But the police car driving down the road puts an immediate stop to that thought. It's replaced by another.

How fucking dare you say that?

Stephen knows what Ryan put me through when we were together. And Ryan is the *last* person I would ever go back to. Even if Earth's survival depended on it.

The way Stephen's hand lingers on Ryan's bicep a couple of seconds longer than one would expect instantly adds fuel to my anger. Stephen has always had a crush on Ryan.

"Wait, is that Gaga?" Stephen drops his grip when the bar door opens and *Bad Romance* leaks out.

Before I have a chance to blink, Stephen has turned and hot-footed it back into the bar without as much as a goodbye, leaving me alone once more with Ryan.

Great.

"How long are you in town for?"

"I leave Sunday."

"That's a shame, it would have been nice to catch up properly," he says, stepping forward.

"Gotta go back for work," I say, retreating and almost knocking the pole over.

"Maybe we should have a Jägerbomb for old times' sake." Ryan lifts a brow.

Nothing good ever comes from a Jägerbomb.

"Who are you here with?" I ask, pivoting the conversation.

"Oh, just my sister. She's having a whale of a time with a bunch of gays on the dance floor." He shakes his head at the thought.

Claire always was the life and soul of his family.

It was part of the reason I stayed with Ryan for so long, despite him not being any good for me.

"Come on," he says, grabbing my hand and sliding his fingers through mine. "Just one."

His hand feels like an old familiar glove. Comforting. Warm.

The squeeze activates a bunch of good memories that I wish I didn't remember.

The surprise birthday party for my twenty-first that he organized with Kelly.

The romantic trip to Paris that he took me on after he'd gone there for work.

But it was just a handful of good moments, and that doesn't make him right for me. My therapist had once told me, *Toxic people are bad people with good moments. Flawed people are good people with bad moments.*

And Ryan was definitely toxic, at least for me.

My phone makes a muffled sound in my pocket, and I instantly let go of Ryan's hand, grateful for the distraction. My heart lift when I see *Skater Boy* appear on the screen.

"Hi," I answer, taking a step away from Ryan.

"What are you up to?"

"I'm in Soho, catching up with an old friend."

He doesn't need to know the truth.

"Great! We're just arriving at a club in Soho to celebrate my number one. You should come."

"Which club?" I put my finger to my ear to block out the sound of a bunch of women drunkenly screaming as they exit the bar opposite.

Alexander's silence gives me a second to look back at Ryan, disappointment etched across his face. It's a complete contrast to the relief I'm feeling inside.

"The Box," Alexander says.

A few blocks away. Perfect.

"Great, I'll be there in five." I hang up and slide my phone back into my pocket.

"That the boyfriend you were talking about?" He nods at my pocket.

I pause for a beat.

I could tell him the truth, but then he might follow me.

Best to be truth-adjacent.

"No, Daniel. His best man has taken him out for one last night of freedom before Kelly ties him down."

It's true, just as it's true that I won't be joining them. I'll be joining Alexander instead.

"Ah yes, the wedding. Please pass on my congratulations to them both. I miss them."

"They miss you too."

Ugh. God dammit.

Why must my mouth answer before my brain has a chance to think?

"Do you miss me?" Ryan steps closer to me, his hand reaching out to grab mine.

"I can't Ryan, I can't." I bat his hand away, turn on my heel, and flee down Frith Street.

"Oh my God!" Carla says.

Alexander's mum's face is a mix of disbelief and disgust as the woman on the stage shoots a ping pong ball out of her vagina and into the crowd.

The Box is crammed to the rafters. Our VIP booth is halfway up on the left, and is packed with Alexander's parents, Alexander, his makeup artist Erica, Rob, and two people I didn't immediately know, but then instantly recognized when she introduced herself as Abbie McCarthy the radio presenter. She's there along with her partner, Adam, who's been filling me in on the latest Formula One standings.

"You ain't seen nothing yet," Abbie says, leaning over to Carla and handing Alex an apple juice before pouring herself another drink.

"What do you mean?" Carla asks, shaking her head.

"It's all shits and giggles, love. Until someone giggles and shits."

And as if on cue, the woman turns around, lifts up her skirt, and proceeds to defecate right on the stage.

Alexander spits out his drink, spattering it across the women at the table in front of him.

The women turn round in disgust until they see Alexander hold his hands up to apologize, and they start giggling. They reach into their ice bucket and start throwing chunks at him.

"What the actual fuck!" He grabs my thigh and rolls his head back in a fit of laughter.

"I knew you'd love this place," Abbie says, lifting her drink in the air and taking a sip.

"It's fucking crazy." He shakes his head at the woman on stage as she lifts herself back upright.

"Don't go getting any funny ideas," Carla says, waving her finger at her husband.

"Not your cuppa tequila?" Abbie says, smirking, as Carla makes a puke face.

I can't even begin to imagine bringing my parents to the Box, yet Alexander doesn't seem to mind.

"I think we better call it a night," Carla says. She brushes down her shorts and stands up, motioning for Bruce to do the same.

Erica coughs to get Alexander's attention, and looks down at my leg. His hand is still resting there and he quickly removes it.

"Dialect coach…" Erica leans over to whisper in my ear.

My back stiffens against the red leather.

Maybe she's seen this before. Maybe she knows.

I thought only his parents, Rob, Paul, Connie, and Lucy knew?

"I think your makeup artist knows," I say, whispering in Alexander's ear.

"She's one of us. It's okay." He takes another sip of his drink.

"A man?" I turn my head back to Erica. Could have fooled me.

"No silly. Gay." He shakes his head as he laughs and puts his drink down.

By my count, that now makes nine people who know about us. His parents, manager, publicist, assistant, Rob, Kelly, Daniel, and now Erica.

"You coming?" Carla asks, looking down at Alexander and me.

I nod, and Alexander and Erica agree too. I'm so beat that I could do with heading back to the hotel. But before I stand up, Erica pulls at my arm.

"We should probably hang back five minutes, then grab a taxi."

She's probably right.

There were hordes of paparazzi lining the tight alleyway when I arrived, and the last thing I need to do is cause any more issues for Alexander or give Paul another reason to hate me.

"I'll see you back at the hotel," I say, standing up to give Alexander a hug. Rob also stands and helps escort him and his parents through the crowd.

My gaze follows him down the stairs as the woman on stage grabs two bottles of beer from a guy next to the stage, making the crowd go wild.

Do it. Do it. Do it, they chant, egging her on.

I see Carla covering her eyes as she rests her hand on Bruce, allowing him to guide her out through the door.

"Two beer or not to beer? That is the question!" Abbie loudly proclaims, as the woman lowers herself down on top of them.

My pant leg puts up a fight as I attempt to remove my jeans. I start wriggling out of them as Alexander turns on the lampshade by his side of the bed.

"You missed the best part," I say, as my legs finally break free. I fold them up and head over to the armchairs.

"I hope you're not into that kind of stuff," he says, grabbing his phone and connecting it to the charger.

"Come on, Ryan, you know I don't like water sports or coprophilia."

"Ryan!" Alexander turns to face me.

"What?" I look right at him, my hand hovering above the armchair, still holding onto the jeans.

"You just called me Ryan!" His words are laced with anger.

My body feels frozen. Every muscle in my body tightens.

Oh shit.

25. Alexander
Friday

Thoughts collide, merge, blend, tangle, separate, and merge again in my mind.

My heart beats against the walls of my chest, like a trapped hummingbird in a glass jar.

Of all the names he could call me, Skater Boy, Chicken Wing, Al, Alex, Alexander, he called me by his ex's name. Ryan. Worse, it's the same name as Samuel's ex. And Samuel had done the same thing right after we'd gotten together.

My body shudders at the sense of Déjà vu.

Rob bursts into the bedroom, scanning every inch of the room, before his gaze land on me.

"Everything okay in here?" He looks between me in my briefs on the bed and Christopher, collapsed into one of the armchairs with his head in his hands.

"He needs to go." I point at Christopher, cutting him a look to let him know I am angry and hurt. His shoulders sag as he lifts his head to meet my gaze.

Rob takes three strides toward Christopher, before Christopher lifts a hand.

"Rob, I'm not going to do anything to him. Can you just sit between us, help Alex understand it was a mistake?" Fear lines his every word, but I'm too angry to care.

"Boss?" Rob diverts his gaze back to me.

"A mistake is messing up the lyrics on stage or forgetting to turn your alarm on—not calling your boyfriend by your ex-boyfriends name." I grip the edge of the bed so tightly that my fingers begin to tingle.

Rob takes a step back, leaning up against the cabinet. The TV on top wobbles slightly before Rob reaches over to steady it.

"Is *that* what this is all about?" Rob asks, raising an eyebrow.

What the hell?

Is Rob taking Christopher's side?

Am I overreacting?

Wouldn't anyone lose their shit if their partner called them by their ex's name?

"Your loyalty is to me!" I poke my finger into my chest as I rise from the bed.

Rob's expression is wiped clean like a chalkboard. It's replaced with the same look he gives me when I go against his command and he's left compromised.

"No. My loyalty is to your safety. And after this week, it seems I need to protect you even more. Not from Christopher. Not from your fans. But from yourself." His deep tone reverberates in my chest.

"It was a stupid mistake," Christopher says, sitting upright. "I promise you, you're the only guy I care about. The only one I want to be with." His eyes are cloudy as they meet mine.

I feel as if the walls of the room are closing in on me, squeezing all the air from my lungs. Both Rob and Christopher stare at me, waiting for a response. But my thoughts are still zooming at a million miles an hour.

"I need a minute." I walk by both of them toward the bathroom, pulling the door closed behind me.

"Leave the door open," Rob shouts, and I release my grip from the door.

The toilet seat stares back at me, and I get an instant flashback to the bottles of Belvedere on the floor. The papers scattered everywhere. Me collapsed in a helpless state after Christopher stormed out.

How is it fair that I'm always painted as the bad guy?

That I'm always the one left in the wrong?

I shake my head, and step toward the sink, trying to control the burning behind my eyes, then turn my focus to the mirror, practicing the box breathing that helps me regulate before I go on stage.

In for four.
Hold for four.
Out for four.
Hold for four.

I complete ten rounds, and then stare at my reflection long and hard. Wondering how many other things in life I've overreacted to. What I've misjudged and flew off the handle over.

I make my way back into the bedroom, where Christopher is now sitting on the bench at the end of the bed opposite Rob.

"Maybe I did overreact."

"You have every right to be pissed," Chris says. "But I promise you, he's a distant memory now. He's in the rearview mirror; you're my dashboard view. My future. Heck, I can reverse and run him over just to prove it to you."

A little smirk appears on his face, prompting an answering smile on mine.

"We good here?" Rob asks, waving his finger between the pair of us.

"I think so," I say, looking at Christopher. He nods.

"Good. I'll leave you both to it." Rob pushes himself away from the cabinet, making the TV wobble again, but this time he leaves it. "Oh, and if you start screaming and shouting for a different reason, a little heads-up wouldn't go amiss." He laughs as he heads to the door, shutting it behind him.

Christopher motions to me to join him on the bench and I sit down beside him.

"We're not very good at conflict, are we." He reaches for my hand.

"No, but then we do get to make up after," I say. I lift my hand but bypass his, reaching for his crotch. Christopher stops me.

"I'm genuinely sorry." He raises his hands to cup my face. "I'm in this for the long haul." The glisten in his eyes causes discomfort inside me, and I fidget on the bench.

I'm so used to resolving conflicts with sex, avoidance, or money that I'm thrown by Christopher's genuine bid for emotional connection.

"You can call me anything, but promise me you'll never call me by his name again," I say. His long dark eyelashes bat up and down, distracting me.

"Sure thing, chicken wing," he says, winking at me before pushing me back on the bed.

Saturday

One more day. One more show.
One more day. One more show.

I continue repeating the words in my head as I brush my teeth in the mirror.

I can't believe that after nearly ten months on the road, I'm actually at the end of the tour. The end of this album cycle. And to top it all off, *My Anchor* is number one here in the UK and in the top five in America.

Not only that, but the live album seems to be going down well online, and I'm due to record the studio version of *Stolen Moments* downstairs in one of the hotel rooms today. Freddy has been there all night, working away on the track.

I did question why we were recording in a hotel room and not a proper studio, since there are so many historic studios here in London, but Paul said time wasn't on our side and that Kanye and Jay Z had recorded their whole album in hotel rooms. One Direction recorded their last album on the road in hotel rooms too. Plus, I guess there's something cool about recording *Stolen Moments* in the same hotel I wrote it in.

Freddy had texted me earlier to alleviate my other concern about the noise, reassuring me that with the room facing into the atrium and not the street outside, we wouldn't pick up anything, and we can use a duvet to soundproof when laying down my vocals.

I return to the room and see Christopher sitting upright, scrolling through his phone. It's a sight I could get used to seeing every day, but I realize that after tomorrow we won't be in the same hotel anymore.

"What happens when we get back to Los Angeles?" I ask, pulling a T-shirt on.

"What do you mean?" He rests his phone on his lap.

"Like, what's your life like back there?"

"As in my schedule?"

"Yeah."

"Well, I work Monday through Friday, the usual hours when I'm in town, and I have to go into the office a minimum of three days a week in Culver City." He stretches his arms above his head as he lets out a yawn.

"What's usual hours? My schedule is all over the place, so my usual hours are anything but usual."

They've been anything but usual since I was fourteen. Even when I was younger and the law mandated it, Paul managed to find a way round it.

"You really do lead a different life don't you?" Christopher says, removing his earbuds and swinging his legs around to get out of the bed and come toward me.

"It's the only life I've known." I shrug.

"Is your life as mad as this back home?" Christopher draws the curtains back to look down at the road below. The faint sound of the fans is omnipresent, as always.

"Oh God no. My place is in a gated area in the hills off Mulholland, and there's quite a few places down in the Valley where I'm left alone." I make my way over to the window to join him, and he puts his arm around me, squeezing me inward as he kisses my forehead.

I've never really been a fan of LA, but it does provide me with a level of anonymity that most other places in the world don't. And that allows me to go about my business and live a somewhat normal life.

"My favorite English pub is in the Valley. Me and my housemate go every Sunday for sausage rolls and a chip buttie and watch soccer. Then we make our way across to the best Indian place in town in the early afternoon."

"A chip buttie?" I scrunch my face up, trying to grapple with the turn of phrase.

Christopher releases me, turning around and gripping my arms.

"Oh my God, you have to try one. It's carbalicious. It's what you'd call steak fries in a buttered roll, and I smother it with vinegar and ketchup. It's an orgasm in the mouth."

"The only orgasm I want in my mouth is that or that," I say. I look pointedly down at his boxers and then over to my iced coffee on the bedside table.

Christopher rolls his eyes and pushes my shoulder as he shakes his head.

"Maybe I'll take you there when we get back?"

"Will you now?" I smirk and head to retrieve my coffee.

"If you'll take me to your favorite haunt?" Christopher turns back to face me.

Christopher's phone begins ringing and I let out a squeal, my cheeks immediately flushing as the noise leaves my mouth. Christopher snorts as he jumps across the bed to retrieve it, answering and putting it on speaker.

"Where are you?" An angry voice echoes out of the phone.

"What's wrong?" he asks, turning back to me and mouthing *Kelly*.

"Everything! The makeup artist has rung to say she's ill with the flu and now I have no one to do our makeup. The wedding dress is too tight, and the shop doesn't open for another hour, so I don't know if they can send a seamstress to alter the dress. And Mum's driving me insane." Panic is etched into her voice.

"It's going to be okay," Christopher says, trying to reassure her. But his expression tells me he's not sure what to do.

"I have an idea," I say, heading to unplug my phone from the charger.

"Who's that?" Kelly asks.

"Hey Kelly, it's Alex. Let me message my stylist and makeup artist, and get them to come help you out, okay?" I'm already tapping away at my screen.

"Oh my God, are you sure?" Hope rises in her voice.

"Of course. They don't have to start work until seven tonight, when I get to the venue, so I'm sure they'll be free to help out."

I quickly fire off a message to Erica and Laurie, noting that

I'll double their pay for the day and any extras they'll need covering.

"You're my hero." Kelly's voice is at a fever pitch.

"What room are you in?" I ask.

"They've put us in the Tower Suite for the day."

I raise my eyebrows at their proximity.

How many is us? How long will they be in there? Christopher will need to be extra careful leaving the room. I glance back down at my phone, waiting for the bubbles to turn into a message.

> ERICA
>
> We're just finishing breakfast; we could be there in twenty. Where shall we go?

"Great, Erica and Laurie will be with you in twenty." I say to Kelly, while giving Erica and Laurie the details.

"You really are my hero," Kelly says, as I throw my phone down and adopt a Superman pose. Christopher laughs at me and pushes me away. "Christopher, can you come get mum and take her somewhere."

"Okay," he says, heading to the armchair to retrieve his clothes. "Give me five." He hangs up and turns to me.

"Thank you for that. This day is already going to be hell having to deal with all my family." He returns to the bed, clothes in hand, and kisses me.

Is it bad that I want to cancel everything and just join him at his sister's wedding?

I've always wondered what an actual wedding is like. The only weddings I've been part of are the lavish ones I'm wheeled in and out of to perform at. In fact, there's a whole lot of things I've missed out on in life. I've missed most of the milestones and celebrations that normal people get to be a part of, either because of work, or because I'll take too much attention away from whoever or whatever is being celebrated.

"What is your schedule like today?" I ask.

"Well, I'm taking care of mum first and foremost. Then I've still got to finish the speech before the wedding starts at three thirty. You?" Christopher hops up and down on one leg, struggling to get back into his jeans.

"I'm heading down to record *Stolen Moments*. Then we'll leave the hotel around six for the show. Maybe you could swing by the room to hear the track before you head down to the wedding?" I pull at the belt loop on his jeans with my finger.

He pauses for a beat, a slight hesitation lining his mouth, and I remove my finger.

"I'm not sure. Between my mum, sister, and this speech, I don't think I'll have the time." His mouth drops into the shape of a rainbow.

"Maybe my parents can take care of your mum for you? It would keep them off my back too," I say. I'm desperate to turn his frown upside down, to get more time with him.

"I'd love to, but I don't need to be footing their therapy bills too." Christopher's face is deadpan as he buttons up his shirt.

"Come on, she can't be that bad."

"Ever seen a tornado, wrapped in emotional guilt? Well, that's my mum."

"Well, they're gonna have to meet at some point if we're to get married one day."

"Married?" Christopher stops midway through sliding a sock on his foot.

"Well, you know. Maybe one day," I say, instantly regretting ever using the word.

It's been four hours since I left the suite to come here and record *Stolen Moments*, and I still can't shake the look on Christopher's face from my mind. The stupid duvet over my head doesn't help. The heavy fabric makes me feel like I'm suffocating, but Freddy convinced me to use it as a makeshift sound barrier to block out any background noise from the rest of the room.

"Once again, from the top of the second verse." Freddy says through the headphones.

The metronome clicks over the production to keep me in time as the last of the chorus from an earlier take plays out, leading into the instrumental for the second verse.

Freddy has done an excellent job with the production. He considered all the notes I gave him last night for what I envisioned the track to sound like and worked through the night to bring it to life.

"Nailed it!" Freddy says, when I finish the second verse.

I fight my way out from under the duvet, flinging it off me and onto the floor by the window overlooking the atrium below. There seems to be a large collection of people by the champagne bar, all in suits and dresses, who I assume must be here for Kelly and Daniel's wedding.

The hotel room door opens, and Rob appears with three Brewed cups as I head over to sit next to Freddy at the desk. His laptop is open, with a mini-electric keyboard in front and Logic files stacked on screen from the recording. A scattering of empty Brewed cups, large San Pellegrino water bottles, and an empty bowl of Chipotle cover the rest of the table.

"Here you go." Rob passes the coffees to Freddy and me.

"Thanks, big guy," Freddy says, nodding, as Rob reaches for his back pocket.

"I saw this in the shop just down from Brewed and had to get it for you," he says. "That way I'll know when not to disturb you." He lets out a chuckle as he swings a door hanger on his index finger.

I grab it from him, reading the sign, and burst out laughing as I turn it over.

Do Not Disturb is written in small letters across the top. Then in the middle, BUSY FUCKING is painted in bold white letters. There's a silhouette of two people going at it underneath.

"This is genius!" I pat Rob on the back and pass it to Freddy for him to see. "You think you could get me a couple more?"

"Sure." Rob smiles at me.

This would be the perfect wedding gift for Kelly and Daniel. And for Christopher to have at his place, too.

Shit, Christopher. What time is it?

I look at my watch: 6:30 a.m. Right! I smack my forehead. LA time.

I grab my phone to see the real time, 2:30 p.m., and call him.

"Have you got a spare five minutes?" I ask as he answers on the third ring.

"We're almost ready to head down." Christopher's response is short.

"I promise it won't take long. I just want you to hear the track and give you something. It'll be five minutes, tops."

The silence lasts for three beats before he answers.

"Okay, where you at?"

"Room 315," I say, hanging up and throwing my phone on the bed before he has a chance to change his mind.

Less than three minutes later, there's a knock on the door and I rush over to answer. Christopher is standing on the other side in a black three-piece suit and a bow tie. His hair is perfectly parted on the right side. His hazel eyes sparkle like the stars in the midnight sky.

"You look so handsome," I whisper, before raising my voice. "Come in."

He walks through, past the queen-sized bed on the right, and acknowledges Rob with a handshake before turning his attention to Freddy.

"Freddy, this is Christopher, my dialect coach. Christopher, this is Freddy my musical director and producer, who you briefly met at Abbey Road the other day."

"Nice to meet you again," Christopher says, extending his hand.

Freddy spins around on his chair, shaking Christopher's hand with a firm grip.

"Can you play him what we've got so far?" I ask, twiddling my thumbs.

Freddy lines up the track, then hits the space bar and turns up the volume on the speakers.

"Take a seat," I say to Christopher, removing an acoustic guitar from an armchair so he can sit. I take the other chair beside him.

My leg bops up and down, not from the beat, but nerves. I'm eager to hear Christopher's response. His head nods up and down, like the label executives do, whenever I head into their offices to play new music.

The track finishes and I turn to him.

"What do you think?" I ask, but before he can answer, I jump in. "It's still got a lot of work to do. We need to add more harmonies, a bass, beef up the production. But the core of it is there."

"It's great," he says, a wide smile across his face.

"Really?" I feel like I still need reassurance.

That's he's not just saying that to appease me.

"Yes, it's really great. You've got something really special here."

I don't know if he means the song or our relationship, but it doesn't matter.

My heart jumps for joy inside.

"Look," I say, grabbing my phone from the bed and opening up Spotify. "The song is at number two globally on Spotify. Nine point two million streams. Crazy right?" I hand him my phone so he can see.

"Watch out, Sabrina!" He laughs as he hands the phone back to me.

Sabrina Carpenter's latest track has me beat by three hundred thousand streams.

"You're a dialect coach, you could help Alex out with his diction, couldn't you?" Freddy breaks into the conversation, as he plays back the second verse.

He's been getting onto me all afternoon about the way I pronounce the word *reunite*. He's made me repeat it so many times to get it right that I never want to hear the word again.

Christopher's body stiffens at the request.

"I'd love to help, but I've got somewhere else I really need to be."

"Do you mind if I just head out for ten?" I say to Freddy.

"Go for it," he says, waving me away.

I grab the door hanger off the desk where Freddy left it and pass it to Christopher.

"Do you think your sister and Daniel will like it?" I ask.

"Like it? They'll love it," he says, laughing as he takes it in. We head to the door, Rob following behind us.

As we make our way down the hallway and to the elevator, I remember that I've not asked how he's doing.

"How's the speech? Did you manage to get it down?" I ask.

"Just barely. I've been fighting fires with my mum all day." He rolls his eyes as the elevator doors open and we step inside.

"Why? What happened?" I reach for the button.

"You don't want to know."

26. Christopher
Saturday

It was bad enough that my mum had to make snide comments about me last night at the family welcome dinner. Now she's gone and offended everyone else, too, including Daniel's mum in the bridal suite. She got on her high horse and started going off about how she's paying for the wedding. Telling everyone what to do, bossing them around like they're her servants.

I'd thought a nice relaxing massage would calm her down while I worked on my speech, but she came back to the suite more enraged than ever. This time, Daniel's mum was on the receiving end of her wrath, who burst into tears when my mum questioned her attire and mothering abilities.

Suffice to say, Daniel's mum didn't stick around, and I'm sure there'll be no love lost there. They didn't like each other much before today anyway.

I've already warned Rob and Alexander about what awaits us behind the door as I knock three times. Rob kindly agreed to step in if things get out of hand.

Kate, one of Kelly's bridesmaids, opens the door and her

mouth gapes as she sees Alexander standing next to me. As we enter, I notice Kelly seated by a table, next to the glass cabinet. The blue and white china vases are thankfully still intact. Erica is nodding as she reapplies Kelly's makeup. Much of it was washed away by the angry tears she cried in the bathroom, where I'd left her when I headed down to see Alexander.

"Where's Mum?" I ask, placing my hand on Kelly's shoulder.

She points to the next room, where I see Kelly's other bridesmaid, Nicole, keeping my mum distracted. I take a deep breath, letting go of Kelly's shoulder, and nod to Rob to follow me.

"Kate, could you keep Alexander company, while I see my mum?"

"Uh-huh." Kate's eyes are like a vampire at sunrise, caught off guard and about to combust. She twiddles with the material of her lilac dress.

I enter the other room and see Nicole nodding and smiling as my mum mumbles inaudibly between sips of her champagne.

"Nicole, could you give my mum and me a moment please?"

Nicole looks at me over her shoulder as if she's just received a pardon from death row. She quickly gets up and heads back into the main room, leaving my mum, me, and Rob, who closes the door after Nicole exits.

My fists clench as I prepare myself for this confrontation. Rob stands guard by the wooden wardrobe.

"What's going on with you, Mum?" I ask, knowing full well what she's going to complain about.

"Daniel's family, that's what. His mum comes in here thinking she's better than us. Judging us. Looking down on me. When they're the working-class family. Daniel's the one punching above his weight." Her jaw clenches as she tightens her grip on the champagne flute.

"Don't you think that's a little harsh?"

"Who asked you?" she says. "And who the hell is he?" She points her glass at Rob.

Here we go. My mum didn't raise me like mothers are meant to raise their children, but she did prepare me for survival. And this is a war I'm willing to wage for Kelly.

"No one asked me, Mum. And this," I say, pointing to Rob, "this is Rob. Head of security. And if you don't get your act together, he'll make sure you don't step foot inside the wedding hall downstairs." I stretch to my full height and cross my arms.

"You wouldn't dare," she says, putting her champagne glass down on the table and pushing herself up out of the chair.

"Ma'am, you need to sit down. Right now." Rob's command startles her back into a sitting position and makes my heart rate spike.

I didn't expect Rob to get into this role, but he does so convincingly. Almost a little too convincingly, which makes me think he's enjoying it. But whatever the reason, it works.

"You need to back off. On Kelly. On Daniel's family. On me. For one frigging day," I say. "Can you just keep quiet, keep your opinions to yourself for twelve hours?" My head pounds. I can't believe I even have to ask this of her.

"Well, if you weren't all such disappointments…"

Rob cuts me a look—*Want me to step in?*—and I shake my head. My mum's love language is passive-aggressive and misplaced disappointment. I bite my lower lip instead, taking a deep breath through my nose, trying to push down the anger and temper my response.

"Do you know what, Mother?" She lifts her head to stare at me. "If anyone's the disappointment here, it's you. You never fail to let everyone and yourself down. This is meant to be the happiest day of Kelly's life, and you've left her out there in tears." I point to the room next door.

"But…" she tries to interject, but I'm far from finished.

"I'm not done," I say forcefully. "You complain that I never come back and visit you, but anytime I'm around you, you put me down. You complain about how I'm not good enough, smart enough, or man enough. Why the hell would I ever want to spend time with you, when all you do is make me feel like shit?"

I glance up at the ceiling, trying to fight back the tears forming in my eyes. Why can't I just have a normal mum?

"Are you done?" Her face reddens, a vein appearing on her temple.

I pause for two beats, deliberating what to do, but I need to defend myself, too, not just Kelly. Wedding or not.

"No, I'm not done. When Dad died, you blamed me for it. And I've carried that guilt for the last four years. But you know what? His drinking and his homophobia killed him, not me. He was the one who decided to storm out. He was the one who didn't want to have a gay son. He was the one who couldn't handle his drink. He was the one who fell down the stairs. Not me. *Him.*"

The tears are now flowing freely down my cheeks, coming from the release of everything I've been carrying, that I've wanted and needed to say, since my dad died.

Rob looks over to me, kindness and warmth on his face.

"I don't have to sit here and put up with this," she says, pushing herself up and trying to get to the door.

Rob takes a step forward and blocks her path.

"I'm going to have to ask you to follow me. I'm under strict instructions not to let you into that room unless you are willing to apologize to your daughter and your son." Rob nods toward me.

"Did you not just hear what he said?" My mum spins back on her heel to look at me. "If anyone should be apologizing, it should be him, not me." She snorts.

"Well ma'am, from where I'm standing, what I can see is

that one of your children is next door crying, minutes before her wedding, because of you. Your other child is trying to tell you about the impact of your behavior and the damage you've caused. But you seem unwilling even to listen or take responsibility for your actions."

My mum starts to open her mouth, but Rob lifts his hand to stop her.

"Now, I don't know about you, but I can't imagine it would look good to all the guests downstairs if the mother of the bride is not at the wedding ceremony." Rob raises a brow. "You have a clear choice here. Either apologize and follow me downstairs to the ceremony and let your children come down separately. Or don't apologize and I'll escort you from the premises."

My mum turns to look at me to see if Rob's bluffing, but I hold firm, arms crossed over my suit jacket. I don't know how Rob has the ability to remove my mother, but given that he has to deal with overzealous fans all the time, I'm sure he'll have no problem taking care of her, just like he did Rita.

My mother turns back to the chair and grabs her clutch from the table.

"I'm sorry," she says, scrunching up her face in a way so I know she doesn't mean it, but I'll take it.

She heads to the door and Rob looks to me. I nod and he opens it, letting her through, and follows behind her, leaving me to take a deep exhale before joining them.

"This gentlemen is going to escort me downstairs while you finish up here," my mum says to the room. She passes Kate and Nicole, who are seated to either side of Alexander, then grabs Kelly's shoulder and whispers something in her ear. I assume it's her feeble attempt at an apology.

"I'll call one of the local security team," Rob says to Alexander as he heads to the main door, opening it and motioning my mum to leave, before closing the door behind him. As it shuts, the tension leaves the space. Like the air being released from a balloon.

"What did you say in there?" Kelly jumps up from her seat, hugging me tightly, while I try not to ruin her beautiful custom-made wedding dress. It's a white off-the-shoulder number that accentuates rather than flaunts her short figure, and now fits her perfectly, thanks to Laurie.

"Oh, I can't take any of the credit, it was all due to Rob."

"Well, whatever you did, thank you." Kelly kisses me on my cheek as she releases her grip.

"And thank you, Alexander," she says, lifting her dress up and walking over to the couch. "Thank you for saving the day and sending Erica and Laurie." She leans over to kiss him on the cheek, too, as Kate and Nicole stare, envy on their faces.

If only they knew the truth.

"What the actual fuck!" Kate says quietly, ten minutes later. Her choice of language is juxtaposed oddly with her posh accent. "How do you know Alexander Morgan?"

Alexander walks slightly ahead of us, next to Kelly and Nicole, led to the elevator by one of his local security team. Kate is doing a terrible job of keeping an eye on Kelly's train.

"We have a few mutual friends in common back in LA. He's been here this week, and we just got chatting one day." I bend to pick up Kelly's train when we get to the elevator.

I'm going to have to keep a note of what I'm telling whom. These truth-adjacent stories I'm telling are going to become harder to remember if I'm forced to tell people how I know Alexander if we're seen together.

"Is he single?" Kate whispers to me as the elevator door

opens. She pushes a stray bit of strawberry blond hair back behind her ear.

"I don't know, why don't you ask him?"

"I just might you know," she says, nudging me forward into the elevator. "It's not every day you bump into a celebrity."

Alexander moves around the elevator to stand beside me as I move next to Kelly to hold her train in place.

The quick journey down to the ground floor is filled with silence. Kate and Nicole almost stumble out and giggle behind their bouquets as they get in front of Kelly, who is followed by Alexander, me, and the local security guard.

"I think you've got a fan," I say, nodding toward Kate.

"Is that so?" He smirks as a little girl approaches.

"Can I get a picture please, Alexander?"

The little girl, no older than seven, is wearing the same Alexander Morgan T-shirt he gave me the first night we spent together. She stares up at him. Her parents wait patiently by one of the giant flower pots opposite the table in the middle.

"Sure," he says, bending down as the girl hands me the camera. Kate comes over to grab the train from me.

The little girl's smile is so wide I'm worried she might combust from sheer excitement.

"Are you getting married?" she asks, when I hand her back the phone.

She looks toward Kelly, who's waiting patiently.

"Oh no. That's my friend's sister getting married," Alexander says, standing back up. "Are you married?"

"I'm seven, silly. Of course I'm not married," she says with an adorable childish attitude.

"Good girl," he says, patting her on the head. "We'll make sure your parents approve of him before you do, okay?" Alexander winks at her parents, while she stares up at him in awe.

The local security guard finally steps over and ushers the girl away before escorting us all down to the Empire Room, where the wedding ceremony is to take place.

Rob stands next to the wedding planner, Stacey, who stands with a clipboard in one hand and speaks into a walkie talkie in her other hand.

"The bridal party is here," she says into it before turning her attention to Kelly.

"You look absolutely stunning," she says, quickly hugging her. "Everyone's in place and ready to go when you are."

"I just need a couple of minutes before we go," Kelly says, turning to Kate and Nicole.

"Of course, take your time," Stacey says, and then notices Alexander and the local security guy as Rob heads over to join them.

"Do you want to head in and take a seat?" she asks.

"We're not staying, ma'am," Rob says, nodding to the local security. The security guard walks away as Rob turns back at me. "Good job up there, by the way. It's not often I'm impressed." He nudges my arm.

"Thanks," I say, unable to look at him. My eyes are beginning to water.

"Actually, Rob," Alexander says, "I'd like to stay and watch just for a few minutes from the back, out of sight. If that's okay? Before I head back up and finish the song." He turns his attention to me.

"I can't see why not, let me double check," I say, and step forward to Kelly.

"Kel, can Alex watch from the back for a bit?"

"Sure," she says, turning to him. "As long as you don't try upstaging me."

Kelly laughs as a smile appears across Alexander's face. She turns to let Nicole pull the veil over her face, while Kate adjusts her train.

"Everyone ready?" Stacey asks, looking around.

Collective nods occur as the photographer for the wedding steps out from inside the room. Kelly asks him to take one picture before she grabs the camera to take one last look. She passes it back and adjusts her dress slightly.

"Ready as I'll ever be." Kelly nods at Stacey as the photographer slides back into the room.

"Right, bridesmaids, assume your positions please," Stacey says.

Nicole passes Kelly her bouquet before she and Kate raise their white and lilac rose bouquets in front of them.

The doors to the Empire Room open, and Kate and Nicole take it in turns to walk up the aisle, leaving Kelly and me alone with Alexander, Rob, and Stacey.

"This is it," I say, grabbing Kelly's hands.

"Thank you," she says, shaking them.

"For what?" I try to meet her eyes through her veil.

"For being my brother. For sticking up for me today with mum. For stepping in and walking me down the aisle. For always being there for me when I need you, even if you do live on the other side of the world. For being the best big brother a sister could ever wish for." She squeezes my hand tightly as a lump forms in my throat.

"Jesus, Kel." I let go to wipe away a tear. "You save this till now, to tell me that."

"Here you go." Stacey steps forward with a tissue.

We've never been sentimental. Humor is our preferred form of communication. But I'd be lying to myself if Kelly's words didn't mean something much deeper. Something that I've been looking for in all the wrong places over the years.

"You're lucky we're heading in right now," I say, dabbing my eyes with the tissue before sliding it in my pocket. "But don't you worry, I'll get you back in the speech. Mark my words."

"We ready?" Stacy asks.

"Ready," Kelly and I say, nodding in unison.

"Good luck you two," Alexander says, approaching Kelly and leaning in to give her a hug.

"Hopefully I'll be in your position next time, watching you two walk down the aisle." Kelly snorts.

"Thank you," I say to Alexander, as he turns to face me.

"No, thank you," he says. He grabs my hands and quickly kisses me on the lips as Stacey turns away to the door.

I'm not exactly sure what he's thanking me for, but Stacey steps back from the doors, which are now wide open, and the sound of Des'ree's *Kissing You* streams out. Kelly pulls on my arm.

"Let's go, pigeon belly," she says, gently whacking my stomach with her bouquet. A stray petal falls away.

We step forward and into the room, and my breath is immediately taken away. The aisle is littered with white rose petals, and a bouquet of white and lilac roses, raised on see-through stands and vases, sits by each row. At the end of the aisle, three candles, all individually enclosed in lanterns, sit at the base of the dais. The chandeliers hanging down from the high-rise ceilings are the same gold as the floor-to-ceiling curtains draped behind the altar and along the right side.

We slowly make our way up the aisle, family members on both sides waving or taking pictures on their phones. Kelly's vice-like grip on my arm slowly cuts off my circulation as we walk up to where Daniel stands patiently with his two best men.

Our mum stands at the front on the left side, unmissable in her oversized hat, and I say a little prayer that she stays on her best behavior. From the look on her face, she seems to have moved on from the altercation upstairs.

We make it to the end of the aisle, and I help Kelly lift her veil before reaching out my hand to Daniel.

"Take good care of her, brother," I say, shaking his hand before turning and making my way to the seat beside my mum. I catch a glimpse of Alexander at the back of the room by the door, waving goodbye.

Thank God that he and Rob were here to help out today. I don't know what I would have done without them. The minister cues everyone to take their seats.

"Dearly beloved, we are here today to join Kelly Marie Foster and Daniel Ashley Reed in holy matrimony," he begins.

The faint smell of burning tickles my nostrils and I try to shake it off as the minister continues, but the scent gets stronger. I look backward to try and work out where it's coming from, then look down to see Kelly's train catching fire from a candle that's been knocked out of the lantern and onto her train.

"Fire!" Aunt Brenda screams from beside me as Kelly looks back. There is horror in her eyes as she sees her train igniting, working its way up rapidly toward her.

I rush up, throwing my blazer jacket on top of the flames. I kneel down to pat the blaze down, Uncle Michael doing the same behind me, while my mother sits there watching it all unfold.

"That's a sign from your father, if ever I saw one," she utters under her breath.

She lifts her right leg over her left and crosses her arms, seemly unbothered, while she looks at my sister. Part of me wonders if she somehow knocked the candle over to get revenge.

She wouldn't though, surely.

Would she?

27. Alexander
Saturday

"I think we got it!" Freddy cheers, his hands raised, as the chords of the outro play out over the speakers.

The track is beyond anything I could have imagined. The backbeat Freddy added perfectly complements the acoustic guitar, keys, and base. Then he added more magic with some ambient sound and synths to tie it all together.

"You, my sweet prince, are the best," I say, high-fiving Freddy.

"And don't you forget it," he says, flicking his long dark hair back over his shoulders and giving me a chef's kiss.

"Let me bounce it out so we can listen to it on our way to the venue, just to make sure we like it before we sign it off. Then I'll fire it across to Nathan for mixing and mastering." Freddy grabs a handful of sour candies from the table and demolishes them in one go before washing them down with a swig of water.

"We gotta go, boss." Rob jerks his thumbs at the door.

"Freddy, you good to meet us downstairs in five? I've got something I need to do first."

Freddy nods as he clicks export on the track and fires up his email.

Rob looks at his watch, then up at me.

"We don't have time. It's already seven fifteen."

"We've got plenty of time. It takes what, forty minutes from here to the O2? And I'm not on till nine, right? That gives us plenty of time. Plus, I'm already ready." I point at my hair and face, which Erica came and did an hour ago.

All I need to do is change into my first outfit and *Hey presto!* Rob shakes his head but waves me out, heading along the hallway and down the elevator to the ground floor.

I quickly check my phone to see if there's any more updates from Christopher, but thankfully nothing has happened since the mini-fire accident he messaged about three hours ago. I slide my phone back into my pocket when I notice the wedding planner standing at the bottom of the grand staircase.

I march toward her, Rob standing guard as I ignore the fans who are loitering in the area.

"Have we missed the speeches?"

"I believe they're just about to start." She lowers her clipboard to study it.

"Great. Is there a way you could slide me inside without anyone noticing?"

Her gaze flicks between me, the entrance, and a side door.

"Err. Well, there is this side room." She points to the door to her right, inconspicuous to passers-by. "That leads into a holding area for the bride and DJ."

"Alexander, Alexander!" The small gaggle of fans calls out, trying to get my attention. But Rob ensures I'm left unbothered.

"I'm not staying for long. I just want to catch one of the speeches," I say.

"Okay, follow me," she says, sliding the clipboard under her arm.

I leave Rob to fend off the fans while I head through the door and into a small room that looks eerily similar to the backstage dressing rooms I've been in over the last year.

I head to the door on the other side and slowly crack it open, to look out into the ballroom, lit with a beautiful lilac tone. The guests are working their way through the last bits of their meals. Opposite of me, a DJ sets up his decks, and in front of him, a technician appears to be working on an LED dance floor.

I scan the room, looking for Christopher, like a metal detector searching for treasure. The sound of clinking glass grabs my attention, and I spot him grabbing cue cards and a microphone before rising to his feet at the middle table next to his sister.

My heart instantly warms at the sight.

"Ladies and gentlemen, distinguished guests, and of course, the happy couple Kelly and Daniel. If I could have your attention for just a few brief moments. I promise to keep this brief, unlike one of Kelly's infamous retail therapy sessions." Christopher coughs twice as the room erupts into laughter.

I open the door slightly to get a better view, feeling safe with everyone's back turned toward me.

"My name is Christopher Foster, and as many of you know, I am the proud brother of the stunning bride, Kelly. I must say, standing here today, I feel like Aunt Brenda at an all you can eat buffet—overwhelmed and yet inexplicably joyful." He points his cue cards at who I assume is the aunt in question.

There's a lightness to his voice, a sense of calmness in his posture.

His effortless charm lifts the corners of my mouth upward.

"Kelly, when you first told me you were getting married, I was momentarily concerned. I mean, who would take care of your extensive skin care regime? Pluck your facial hairs for you, squeeze your zits?" Christopher pauses as Kelly whacks him in the leg, to more laughs from the crowd. "But then I met your beloved, Daniel, who I must say is the perfect match for you. I mean, he's no match for me, but is a perfect match for you nonetheless."

That cheeky grin of his rises as he shrugs his shoulders like —*Hey what can I say?*

"Daniel. Remember marriage is about compromise, and when I say compromise, I mean agreeing with everything Kelly says. Just think of it as a learning exercise in patience. After all, you are doing the Lord's work."

The warm feeling inside my heart washes all over my body as I watch Christopher get the crowd to eat out of the palm of his hand. He takes a short pause, allowing the laughter to ring out.

I desperately want to catch his attention before I have to leave, but this is his moment in the spotlight. His turn to shine, not mine. And so I patiently wait, holding on to the doorframe with my hand.

"I'd also like to remind you that all sales are final, and you won't be able to return or exchange Kelly now that you've signed on the dotted like. So, good luck with that." Christopher turns his attention from Daniel back to Kelly.

"Kelly, as I look at you today, I know our father would have been proud. Proud that he no longer has to fund your limited-edition handbag collection. But, all jokes aside, I wish he was here to see how beautiful you look today." Christopher reaches for Kelly's hand, lifting her up for everyone to see.

I manage to catch Christopher's eye as his gaze moves across the room in my direction. I wave at him crazily, like one of my fans in the front row. He acknowledges me with a nod and a smile before returning his attention to Kelly.

"Before I wrap this up, I just want to leave you with a quote from an ancient philosopher. Love is like one of Kelly's farts. You can't see it or feel it, but you always know it's there."

The crowd bursts into applause as Kelly shoves her brother into his chair. He puts his arm around her before grabbing his glass of champagne, lifting it high.

"To the happy couple. May your marriage burn strong and bright and not go up in flames like Kelly's wedding dress." Christopher drops the mic and his cue cards and knocks back the champagne in one.

As everyone turns to talk with one another, Chris gets out from his chair. He works his way through the tables, giving high-fives to various people before he slides into the room with me.

"That was amazing. I don't know why you were so worried about your speech," I say, closing the door and hugging him.

"Well, what can I say, move over Alexander, there's a new star in town." He stretches his arms out wide as he steps back from the hug.

"You never told me you were a stand-up comedian." I dust off bits of ash from his suit jacket.

"Well, if there's one thing us Brits can do, it's humor," he says, taking a bow.

"Well, I can think of another thing," I say, grabbing at the band of his trousers.

Christopher coughs and I let go as Stacey reenters the room.

"Don't you have a show to be getting to?" he asks.

"Yeah, but I didn't want to miss your speech, and I'm so glad now I didn't." I reach out to adjust his bow tie.

God, he looks so handsome.

"What time will you be back?"

"I'm not sure. They want to do an end of tour wrap party for the crew, but I'll message you when I'm en route, okay?" I grab his shoulder and shake him.

"Okay," he sighs.

I don't want to go either, but after this last show we can spend more time together.

"Right. Go enjoy yourself." I tap my finger on his nose and motion him back out the door into the ballroom. Then I turn back to Stacey, who walks me back out to Rob. He's standing with Freddy, who is ready to go.

One more show.

One. More. Show.

The backstage bar is a buzz afterward. There's a celebratory atmosphere now that the tour is officially wrapping. I get several hugs and high-fives from the band and the crew, along with a few tears.

Nathan is jubilant at the studio version of *Stolen Moments*.

Lucy and Erica are both excited to finally get back to their own beds.

My parents are happy to be off to see Windsor Castle tomorrow.

Paul pauses us mid-conversation to gather everyone around and have one final team talk.

"One hundred and twenty-two shows, over ten months, across five continents, with nearly one point eight million tickets sold. None of this would have been possible without every single one of you in this room. So, thank you," Paul says, to cheers and raised glasses.

Paul motions me to come forward as Lucy brings out a plaque from behind the bar.

"Alexander, you are the hardest working person I've ever met, and I know this tour and I have been tough on you, but I'm so proud of the work you've put in, and for the man you've become."

Paul shakes my shoulder.

This breadcrumb of praise stirs up emotions in the pit of my stomach.

I swallow down the feeling, not wanting to get overwhelmed in the moment, or too comfortable and familiar with Paul's praise.

Why can't he be like this more often?

Like fifty-fifty percent asshole, rather than ninety percent asshole and ten percent caring.

I sigh and let my shoulders drop as Paul continues.

"This plaque is in acknowledgment of the amazing achievement you've just pulled off, and what I hope will be eclipsed when we all head out on the road again in the future." Paul wraps up to cheers from everyone.

Lucy hands me the impressive plaque. It's a photograph of me standing on stage, the sold-out crowd from Madison Square Garden behind me, with all the incredible stats Paul listed underneath.

I place the plaque down on the bar and quickly hug Paul and Lucy before turning to everyone.

"I'm not big on speeches, as many of you know," I say. "But I just want to take a moment to thank each and every one of you for all the hard work you've put in over the past year to bring this show to life. It takes a village to raise a child, and many of you here have literally helped to raise me. Not only into an adult, but up through the stage and out into the crowd." I nod at the toaster-lift operator as I grab a Fuji water from the bar. "You are my heroes. You are the ones who help to bring my dreams to life every night on stage, and I can't thank you all enough for everything you do."

"Alex, Alex, Alex," the crew chants as I wrap my speech up and hold my water up in the air.

It feels wholesome being surrounded by everyone. My parents look on, my mom clutching her hand over her heart while my dad's arm is thrown over her shoulder. Connie and Laurie toast each other with their drinks.

My eyes well up, but I blink it away and take a sip of water.

I've done it.

I've made it through the tour, despite all the hurdles.

I let out a deep breath.

Now I can head back home to America. Switch off and just be Al for a minute.

"How you feeling, kiddo?" my dad asks when he reaches me, ruffling my hair.

"Exhausted. I just wanna get back to the hotel."

"You don't fancy another night at that Box nightclub?" He lifts his brows.

"Not on my watch," my mum interjects, whacking him. "Let's get you back, son." My dad rolls his eyes as she loops her arm into mine, and I nod to Rob.

I feel a bit guilty for slipping out, but I've said my bit and spoken to most people in the room. Plus, this wrap party is more for them than me. And right now, there's somewhere else I'd rather be.

It's almost 12:30 a.m. by the time I make it back to the hotel. Rob calls ahead to make sure there's extra security at the back door so I can get inside quickly and straight to where I want to be—with Christopher.

As much as I enjoyed the last show, my mind was back here

with Christopher. I dreamed of us in each other's arms, gliding across the dance floor while the music played.

Christopher had said he'd wait for me when I texted that we were en route to the hotel, but my fans ambushed the car when we left the arena. It took Rob calling the security from the venue to clear the way, and it delayed us by half an hour.

Rob follows me into the ballroom, but the room is vacant. Empty glasses of wine and champagne sit alongside half drunk bottles of beer on the tables. The DJ booth is already packed down; someone left their blazer hanging over the back of one of the chairs.

I reach for my phone and call Christopher, wondering if he's already back in the room, when I hear a ringtone coming from another suit jacket, this one hanging from the back of the chair he was sitting at earlier.

Hmm.

I hang up my phone and make my way over.

He can't have gone that far without his jacket.

Rob offers to head back out to the main entrance of the ballroom to look around, while I sit down in Christopher's seat. I pick up an unused fork and cut into a slice of wedding cake, left untouched on a small plate. The sponge and strawberry jam and cream gives me a sugar rush as soon as I take the first bite.

"There he is," I hear Christopher call out, arms wide, as he enters the room.

Rob laughs behind him as Christopher stumbles through the tables toward me, looking slightly worse for wear. His bowtie hangs down on either side of his collar, right above his unbuttoned waistcoat.

"Sorry I took so long to get here," I say, getting up from the table. I feel a little underdressed in my black jeans, white vans, and white T-shirt.

"No worries. I had to put my mother to bed. She was all over the place by the end of the night." He rests his hand on the table when he finally reaches me before planting a wet kiss on my lips.

Rob glances at me and I give him the thumbs-up before shooing him out of the room. I want a moment alone with Christopher, just us two.

"How was your last show?" he asks, grabbing my hand. He pulls me to the dance floor.

"It was good," I say, nodding at the back of his head.

"Only good?" His face scrunches up when he turns to face me.

"Well, I'd rather have been here with you, if I'm honest. I was thinking about dancing with you, and I'd hoped I'd get a moment with you tonight, but it seems we're out of luck." I nod at where the DJ setup was.

"Fear not." Christopher raises his finger. "I have the answer."

He dashes back over to his chair, waving his phone in his hand as he returns. He types something on the screen before he places it on a table next to the dance floor.

"Sir," he says, bowing. "Would you do me the honor of dancing with me?" He stretches his hand out toward me.

My chest feels like a shaken soda can—too much fizz—nowhere for it to go.

I reach for his hand as he extends his other to press play on his phone.

"Let me be your hero," he whispers in my ear as the opening line of Enrique Iglesias's *Hero* plays. I rest my head on his shoulder as he tenderly holds my sprained hand in his. His other arm goes across my back.

I soak in each moment as we gently glide across the dance floor.

Our feet move slowly in time; the sound of his heartbeat is

soft in my ear.

My chest rises and falls in unison with his.

He spins me outward, as the song hits the instrumental part, before rolling me back in, catching me in his arms and leaning in to kiss me. The taste of lime is on his lips.

I tilt my head backward as he holds me, and decide I could get lost in his arms, in those hazel eyes, forever. He pulls me back up and in for another kiss, but I jolt as I hear a creaking sound behind us, snapping me out of the moment.

In a panic, I look at the door I came in through, but it remains closed. I know that Rob is outside guarding it, so no one can enter, but paranoia still creeps into my head.

"Did you hear that?" I ask Christopher.

"Hear what?" he asks, turning back toward me.

I shake my head. It must be my ears playing tricks on me, or maybe it's the tinnitus.

I lean back into Christopher, placing my head back on his shoulder, and for a moment I let myself dream of a life where we can be just two guys dancing together and no one bats an eyelid or makes a fuss.

As the last line of the song plays, Christopher slows to a standstill, grabbing my face in his hands and singing along with the last line. He goes in to kiss me, before stopping himself. His shoulders and chest jerk and a pale look comes over his face.

He lets go of me and runs toward the table, but stops just short and vomits all over one of the chairs. He reaches for a napkin to wipe himself clean before turning back to me.

"Come on," I say, heading over to him. "Let's get you back to the room."

I help him to the door and pick up another napkin, just in case he goes for round two. It's nice not to be the one who's a hot mess for a change.

Another hour has passed by the time we get ready for bed.

Rob had to call on local security to help us back to my room, to avoid any suspicion. And Christopher takes an extra-long shower before I jump in after him.

"God, your fans are extra loud tonight," Christopher says, drawing the curtains closed before climbing into bed with me.

"Here, put these on," I say, giving him my earbuds from the bedside table.

He grabs them, letting out a yawn as he puts them in.

"I'm going to set my alarm for eleven. That works for you, right?" I scroll down through the alarms I have stored, and switch on the appropriate one.

"My flight is at three," he says, snuggling down into the pillow.

I turn and plug my phone into the charger, switching off the lamp before turning back and snuggling into him. For once, I'm the big spoon to his little spoon. I breathe in the scent of his hair and wonder how I got here.

I had almost given up on everything.

Then Christopher came along like the breaking of dawn, brightening the darkest of days.

"Thank you for saving me," I whisper into his ear.

The soft exhale of his breath tells me that he's already fallen asleep.

I roll back slightly, letting go so I can study him. I try to memorize every detail, the mole on his back, the curvature of his spine. The way his hair falls naturally to the left. I take a mental snapshot, wanting to remember this moment, before rolling back up against him.

"Thank you," I say again, kissing the back of his head.

28. Christopher
Sunday

I'm startled awake by a soft grip on my arm shaking me back and forth, followed by a high-pitched feminine voice.

"Excuse me, sir."

"Stop messing with me!" I try to bat Alexander away before reaching up to remove the earbuds from my ears. My head is pounding, and I'm not in any mood for his humor at this godforsaken hour as I try to pry open my eyelids.

Surely it can't be time to get up already?

"Check out was half an hour ago, sir." The voice is louder now, and a shadow moves in front of my face as my eyes start to focus.

My heart jumps into my throat when I see not Alexander, but a woman from housekeeping, standing beside the bed.

"What time is it?" My words trip over each other as I jolt upright.

I immediately regret the motion as a surge of bile rises with it.

"Twelve-thirty, sir." Her arms are now crossed, her fingers tapping on her arm.

I swallow the bile down, and fling my legs out of the bed to stand upright. I immediately grab the duvet to cover myself when I realize I'm completely naked. The woman diverts her gaze to the windows, the curtains still drawn.

Fuck.

Think Christopher, think.

Pack.

Taxi.

Run to check in.

Some of Alexander's clothes are still scattered across the floor, including the white T-shirt he wore when I was dancing with him last night. Or did I just dream that?

Come to think of it, where is he?

"Alex?" I shout, heading into the bathroom, but there's no one inside. His toiletries are gone. A rising sense of dread heats my body. I glance into the walk-in wardrobe, but his suitcases and clothes are all gone too.

"Alex?" I shout, moving into the lounge.

"There's no one else here, sir," the woman calls out to me.

Fuck. What the hell?

My phone! Where's my phone?

I rush back to the bed, but my phone isn't on the side table.

Think Christopher, think.

I rub the back of my neck, sweat dripping from my hair.

I reach for my trousers next to the bed. Nope, not there.

My suit jacket.

I rush over to where it's hanging over an armchair, almost tripping over my shoes in a mad dash to find out what the hell has gone on. I pull out my phone, and my hope turns to despair when I repeatedly press the screen and side button. It refuses to turn on.

Ugh.

"Do you need any help, sir?" The housekeeping woman puts

an armload of towels down on the bed. She still won't look in my direction. I reach for my boxers, stepping into them and pulling them up.

"Could you type BA210 to Los Angeles into your phone please? And let me know if the flight is still on time?" I frantically grab the rest of my clothes and throw them on.

"It's delayed, sir. Departing at three-fifteen." Her gaze collides with mine when I look back to her and reach for Alexander's T-shirt, sliding it over my head. The smell of his Creed aftershave lingers in the cotton.

I exhale.

At least one thing's working in my favor today.

"Thank you," I say, sliding into my shoes. I grab my blazer, shirt, and bow tie, and make a beeline for the main door. I close it quickly behind me, and then am stopped by something dropping to the floor.

A door hanger.

The same door hanger Alexander gave me for Kelly and Daniel yesterday.

We've Made A Mess stares up at me.

Wait, was it that side or the other side on the door? I reach down to pick it up, flicking it over to the *Busy Fucking* side. I stiffen as I flip the door hanger back and forth.

You don't have time to think about this right now, you just need to get to the airport, I think. I shake my head as I take the twenty steps down to my room. I shove everything into my left hand and pull out the door key, waving it frantically over the card reader. The light blinks red.

For God's sake.

I wave at another housekeeping staff member down the hallway, motioning at him to help me. He looks at me oddly as he approaches. My disheveled appearance probably makes me look like I've just escaped an asylum.

"Can you help me get into my room?" I plead, waving my key over the door.

He hesitates, pulling at the master key clipped to his waistband.

"Please, I'm going to miss my flight." My jaw tightens as I tap the key on my hip.

I do not have time for his hesitation.

The guy relents and taps the key to open my door.

"Thank you," I say, banging the door open.

Thankfully, I'd packed all my bags before the wedding yesterday, leaving them all lined up by the desk. My family used to mock me for being overprepared as a child. Sometimes I'd pack days before we left. But right now I'm grateful that it's one less thing to deal with.

I strip out of my clothes and shoes and change into the sweatpants and polo shirt I'd left on the armchair, before unzipping my suitcase and throwing everything else in.

I grab my rucksack, pull out my sunglasses to get some relief from the sun pouring through the window, throw on my baseball cap, and do a quick scan of the room and head to the door. I rush down the hallway and furiously stab the elevator button.

Come on. Come on.

When the elevator finally arrives, it's full, but I don't care. I push my way in, much to everyone's dismay, and let out a deep exhale.

Why would Alexander leave without saying goodbye?

We were supposed to fly at similar times.

The doors open on the ground floor and I burst out, turning left and almost running through the hotel, swerving past people and out of the back exit to the taxi rank.

The exit is completely quiet aside from someone walking their dog.

There's no screaming fans.

Stolen Moments

I open the door to the taxi, lift my suitcase in, and fling my backpack on the seat, closing the door behind me

"Where to mate?" the taxi driver asks.

"Heathrow. Terminal Five." I reach for the seatbelt.

Forty minutes later, I'm standing at the check in desk, taking deep breaths. The drive was both slow and painful with this hangover. The drive was made even worse when I realized the taxi's USB port was broken, leaving me unable to charge my phone and none the wiser about what happened. The only plus was that I didn't puke.

"The flight will be departing from gate B46, and you have access to the BA lounge, which is located at either end on the other side of security." The check-in lady passes back my passport with my ticket as my luggage disappears down the conveyor belt.

"Great." I grab the passport, tapping it twice on the counter before hotfooting it through to security. I'm eager to get to the lounge to charge my phone.

Thankfully, the security line isn't long, and after a brief stop to scan my ticket at the BA lounge entrance, I'm at the bar. I pour myself a Bloody Mary to take the edge off my hangover and head over to one of the seats.

I rummage through my bag, pulling out a pack of ibuprofen and the USB cable, and grab my phone to plug it in, then pop two pills and wash them down with the drink.

I tap my foot impatiently, waiting for the phone to start.

Fear creeps into my thoughts while I wait.

Did I say something that caused Alexander to leave without saying goodbye?

Did I do something to piss him off?

I'm sure I remember everything that happened last night, but what if I did?

Then my fear switches up a gear, turning into anger.

What if this is what Alexander does? What if he just hooks up with a guy and then ghosts them, everywhere he goes, disappearing without a trace. I tighten my hands around the arms of the chair.

But, if that were the case, it doesn't make sense that he was talking about going out on a proper date when we got back to LA. I reach for my drink, taking another sip to distract myself from the fact that my will to live is charging faster than my phone.

The Tabasco sauce hits the back of my throat, its peppery taste offsetting the copious amounts of vodka I free poured into the glass. It overwhelms my tastebuds, but simultaneously soothes my head and stomach. Maybe it's psychosomatic, but whatever it is, it's doing the trick.

My phone finally comes to life, and I drop my glass on the table, retrieving it and waiting for the Apple sign to disappear and the home screen to load. Hopefully there will be a message from Alexander that clarifies what the hell is going on.

That he's okay.

That we're okay.

Messages start to pop up. There's a dozen missed calls from my sister and three voice messages, and over fifty WhatsApp messages. But nothing from Alexander.

I reach for my chest, rubbing it to settle my worry. After what happened at the start of the week, my mind instantly fears the worst.

I pull up his number and call him.

The number you have called cannot be reached at this time. Please try again later.

I dial twice more and am greeted by the same message.

My breath becomes shorter and shallower each time.

Think positive.

This can all be explained.

Stolen Moments

He must be on a flight if it's going straight to voicemail.

Maybe something happened and he had to head back home early.

Just as I begin to look at my messages, Kelly's name flashes up on the screen.

"Hey," I answer, but Kelly immediately cuts me off.

"Oh my God, I've been trying to get hold of you all morning. I even knocked on your door and on Alexander's door, but there was no answer. Are you okay?" The concern in Kelly's words does nothing to settle my breathing.

"Sorry, my phone died. I overslept and nearly missed the flight. I'm at the airport now and only just managed to get my phone back up and running."

I let out a deep exhale, trying to slow my breathing, and reach for the Bloody Mary.

"Wait. You haven't seen?" Her voice goes up an octave.

"Seen what?" I place the drink down and my breathing picks up again.

What am I meant to have seen?

"It's all over social media and the news. Are you with Alex?"

I look at the TV, but a soccer match is playing on screen.

"No. I was woken up by housekeeping. He was gone. Why, what happened? Is he okay?"

Kelly falls silent. Images of the paramedics running past me in the hotel run through my mind as I pull the phone from my ear and fire up the news app, searching for Alexander Morgan. My heart is now beating so fast, it might actually qualify as a medical event.

The results load, and my heart stops cold:

> *Alexander Morgan Caught Kissing A GUY In London.*
> *Alexander's Stolen Moment With A Mystery Man.*
> *Pop Star Alexander Morgan's Secret Life Exposed.*

"Oh my God. Oh my God." I scroll down to see even more headlines. The faint sound of Kelly's voice comes from the phone, and I lift the phone back to my ear.

"Are you still there?"

"I'll call you back."

"But—" I hang up before she has a chance to say more.

I go back to the top of the feed and click on the first article.

Alexander Morgan caught on camera locking lips with a mystery man in a London hotel. The caption is under a picture of him kissing me. The back of my head conceals my identity, but Alexander's face and hair are instantly recognizable, making it indisputable that it's him.

My spine stiffens as I continue to read through the article, and it takes all my self-control not to scream. I swallow down the boulder-sized lump in my throat.

I close the app and try calling Alexander again, getting the same voicemail message. A boarding call plays out for my flight, but I ignore it.

There must be some way to get ahold of him.

To find out what happened.

Social media!

Surely there will be videos of him leaving the hotel that will help me piece everything together. The algorithm must remember my search history because the first video that pops up as I open the app is of Alexander leaving the hotel. He's flanked by security as he gets into a car, head down with a hoodie on—my hoodie—as Rob gets in after him.

Surely that's a sign? A signal that he's sending to me?

I look at the time stamp on this video and subsequent videos of him leaving the hotel, and they all seem to be posted between six and seven hours ago, which must mean Alexander left the hotel around seven this morning.

But how the hell did I not hear him leave?

Stolen Moments

I'm such a light sleeper.

I continue doom scrolling, finally stopping on one of him walking through the airport. The paparazzi are snapping away and yelling at him. *Are the rumors true, Alex? Are you gay?* Alex keeps his focus locked on the ground as Rob does his best to protect him. I swipe up one more time and stop on a video by Hollywood Exposed that already has thirty-five thousand likes.

Alexander Morgan finds himself embroiled in a new scandal this morning, just days after rumors of an alleged affair between him and Rita Watson. A video has emerged of Morgan kissing an unidentified man at his hotel last night in London.

Grainy video cuts in, showing Alexander and me dancing, Enrique's *Hero* just about audible in the clip.

Another lump forms in my throat.

He was right.

That sound must have been someone sneaking in through the side room to record that video.

But who is this mystery man? Is Alexander Morgan gay? Bisexual? You know what to do, followers. Let's solve this mystery!

The video loops back to the start and I click on the comments, immediately regretting it when I see a load of vile slurs and rampant speculation about who I could be.

Whoever he is, he needs to keep his hands off MY man.

It looks like Asher Angel.

No way it's Asher, it's probably some deadbeat guy.

I keep on scrolling, but pause when I come across one message.

It looks like that guy who walked in with his girlfriend the other day.

Fuck.

The comment only has a couple of likes, but it won't take long for those keyboard warriors to track me down if anyone from the wedding tags me in a picture from last night. I quickly go through all my social media profiles, double-checking that my accounts are set to private, and pull my baseball cap down even lower.

No one seems to have glanced my way. They're all lost in their own conversations and digital devices, but I can't be too cautious.

Surely, this can't be happening. It must be a nightmare.

A quick pinch of my arm confirms it's not, just as the last call goes out for my flight.

Fuck.

I pull the charger out from the socket, down the last of the Bloody Mary, and throw on my backpack as I head to the exit. I make my way through the terminal and toward the gate.

When I get to the top of the escalators, I'm greeted by a newspaper stand and an image of Alexander staring back at me from the front page. It's the same picture I selected from the *Men's Health* shoot. Underneath the photo are four simple words: *Is Alexander Morgan Gay?*

I fight for breath, the force of seeing the image crushing my chest, and debate whether or not to pick up a copy of the paper in the time it takes me to blink.

I grab a copy and shove it under my arm before turning and heading to the gate. The last few people are lining up by the desk, handing over their boarding passes.

I suddenly feel a shooting pain from my bladder, desperate to be relieved, but I take a deep breath and ignore it. I just want to get on the plane. Get back to Los Angeles and get ahold of Alexander.

"Ticket please," the man at the desk asks when I get there.

I reach into the pocket of my sweatpants to retrieve my passport, but it's not there. My other pocket, holding my wallet and the earbuds that Alexander gave me, doesn't contain my passport either.

The earbuds.

The fucking earbuds!

Did he give them to me knowing they would stop me from hearing him leave?

"One moment," I say, stepping aside.

Be calm. Think. You had it at the lounge, and you also had it when you left for the gate. It can't have gone far.

"Looking for this?"

I turn to see Connie holding my passport up in her hand.

She wears the same look of disdain on her face as when I called her Bonnie.

"Thank you," I say, stretching out my hand to take it as she hands it over. "Are you on this flight too?"

"I am," she says, motioning me forward to the desk.

My shoulders relax at her two-word response. Finally, someone who can help fill in the blanks. She may not have the answers to all my questions, but at least she'll know the answers to most.

I hand my ticket over to the man at the desk, who quickly tears off the stub, hands it back and points me to the bridge to board the plane.

"Where are you sitting?" I ask, turning back to Connie as we walk down.

"I'm in 12A," she says sharply.

"That's next to me," I say as we get to the airplane door. The stewardess greets us with a warm smile, checking my ticket and pointing me to the left.

"I know." Her tone is darker now, causing my muscles to tighten.

How does she know? And come to think of it, how come she's on this flight and not with Alexander and the rest of his team?

I empty the flight essentials from my bag onto my seat, charger, sleeping mask, ibuprofen, and stow my bag in the compartment above my head. Connie does the same, offloading her laptop, reading glasses, headphones, and a folder. The same color folder as the one Paul used for the MNDA.

"Could I offer you a glass of champagne, sir?" a steward asks, tapping me on the shoulder.

"You don't happen to have a Bloody Mary, do you?" The effects of the previous one and the two ibuprofen are quickly wearing off.

"Certainly, and for you, ma'am?" He turns his attention to Connie.

"I'm good, thanks."

The steward walks away as the rest of the passengers settle into their seats, and I turn to Connie. There's a plethora of questions running through my head.

I want to ask the most burning question, but I'm mindful of prying ears and opt to speak in code, going for a low-hanging fruit.

"How come you're on this flight? I thought you'd have left with everyone else."

"That was the plan, yes." Connie takes out her reading glasses from her case and puts them on. "But then things changed this morning, as I'm sure you are *well* aware."

Her veiled swipe of passive-aggressiveness, coming as she slams her glasses case shut, makes me feel like I'm responsible for this, rather than a victim.

Cabin crew, boarding is complete. Close the doors and cross check.

Connie glares at me and reaches for the folder. I start to ask another question, one of the dozen I still have, but decide against it. Instead, I start to take my seat, but she reaches for my arm and stops me.

"Before you get off this flight, I'm going to need you to read through what's inside, sign the documents, and hand it back to me." Connie passes me the folder.

Her jaw clenches so hard as I take it that I can hear her teeth grinding.

I want to speak, but my voice cracks. Like I've lost all ability to voice my thoughts.

Connie shakes her head at me, turns, and slides into her chair. She grabs her headphones and slides them on.

Point taken.

"Here you go, sir." The steward returns with the Bloody Mary. "I'm going to need you to take your seat for takeoff." He points to my place.

I nod and sit down, placing the folder to the side along with the drink, and fasten my seatbelt.

I take a deep breath. Then another. And another. And then reach for the folder.

Resting it on my lap, I slowly open it to the documents inside. My jaw drops as I take in the first line.

29. Alexander
Monday

The atmosphere in the green room suffocates me, like I'm being buried alive, but the dirt isn't just my own thoughts, but everyone around me who is making a fuss about this TV interview with *Behind the Scenes*.

Erica applies another layer of makeup.

Laurie holds up several clothing options to choose from.

Paul and Connie continue to explain the "strategy" to me.

Lucy runs in and out of the room fielding calls.

Rob stands guard by the door.

"I need a minute." I bat away Erica's brush as I get up out of the makeup chair and head toward the restroom.

I try to close the door behind me, just to get one moment to myself, but Rob's glare—not a chance—stops me from doing so.

God forbid I have a few seconds of privacy.

Everyone is worried about me. I've caught their sideward glances, the awkward silences. I even overheard Paul say *suicide watch* to Rob yesterday, when they thought I was listening to music through my headphones.

I turn on the tap and let the familiar feeling of cold water wash over my hands. I lean over the sink to splash my face. It's the only thing in the last thirty-six hours that seems to calm me down, other than Ambien.

I'm not allowed to go for a run.

Box breathing no longer works.

Even my ADHD medication isn't helping me focus.

I thought I'd left all these scandals behind me. That I'd finally turned the page after Rita Watson's team issued a statement about her entering a treatment facility on Saturday. But no sooner had that news broken when this story dropped and blew up in my face.

What's worse is that I don't even know how bad everything is. Paul took my phone from me, telling me it was to protect me from reading everything that's being posted online. But I think it's just to stop me from contacting Christopher.

To continue to punish me for breaking out of the hotel on Thursday.

I lift my head back up from the sink, turn off the tap, and grab one of the white towels on the side. I dab at my face and take in several deep breaths before dropping it and looking at myself in the mirror.

Guilt comes out through every pore of my face.

I didn't even get a chance to say goodbye. It all happened so quickly. One minute I was asleep, the next I was being woken up by Rob. He'd covered my mouth to stop me from speaking. Then I was moved out into the office on the other side of the suite while Lucy packed up all my stuff, tiptoeing around in the dark so as not to wake Christopher.

Neither one told me what was going on, other than saying it was an emergency. Lucy threw me some clothes to change into —Christopher's hoodie, a vest, gray sweatpants, socks, and my black vans.

I tried to go back to the room to get my phone, to say

goodbye to Christopher, but Rob refused, not even letting me leave a note. That's when I knew something bad had gone down.

It was a military-style operation getting me out of the hotel. There were decoy cars at the front and back while we slipped out of the side entrance. It was the same one Rob had let me in when I fell off the wagon a week ago. Lucy gave me her Bose headphones to slip over my head just before we left. As Coldplay's *Speed of Sound* played out, Rob used the local security guards to shield me as I got in the car.

My legs were twitching, my fingers tapping on the arm rest, as we made the drive to the airport. The swirling fear inside my chest churned and turned into anger by the time we got to the terminal. The last thread of my patience snapped at Paul and Lucy's deflections when I tried to find out what was going on.

We just need to get through to departures.

We'll tell you everything once you're on the plane.

Don't worry.

I finally blew, refusing to leave the car until someone told me what was going on, and I even threatened to fire them all on the spot, which seemed to do the trick. But what I heard, what they showed me, sent me spiraling.

Someone had leaked a video of Christopher and me making out in the ballroom. It had already spread like wildfire all over the internet and to the press. Rumors were flying that I was gay and many were wondering who the mystery guy is.

I demanded to have my phone back right there and then, to call Christopher, but Paul flat-out refused. He said they hadn't ruled out whether Chis had been involved with leaking it.

That's when the panic set in.

Had this all been a setup?

Had he pulled the wool over my eyes?

When we hit the ground in LA, it was like a circus. The terminal was swarming with more paparazzi than I'd ever seen in my life. They were snapping away at me like vultures. Thank God I'm not epileptic.

The team decided it was better to put me up at a hotel than have me go home.

At the hotel, they could keep an eye on me.

And, as it turns out, lay out their plan.

They wanted to claim that I was rehearsing for an upcoming film with a movement coach, and that the whole thing was being filmed for preproduction. If I did a sit-down interview, I could use it to explain away the rumors and announce my first feature film at the same time.

When Connie joined us at the hotel that evening, Paul didn't miss the opportunity to let me know that he and Connie had been working nonstop since the scandal broke. Connie had caught a later flight to "clean up the mess," as she put it. She'd been fielding calls from all over the world. Demands for a quote, a response to the scandal. All the big-name interviewers, from Oprah to Piers Morgan, were requesting interviews, expecting a coming-out story.

Connie focused on finding easy hosts whom she and Paul could control. They finally settled on Roberto Gonzales from *Behind the Scenes* to do the interview.

Meanwhile, Paul was busy green lighting the whole movie, without so much as a consultation with me. He fast-tracked the conversations with Jackal Entertainment, officially getting them on board as the production company and hiring Alfonso as the director and producer.

Things escalated quickly from there. Like a runaway train with no brakes.

I pushed back, saying I hadn't even read the script yet.

Paul berated me for not making the time for it. For being "too busy."

I fought back at the insinuation.

Then Rob came back into the room at the perfect time to confirm that it was a fan who had broken into the Landmark's ballroom and taken the footage.

I cursed Paul for planting a seed of doubt in my mind about Christopher.

Rob had to hold me back when Paul labeled Christopher as collateral, dismissing him as nothing more than a whirlwind fling that I'd quickly forget about.

That's when the red mist hit.

"It wasn't a fling," I snarled, taking off my baseball cap and throwing it at him. "He is my boyfriend. We're meant to be together. Like star-crossed lovers."

"That worked out really well for Romeo and Juliet," Paul snorted. "One was ostracized from their family. Both of them ending up killing themselves, three days after they met."

Connie sat there watching it all unfold, drinking her Diet Coke, like it was a reenactment of an episode from Real Housewives. Then she spoke up.

"It's all handled now anyway. The interview will clear all this up. The movie is moving forward. And Christopher has agreed to go along with the story."

"He did? What story? When did you see him?" I'd asked.

"I flew back with him. He signed another agreement stating he'll honor whatever story we put out. He agreed to cut all communication with you to ensure this scandal dies out." She waved her hand with a whimsical, blasé attitude as she explained it all away, like I was some fly who was bothering her.

"But why would he do that? Why would he be so willing to cut me out of his life, especially when we just agreed to be together?" I'd asked out loud.

"Money talks, darling," Connie had said, rubbing her thumb and fingers together. "Everyone has a price."

A knock on the doorframe snaps me out of my trance. Erica

stands behind me. The towel to my left is covered in bronzer, and I'll need to sit down and have more makeup applied.

"You ready for me to finish up?" Erica asks, stepping forward. She rests her hand on my shoulder.

My eyes start clouding up and my shoulders drop.

Everything has moved so quickly.

The damage control always seems to protect me, but causes untold harm along the way to others. To Samuel. To Rita. And now to Christopher.

"You don't have to go through with this, you know." Erica squeezes my shoulder tightly. "There's still time to pull out."

I lift my hand to wipe the tears falling from my eyes.

I had thought about just that. About leaving the building and locking myself away at my house. About telling the truth, *my truth*, live during the interview. But Connie made sure that the interview would be prerecorded, and that Paul got final sign-off before its broadcast.

"I don't have a choice," I say, turning to face her. I shrug my shoulders and head back out to the chair.

Lucy comes back into the room as I sit back down in the makeup chair, and hands Connie a pile of papers. Connie motions to her to pass them around to everyone. Paul takes a copy and Lucy hands one over to me.

"This is the final press release for the film. Everyone has signed off on it. We'll go wide tonight as soon as the interview airs," Connie says as I look down at it.

Alexander Morgan set to make his feature film debut in psychological thriller Disposed. *Set for release next fall in association with Jackal Entertainment and Universal Studios.*

I read the headline and press release, trying to take it all in, but the words blend and blur into one. I'm unable to absorb anything on the page.

"Chin up," Erica says, lifting my chin and sliding a towel into the neck of my white T-shirt so she can smooth out the tinted moisturizer from my jawline to my neck.

Paul stands up and heads to the table by the fridge, grabbing himself an apple and taking a bite.

"I spoke to the label earlier," Paul says. "*Stolen Moments* the live version is now at number one on both Spotify and Apple, and they want to fast-track the studio version. They plan to drop it in an hour, along with a premiere on KIIS. They also want us to shoot a music video at the end of this week, to capitalize on the momentum."

He smiles toward me, igniting a burning fire inside my stomach.

"You mean, take advantage of the pain we've inflicted on both Rita and Christopher," I say. My grip tightens on the wooden arms of the chair.

"Rita wasn't well, Alex. And as for Christopher, well everything will be sorted after today's interview. Don't forget he's been financially taken care of too." There's now a stoic look etched across Paul's face.

Two days ago, I was looking forward to taking a well-deserved break from being out on the road for the last ten months. Actually, come to think of it, I've been working nonstop for the better part of the last eighteen. But now it seems like my workload has increased, not decreased. There's no break in sight between now and Christmas.

"The money's been wired through," Lucy says, looking up from her phone toward Paul.

"See, Christopher's been taken care of." He points at Lucy while looking at me in the mirror.

A knot forms in my stomach, just as a knock comes from the door.

Rob opens it to a man dressed in black standing outside.

"We'll be ready for Alexander on set in five minutes," he says.

"Great. Thank you." Rob nods and closes the door.

Connie gets up and grabs a Diet Coke from the fridge.

"Right." She turns to face me, pulling open the tab and taking a sip. "Let's go over everything one last time before we head out."

I roll my eyes, and catch the smirk on Erica's face in the mirror.

"What's the name of the film?"

"*Disposed*," I say, bluntly.

"What's the film about."

"It's a psychological thriller set in New Mexico at the turn of the century, where a guy seeks revenge on a town that destroyed his family." My voice is so monotone, it's flatlining.

I feel like I'm a child in school, being made to recite times tables back to the teacher.

"I hope you're not planning to answer these questions as flatly as you're answering them now," Paul interjects.

"Oh, I'm sorry. I didn't realize the cameras were rolling."

"Now, now boys." Connie looks back and forth between us as I let out a sigh. "Let's just focus on getting this done, shall we?"

I let out another deep breath as Paul returns his attention to his phone and Connie continues questioning me.

"What drew you to this role?"

"I always wanted to be an actor when I was growing up, but I ended up pursuing a career in music instead. Then a few months ago, I got approached to do a film, and when I read the script, I fell in love with it."

The irony is I still haven't read the script, I'd acquired the rights to the book, and I didn't grow up wanting to be an actor. That came when I was older.

Connie leans back on the table, setting the Diet Coke down to take her glasses off and look at me, as if that makes her able to understand me better.

"Now, Roberto has been briefed not to ask you any direct questions about your sexuality, and if there is any hint we're heading in that direction, I will jump in. However, we do need to address the footage that leaked and shut down the rumors." She reaches for another piece of paper.

I still haven't seen how bad things are. Paul is still holding my phone prisoner.

I want to see what's been written, to defend myself against what is being said. But I know that will only make things worse and feed the trolls.

"I appreciate that you've turned down the offer to have us contract someone to assume the role of your girlfriend for the next year or two. With that in mind, we will continue with the narrative that the person in the video was a movement coach, hired by the production company to prepare you for the role, before we pivot to cover one of the key points we want to get across: How excited you are to begin shooting the film this summer and your gratitude to the fans for making *Stolen Moments* the number one song in the world."

I shake my head. Not in disapproval, but at how good she is at all of this.

She frames it all in a way that helps protect me and promote me, all in the same breath. Yet I can't help but feel wrong about what I am doing.

I'm lying to the world about who I am.

Lying about what happened with Christopher.

All to protect my image.

It's an image I barely recognize when I stare at myself in the mirror.

Another knock sounds at the door, and Rob heads back over to it.

"Ready guys?" he asks, as he opens the door.

"Yep," I say, reluctantly lifting myself up.

"Great to see you, buddy. How was Europe?" Roberto asks, hugging me.

His Hollywood smile momentarily blinds me when I step back. The audio guy fits the microphone on my T-shirt, sliding the cable underneath and plugging it into the pack before handing it to me to slide into the back pocket of my jeans.

"Eventful," I say, eyebrows arched, already regretting being here.

I sit down and make myself comfortable. It's not too dissimilar to what I would expect a therapy office to look like. A box of tissues and a water sit on the table beside me. There's a matching cream armchair opposite of me for Roberto. A green screen wraps around the set behind us, which they'll no doubt superimpose some form of comfy room onto.

Erica steps on set to make last-minute touch-ups to my hair, and she pulls a sponge out of her bag to dab at my forehead. Paul, Connie, Rob, and Laurie stand by the TV monitor behind the cameras.

Erica pulls the sponge away and leans in.

"My car's out back if you want to make a dash for it," she whispers into my ear.

She pulls back and looks at me, her eyes narrowing.

I pause for two beats to consider it, before ruling it out. It will only make things worse. Get spun out into an even bigger story.

I'm in this now.

I'm committed.

I just have to get on with it.

"I'm good, thank you."

Erica nods and leaves me on set.

"We ready?" the producer shouts from behind the camera.

Roberto looks up from the cue cards in his lap and nods.

My mind starts racing and I start to question everything.

Am I ready?

Do I really want to do this?

What if it's all a big mistake?

How long can I keep this lie up for?

What happens if something else comes up down the road?

What if this is finally my chance to tell the truth, no matter what the consequences are?

My leg twitches and I glance at the exit sign *Dramatic Exit*, above the door to my right.

"And we're recording in three, two…"

30. Christopher
Monday

The last place I want to be right now is sitting in this meeting, nursing my wrist. I've been pretending that it is the reason I missed last week's call, even though it was all Alexander's fault. In fact, everything the last few days has been his fault.

I play with a loose thread from the wristband I picked up from CVS, trying to garner sympathy from the HR representative who is sitting directly across from me in the meeting room, next to Pietro.

"Taking everything into account you've outlined today," the representative says, sliding back the paperwork I got emailed from the hospital, "we've decided that a verbal warning is the outcome from this process."

My shoulders slump and I let out a sigh.

The last thing I needed after the past forty-eight hours is another blow.

"And the Brewed account?" I ask. I turn my gaze to Pietro.

"Given the impact that you not attending Thursday's meeting had with their team, we are going to keep the account with Tony, who managed to save the meeting and stop it from turning into a catastrophe." Pietro's body stiffens.

Right, Pietro, say how you really feel.

I can feel the sense of injustice rising inside of me. I've been working hard at this company for the last five years, the last three of them here in LA. And because of one slip up, when I was on leave no less, I've lost my main account and gotten a verbal warning. But I force myself to swallow it down.

I still have a job to come back to.

I can still live in America.

"Okay," I say, lowering my head and grabbing the papers. "Thank you for your time today."

I get up, let myself out of the meeting room, and head back to my desk. Tony and Sara look smug, sitting opposite of each other at their laptops.

Clearly, Tony already knows he's got the Brewed account, and by proxy, given that he and Sara are definitely fucking, she'll know too. But I need to play the long game here. I plaster on a smile and act as if everything's okay, something I've been forced to do for two reasons today, and bide my time.

HR works in the best interests of the company, never the employee, and loose lips sink ships. It's only a matter of time before someone's loose lips speak to HR about the Tony/Sara ship, and wipes the smug looks off their faces.

"Everything okay?" Tony asks, turning to me.

I meet his gaze through his Harry Potter-framed glasses, then note his patchy stubble, messy hair, and the two-sizes-too-small black T-shirt that reveals a potbelly.

They say you shouldn't judge a book by its cover, but given that we work in marketing, the cover looks less homeless chic and more homeless geek. And it's definitely not what you'd expect from an account executive who is working with one of the biggest brands in the world.

"Couldn't be better," I say, flashing him a fuck off smile.

Bide your time.

"What are you up to tonight?" Sara asks, getting up from her chair and opening the filing cabinet behind her.

Her short tennis-style dress, provocative to say the least, rides up even further as she bends down to get a folder out of the cabinet. Out of the corner of my eye, I catch Tony staring at her like a piece of meat.

"Just a chill one. What about you two? What are you up to?" I ask, reaching for my bag and unplugging my laptop from the charger.

Sara freezes in position. She keeps her back turned away from me, clearly an attempt to hide whatever expression has appeared on her face that will give away what I already know.

"Off to play tennis," Tony says, twiddling with his glasses.

He always does that when he lies.

I wonder if he knows that's a tell.

"You should play mixed doubles," I say, after an awkward pause when Sara returns to her desk. "Looks like Sara's already dressed and ready to go, and you'd both make a great... team."

Sara's cheeks immediately flush as her gaze darts to Tony, then to her laptop.

"Right, I better go," I say, sliding my laptop into my bag and getting up. "Have fun."

Julie, Pietro's assistant, waves goodbye at me and shouts, "Lunch tomorrow?"

"Absolutely," I say, waving back.

That is, if I make it through tonight.

Forty minutes later, I unload my shopping basket onto the conveyor belt. Although I might be able to mask how I'm really feeling to the world underneath the guise of a smile, my shopping choices clearly aren't hiding anything.

"Tough start to the week?" the cashier asks, scanning each item through and placing them in a brown paper bag.

"What gave it away?" I ask, laughing at my purchases.

The two tubs of Ben & Jerry's ice cream.

The tub of pringles.

The chicken tenders.

The six-pack of Corona.

Thankfully, I managed to pick up some healthy items too. Spinach, avocado, bananas, and berries, but I'd be kidding myself if I claim I'm going to eat any of them. My housemate Andrew will probably end up eating it all instead.

"That'll be ninety-one dollars and seventy-two cents." The cashier places the can of pringles into the bag while I take out my wallet. I show him my driver's license so he can verify I am indeed over twenty-one before tapping my Wells Fargo card on the card reader.

A flashback to the flight home to LA almost knocks the wind out of my lungs.

Filling in my bank details on the paperwork and signing the numerous pages.

They were a renegotiation of the terms Paul had made me sign, but with no negotiating.

I shake my head, shoving my wallet back into my pocket. I grab my bags and head to my car, throwing the bags in the trunk of my jeep before jumping in the driver's seat, turning on the car, and cranking up the air conditioning full blast. I wave at another driver, waiting with his indicator on for my spot, to move on.

He throws his hands up, but I give him a death glare. He really does not want to pick a battle with me, today of all days. I grip the steering wheel and let out two deep breaths as he moves on, before pulling out my phone and firing up the Wells Fargo app.

The money wasn't there earlier, and I have a rousing suspicion that Connie has pulled a fast one on me. She's bought my silence, but without the payment. She said the money would be there by 4 p.m., but when I checked just before heading into the HR meeting at five, I didn't see the deposit.

I hold the phone up to my face, the app opens and loads, and I close my eyes.

I wish I'd never met Alexander Morgan.

I wish our paths had never crossed that first night in the lift.

I feel like I've been stabbed in the back. Not with a knife, but an axe.

But maybe I dodged a bullet, or more aptly, a cannonball.

I also *don't* wish that I'd never met him.

I don't.

But I do hate the way I'm feeling right now. How all of this has left a bitter taste in my mouth. Like a shot of tequila, but without the warm feeling and buzz inside.

I open my eyes, and let out an audible gasp.

Checking Account
$108,274.52 available

I rub my eyes to make sure they're not deceiving me.

I've never seen that much money in my checking account in my life.

Sure, after Dad died and the inheritance money came through, I had a nice little bump in my UK account that I've put into savings for a downpayment on a house. But that figure. It blows my mind.

Yet, I can't help but look at the money and feel cheap. Like I was an escort, paid not for sex or company, but to ensure I left afterward. I never would have taken the money if Connie and the documents weren't so convincing.

This scandal will ruin Alexander's career.
If it comes out that Alexander is gay, he will lose everything.

And she'd asked what would happen to me. Was I prepared for what would unfold if my identity was revealed? The trolls would tear me apart. The press would comb through every part of my life. They'd air all my dirty laundry for the world to see.

And then she delivered the ultimate blow.

Alexander was on board with it.

He wanted to pay me off. To make all of this go away. To give me one hundred thousand dollars so that I'd go along with whatever narrative they put out and never discuss it with anyone.

I wanted to speak to Alexander. To hear it directly from him. But Connie told me that wouldn't be possible. Now all I have left from our time together is this hush money, his white T-shirt, the door hanger, and those poxy earbuds.

I pull my seatbelt on, and move the car into drive when the radio host stops me in my tracks.

"And now, the moment all you Morganites have been waiting for. The world premiere of Alexander Morgan's brand-new single. The studio version of the live track that's currently sitting at number one on Spotify, *Stolen Moments*."

I pull out of the parking spot and work my way up San Vicente and onto Sunset Boulevard while the song plays out. My hands begin to burn from the tightness of my grip on the steering wheel. When I stop at a red light, a huge billboard of Alexander stares back at me, naked except for a pair of Hugo Boss briefs.

Really?

Are you fucking kidding me?

Is it going to be like this everywhere I go now?

I change the station, the song too painful to hear, and opt for the soothing sounds of KOST 103.5 FM instead. Kelly Clarkson's *Behind These Hazel Eyes* plays out.

"You're right, Kelly. You're right," I say out loud, as I pull into the garage underneath my apartment. Alexander won't get to see any tears I cry behind these hazel eyes.

"Who broke your heart?" Andrew shouts from the kitchen.

He's rummaging through the shopping bags to see what I got while I relieve myself in the toilet. His voice is barely audible over the NBA Finals blaring in the background on the TV from the lounge.

"How long have you got?" I say, returning to him in the kitchen.

"So, how was London?" He tilts his head sideways as he pulls out the pringles can and helps himself to a handful.

When I finally got back last night, Andrew wasn't home. He was staying over at his partner's house, who he's been with for nearly six months now, a new record for him. Andrew and I started out as friends with benefits when we first met two and a half years ago, but over the last eighteen months, our relationship has evolved. We moved in as flatmates a year ago and now he's one of my closest friends.

"A roller coaster," I say, grabbing two spoons from the utensil drawer and the Ben & Jerry's cookie dough ice cream from the shopping bag.

"You want some?"

"When have I ever said no to ice cream?" Andrew says, laughing. He grabs the bottle opener and two bottles of Corona before heading back into the lounge.

Connie had mentioned that Alexander would be doing a sit-down interview today to shut down all the speculation, but hadn't given me any further information.

After some investigating, I'd figured out the interview was with *Behind the Scenes* and would play at eight o'clock tonight. Which meant I'd be home to view it. I'd hoped watching it would give me some closure, but if my reaction to the song on the radio and the billboard I saw is anything to go by, I don't think it will.

Then there's the issue of convincing Andrew to watch it.

I've been trying to work out how to approach this, especially since watching the NBA Finals has become a new tradition. It's something we both do when we're home during playoff season. Andrew even dons his Laker's jersey, revealing toned arms that remind me of Alexander's.

Clearly, I do have a type. Shorter than me, muscular, into sports, and with that pretty bad boy look.

"Do you mind if we flick over to NBC at eight?" I ask, popping the lid off the ice cream and leaning across the couch to offer him a spoon.

"What's on at eight?" Andrew puts his Corona down and takes the spoon, digging in extra hard to get a large scoop of ice cream.

"It's one of my sister's favorite artists. He's doing an interview, and she wants me to text her all the details as soon as it airs."

I move myself back, hiding my discomfort at concealing the truth. I reach for the other spoon, taking a scoop of the ice cream and swallowing it down along with my guilt.

"Can't we just TiVo it?" He looks at me, his face crinkling.

I knew this would be his answer and thank God I planned for this. I have a backup plan that will work. Call it emotional blackmail if you will, but desperate times call for desperate measures.

"Remember when you broke up with Michael and all you

wanted to do was cuddle up on the couch and watch Disney films? We skipped two NBA games last year so you could pretend to be Jasmine and that Aladdin would come rescue you."

"What does that have to do with this?" His brows furrow.

"Well, I'm just asking for thirty minutes tonight for you to cuddle up with me on the couch and watch the interview. If not for me, then for Kelly." I break away from his stare to put the tub of ice cream down and grab the other Corona, taking a swig.

"Okay," he says after a short pause. "But I don't want this becoming a habit."

"It won't," I say.

The next twenty minutes pass tediously. I pick at the label on the beer bottle, waiting for the clock on the wall to hit eight, before I reach for the remote.

The program credits start, and I inhale so deeply that it startles Andrew.

He shakes his head as he reaches for his beer and takes another sip.

After a brief introduction from the host, the camera cuts to Alexander sitting across from him, and my heart skips two beats. His face looks even more beautiful on screen than it does in person. The white of his shirt brings out his tanned skin and blue eyes. His hair is on the stylish side of messy, in complete contrast to Tony's hair.

"Your sister's got good taste in men." Andrew raises his brows at me.

"He's alright. Had better." I wink and nudge him with my elbow.

Andrew laughs and grabs another spoonful of the ice cream that now sits between us. I lower my head to his shoulder, grateful not to be going through this alone. I'll do anything right now to make the pain of watching this more bearable. Even if it means flirting with Andrew.

With the pleasantries over, the host readjusts himself in his chair, and I get a sense of where this conversation is starting. My shoulders tense up, bracing like I'm watching a suspense scene in a horror film.

"There's been a lot of speculation going around the last couple of days about the video that leaked online of you with another man, and I wanted to give you the opportunity tonight to address the speculation directly." He points his cue cards at the camera.

A ping sounds from Andrew's phone, and he picks it up, thankfully distracted from the clip I've now seen a hundred times of Alexander and me. The last thing I need is Andrew finding out about this. I love him, but his lips are as loose as his asshole, and if he were to find out, half of WeHo would know before the night is out.

"Wait, he's gay?" Andrew asks, when he finishes responding to the message.

"Shh," I say, whacking his arm.

I'm keen to hear how Alexander addresses what happened between us, and I don't need any interruptions.

I can tell Alexander is uncomfortable by the way he fiddles with his watch, which helps soothe my racing heart.

"I appreciate that there's a lot of speculation about my love life, my personal life, but that speculation over this last week has already caused a lot of damage. Rita Watson's family had to sit by while the press and people online vilified her. She actually needed our support and understanding."

There's a sincerity in his voice that pulls at my heartstrings.

To have to go through this. On national television.

I shake my head at the thought of being forced to do the same.

"As for the video that leaked online, what the footage didn't capture was the camera crew in the ballroom. We were filming a scene I was rehearsing with a movement coach for an upcoming film I'm going to be shooting at the end of summer."

My heartstring snaps.

So that's how they're going to spin this.

I've gone from dialect coach to movement coach. From stranger to hookup guy, from boyfriend to discarded, all in the space of two weeks.

"A new film?" the host acts surprised.

Like he's not in on this whole masquerade.

Three fast blinks and a twitch in his lip, and Alexander's face shifts ever so slightly. He's more stoic, more composed. It's the way he acts whenever he's confronted by someone he doesn't know.

"Yes. I wasn't planning to announce it until we began shooting, but I'm going to be starring in my first feature film, called *Disposed*. It's a psychological thriller, set in New Mexico, about a man that's seeking revenge on a town that destroyed his family."

That's it.

That's all I get.

Is that all this relationship was to him?

I'm barely a footnote in this conversation.

And as for the title of the film! Doesn't look like he'll need to do much rehearsing at all to get into character. He's clearly already skilled in the art of disposing things he no longer needs or cares for.

"You know what, let's switch back to the finals. Kelly can find out what he says online," I say, pushing myself up off the couch.

"You sure?" Andrew leans forward to grab the remote.

I look at the TV one more time, and the thought of listening to another word of what Alexander has to say makes me want to grab the bottle of beer off the table and throw it at him.

"Yeah," I say, picking up the beer and gulping the last of it instead. "Want another one?"

"Sure, why not." Andrew flips back to the NBA Finals as I make my way into the kitchen.

I grab two beers and a lime from the fridge and take a moment to rest my arm on the door. The cool air helps cool me down. Maybe it's for the best. Maybe this wasn't meant to work out after all. And at least I still have a roof over my head and I'm one hundred thousand dollars better off. It could be worse.

I close the fridge door and head over to the counter, setting the bottles down and picking up a knife to slice the lime into quarters. I pop the bottles open and slide the lime slices in.

"Chris, your phone's ringing. It's someone called Skater Boy?" Andrew says from the lounge, and I freeze. My hands lose their ability to function, and I drop both Coronas. The glass smashes and the beer spills out all over the floor.

"You okay?" Andrew comes into the room, sprinting toward me. "Is Skater Boy the one who has you all up in your feels, buying ice cream and beer?"

I shake my head.

"Sorry, I thought I saw a spider," I say, stepping carefully out of the mess and grabbing the kitchen roll to clean it up.

I avoid Andrew's gaze as I try and compose myself. He goes to the fridge and retrieves the last two beers, popping the lids off.

I haven't heard a word from Alexander in nearly two days, and now he calls me.

Now he decides to get in touch.

Fuck him.

My breath is short and shallow as I pat down the floor and then pick up the glass shards.

"Come on, let's leave that till the game is over," Andrew says, pulling at my arm.

I get up and take a beer off him, then follow him back to the couch, settling down and grabbing my phone.

The missed call notification stares back at me from the lock screen. The temptation to call him back is strong, but a bigger part of me wants to just end this chapter with him. Draw a line under everything and begin anew, hard as that may be.

As I put the phone back on the table, another notification pops up.

Voicemail

My whole body tenses at the sight.

I will my body to relax, just as Andrew becomes animated and starts shouting at the referee.

A doctor told me once never to pick at a scab. If you do, it will never heal. But the itch is there, and I need to scratch it. To hear what he has to say.

But what good would that do me?

I'm already a footnote in his narrative, as evidenced by the interview.

I've been silenced by Connie and a hundred thousand dollars.

But maybe I should listen to the voicemail. It's not like I have to respond to him. And unlike a call, it's not like he'll be able to ask me any questions and catch me off guard.

I get up and make my way to the toilet, taking my phone with me, and sit down. I open up the voicemail and immediately notice the length. Shit. It's a long message.

Maybe this isn't such a good idea.

Maybe I'm reopening Pandora's box.

I let my finger hover over the red delete button, but I can't bring myself to do it. The curiosity about what he's said is too much to take.

I take a deep breath and remind myself that this will help answer some of the questions I have, and maybe give me some closure that the interview didn't.

I press play.

"Hi Chris. It's me..."

To be continued...

To hear the voicemail Alexander left for Christopher head to www.abjackson.com or scan the QR code below.

To get your copy of the second book in the trilogy, **Stolen Hearts,** scan the QR code below.

You can listen to all of Alexander Morgan's songs featured in this book, including **My Anchor, It's You That I Need, Compare To You, Tonight, I'm Gonna Fly** and **Stolen Moments** by heading to Spotify, Apple or Amazon or scanning the QR code below.

To get a **FREE** copy of the prequel novella **Stolen Nights** and learn about the eventful night Alexander lost Samuel head to www.abjackson.com or scan the QR code below.

Also, if you enjoyed this book, please review and rate it. It helps more readers like yourself discover this book.

ACKNOWLEDGEMENTS

Truth really is stranger than fiction! In the writing of this book along with the subsequent two in the series, it has been both a cathartic and retraumatising experience in equal measure, and I am glad to let it go, and have this out there in the world.

It can take a village to raise a child and it can often take a village to help bring a book to life, even though the process of writing a book itself is a very solitary experience. And so, there are a few people I would like to take the time to express my eternal gratitude to.

Leah Stockford. You were there at the conception of this book and have always been a supportive and great sounding board for everything I do in the realm of writing. Thank you for encouraging me to write this story and for being there throughout. **Kelly Thatcher.** Thank you for being my sassy pocket-sized sidekick, for coming and doing the rekkies with me, to remember where things are located at The Landmark hotel, and for pretending to be engaged so we could access the ballrooms. **Stefan Demetriou.** Thank you for always being a sounding board on all my creative projects, for being there with me at The Landmark the night I completed the first draft, and for all your invaluable feedback to tighten up the story and bring it to life. **Dakota Nyght.** This book would not be seeing the light of day without you. Your editing skills have really helped me to push my writing even when I didn't want to, and to help me view things through the lens of the reader, so that I don't get lost in music industry babble and confuse readers with too many characters that would usually fill a popstars world (shoulder shrug). **Matt Crossey.** Thank you for being one of the first people to believe in this project. For opening my eyes and ears to the world of book publishing and for becoming someone I now consider a dear friend. **Sam Hurst.** What can I say. Thank you for helping bring the music portion of this book to life. When I envisioned the songs for this book, I never could comprehend I would be able to co-create music that could sit alongside pop songs and sound like they fit in. It is a testament to how great a musician you are, and I am excited for what the future holds for us. **Scott Curry** and **Christina Calderone** at Spotify. Thank you for all the laughter from London to Las Vegas, for encouraging me to step outside my comfort zone and to bring these books to life. **Goodness Victor, Mark Butterworth** and the Spotify publishing team, thank you for giving me the opportunity to write and record songs in your recording studio. This book is only half of this project, and without your support, the songs that accompany and compliment this wouldn't exist. **Jin Jin,** my forever fairy god sister. Thank you for continuing to show me what kindness is, and how we can uplift people without that impacting our own journey. **James Phillips.** Thank you for sharing in my joy, frustration, confusion and more in the process, and for always making me jump. And finally, to **Sk8er Boi**, this book wouldn't exist without you.

ABOUT THE AUTHOR

A.B. Jackson is the pen name of Jack Williamson, a former music industry executive who spent over two decades living life backstage—touring the globe with chart-topping superstars and navigating the wild, unpredictable rhythms of fame. After years immersed in the spotlight's shadows, he traded stadiums and arenas for introspection, pivoting into a powerful second act as an author, songwriter, and practicing psychotherapist.

Blending sharp insight with raw emotional truth, Jackson brings a unique voice to contemporary fiction. *Stolen Moments*—the first book in the *Stolen Romance* trilogy—marks his electrifying debut as a novelist. While this is his first foray into fiction, he's no stranger to storytelling: under his real name, Jack Williamson, he authored two best-selling non-fiction titles, *The Shitty Committee* and *Maybe You're the Problem*—both praised for their bold honesty and emotional depth.

For exclusive content including free novellas, bonus epilogues, merchandise, and early access to upcoming releases, visit www.abjackson.com and join his mailing list.

BV - #0273 - 081225 - C0 - 216/138/24 - PB - 9781738530595 - Matt Lamination